Not Without You

STEPHANIE LOGUE

This is a work of fiction. Names, characters, places, and incidents either are the product of the author's imagination or are used fictitiously, and any resemblance to actual persons, living or dead, business establishments, events, or locales is entirely coincidental.

Book Design by Pixelstudio and Stephanie Logue.

Copy editing by Meg Clifford.

ISBN: 979-8-218-45768-6

For all the girls who keep trying.
For my parents, from whom I learned how.

Spirit of my silence, I can hear you
But I'm afraid to be near you
And I don't know where to begin

"DEATH WITH DIGNITY" SUFJAN STEVENS

I FOUND MY MOM'S BODY IN THE BATHTUB THE DAY I graduated from high school.

I'm not trying to be shocking or macabre about it, but Ginny says you start the story where the story starts, and where it starts is that I found my mom in the bathtub.

The day before Mom took her own life, she made me promise I'd use every bit of scholarship money any university offered me. I assumed it was so I'd never feel like I owed Dad anything, but Mom shook her head, vehemently, and gestured at my legs from under her afghan. She was 49, acted 86 (low iron, she claimed), and looked about 32 with her high cheekbones and blonde waves. She was beautiful. "You fly, Birdie," Mom said, like she always said before a race. "I see it every day"

I grinned, rolled my eyes and double pinky swore to her that I'd accept every scholarship, and left for a run.

The next morning, I found Mom in the bathtub.

Mom didn't mean for me to find her. The depression silenced even the thought of me. That's what I believe. She wouldn't leave me with all of this, and everything else, not on purpose. Her pain was greater, bigger, than everything.

Even me.

My high school diploma turned up in the mail a week later, the day after Mom's funeral, with Principal Smitz's sympathetic platitudes in block letters on a Hallmark. I tossed the card in the trash, the diploma on the counter, and tied my running shoes tight enough to numb my toes.

At least Principal Smitz sent a card. My best friend didn't even come to the funeral.

That's Ginny's MO though. I'm the runner, but Ginny's the one who runs away. I trail behind: fixer of bad haircuts and awkward blind dates, comforter of bad algebra grades, confidence builder as she reads her short stories aloud at open mics.

But this wasn't fixable. It's laughable how unfixable a dead mom is.

My mom, though? Mom was my fixer. When she had the right cocktail of drugs keeping her brain clear, she was warmth. Safety. My net after meets or my own shitty grade. Her heartbeat was the first one I heard, and even now, I can feel it, her, sometimes, I swear it. She didn't mean for me to find her. Maybe she meant for it to be Dad, or she thought that when she left the earthly world, she'd turn to dust, or evaporate, or there'd be a snag in the fiber of how time works and there'd be no reason for me to stumble into her bathroom at 9:04 am looking for the extra-long bobby pins to attach my grad cap to my blowout and find her, long since bled out in water gone cold.

Mom tried to stay. And she did so, so good. She didn't mean for it to be me.

But it was me.

And it ripped me open.

Part 1

THERE IS NOTHING TO SAY...

CHAPTER 1

SWISH.

Tap.

Swish.

Tap.

The steps come easily when I'm alone. Comfortable. Even. Hypnotic. I'm under no pressure to race. Don't misunderstand—when it's time to go, I'm off with a flick of a ponytail and disappear before you even realize I was here. I decided this summer that's my super power: not speed, or endurance, but my ability to cease existing in any given space. My legs get me up and get me out. Running is my reality. My escape. My place to think.

My only good reason to get up in the morning.

And what I wish I was doing right now.

Everything else? Mind-numbingly boring. Scoop-my-eyes-from-my-head-to-feel-anything-at-all boring.

"Lou." Annabella, my roommate of six days, has a hold on my foot. Her tug is gentle. So's her tone. Her message is not. "You can't be late."

I press my face into my pillow. Inhale. Pretend to drift into a deeper sleep at 7:50 in the morning. Our dorm hallway buzzes, alive, and is loud—kids—students, whatever we are—calling good morning, complaining about early Geography 101 labs, retelling last night's stupid shenanigans. Like I can sleep with my roommate hanging off my ankle and the noise pollution leaking into our room, but I wait Annabella out, and she releases her skinny fingers from around my crew sock.

I try to not miss human touch as soon as it's gone.

Annabella doesn't know I've been awake since four. She doesn't know I spent forty minutes in the bathroom finger-combing the fried bleach-blond at-home dye job I did the night before she moved in, snipping away crusty, dead ends with kitchen shears I found in the building's kitchenette. A half hour zombie-walking the dorm hallway with only the neon fire escape sign glaring off the linoleum. I floated into our room and up the loft bed ladder like a ghost around the time she started to stir, and assumed sleeping position: back to the room, fetal curl, check.

We've lived on a campus for a week, but already I've memorized the pattern the rising sun treks through the university-issued blinds, the light so pale it's basically white. Sleep in an anomaly here. It was all summer too, but Dad hardly realized I was in the house, let alone that I was a newly-minted insomniac. Annabella is already more tuned in.

Someone turns on a shower down the hall in the bathroom. Pipes in the ceiling screech to life behind a stain shaped like a million foreheads smacking into it from startling awake in a loft bed. Below me, Annabella doesn't make another sound that isn't premeditated and slow, like she would rather run wind sprints uphill or recite extra Hail Mary's after confession than try to wake me again. She's a church mouse right down to the choker with a tiny gold cross nestled against her windpipe. It catches the light sometimes, like Jesus himself shines from it.

Annabella moves around our room like a premonition: snaps her laptop shut, opens the microwave with her hot to-go oatmeal right before it beeps. Shoes on, spoon grabbed, backpack zipped. "Lou." Her hand is on my quilt, inches from my shoulder. Annabella easily clears six feet tall. Probably how she runs fast. Big-ass strides. She's a gazelle on the course. Like she's not even trying. "Come on. We're both in the Rotunda this morning. I'll wait and walk to class with you."

My tongue presses against my teeth to speak. I can't squeeze my mouth enough to say no.

Annabella waits a beat and pats my quilt, her fingers brushing my shoulder. Perhaps on purpose. Perhaps not. She glides out the door—the rambunctious clatter of freshmen on their own for the first time seeps into our room—and shuts it, stilling, if not quieting, the world.

Safe to move and not be caught as a liar, I look at my phone. Two minutes after eight. She's late. If Coach finds out, she'll have Annabella's ass. Let alone mine when she hears I skipped Comp 101 entirely.

I itch to get out of bed and pull on my shoes. I have other things to do.

Outside, it's end-of-summer sticky. The gross kind that pools inside your elbows and makes your skin squelch when you shift. The soupy air is heavy enough to cradle me mid-stride, and lift me far, far away. Where would I go? I wonder, walking the opposite direction of Composition 101, the class I'm skipping. I pitch forward into a stretch.

Hamstring: Key West. Glassy water, more swamp than land. Every other true crime murder goes down in Florida. I bet there are lots of ripped men looking for alibis. I'd make a good alibi.

Calf: Alaska. But only the time of year when the sun is up 24 hours a day. It's easier to pace hallways in daylight. Less creepy.

Glute: What about Sydney? To them, the world is normal, even as they cling to the earth by their shoes, upside down. Dangling like bats. And they don't even know it. Nocturnal and barely hanging on. Sounds familiar.

Or maybe people in the northern hemisphere are the ones hanging on for dear life. Which part of the human condition is scarier? Dwelling on that string of gravity that keeps us from flying off our spinning rock? Or the general consciousness to live our lives and not fixate on the what-if every damn minute. Acute fear or complete ambivalence?

God. I need to go back to bed.

I zigzag between girls in fuzzy beige pajama pants and more girls in bike shorts and ice white, thick-soled sneakers. Bros in mesh shorts and hoodies who brood down sidewalks, their earbuds peeking out. Thousands of kids rich on student loan cash, flexing through rap lyrics they have no reference for, caffeinated by seven-dollar matcha lattes for the semester's first French quiz.

I set towards the Campanile on the edge of campus. My bones settle into the rhythm of my feet pounding the pavement.

Swish.

Tap.

Swish.

Tap.

I inhale, my heart leads the way and—

There it is. Adrenaline surges. The only good reason to get up in the morning.

Rude.

Go away, I think.

And true to character, even in my head, Ginny listens, and goes away.

I pick up my pace, but it's fruitless. I'm not leaving her behind.

The Campanile's bell tolls: nine dings reverberate through the sea of brick buildings where smart things are discussed, regurgitated, slept through. Campus takes a deep breath and exhales students into the wild again. I pass the bike shorts and bros and slow as I take the steps two at a time to Pierson Hall's front door. My shoes squeak on the linoleum, but I'm just a footnote in the chaos of comings and goings. Sweat coats my arms from my sprint down Medary. Feels like I accomplished something, at least.

Annabella nearly flings a shoe across the room when I walk in. Her other shoe is double knotted on her foot, safe from a startled throw. "I thought you left already," she says, tying her laces, pretending she didn't spook harder than a sleeping cat next to a robot vacuum.

"Left for where?" I nudge our door shut and pull off my gross tank.

Annabella stands, confused, her cleats tied together and looped over her wrist. Dread pools in my gut. "Practice. Have you already trained? Today's the ten miler Coach harped about all week."

Shit.

I shrug my shirt back down and grab my gym bag. What I would give for a breeze to scoop me up and drop me over Australia right now.

CHAPTER 2

I AVOID THE COFFEE SHOP IN THE STUDENT UNION FOR exactly eleven days. It isn't long enough. Coffee shops pretend they're about serving people with curated taste, but that taste better be bitter. I'm bitter all the time now, but flowery drinks are my jam, and I need one. Badly.

The guy behind the counter looks vaguely familiar. I've barely ventured outside my room for food, and besides, baristas look the same in their black beanies and flannel and autumn-colored aprons. But this guy is staring. He knows me, and I hate it. It gives me the willies. "Medium chamomile tea latte, please."

He punches my order in, eyes narrowing as he stares harder, forcing his brain to place a name to my face.

I pay. Step aside. Stare back.

Creepy Barista says my name when my drink is up. Recognition spreads over his face like butter. "Lou! That's it."

I ignore him, and open the cup to check for steamed milk; they always forget the steamed milk.

He leans close, his face contorted into overt sadness. "Sorry about your mom."

Heat curls into my palm. I click the lid on and fight to breathe past the clog in my throat. "I don't know what you're talking about."

His eyebrows crash into each other like a couple cumulonimbus clouds. "Sorry. You look like this girl my brother ran cross country with from Aberdeen—"

"I've never run a day in my life." I lurch backward, clutching my cup to my chest.

"My bad," he calls, his voice reverberating off the high ceilings past the coffee counter.

I peel away, certain I leave a black squeak mark on the over-shined floor. Into the sea of students, I disappear Fast. Faster, oh my god, gogogo, I run.

Right into a hobbit.

Truly. I smack right into a hobbit. A hunched-in-half, red-haired hobbit covered in tattoos. My cup's lid pops off. Tea and milk spikes and splashes, mostly on him.

"What the hell?" He jerks up, my precious tea streaming down his neck. Okay, not a hobbit. Just a weirdo sitting on the edge of the Union foot traffic, strumming a guitar. A guitar?

"What the *actual* hell?" I spit back. A splotch of tea blooms across my hoodie, like a map of the infested country you see in movies about the plague. "Why are you on the floor?"

Hobbit Boy shakes out his hair. Droplets scatter like confetti. Tea soaks his t-shirt from collar to armpit. People pass, unnerved. Junior year in the lunchroom, I dropped a tray of chili and a cinnamon roll seconds after paying. The clatter of plastic on linoleum inspired hoots, clapping, and necks stretching to look for the guilty party. I did an extra cute curtsey to deflect, but my palms shook so hard Ginny folded them between hers at our table.

Here, no one cares. For once, I'm grateful.

"You stop when inspiration starts." Hobbit Boy flips up his auburn curls. Gray eyes. My stomach jolts like it did the first time I saw my yet-to-be ex Milo in his baseball jersey and his cleats crunching over concrete like it was made of Rice Krispies.

But a musician? Absolutely not. My quota for artistic people in my life is long-filled.

"Whatever." I step past Hobbit Boy and his guitar case—another trip hazard—and try to not slip in the chamomile river snaking past our sneakers. "I have class." With a fistful of napkins swiped from a nearby table, I mop the tea from the floor the best I can, shove the napkins in my cup, and drop it in a garbage can. I hand him a stray napkin I don't use.

"Wait." Hobbit Boy clicks his guitar case shut and slings it over his shoulder, hot on my heels. "This isn't coffee. What do I smell?" He dabs his hoodie with the napkin like there's any saving it.

"Dreams and misplaced ambition." I push open the Union doors.

"Seriously." He keeps up. Impressive. Most people don't, unless I let them. "Is this tea?"

"Chamomile."

"Nobody drinks chamomile."

"Then I guess I'm nobody."

Hobbit Boy looks at me. It's a side-eye, and it's sharp, but weirdly warm, and what is it with complete strangers thinking they know me this morning?

Hard pass. "I'm late for class."

"Me too."

"If I hadn't run you over, you'd still be on the floor with your feelings strumming your guitar."

"Don't talk shit about feelings," he says. "Besides, what did I just tell you? When inspiration starts, you stop."

"Now you're following." I peek at him. He's smiling. When did someone last smile at me? Not a sorry-your-mom's-dead smile, but a real smile. I focus forward on the bank of glass doors to the Wellness Center ahead. Coach is in there, probably in her office, probably plotting our next hell run. Or conjuring up evil spirits. Something super annoying, regardless.

"Let me amend my original statement: when inspiration starts, you follow." He darts ahead of me and yanks open a door.

"I have class," I repeat, slipping past him.

"I do too." Hobbit Boy follows me. "Wellness 101. Let's go memorize signs of heart attacks and volleyball rules. I'm sure the TA has a pastel pink worksheet and is waiting with baited breath for our arrival."

"You're in my class?"

"I am, yeah." His smile fades, and my heart pings. "I can't believe you don't remember all this," he jokes, trying to come back from my accidental burn.

I grind my lips between my teeth, the guilt real. "I'm sorry."

He shrugs, and his right shoulder darts higher up to his ear, and his lips twist into a smirk, recovered. "You'll remember me now."

We cut through a gym and under a volleyball net. Hobbit Boy jogs ahead and makes a production of opening the classroom door. The TA looks up from her attendance list on her tablet as we snag the last two chairs in back. "Why are you dripping?"

"Chamomile tea," he answers cheerfully, swinging his guitar case against the wall next to a fire alarm pull. To me, he says: "I'm Archer, by the way."

"Lou," I almost say. I want to say it. It tickles my throat and curls my tongue into place. But my own name dies on my lips.

I shake my head and look to the front of the classroom.

~

I smell Annabella before I see her after her shower: coconut and vanilla body oil and blueberry shampoo waft down the hall ahead of her. She falters in the doorway, her wet curls clumping to her elbows. I'm on the futon, back in the shorts and t-shirt I'd slept in. My psychology textbook is open and heavy in my lap.

"I gotta go," she says into her phone pressed to her ear. "Dinner. Six sharp. Yes, the diner. I'll be there." A long pause. "Yes. I swear I will be at the show tonight. Bye." She plops to her desk chair. "Sorry. Didn't mean to interrupt your studying."

Studying implies enlightenment, none of which is happening here. "You didn't."

The book was for show. I left it splayed on the futon while Annabella was showering so when I heard her flip flops squelch back to our room, I could dive back to it like I'd been reading the whole time. In reality, I couldn't sit still. My legs begged me to keep moving, even after my self-imposed fifteen miler today. There were string lights to flip on under our lofted mattresses. Circles to plod in our area rug. A sloped tower of hoodies in my closet to refold.

Now, transferring my tight stack of sweatshirts back to my closet, I notice a small, hand-sketched drawing of an anatomical heart on Annabella's desk. Bright pink pansies and snow-white daisies pop from the right and left atriums. Daisies surrounded by leafy greens burst from the aorta. Tiny script winds up the side: You Make My Heart Bloom. It's framed and tucked behind Annabella's open laptop. Like she'd pulled it out, studied it, and didn't put it all the way back.

"Correct me if I'm wrong..." Annabella crosses her legs on her desk chair. "But I just got two words out of you in a row. I think it's a record."

In my previous life, I would have smiled.

But in my previous life, I would have said more than two words in that sentence. "Maybe."

Annabella slides her elbows to her desk. Her eyes dart to where I know the framed heart is. She inches it farther behind her computer. "Do you want to go out with me tonight? Dinner?"

Ask her about the heart flowers. Who's the boy?

I shake my head, but Ginny clings on. Annabella's face relays that I'm saying no to her though, so I let her believe it. "I should keep studying."

"A concert too." Annabella is stubborn. A foot shake to wake me. An invitation to get out of our room. "Nothing big. Just a friend from high school—"

"I said no thank you."

Louise, that's rude.

Annabella's hurt evaporates quickly and drifts into the air. Faster than Ginny's ever did. "Call me if you change your mind."

I won't.

I pretend to read my textbook. Annabella looks at her laptop and clicks, looping the ends of her hair around her knuckles. We fall to silence.

~

I sleep fitfully. The room's too hot, and I've long since kicked off my quilt. Underneath my belly button, my insides twist and shrivel like a dead cicada in September, curled up where the grass meets the sidewalk. It wakes me from the hazy dream I'm circling the drain in. I process my damp underwear and swipe underneath the elastic. I lift my finger to the lamp light I left on for Annabella. My period.

I swear and slither off the loft.

The bathroom is empty, the line of stall doors open. It's Friday, I remember, locking a door. Everyone's out. I wiggle out of my shorts and pull down my underwear. At least this pair is old. Red splotches stain the cotton, a painting gone awry. The blood is bright and, without a chance to soak into the cloth, gleams beneath the shitty dorm bathroom light. I blink, and I'm taken away.

Dad and I are led into a greige office with one window to the street by the funeral director in a heather gray suit that looks too warm for June. A bead of sweat creeps out of his hair. Unbothered, he launches into his speech about sympathy and "support in this trying time," and latches onto me with his round pity eyes, darting to his massive desk, and peeking back up to me, as if I'm glass. Like I'm the one about to break here.

"Is there a poem or a short reading she loved?" Big pity eyes.

"Would she have preferred a ceramic or brass urn?" Big pity eyes.

"What songs might your mother have wanted?" Big pity eyes.

Big pity eyes, all day. Poor little Lou, momless, and saddled with this jokester of a dad, bouncing his knee away next to her. My mother's body is at the crematorium. A two-person biohazard cleaning crew is in my parents' master bathroom wiping, scrubbing, removing any trace of my mother's blood so we don't have to. Dad managed to leave his phone in the car, but he keeps flexing his fingers as if he's reaching for it.

The funeral director is softly rattling off songs. My ears cling to a title, and I repeat it, just to move on. "'Blackbird' is fine."

I jerk a wad of toilet paper off the roll.

The tiny chapel has cheap pews and a non-denominational altar stained in oak at the front of the room. Heavy, dusty rose curtains bunch over walls, dragging to the carpet, and I can't tell if they're blocking the view of the road, or meant to stifle cries from the business side of the funeral home. It smells like old lady in here, like funeral lilies. Like candle smoke and incense smoke and cigarette smoke. Mom deserved better than this.

I deserve better than this.

My black opaque tights were a wholly stupid choice for the funeral. I own one black dress, but it's short and left over from the winter formal with Milo.

The only way Mom let me out of the house that night was to pair it with these wool tights. "You'll be cold anyway," she'd reasoned, tossing the pack on my bed next to the dress as I emerged from my bathroom, my hair piled into a towel barely balanced on my head. I'd agreed, even though we both knew her motivations were for naught; later that night, I'd help Milo peel the tights from my thighs as his lips traced down from hip bone...

I scrub at my panties. The dry toilet paper pills, then tears.

I'm alone in the front pew, rubbing my fingertips into my shin, trying to scratch without pilling the tights. Dad's in the back, his realtor voice loud even when trying to be quiet, greeting people—a lot of colleagues, a lot of people he's sold houses to when he should have been home, watching with me as Mom started wearing long sleeves again, even in the spring. As her eyes lost their luster.

"Hey." There's a hand on my shoulder from the pew behind me. His thumb squeezes into the place on my neck where he used to playfully nibble.

"Hi." I'm relieved he's here. We've been done for weeks—he saw a future I didn't, but he told me to keep the promise ring. I wish I was wearing it now, not for all that it implies, but because towards the end, it morphed into a fidget toy. I'd spin it around my knuckles, the diamonds too little to even glitter, and feel a little stress crack off my chest. "Nice tie," I say, nodding to the maroon-and-gold-checkered silk looped under his chin. I'm pretty sure he borrowed it from his dad. It looks like his dad.

A swell of gratefulness fills my chest and steals my breath for a moment.

"Thanks." Milo flips the end of the tie between his fingers. Behind him, I watch his dad clap my father on the shoulder. His mom is teary and armed with a ball of tissue as big as a baseball. He's so lucky. Does he know?

The line behind Milo's parents is long. It stretches out the funeral home door, based on how the weak sunlight is pulling across the ceiling in the lobby. "Is Gin here yet?"

His eyes dart up—normally a perfect shade of moonstone, today they are closer to navy. "No."

I nod and shift my body forward. Mom's urn is on the table next to the altar. I'd decided on ceramic, without waiting for Dad's input. It looks nice, but doesn't look like her. None of this does.

Toilet paper shreds over my panties. My fingertips are pink from effort. I step out of my panties and crumple them up in the tin garbage can drilled into the wall. I clean up. I go back to bed.

CHAPTER 3

"McKINNLEY!"

Annabella and I both spike to attention. Last Annabella saw me, I was tying my shoes on her futon, deeply considering skipping practice and returning my scholarship. Last Coach Stevens saw me was yesterday as I lost my train of thought and stared into my locker for too long.

Mom's pinky promise is the only reason I showed up today.

I step over my teammates stretching in the grass under a huge oak tree behind the Wellness Center. "Someone's in trouble," Emily fake whispers. Sara knocks her elbow. Maddie's mouth turns into a tunnel big enough for a train to roll through. Their giggles rise like hot air.

Bitches be bitches, no matter where you are.

Coach waits in the stark sunlight, basically vibrating in anger. Her glare is as sharp as her chin, and she points to her office. She follows me through the locker room to guarantee I arrive at her intended destination.

Her office door slams, the crack of wood on metal painful in my ear.

Fuck.

"You know your time on the 5 has spiked since the day you got here. This is not the woman we recruited last spring…" Coach's yelling style means enunciating weird syllables and waving her arms, as if attempting to take flight. I quit listening. The ass chewing is for her, not me.

Rather, I look around her office. Ratty Venetian blinds turn sunshine into slats. No curtains. A huge print schedule of our meets; the next is Saturday. Jackrabbits. Gophers. Coyotes. Bison. Our mascots are so Midwestern zoo it hurts. Coach is married, based on the photo on her desk and the thin gold band on her finger. Her wife is pretty. Brownish-grayish barrel curls frame her face, and she smiles with her eyes. I bet she's a kindergarten teacher or a manager at Pottery Barn. Or owns an Etsy shop and sells hand-crafted mug koozies.

"...your scholarship." Coach drags her palms down her cheeks, and something about her face eases. I think it's her jaw unclenching. I tune back in. "Listen. I know you're grieving. I truly cannot imagine."

I focus on my hands in my lap. Dad told her. It was the one parental thing he's done in years. Move-in weekend, Dad requested a meeting with Coach, and when they went into her office without me, I straddled a bench in the locker room, thinking about how I could not possibly feel more and less like a child at the same time.

"But." Coach's jaw clench is back, but less intense. "Your effort sucks, and it's damn obvious you could care less, but I see something in you. God help me. It's not about your 400 time or your split on the 6. I don't know what it is." She pauses and I see a sliver of something. Careful contemplation? I don't know. But it isn't pity, and for that I'm grateful.

"You best thank your lucky stars because you have one more chance. One." Coach shoots her pointer finger into the air like a flag, as if a visual representation of the number of my chances left will light a flame. "One. Now get out."

Out, I get.

Outside, the squad is gone, well on their first lap around campus before heading to the golf course to do hill work. I look down the path the girls ran.

The locker room door swings open. Annabella bounces out, her right arm crossed in front of her chest, stretching her shoulder. "It must not have been bad if she let you out already."

"Did you wait for me?"

"I had to pee."

"You waited for me."

"What's the big deal if I did?" Annabella sets off, her hot pink soles caked with dirt from yesterday's mud day.

What's the big deal? I'm a loner now. A baby introvert. I can't let anyone in—no one should want to be in, anyway.

I can't risk more loss.

That's the big deal, Annabella.

In my head, Ginny nods with authority.

Annabella jogs down the trail. My stomach lurches as if she's lassoed me and is running away with the rope. I led Ginny through the halls of our high school, Milo to the backseat of his car, my teammates to the finish line. I don't know how to follow. It's not me. I need to go back to Coach's office and quit. I'm not part of a team. Not anymore.

I don't know how to do this, now.

"Lou!" Annabella trots backwards, balancing on the balls of her feet. Her hand is angled at her eyebrows to see me through the hot, hazy sunshine. "Come. On."

To be clear: I'm following no one.

This is my decision to take the team's trodden path.

So what if it's behind Annabella?

"Let me get this straight." Annabella tugs her neon purple scrunchie onto the top of her skull on our walk back to our dorm. Her curls burst out like a firework. "You have one last chance. And it's Saturday's meet."

"Seems so," I say. Coach trapped me in the locker room after the showers to clarify my One Last Chance parameters. "I show up or I'm out." I unlock our door and we pass through.

"What's 'show up' mean?" Annabella drops her gym bag on top of her hamper and collapses to the floor. She lifts her leg skyward and stretches. "Like have a good race or have the best race of your life?"

"I was afraid to ask." Coach's jaw clench rivals that of a hungry T-Rex, or any number of actors on afternoon soaps. I unzip my bag and dump it over my dirty clothes.

Annabella props herself up on her elbows. Her cross necklace gleams at my eyeball: Jesus says hi. "My next question, now that you're speaking in full sentences: I'm meeting a friend at the dining hall before Bible study. Want to come to dinner?"

Her persistence is annoying. A little charming. But mostly annoying. "No. I should study." Those Wellness 101 worksheets won't do themselves.

"You sure?" Annabella tugs her hair again. Her curls lump to the side, and she yanks out the scrunchie. "It's my best friend from high school. I swear he's entirely harmless."

"The 'he' makes me even less inclined."

"Me too, if it wasn't him." Annabella looks at me through a stretch. Why do people keep studying me like I'm a lab rat or a YouTube sensation? "We'll talk later?"

"Probably not." But I smile.

Annabella smiles back.

~

Social media is stupid. We let it tell exaggerated stories. People—couples—are never as happy as they claim to be.

Except these two, filling my phone screen.

They're on a carousel, backlit in ripples of color and plexiglass ponies. I can count Ginny's molars, and I've never seen Milo's heart eyes be so ... heart-y. Their hands are clasped at her hips, her braid is unweaving, and the filter has been notched up just enough to bring out the flush in Milo's cheeks.

I will not like this photo. On principle.

"Who are they?" Archer slides into the seat next to me in Wellness 101. He investigates the picture, nose-to-nose with Ginny. I pretend she goes cross-eyed from Archer's proximity. "Is anyone actually that happy?"

"I think they might be." I thumb back to my lock screen. "You're nosy."

"It comes naturally."

The TA drops two worksheets (hot pink) on our table. "Do these with a partner. Don't forget to put your name at the top for credit."

Archer swipes a sheet and scribbles his name at the top. His handwriting fits his vibe: pointed peaks and meandering valleys. He glances at my sheet. "I see you're still nameless."

"What did I just say about being nosy?" I scratch my shoulder and read the sheet. FARM FRESH FRUITS – WHAT'S AVAILABLE AT YOUR LOCAL FARMER'S MARKET. It's a crossword. "Is there a farmer's market near campus?"

"It's a few blocks from my apartment." Archer looks away from my shoulder, chews the end of his pen, pretending he's deep into the prompts.

"You live off campus?"

"I have to answer questions and you don't?" Archer taps his pen on my worksheet. "Four down, three over is watermelon. 'Fruit, green, red, large. Harry Styles single.'"

I write down watermelon. Scandalous pick for a 101 course—the TA has to know what Harry's singing about, right? "'Starbucks unleashed this latte flavor on us in 2003' is obviously pumpkin."

"Pedestrian."

"Gross."

Blueberries, grapes, and apples are nailed in a hurry. Papaya, mango. Avocado. ("'Frequently found on toast?'" Archer scrunches his nose. "Not in my kitchen.")

"'Part of the rose family,'" I read our last clue. "I don't know."

Archer closes his eyes. No, he squeezes them shut, and doesn't write the answer down as he says it. "Pear."

I count the boxes and look at the letters filling adjacent slots. Pear, it is. "How'd you know that?"

"Alex Trebek was my de facto babysitter." Archer rubs the butt of his palms into both eyes, scribbles pear, and leaps up to slap his worksheet on the TA's desk. Her stare stays fixated on her phone. Archer cracks his neck and turns. "You gonna write your name on the sheet?"

"I will. Stop creeping."

Archer sits and makes a point of opening a tattered, spiral-bound notebook. Tiny words in his handwriting wind and mold into haphazard shapes on every page, separated by heavy-handed lines. Big x's cut through entire sections, arrows and circles pulling the maze of letters together. I yank my eyes back to my paper and scribble Lou on the corner. At the TA's desk, I make a show of sliding my sheet in the middle of the stack, so Archer can't find mine.

His eye roll is gargantuan, but so is the way his smile tilts on his lips.

Class ends. We move to the door. "You don't have to tell me," Archer says. His guitar is with him again today, the case handle stretching over his shoulder. "I'll just call you Chamomile."

"Lavender Chamomile," I correct.

"Sounds like a psychic's name."

"Or a porn star's. I should just claim it as mine now."

"It tells a story, for sure." Archer pauses underneath the basketball hoop in the gym. "That's what names do."

Our classmates rush by us, water to our rocks. I'm rooted, somehow. "How's that?"

"I know a girl." Archer winces, then amends. "I knew a girl. Her last name is Birne. It's German for 'pear.' In eighth grade we were really into etymology, so in English she did this research project on her last name, and how our names are bigger than us. Pears symbolize grace. Pear trees bring inner peace. Fertility, wisdom. Sweetness. All these good things." Archer pushes his lips to one side of his face. "Affection."

"Yeah?" I'm invested in this girl. Or maybe it's the way his voice makes my lungs relax like the iron band around my chest is opening.

Can't be. I'm definitely invested in the pear girl's story.

"Turns out," he continues. "In Chinese, the word 'li' means 'pear' and 'separation,' so it's recommended that to not be separated from your beloved, lovers shouldn't share a pear."

"Let me guess," I say. "You and this girl shared a pear."

"Oh yeah, we totally did. Pears are great." Archer shrugs and squints. "But that's not why we broke up."

Shit.

"You didn't know." Archer reads me, as if he just knows how, and rolls his flannel sleeve up to show me the inside of his wrist. Another tattoo disappears under his cuff, but the one I'm supposed to see is on full display. Half a pear is etched through the freckles, oblong and awkwardly lumped, its stem hosting two tiny leaves. Yellow-green rounds the pear for depth, a slight shadow stretches behind to ground it to Archer's skin.

The iron band loosens again, but this time it nicks my heart. "It's beautiful."

"Thanks." Archer shakes his sleeve down.

I look at him, in his flannel and dusty Vans. Jeans with a torn hem trailing behind his shoe like a little white worm. Curls for days, an arm of tattoos. Clever as hell. Guitar strapped on his back and another girl in his heart. He won't get too close. He's safe. He's as safe as they come. "My name is Lou."

Archer smiles, slowly, and then full force. "Ted."

"Wait. What?"

His goofy giggle fills the gym. "I'm kidding. It's Archer."

CHAPTER 4

MY ONE LAST CHANCE. MEET DAY.

Steam rises from the golf course grass. Sunlight streams around trees and peeks through branches to watch my impending failure.

Great foreshadow of your manifested doom. Do you mind if I borrow that for my next piece?

Great. Ginny's accounted for.

Joining Ginny to watch me fuck this up: Emily and Sara. My read on Sara is that she's the mean girl assistant and Emily runs the show, but with their matching high ponies and sunblock-shiny shoulders, I hate them equally. Emily lurks behind Annabella, stretching and double-knotting her cleats, passing me smirky side-eyes. Sara turns up with two frosty jugs of water. As they sip to avoid bloat pre-race, Emily whispers at Sara and lets her stare burn my cheek. Sara giggles. Emily's grin looks like the closing shot in a horror flick about a jailed cult leader harboring dead-body secrets. Or straight-up Hannibal Lector.

I really hate her.

My uterus is also announcing mutiny. Steely cramps woke me from a dreamless sleep around five. Annabella snored on, curled up tight in the corner of her bed. My period's always unreliable, but stress makes it even more so. It's light for days and then rages back like an animal hell-bent on ruining my underwear and my day.

"Don't forget the second hill right after marker two. It's steeper than you think," Annabella murmurs as much for herself as for me. "And the sharp corner by the gardens right after."

Sweat seeps under my arms. I think about my tampon jumping ship mid-stride. And the bitches whispering and screwing and unscrewing their water bottles behind me. A flurried whisper of words I can't make out crashes into my ear drums and bounces around my brain.

The golf course tilts.

I wave my arm out to catch anything steady, and brush Annabella.

"It's all a mental game, and they're experts at playing it." Annabella says, reading the situation, or my mind. Bent in half in a hamstring stretch, her voice is muffled. "You're here. That's half the battle. Be *here*."

I lift my arms over my head, as if that's what I meant to do. My uterus makes a play to crash out between my knees. "What's the other half?"

Her ponytail arches as she swings up. "Does anyone ever know what the other half of the battle is?"

Annabella and I are scheduled for the second race; five girls from each team run an 8K (which I can do in my sleep, but so can everyone else here.) Coach sends the first team to the starting line. The rest of us edge the course to cheer. This is unnatural, the circus of caring for the sake of it. In high school, with cross country, track, even dance, I only wanted—needed—to keep my itchy legs moving. I didn't connect with the girls. No need. I had my team. She lived across the street from me. She had my back.

I thought, anyway.

Focus.

I bend to the crowd, searching for Ginny's frizzy, dirty-blonde waves. Her voice is solid, like she's next to me, about to link her arm through mine and yell generic encouragement.

I'm not here.

"What do you think your time will be?" Annabella's eyes are glued to the trampled grass on the course.

"I'd be happy at 25 minutes."

"Me too."

"Liar," I want to say. "That's such a shitty time." The sun creeps higher, light slicing between the leaves. Waiting. Little spotlights ready to watch me fail.

Her voice is soft. **Stop it.**

Annabella's palm is like ice on my shoulder. How? It's 85 degrees and the humidity is making stray hairs stand up like we're Troll dolls. My fried ends are entirely static. I feel like a lightbulb, shoving the heat out. "We should go to the line." She steps closer. "Are you okay? You're flushed."

"It's hot." I swipe my forehead. A sheen of sweat slicks the back of my hand.

"Get water before we start." Annabella lets me go and arranges her face into competition mode. She's done looking out for me until the finish line.

At the starting line, Annabella and I separate. Coach stares at me from the side. No emotion on her face. No encouragement, no anger. Just... blankness. Like she knows how this will end.

Stone cold.

Annabella, Emily, Maddie, Sara, and 15 girls from the Midwestern zoo mascot teams jostle to the front with me. Elbows pointed, we dig in our dominant feet, ready to peel out. As is tradition, at the last minute, I raise my arms to tighten my ponytail. It throws off competitors. Distracts. What's Lou doing now, they think, as they blink to get back into their headspace. It always works.

Always.

Don't fuck this up.

Pop.

Girls trample past me at the gate, blowing up dead grass.

Swish. Tap.

Swish. Tap.

Something's off.

This doesn't feel good. This is supposed to feel good.

The air is thick. My knees are jelly, and my shins crank forward blindly, dictating uneven steps on flat ground. My feet pound on the trampled path, but in no discernible pattern, let alone grace. No control. Each step lands different, as if each is going in the opposite direction.

Swish...Tap.

Swish..........Tap.

Swishtapswishtapswishtap.

This body isn't mine. I'm not this sloppy.

The slaps of a million coordinated steps are too far away to hear. The girls are distant, climbing the first hill and disappearing off the other side like lemmings. My eyes switch to telescope vision and their jerseys are fuzzy dots way out in front in the trees and I'm back here in the dirt and my lungs are wrecked, and—

You're losing them.

Your effort sucks.

Why do you bother?

And finally:

What happened to you?

I crawl to a bush as clear bile spews from my mouth, pooling, dripping off leaves. Slime leaks between my knuckles, sliding to weeds.

"It's okay." A hand claps my spine. A real voice. "You're okay."

"Keep going." I clear my throat. My throw up is mostly water, bits of undigested toast oozing to the dirt. "This isn't worth it."

"Em and Maddie have it. I was never gonna place in this heat. We'll still get the points." Annabella kneels, holding my elbow. Her voice is gentle. "When you're ready."

I gulp air and listen as hard as I can, but Ginny's happy with her work. She's gone. "I'm ready."

At my insistence, Annabella races down the trail ahead of me. Sweat—and not the satisfied kind—clings to me as I jog. There's no rhythm to seek, no pace to keep today. Just me. Fucking it up.

I cross the finish line over four minutes behind everyone else. Coach stands to the side, seeing right through me. Emily's in the shade by the finish line, splashing water from her bottle on her face. She winks. And I want to crush her face into the ground.

My stomach churns again.

Annabella comes out of nowhere and drapes an ice-cold, stiff towel over my head, blocking me from prying eyes. "Take my hand. We're going to the medic."

"Panic attack?" Annabella passes me a fresh t-shirt from my bag as the medic leaves the hospital tent. "Are you prone to anxiety?"

I ignore her question and swap my gross jersey for the clean shirt. What I really need is a shower. "How'd we do?"

"Two out of three are ours," Annabella means the team. Obviously. "That should ease Coach's anger."

"Shit." I drag my hands over my eyes. Can I hide under the medic's cot with the scratchy army green blanket until at least Thanksgiving? "She's gonna kill me."

"Worse." Annabella's face is stoic. "She'll kick you off the team." She tugs me up, and I let her. "Let's get it over with."

The sunshine is relentless. Coach and the medic wait for me underneath a tree. Annabella shoves me forward, the third point in a triangle of people who "have concerns on my performance."

At least I'm in the shade.

"Thanks for your help." Coach dismisses the medic with a killer flick. He pats my shoulder and leaves. Traitor.

Coach positions herself across from me, shoulders square, jaw square, clipboard square. Lots of squares. "Is this your first panic attack?"

Um.

My first was Milo-adjacent. Christmas Eve morning. He never knew.

Mom walked in on my second in the spring, after I watched Ginny leave her house on a Saturday afternoon. She was on her phone, her giggles spiking to the sunshine. It was foreign to hear her laugh without mine accompanying hers. Ginny hop-skipped to her shitty Honda and swung in so hard her ponytail bounced to the sky. Carefree without me and my drama. My view pixelated and my knees locked and I was already on the floor when Mom padded by on her way to get tea. I combed her fleecy white slippers free of fuzz to get my breath back as she sat next to me on the cold tile.

The last one: I was alone in my car.

"Do I buckle you in?" I ask Mom's urn.

The words are out, and I feel fucking dumb.

I am fucking dumb.

I don't know where to go, or where to take her, now. Dad's long gone, Ginny never showed, and I'm still here.

You're gone now, too. Where do I go, Mom?

The tears are fast and hot. And I know I'm screaming, but I can't hear my own voice, just feel my jaw unhinge like a snake about to swallow its prey, or like a girl is just starting to mourn her mother.

No one saves me. No one wiggles my door handle or peers through the windshield to locate, to silence the screaming.

No matter. Maybe I'll die too, if I carry on long and loud enough. Maybe I don't even mind.

"No," I say now. "Not my first."

Coach's jaw relaxes. Kind of. Her face is destined to be full of corners. "I'm not kicking you off the team. I want to keep you close, because you're not doing this alone. You are, however, going on probation. I'll be in close contact with your academic advisor to monitor your grades and class attendance. You will still train, but on your own time and you won't run in any more meets this year." Coach adds, casually: "And you're seeing a therapist."

"No!" I recoil. "Definitely not."

"Not negotiable." Coach flips a few pages up on her clipboard and slips out a business card. "Dr. Stellan is on campus and she's a runner too. You will see her, your attendance will be noted, and maybe, maybe, at the end of the semester, based on your general progress in these areas, I'll consider rolling back your probation."

Coach presses the card into my hand and taps her finger on the cardstock. Her nail is as square as her face. She shifts, itchy to be on her way, back to her successful girls. The women without mommy issues who she trusts not to puke stale toast into the greenery. She pauses, takes me in. My breath is rank, sweat crusted over every joint and my eyes feel sunken into my skull. "Do you want this?"

No one's ever asked.

When you're good at something—so good you win awards and scholarships and money without even trying—people assume it's the only thing you want. You silly girl, I'd imagine them saying—you can't possibly consider wasting that natural potential, that talent, that drive.

But I can. And I do.

"You fly," Mom had said.

I don't. I really don't. I just run really fast. But I can't tarnish her words with anything less. That's an abyss I won't climb out from.

"I need committed athletes. Who will put forth the necessary effort." Coach's voice is low. The breeze rattles the leaves. I have to focus to follow her words, as every leaf begs me to watch it rustle. "I'll ask again. Do you want this?"

I look up from Dr. Stellan's card. "Yes."

CHAPTER 5

"I'M SHOCKED I TALKED YOU INTO COMING OUT."

Annabella bounces into a booth at an admittedly cute diner downtown. Her hair is damp and smells of blueberries. It's nice. She grabs menus from behind the condiment rack and slaps mine in front of me. "We ran hard today. I vote for milkshakes."

"You ran hard today," I correct and curl my legs into a pretzel on the nylon seat. "I barfed for a while and stumbled in a big circle."

"Stop." Annabella's menu blocks her face. I only see the crown of her head. "Definitely a strawberry milkshake."

"Am I a fun-hater if I get tea and peanut butter toast?" Who am I? Monumentally losing races. Refusing ice cream. Asking what to order. Lou from a year ago wouldn't recognize Lou today.

Annabella slaps her menu on the table. She shakes her head emphatically. "Crap, I forgot. Get what you need to feel good." The diner door squeaks open. Annabella flops from the booth and waves madly. "We're over here."

"Hey—sorry I missed the race this morning! This melody was in my head and I had to—" Van sneakers skid to a stop at our booth. A guitar case flies past my shoulder, not ready to stop yet. Pear tattoo at eye level. "Lou. What are you doing here?"

I look up at Archer. His curls spring in every direction. "What are *you* doing here?"

Annabella grabs Archer's guitar case and sets it at the end of the table against the window. Archer slides in beside her and swipes her menu away. He knows her. Really well.

"I followed her to school." Archer digs his elbow into Annabella's ribs.

She grunts and slaps him away. "Aforementioned bestie. Though it's conditional."

It's definitely not conditional. Their energy is cozy, like a million invisible strings tie them together, into knots that can't—that shouldn't—be undone. His shoulders don't hunch when she's next to him. And Annabella's smile notches up.

Two sets of eyes stare at me. It's too much. Instantly too much. "I'm gonna go."

"Stop." Annabella grabs my wrist. "Stay."

"I'll go." Archer moves to the edge of the booth. "I don't want to scare you away."

"I'm not scared."

"Okay. Well. I just don't want to inspire a dead sprint out of here."

"Wouldn't be the first time a girl ran away." Annabella pokes Archer's arm. He grabs her fingers and twists, a light defense, and slowly scoots back into his spot. He's watching me, like I still might run, and it's nice, being cradled in a gaze like this.

"I thought when inspiration starts, you follow," I say.

Archer smiles.

Pinpricks of electricity cascade down my neck, bounce off vertebrae, and spin, collide, fall. Like the guy who jumps off the back of the Titanic, slams into the gigantic propeller, and is flung into the ocean. Probably dead before he hits the waves. That's me. Dead before I hit the waves.

Annabella releases my wrist, looking from me, the flight risk, to this hobbit-turned-charmer. "I'm missing something."

~

"What's the deal with the guitar?" An empty plate that once held French fries and my peanut-butter-slathered toast sits between Annabella and me.

Archer blinks rapidly at me over his coffee, as if my question is absurd, rather than his late-night Americano. "Show respect. Her name is Matilda. And she is my greatest tool, the catalyst to making my dreams come true."

Annabella slurps at her milkshake dregs and pets Matilda's case with reverence.

"She goes everywhere with me because. Well. You know." The skin around his eyes crinkles.

It's cute.

Ah, crap.

"Wait, you were writing a song when you missed Lou's One Last Chance run?" Annabella licks whip cream off her straw, immune to his eye crinkle.

"I meant to be there." Archer looks at Annabella. "Why didn't you tell me your roommate is on the team? And it's..." Archer glances at me covertly, like I won't notice. "Lou."

She shrugs. "Why didn't you tell me the goddess from your Wellness class is actually a damn goddess? Communication is a two-way street, my friend." Annabella winks at me as Archer's face turns pink.

Look at them. They're us. Well. Who we were. When we didn't suck.

I wave Ginny's voice away, like I'm swatting at a fly near my ear.

Archer leans on his cheek on his hand to hide at least half of blush. "The women in my life are enigmas."

"And the men in ours are dramatic." Annabella retorts.

I laugh.

Annabella looks stunned. "She laughs. I wondered."

"Laughing is overrated." Archer says.

"She's had a day, Arch." Annabella smacks his shoulder with the back of her hand. "Rein in the sarcasm."

"I'm not being sarcastic—"

"It's fine." My ears are ringing, unaccustomed to my own laughter. "He's right. Unless something is truly funny. Which is rare."

Archer scoots forward in his seat, a French fry dangling from his fingers like a toothpick. "Thoughts on talking dog videos?"

"Eh."

Annabella narrows her eyes in competition. "Cats knocking full water glasses off counters."

"I'm not much of a pet person."

The stakes skyrocket. Pandas tumbling down hills in a blur of black and white somersaults. Giggling babies. Viral dances gone wrong. Viral trends gone wrong. Children dressed up like old men. Babies who laugh like old men. Fails, the whole lot.

"I got it, I got it." Archer snaps his fingers and points at me. "People. Falling. Down."

"How old are they?"

"Our age. I'm not heartless."

"Do they get hurt?"

"Probably not."

"Are they doing it on purpose?"

"Obviously not."

The image of someone tipping over, bound by their own clumsiness, makes my ribs itch in a way that makes a giggle begin to curl upwards. Archer got me. "Yes."

His smile is back, the slow-and-then-full-force one. He wraps his arms around Annabella, crushing her into his chest. "AB! We found one! She can stay."

Annabella shoves Archer off her. "Lou can stay anyway." She holds a flat palm up at Archer's face and mimes apologies to me. "Let's do more speed rounds. International Pop Star Dreamboat Dalton Rogue: yay or nay."

A yay pops out before I can stop it. Dalton Rogue is known for trucking his guitar everywhere. My cheeks are on fire.

"I can see that about you." Annabella notes. "I'm a nay."

Archer sips his coffee. "Shocking."

Annabella glares at him. Her silent shut-the-fuck-up is palpable.

I remember her hand in my elbow as she helped me up from the course this morning. If my clear puke grossed her out, she hid it well. "You know, I think I'm nay too. Overrated."

Archer's mug clatters to the table. "What do you have against ruggedly handsome singer-songwriters?"

"You can stay into Dalton Rogue. But thanks for the backup." Annabella offers me a high-five and bounces in her seat to make our hands smack together. It's loud, and it's warm, and it cracks my heart open.

"Are you sure you don't want to head to Haven with us?"

We're outside the diner. Archer's guitar—sorry, Matilda—peeks over Archer's shoulder like a friendly giraffe that follows him everywhere. Annabella's hands are shoved in her back pockets. While we were inside, clouds crowded in the sky and now a late summer mist fills the evening, killing the heat and this terrible summer. Finally.

"No." I step backward. "I should go back to the dorm and sleep. This morning was a lot." That part is true. But also: Ginny's dad owns a coffee shop. Seen one, you've seen them all.

"There's an open mic tonight," Archer says again, like I didn't hear him the first time while we paid for our food. His eyes are so bright it's almost uncultured. "In case you change your mind."

"Noted." I might go with them sometime. But not tonight.

Annabella pushes Archer down the sidewalk, turning his shoulders to walk the opposite direction. "Text when you get home. I don't want to worry."

"You know I'm not gonna, right?"

"Think about it," she yells, a half block between us now.

I turn the corner back to campus, Annabella's request fresh in my ears. I know it's what people say to each other, but it feels nice.

I asked you to call every day this summer.

You wanted me to call you for you. Not the same thing, Ginny.

It's still all about you.

She's never this honest in real life.

The last block before campus is student rental housing. The first house is more chipped gray paint than anything else, and they only devolve in quality. Front porches slope to weedy yards. Cars line the street, divided between the curb and gravel driveways. Mismatched curtains fill the windows. The properties are owned by lazylords, cashing in on students who need a roof and space for their extra beer fridge.

On the last house, the screen doors whips open, begging to crash off the hinges. A guy clamors down the front steps, car keys rattling in his hand. He sees me and stops. "Hey. You live here?"

"No." I pause, startled. I've gotten used to being invisible.

"Too bad." The guy's smile is full of straight white teeth. His dentist must be proud. "Where are you going?"

"Home."

He shifts his head to the side, flips his hair. "You look familiar."

"You don't." But he does. He looks like he spends days at the gym and nights flossing. He's hot. Conventional farm boy hot. Ripped in the exact right places.

"I'm Chris." The guy switches his keys from one hand to the other and holds out his hand. We shake. Warm skin. Trimmed and shaped nails. He'll do.

"Lou." Archer would be pissed at how easily I give this guy my name.

I don't know why I do.

"Short for Louise?"

I hear Gin take a deep breath to launch into who exactly gets to call me Louise. I clamp her down. "Lou is fine."

"Yeah." Chris steps closer. "She is."

"Seriously? Has that line ever worked for you?"

Chris' face is rosy. Shame looks good on him. "That was bad."

"Extremely." I don't move.

"I'm going to a party." Chris points to a Chevy pickup parked on the street. Of course he drives a pickup. Of course it's cherry red. "You wanna come?"

Ax Annabella and Archer, and the day sucked. The week sucked. Everything's sucked for a long time. And a cold beer would taste good.

"Let's go."

My underwear is on backwards. Cocktails mixed in a cooler in a bathtub gave me the spins last night, but now the front of my underwear pinched my ass until I woke up.

I look at Chris. He's drooling into his pillow, out so hard he might not come to until noon. He'd been good. That's probably all that could be said for me either. It was consensual. It scratched an itch.

Never mind. I rocked his world.

Shame looks good on me too.

Dawn peeks around his curtain (a faded Vikings sheet with a tiny purple helmet pattern that I bet his mom picked up from K-Mart when he was in third grade) and I wiggle on my shorts and tank. The condom wrapper landed in my sneaker. There's a souvenir. Oof.

Clothed, I sneak out the bedroom door. Chris rolls, stuffing my pillow under his arm.

I open the fridge in the kitchen (not the beer fridge—that's a classy addition to the living room) and grab a sports drink. The screen door slams when I leave, and I don't try to stop it.

Campus is quiet in the blue light. Cold, lonely. The Campanile stretches to the blank sky, its bricks gray without bright sunlight.

I hope Annabella crashed at Archer's.

Though I've had plenty of practice at going undetected lately. A life hack I picked up this cursed summer: how to slip into a house, or past a carousel, without bringing attention to yourself when your ex-best friend and ex-boyfriend are kissing. Tiptoeing is pointless. The key is to walk with your whole foot, quickly, like a ghost and barge in on the kissing people before they have time to present excuses.

Not that I care about kissing. Ginny and Milo make way more sense than Lou and Milo ever did. My two favorite people—of course there's a love connection. It tracks.

It's that the kissing was why she wanted me to call her back. Like it was the only thing worth catching up on.

Ginny used to be more than Milo's girlfriend. She loves the way light filters through neon green leaves in June. She sits under the oak in her backyard and stares up, trying to describe how the veins meander through each leaf differently, the way each snowflake is new. She loves her dad's blueberry scones. Says the crystallized sugar smells like life. She shuddered when I picked out lipstick for her. She hates loud engines on too-big trucks and olive as a color and olives as a food. Her bed is warmer than mine. She cheats on choose-your-own adventure books, not to get the happiest ending, but to find the intriguing plot. Ginny's a writer—she's always looking for the best story.

She got the story, in the end.

I don't care that she fell in love with my ex-boyfriend. I care that I hadn't talked to her in two weeks when Mom died. I care that I couldn't hide in her house as they took Mom's body away. I care that she never showed up after.

I care that being a best friend, to her, was conditional.

~

Annabella pops her head up like a chipmunk from her loft, her hair swaying like a not-evil Medusa when I walk in. She's as disheveled as a brunette Barbie who spent the better part of her life on her Malibu Dream House's floor in mismatched clothes and missing a shoe. But she's not the one hungover as hell. "Busted."

So, so busted.

"You didn't text."

"I told you I wasn't going to." I take off my shorts and climb up the side of my loft. Our beds are perpendicular, squashed into the far corner of the room. Annabella's head is two feet from mine.

She flips to her stomach. "I know you didn't, but I hoped you would."

"I got distracted."

"That's one way to put it." Annabella pulls her phone from under her pillow, scrolls, and shoves it in front of my face. "Dancing. On probation!"

I vaguely recall smutty house party dancing. Somebody boosted me onto a kitchen island with Chris and his gyrating hips. His hips bounced off my ass and reverberated deep in my bones, and it felt good. Later in bed, he and his hips did the same move, and I have no regrets. "Where's this posted?"

"TikTok. You went to a frat party?" Annabella stashes her phone under her pillow. "Who's the guy?"

My throat hurts. I should've brought water to bed. "His name is Chris. I met him walking home."

"And...partied with him?"

Oh, Annabella. More than partied. He has a scar on his left pec. It isn't sexy or anything, it's just a scar, probably from a fight with a house cat or he was drunk and fancied himself an MMA fighter. Now it's all I see behind my closed lids. A stranger's scarred up pec. "You think Coach will see the TikTok?"

"Do I think she peruses apps she's never heard of, antsy to bust her student athletes? No." Annabella throws her hands over her head. They bounce off her mattress and jiggle mine. "Do I think she's got binoculars focused on you right now? Yes." She sighs dramatically. "You know, at first I wasn't sure about our room set up, with my head close to yours, but I like it right now. I can be the angel or the devil on your shoulder, metaphorically."

"Sort of literally, even." I picture Annabella perched on my shoulder under a halo and Party City angel wings. A tiny Annabella yanking my hair until I make the right decision would probably be helpful.

"We'll call this the Meeting of the Minds," Annabella decides. "Where advice is given and received."

"I feel like you have advice you'd like me to receive right this second."

"Funny, I do. Call the therapist Monday. Right away. Not because you had a random hook up—you do you—but because Coach told you to."

My pillow is cradling my head just right. This is a tomorrow problem. "I promise."

"You mean it?"

"Yes." I roll to the wall.

"I'm pretending you're returning my pinky promise right now." The sun slants into our room to perfectly project the shadow of Annabella's outstretched arm and extended pinky next to my face. She wiggles her pinky in and out for dramatic effect, and her shadow dances along.

"It looks like a horny hummingbird."

"You look like a horny hummingbird."

I yank my pillow from under my head and smash it into Annabella's giggling face.

~

Dr. Stellan picks up her phone on the second ring, and in a no-nonsense, but tiny, sweet voice confirms 9:45 Tuesday morning literally has my name written all over it on her calendar. "I'm looking forward to hearing your story, Louise."

Makes one of us, Dr. Stellan.

Her office is on the edge of campus, tucked on the third floor of an ancient, forgotten dormitory that allegedly once housed professors who didn't want to be found. And it's haunted. It's fitting that Student Health is hidden. Shame in shadows, and whatnot.

There's no elevator, because why would there be in a building constructed when buffalo still roamed the prairie? I take the steps two at a time. The squad is east of campus running a dried-up creek bed. Maybe this is Coach's actual plan—make me run steps as punishment and talk to someone. Endurance over pace. She is brilliant. (And the worst).

Dr. Stellan meets me in her office's doorway. "Oh! You're early. And you're not even winded." She nestles an aqua mug in her hands like a newborn baby, the tea bag string between her knuckles. "I need to do more endurance training. How is this building ADA compliant? Spoiler: it's not." She smiles, teeth all the way back to her tonsils. She's young. Only a decade older than me.

A clipboard with a questionnaire is placed into my hands. "I ask that you fill this out before we begin. I want to know a little about you before we get started. If a question is uncomfortable, skip it." Dr. Stellan grabs a pen. "Take your time. I'll warm my tea. Do you need anything?"

I sink into the couch. "No."

"Give me just a second."

I scan my survey, and fill in what I want, per instructions.

Age: 18

Year: Freshman

Referral?: Against my will.

Why Are You Here: Coach forced me.

Are you a harm to yourself or anyone else?: No

At least there's that.

When Dr. Stellan comes back, I'm doodling on the survey, less than half the questions answered. The margins feature a wave pattern corner to corner across the top. I'm layering in sea foam with a spray of dots, and thinking about adding a mermaid, but a mermaid could signify something major to set off Dr. Stellan's therapist-Spidey-sense. Like drowning. Or swimming. Or escape from this life into something else.

Steam spirals from Dr. Stellan's mug as she reads my answers. She looks like a coffee commercial from the nineties, with the sunlight flooding in from the ancient windows backlighting her chair. The best part of waking up.

I look around while she (probably) reads into my waves.

An ancient radiator coated in chipped white paint gurgles, with an empty bucket underneath to catch drips. I bet it bangs like a drum major when frost lines the windows. Yellow seems to be Dr. Stellan's comfort color. Golden throw pillows with white fringe sit sunny on the couch. Butter-tinted curtains trap the cheer and hold it ransom. A cozy yellow Chevron-patterned blanket is tossed on the couch arm casually, like she didn't karate chop the folds into place as I huffed up the steps. Clearly a millennial, even her flats are velvet mustard, I see as I perch on the couch cushion, the best student in class. Her legs are crossed at the knee; I sit with my heels pressed to the floor. "Louise," Dr. Stellan opens. "What do you prefer I call you?"

The name question. Always the name question. I've never said my own name more than I have here. "Lou."

"Lou," she repeats, her voice sweet, like a cartoon princess. Do woodland creatures follow her home from her runs? "Call me Meghan. I try to keep it casual."

"Is it because you're not really a doctor?" I blurt. The yellow is disorienting. I feel trapped on a yellow brick road from hell.

"I'm a real doctor." Meghan doesn't sound mad, or surprised. She points to the wall behind me and lo and behold, framed diplomas, the PhD dated last May. While I was losing my mom and best friend and myself and self-medicating with dumb boys in humid basements at boring parties, Meghan was productive with her life. Good for her.

"I'm new to campus. Still learning my way around." Meghan sips her tea. "Liz was a wonderful friend to me right out of the gate. When I moved to town, I looked for running groups, and Liz reached out to me."

"Liz?"

"Coach Stevens, sorry." Meghan sets her mug on her end table. It holds a succulent and a miniature gold-leaf picture frame featuring a cat with gray eyes staring into my soul. She's a cat lady. Makes sense. "You're new to town too, right? Freshman?"

I bob my head.

"Do you live in the dorms?"

Another bob.

"With a roommate?"

BobBobBob.

"What's her name?"

Annabella wished me luck this morning, as she bounced off to run the creek bed. She seemed free, heading out alone. "You're going to your appointment, right?" she'd said. I hummed confirmation from my bed, and she lunged at me, her right pinky extended. "I need you to pinky swear it, Lou. It's the only way."

We linked pinkies, and Annabella nodded hard. "Horny hummingbird for takeoff."

"Annabella," I answer Meghan. "She's on the squad with me."

"Are you getting along?"

"We are." I'm surprised to say it. I never imagined a roommate, outside of Ginny.

Meghan looks thoughtful. "Do you hang out with anyone else?"

Archer's face springs to mind, all crushed curls and pastel worksheets from hell. "No."

"It's still early in the semester."

Meghan's taking notes—pencil on loose-leaf paper in quick caps. It'll be like she's yelling back her thoughts at herself later. I can make out ANNABELLA upside down.

I crack my neck for release.

"Before we get too far, should we establish ground rules?"

"What do you mean?"

Meghan re-crosses her legs with the opposite foot in the air. "We need to decide what our goal is during our conversations. Are you struggling with time management? Are you thinking this university, or the team, isn't the right fit for you? Or do you have an outside issue that we need to work out together?"

I frown. "How much do you know about me?"

"Just what Coach Stevens has shared. You had a panic attack during a meet. You aren't connecting with anyone outside of your roommate."

"How much of what we discuss will be reported back to Coach?"

"Absolutely nothing. Every single thing you say in this room is confidential, Lou." Meghan's eyes bore into me. "This isn't a spy mission. I'm not on Coach Stevens' payroll. I'm here for you. The only thing I'll ever tell her is confirmation that you show up."

I stare at her. I know the pastel pillows and the tea and the sunny space is supposed to make me trust her. It's a strategy. People have a hard time unloading to therapists. Hey, stranger with letters behind your name—listen to my story and put me pack together, please.

Meghan sits and looks back. Not rudely or anything. Gently. Like Princess Ariel, post Ursula-human-legs-black-magic. She'll wait. She'll wait all day. Or at least to the end of the hour.

Talking to a Disney princess probably isn't the worst.

"Do you want to get started?" Meghan asks.

Bob.

Bob. Bob.

CHAPTER 6

I DON'T TRAIN AFTER MEGHAN'S APPOINTMENT.

By dinner I regret it, especially when Annabella rolls in, her limbs languid like she had the most relaxing run of her life.

At bedtime, she's crawling up her bed, Bible in hand, and turns on her mini booklight. "Will this bother you? I can go to the lobby to read."

"No." I collapse into my pillow stash like my exhaustion is real. "You're fine." And she is; the room could be pitch black and I wouldn't sleep for hours. Meghan and her tea cup and her laugh that sounds like glitter click through my head on a reel. I wish I would have run her off today.

But I didn't. And now Annabella's light is long off and it's midnight and I'm staring at the place on the wall that I know the sun will touch in the morning, telling me when it's socially acceptable to rise.

I dig my phone from my quilt and Google "signs you have depression." Butterflies scale my throat — know the answer, but I make the internet give me hints anyway.

Sign 1: Do you make impulsive decisions you might not have a year ago?

Chris is the only face I remember, and that's because he was recent. There are other faces though, rejected by my memory, marked only by their universal scent of smoke and sunscreen.

Sign 7: Do you have problems sitting still?

One night I walked home in a pair of six-dollar Old Navy flip flops I stole from a girl passed out on the couch because it was too dark to find my Toms. I literally ran home in a stranger's shoes.

The last question is a total dick:

Sign 15: Do you worry non-stop about unrealistic consequences for minor problems?

Who doesn't? Mom took an Ambien every night. And a blood thinner every morning with her Earl Grey. I worried that she would fall asleep in her nightly bath. Or drive to the grocery store and hit a stray toddler or an old lady in the crosswalk. Or find out that Dad is sleeping with yet another woman. Or bake my favorite snickerdoodles to make me happy and forget the oven and burn down the house and I would notice Ginny watching the rest of my world burn from her side of the street and do nothing and then—

The reality is worse. I worried Mom would forget that her blood thinner makes it easier to bleed out, faster. When she started tracing her old scars from her college days, etched along her wrist when she thought I wasn't watching. When she stopped tracing her veins with her fingertips, and replaced her nails with the knife she used to slice my apples into wedges with, well.

Minor problems. Yeah.

Depression is a bird's nest of tangled, sinewy sticks and weeds weaved in soggy mud and bird crap. I watched Mom. She swayed her like she was on a deck that wasn't rooted to the lake bottom.

And it took her.

If Meghan's doling out diagnoses, I hope for anxiety. A few wires are crossed, and little pills will pull them off my brain, taut, straighten them into a neat pattern to match normal brain wires, gently pat me back together, and send me on my way.

If I am treated for anxiety, hopefully that will keep the depression away. It seems, to me, that one precedes the other: a root to the tree. If I get the anxiety calmed, maybe the depression won't find a way to grow, and I'll never have to talk about finding my mother in the bathtub.

Probably not how this works.

After two sessions, Meghan prescribes me Xanax. "Grab it in the Student Health pharmacy downstairs when we're done. Do you have questions?"

I shake my head, Meghan releases me to the pharmacy, and I find myself at the dorm without remembering the walk over.

We left our windows open back in the dorm. The blinds rise and drift down with the cool breeze like the room is breathing. I make sure Annabella is gone and pull the orange bottle from the envelope. The pills are white, with miniscule numbers stamped on the top. I study the tiny valley carved right down the middle for longer than necessary. Stop being dramatic, I command. Mom started these when you were seven. Same pill, higher dose. I ignore the chalky, sour casing and reach for my cold tea from the morning.

I picture Meghan flipping open my skull and pulling my rogue brain wires straight with her rose-colored fingernails. The pill tastes foul. Tomorrow, I'll take it with hot tea. I tuck the orange bottle in my backpack drawer.

"Now, I wait," I say aloud to no one.

~

Fresh from French, my stomach growls as I unlock our dorm room. "Hey, do you wanna get—"

Annabella has a guest. They sit close on the futon, hands on shoulders, knees crooked over laps. Annabella's head rocks back when I walk in. They'd been kissing.

The drawer of the flower heart.

The one whose heart blooms.

She's a girl.

I shut the door.

"Hi." I drop my bag on my desk, attempting nonchalance and landing in the neighborhood of weirdo. The heavy undercurrent of sexual tension is about to engulf the room. And I galloped right in. "I came back to study and grab dinner, but I can go to the library."

"No, this is your room too, right?" The mystery girl smiles, her brown curls tumbling over her shoulders. Big, fat barrel curls combed out—the product of a curling iron and great hairspray. I haven't done my hair since I moved here, but it would probably break off in chunks from the bleach. My heart pangs. I miss my blowouts. They made me feel like the baddest bitch. "I'm Zoey."

"Lou." I need a nametag.

Zoey waits for one of us to speak. I fiddle with my backpack. Annabella's eyes are big enough to fall out of her face. "Do you need a Xanax? I just got a prescription for it."

The dam breaks. Annabella's laugh fills the room. Zoey exhales and pulls Annabella to her feet, and I trail them out the door into the early October twilight to dinner. Why was she nervous to tell me?

What makes us whole is terrifying to announce, Ginny whispers.

~

I like the sounds Archer makes as we walk to class. His shoes scrape the sidewalk as he drags his right heel harder than his left. Matilda's case rubs against his hoodie of the day in a swoosh. His car keys jangle in his right pocket. The tiny melody of whatever he's listening to before I walk up leaks from the headphones bouncing along his collar.

Outside of hello, he never speaks first. He lets me determine the rhythm of conversation, and we go from there.

And once I start talking, I can't stop. I want to know if he chugs his Americanos from the coffee shop because they burn the coffee, and why his sweatshirts have chewed-on cuffs. Why he doesn't seem to believe in regular haircuts, and why he toasts his Pop-Tarts like a heathen with a perpetually scorched mouth. I want to watch his smile lift first on the right side, and find out what's funny enough to make his nose crinkle in a laugh.

When I don't see Archer in the Union, I wait as long as I can. My chamomile tea cold and with only a few minutes to spare, I dart to Wellness alone, my tea sloshing in the cup. Where is he?

As the TA closes the door to start class and I stare at Archer's empty chair, he rushes in, clutching a pile of papers. The edges ruffle out like an already-read newspaper.

"Nice to see you today, Archer." The TA's tone is dry as she sticks a pencil in her bun.

"Thanks! I shamelessly used your code on the copy machine in the work room."

She rolls her eyes and starts passing out worksheets.

Archer slides the first paper off his pile and slaps it on the table in front of me. He beams, waiting for my reaction.

It's a lime-colored flier. Clearly, he got into the TA's paper stash too. "Battle of the Songwriters. Sing, sing, sing!" I look up. "Are you...singing?"

"I am." Archer's wound up, as if someone pulled his string and he's spinning away. His hair is pointing to the right, and I imagine him next to the copier, waiting for the machine to spit out these flyers, and him tugging his hair with his hand and tapping his foot. "When you sign up, you promise to market it, and social media will be overrun with ads for this, so I decided to go the old-fashioned way."

"You'll be great." I put the flier back on top of his pile. Ginny read her work at the open mics at her dad's coffee shop. She's a prolific writer, but it was easier to read Ginny's work than listen to Ginny read it. I have no idea how—it lost her voice, when it was her voice reading. Though, I was the only half-listening because I was surveying the crowd, ready to take out anyone who smirked out of turn while Ginny read.

Archer gives me the highlighter green flier again. "This is for you. I want you to come."

"Archer—"

"Please?" He interrupts earnestly. "You haven't seen me play. I know I just learned your name, but we might be friends, and it's important to me that if we continue to grow our relationship you see this part of me."

"Grow our relationship?" I latch onto his awkward wording to distract him. "Is this a dating app?"

Archer leans in. Not too close. But closer than he ever has. "Do you want it to be?"

The air crackles.

I clear my throat. "What would it be called, Romeo?"

"Give Your Local Singer/Songwriter a Chance."

"You'll need to make that an acronym." The TA drops her last two worksheets in front of us, clamoring into our spell. "First, fill out questions about average and spiking heart rates, then proceed with flirting."

Archer blushes to his ears.

I smile and write my name at the top of the worksheet. "Are you good? Annabella says you are."

"Annabella can't lie. Catholicism prohibits it." Archer doesn't bother to start his worksheet. He taps his pencil's eraser on his bottom lip. "But yes. I am. The show's a week from Saturday. Please come."

Standing shoulder to shoulder in a cramped all-ages bar downtown. Sweaty people swaying on hard concrete to off-tune singing about first love and high school exes. Hard pass.

But sitting in Wellness 101 now? Archer's bottom lip slips between his teeth. His foot slowly knocks against my chair. The vibration sends blood zipping through my veins. I want to get up and run a 100-yard dash with this new-found electricity.

Speaking of spiking heart rates.

"Okay," I agree. "I will."

~

I begin my loop around campus, trying, and failing, to forget the way Archer's side gaze pulled the blush to my cheeks. He spent the rest of class looking at me like I'm a Picasso and all my features are in the wrong place, but he doesn't care, because the painting is still whole.

I'm going to need a cold shower after every Wellness 101 class.

He's cute.

I'm not on the market, Gin.

He could write a song about you. He probably already has written a song about you.

He has a tattoo dedicated to a pretty recent ex. I'm a disaster on day twelve of Xanax.

Maybe that's the best place to be.

Says the girl who's fucking my ex-boyfriend. Seriously?

It's harsh. I don't mean it. But it makes her voice evaporate.

I want to apologize immediately.

"Hey! Lou, right?" Thumping footsteps bang up behind me.

A scream dies in my throat when I see it's only Chris. I skid to a stop, my breath out of whack. "Jesus. Not a chill way to approach a girl."

Chris waves to the direction he'd come from. "I yelled your name from across the street. You weren't stopping." He steps closer, peers at my ears. "Are you wearing ear buds? You looked like you were talking to someone."

I wipe sweat from my cheeks. "What do you want?"

"You ran out of my room the other morning." His hips are inches from mine. A nice hip cut lurks under his jeans and hoodie, and it'd been fun to press my thumbs against his skin right there, but the way he snuck up on me makes his hips approximately 85% less alluring. "I was gonna ask you to breakfast."

"Were you?" His hair is lighter than I remember. In the sun it's blonde. Dark blonde, but blonde, and crunchy from too much gel.

"Yes!" The word is forceful. "I wish you hadn't left."

"Okay. Well." I turn back to the direction I want to go. "Thanks for saying you would have bought me a muffin, or whatever."

I take off before he gets another word in and cut across a parking lot for extra space between us.

He's not cute.

Maybe earbuds will tune her out too.

CHAPTER 7

"DAY FOURTEEN OF XANAX." MEGHAN'S TEA SMELLS LIKE berries today. "Having any side effects? It can cause drowsiness, for starters. If you're experiencing anything, tell me."

"I'm okay."

She looks at me for a beat. "If that changes, let me know."

I nod.

"So last time, we talked about the transition of moving into the dorms, getting to know Annabella, adjusting to life away from home." Meghan is ready to needle at my deepest, darkest scars. I imagine her cracking her knuckles, ready to peel back my drama, my trauma. "I'd like to hear about your parents today."

"Why?" I'm being obtuse. I won't blame it on my parents, but Mom's Xanax prescription was twice as strong as mine, and Dad wouldn't have realized she sought treatment if health insurance statements weren't emailed to him once a month. They were barely friends, let alone married.

"What do they do?" Meghan presses by my question. "Were they young parents? Older parents? Have you talked to them since you started classes?"

Here we go.

"No. Dad's in real estate. He's never home." Dad fielded phone calls from clients the day he moved me to campus. He told them why he was unavailable, making me the burden, rather than the Bluetooth beeping on the speaker the entire drive. "He specializes in wealth management properties. He sold this insane lakefront property that's in architecture magazines to my ex-boyfriend's parents last year. If I wasn't here on scholarship, that sale alone would've paid for this semester."

"What about your mom?"

"She's dead."

Meghan blinks. "I'm sorry to hear that. When did she pass?"

"The day I graduated from high school. A few hours before the ceremony." That's what the coroner estimated. I found her about twenty minutes before I was supposed to leave, frantic because my hair was half done.

"Oh." Meghan's finger twitches. She stills it on her knee.

"It was suicide." I know she wants to ask. "She'd been cutting herself again. You can write that down if you want."

"No need." Meghan scoops up her paper and pen and drops them to the floor.

I pull an overstuffed yellow throw pillow into my lap. "Dad and I aren't close. Mom had her own prescription for Xanax. She slept a lot."

"You said last time you're an only child."

"Yes."

"It sounds like your Dad isn't always available to you." Meghan shifts in her chair. "Who is your support system?"

"Deep breaths, sweetheart," Mom says, twirling a lock of my hair around her finger. "I'm right here." We're on the kitchen floor. Ginny's driven away now, taking her giggles with her.

I look down. My hand is in Mom's. I pretend I can't tell her knuckles from mine, but I can.

"Should we order dinner in? I can make snickerdoodles, and you can pick a movie. Your father is in Cincinnati until Thursday."

We both know Cincinnati is code for Marissa, Dad's new secretary.

I nod, and move to stand, but Mom holds on. "This is nice," she says. "Let's stay here another minute."

"My mom was." My nails jab deep into the pillow and it puffs out around tiny half-moon welts in the fabric.

"Who else?" Meghan's voice is soft. "You mentioned an ex-boyfriend a minute ago."

I shake my head.

"What about friends?"

Double headshake, short, but so aggressive I have to tuck my hair behind my ears again. My hands ache from squeezing the pillow. I let it go, and it begins to fluff out around the ripple.

Meghan watches me. "Do you want to sit with me in the quiet? You can read or do homework, or just close your eyes and I'll sit at my desk and catch up on charting. It's a beautiful day. I'll open the windows."

I press my palm flat into the pillow to hide the new scar. Meghan pushes the window up, and earthy caught-in-a-sunbeam air blows life into the room.

~

"Meghan gave me this," I slide the worksheet across the table to Annabella. Turns out freshman year is reduced to a collection of Easter egg-colored worksheets. This one's delicately titled TURNING UNHEALTHY COPING STRATEGIES INTO HEALTHY OPPORTUNITIES.

Annabella reads it and munches on a French fry. She met me at the diner after her Wednesday Bible study. The good book tilts out of her bag next to her hip. It's leather bound, with wildflowers engraved in the middle of the cover. "Is Meghan suggesting you have unhealthy coping strategies?"

"Shocking, right?"

"Are you going to fill it out?" Annabella doesn't look from the sheet and feels around the table until she finds her cheeseburger for a bite. "Or do you have to fill it out?"

"It's mandatory." I push my empty plate to the end of the table. "We're going to use it as a kick-off for our conversation on Tuesday."

Annabella hands me the worksheet. "Make a copy of it before you start it. We can give it to Archer and have him realign his priorities."

"What do you mean?" Outside of his drop-everything-to-sing-about-feelings schtick, Archer seems like he has his shit together.

"Dude's only going to one class right now. Spending his time holed up in his apartment songwriting. And planning that Singer/Songwriter showcase."

I stuff my worksheet in my bag. "Are you going?"

She bounces back in her seat, eating another fry. "I genuinely do want to, but it's cute you think I have a choice."

"Can I..." Oof, this is hard. "Can I go with you?"

Annabella's lips twist together. She looks like she's in on a secret. "You most certainly may."

Too late, I remember Zoey. "I mean, unless you and Zoey are making it a date."

Annabella's smile is small. "That's nice of you to say. Zoey's going to school in Minneapolis. She's a sophomore in their pre-pharm program. Or, like, bio-chem right now, but she's into pharmacology too. She was home over the weekend to visit her family and she came up to see me."

"Long distance. That's hard." Like I have any idea. "How did you meet?"

Annabella looks at her plate.

"You don't have to share—" God, making friends is hard.

"No one's ever asked me that." Annabella looks up, her eyes clear. "You and Archer are the only ones who know about us, and Archer was with me when I met Zoey."

"Oh?" I try hard, but fail, at a casual tone.

"My family knows I'm a lesbian," Annabella fills in quickly. "They just don't know that I'm with her. They've never met." Her wince crinkles up to her eye. "It's one thing for a Catholic mother to accept the abstract. It's another for the proof to be asking her to pass the pepper at dinner."

"Oh."

"It was at a concert, by the way," Annabella continues. "A Christian folk show in downtown Sioux Falls. Zoey was there with her youth group, and Arch begged me to go. I don't remember where Cadence was—maybe she met us later? Anyway. It was like a movie. Eyes locking across a room." Annabella's cheeks are pink. "It was perfect."

I file Cadence's name away. "Sounds like the best rom-com."

"It was." Annabella clears her throat, a sign, I'm learning, that she's antsy to change subjects. "Archer likes you. But you know that."

I stay quiet.

"He put his whole heart in pretty quickly," Annabella says. "It takes him a long time to decide he likes someone. And it didn't this time, with you. He blinked and now it's Lou-time, all the time."

I know. I have for weeks, as Archer sinks in under my skin and I've carried him around. Gotten used to the way his eyes reflect in my memory, and how I can already pick his steps out of everyone else's on the sidewalk.

Annabella funnels air in through her lips. "I'm telling you this for your sake. You can get out now, if you want."

"Thank you?"

"I really like you." Annabella sits up, waving away my glib response. "I'm glad we're roommates." She sticks another fry in her mouth. "Don't mess around with my best friend and his heart."

I stick my pinky up to her. "I won't mess him up. If things get weird, I'll bail."

"Well, don't ghost us either," Annabella hooks her pinkie through mine and holds on tight. "I like having you around."

Later, Annabella and I lay in our beds under the covers, our heads at the perpendicular axis. I'm scrolling aimlessly, shopping for a new pair of cleats. As if new shoes can earn me my place back on the team. As if that's what I want. Annabella's reading light shines over her left shoulder, casting her shadow huge against the wall over the television.

She sighs, clicks the lamp off, and the Bible thumps shut. I hear it slip into the space between our beds.

"Can I tell you more about Zoey?" Annabella's voice is quiet; I think she's flat on her back. Her words aren't muffled.

"Yes." I tuck my phone under my pillow. The only light in our room peeks through the blinds from the campus security lamps that line the sidewalk.

"She approached me first. That night, at the concert I told you about. She was braver than me. Still is. And she's warm, her skin, you know? No matter where we are, her skin is warm."

Annabella rustles and flips so her face points to the top of my head. "It was snowing. Arch was distracted by Cadence and Zoey came to say hi. She asked me to grab coffee. We walked to my car in the snow. The fat snowflake kind. You know?"

I do.

"We went to this coffee shop downtown that we both loved and had never seen each other at. And we sat in the window and watched snow pile up. We talked forever. About how free I feel when I run, about how she wants to help people feel comfortable in their own bodies. It was the most honest I'd ever been with anyone else except for Arch...and that took us years. It was instant with Zoey." Annabella murmurs. "I love her, and she loves me, and my parents don't know she exists."

"That's okay." My throat is tight. I hope I sound empathetic.

"It's not, Lou." Annabella says quietly. "I want them to know her, because to know her is like knowing part of me. I want them to know Zoey. I want my sister to know Zoey."

"What's stopping you?"

"My dad's a doctor. My mom stayed at home all these years. Supporting us, and the Church. The community that she holds close to her heart is already side-eyeing her because of me..." Annabella flips, and I think she's facing the ceiling again. Words crowd in her throat, elbowing each other, tumbling out of order. Fighting to be heard. "Humans are nowhere as forgiving as we're called to be. And bringing a real girl home will make my mom suffer."

My hand darts under my pillow, crosses our mattresses, and lands on her shoulder. Annabella catches my fingers and holds on. "You aren't alone."

She grasps my hands. "Thank you. Neither are you."

~

Dad's missing, but what's new. Mom and I are still doing our annual Christmas Eve viewing of It's a Wonderful Life *on the couch. I snuggle into her shoulder and try to be enough as my phone buzzes under our blanket.*

MILO: *Come outside. I have your gift.*

I leap up and Mom laughs as the blanket parachutes back down over her lap. I picked earrings out with Gin around Thanksgiving: diamond studs. Perfect amount of sparkle and class.

Milo's on my front stoop, his cheeks ruddy from the chill. Mistletoe dangles from his fingertips above our heads. "Come here." He pulls me outside. "I'll keep you warm."

Clumpy snow falls in balls of glitter. One lands on his nose, and he pats it away with his mitten. Giggling, I unzip his parka and burrow in and line his jaw with kisses. His stubble makes my knees weak. We're such adults with diamond earrings and faint five o'clock shadows. I can't wait to show off the diamonds in my track team group text: look how loved I am. How special I am. "Can I have my present?"

"I should have led with that." Milo rolls his eyes, but his smile doesn't waver. If anything, it gets bigger. Away goes the mistletoe, out comes a jewelry box with the store's logo stamped on top in gold foil. My heart takes flight. Exactly what I want.

"Don't get too excited. Consider this ... a promise, of sorts." He cracks open the box.

It's a ring. White gold, ten baby diamonds pressed into the band. Sparkles like the snow.

This isn't what I asked for. This isn't it at all.

My lungs crumple, then shut.

Milo mistakes my silence for glee. He slides it on my right ring finger; it fits perfectly. How does he know my ring size?

Gin. I look across the street. She's framed in her bedroom window, gleeful. She sees me see her and drops to the floor.

"...wear it however you want, babe. No pressure." Milo's hands shake. Of course there's pressure. You don't hand out diamond rings without wanting something in return.

I send Milo home promising I'll call later. In the house, Mom's at the part in the movie where George hurries to the bridge and begs the angel for his life back. "Come show me your earrings!"

I pretend I don't hear her and dash upstairs.

My heart is banging. It tries to squeeze between each rib and send every drop of blood to my head, all at once. I sink to the carpet and shove the ring box under my mattress and press my cheek to the carpet and tears stream and I don't know who to call or what to do or how to get up and I stay there by myself on my bedroom floor.

My first panic attack.

Desperate.

Sad.

Alone.

CHAPTER 8

RIGHT ON TIME, ARCHER SWINGS IN NEXT TO ME ON THE sidewalk outside the Union pointed to the Wellness Center. "Lou," he says, hiking Matilda up his shoulder. "How's your morning?"

"Fine." Dream or memory or maybe both, the aftermath of Milo and the ring hangs low and too close. At least Ginny hasn't chimed in yet. "Yours?"

"Good, now." Our steps match all the way to class.

Our TA drops the worksheet of the day on our tables. Today, burnt orange. The pumpkin spice of worksheets. "Hope you did your reading for today," she's saying, her voice bored. "Important topic."

"Did you read it?" Archer stage whispers in my direction.

I shake my head. My worksheet floats down like an autumn leaf and I flip it over: Mental Health and You. Down deep, my stomach twists, and I know what I'm going to see before my eyes get to the next line. Buzzwords: Stigma. Experience. Awareness. Condition. The national suicide awareness hotline.

Her blood has been out of her body long enough to be maroon, garish on her pale skin. Most of it slid into the bath water, but one wrist still floats, the gash pointed to the ceiling.

I'm halfway to the Wellness Center's front door before I realize I left.

Archer skids out behind me and Matilda's case bangs into the doorframe. "Hey, hey, hey." His voice is too loud. The sun is too bright. Every nerve feels like it's trying to slither out of me.

"Can you say something, please?"

My skin is still trying to turn itself inside out. And his voice is far away, but my focus lands on his 'please' and, for now, it tethers me to gravity. "Archer."

"Yes?" He pops into my line of vision, wired, like his pants are on fire.

"Take me off campus," I say.

Archer's eyebrows squish together. "Okay."

I don't mind when he grabs my hoodie sleeve and pulls me along behind him.

Bumper stickers layer Archer's Bronco's dimpled back bumper. Hobo Day - Get Crunk! Obama: Dare to Hope. Make Music, Not War! Songwriters Do It Best.

I'm sure they do, Archer.

He beats me to the passenger side and jiggles the door until it gives. "She's old. She needs a special touch."

"Exactly how old?" I toss my bag inside and climb in while Archer circles the hood and gets in the driver's seat. He lovingly sets Matilda in the backseat.

"Don't be an ageist." The Bronco roars to life with the key turn. "Good girl," he pats the dashboard. "She's is a young 22 years old."

The walk to the parking lot was long enough to steady my breaths. Focusing on a conversation is hard, but getting easier with each sentence. "This thing is old enough to drink?"

"She prefers to be filled half a tank at a time, but yes." Archer backs out of his spot. "Where to?"

"Just drive around." I crank the window down. Air. I need air.

"Can do." Archer turns right out of the parking lot, and we drive past rows of dorms, buildings full of classes, and the horse stables. On the highway, Archer accelerates and the engine thunders like it might crash into the road. I twist to feel air rush over my forehead into my hair.

Miles and minutes pass. I peek back at Archer and he drives with his right wrist at noon and his left hand dangles out his window. Sun glints off his skin and black t-shirt and I want to scoot to him, but I blink and see bathwater and I stay put. I need distraction. "How do you and Annabella know each other so well?"

"We dated," Archer calls over the wind.

"What?" Found my distraction. "But—"

"True story." Archer looks down the highway at the wide-open space. "AB began to realize it about herself the same time we dated. We kissed once. It was the weirdest experience of my life. And hers too, she said. We were fifteen, anyway. We were kids."

Aren't we still, I want to ask, knowing the answer is a resounding no.

"We were always close friends, and we lasted like two whole weeks as a couple. We broke up at our freshman homecoming dance. Very dramatic," he says, and if I could laugh, I would. "That night I missed talking to her before bed. It was my favorite thing about dating her—her voice in my ear, at night. That's when secrets are exchanged, you know? The most intimate things are said, the paths to hearts laid. I called her to say goodnight anyway. And she still picked up."

"Anyway. She met Zoey. I was with Cadence for years." His fingers bend over the steering wheel as we zip past a combine harvesting in the field. Dust churns around the combine's tires. The sun is turning the sky pale blue, and Archer squints into the light. "So do you want me to ask what made you sprint out of the classroom like your hair was on fire, or do you not want to talk about it?"

I blink. For a minute, I'd forgotten. It was the most peaceful I'd felt in weeks, getting a snippet of Annabella and Archer's origin story. But of course he'd wonder. How could he not?

I open my mouth to spill it, all of it, and he glances at me, his gaze drifting to my mouth. His lips curve upward and he looks back to the road, taps the brake, and hits the blinker. There's a gravel lot ahead, just off the highway, with a tin building on one side. "I'll buy you lunch," he sings, and a smile trips onto my face. We leave my mom and Ginny in the rearview, for just a second.

"It's a bar!" I slide out of the Bronco. "Will they let us in?"

Archer digs his heels into the gravel and yanks the rusted metal door open. "They don't card. And it's quiet. I've done a couple gigs here."

Inside is a typical roadside bar lined with stools, liquor, and keg pulls. Tables, dart boards, and a pool table fill the back. A handful of people mill about, and sunshine struggles through the cloudy front window. It's trashy and smells like several generations of cigarette smoke.

It's exactly what I need.

"Cheeseburger and fries?" Archer asks me. I nod and sit in a metal café chair.

He catches the bartender's eye. "Bill, can we have two cheeseburgers, fries, and Cokes?" Bill nods and walks to the kitchen.

"So," Archer segues back into our conversation, sitting across from me. "You don't have to tell me, but if you want to, I'm a fantastic listener."

"My mom took her life in May." Turns out that ripping the bandage off is easiest. Of course, that Band-Aid only applies to whoever I'm telling. I never got a Band-Aid. I never got anything to stop the bleeding. I would've needed a tourniquet. Or a time machine to stop her.

"Oh, wow." Archer hits the same facial expressions everyone does. "I'm so sorry."

"Thanks." Now's when it gets awkward: the how, the why, the did you know she might do it?

Archer tilts his head to his shoulder. "How are you?"

"What?"

"How are you?" he repeats. Bill sets down our Cokes in red plastic bar glasses, and moseys behind the bar again. "You sprinted from our classroom. I'm betting you're not great." Archer rips the top of the straw wrapper off, and pounds the bottom of it on the table so the straw flies out.

"I am...not great." I hand him my straw. "Do that trick again."

Archer does the trick again, and pops my straw in my Coke. "What trick?"

I smile. He smiles back.

In the back, someone breaks a cluster of balls on the pool table. The sound cracks through the bar. I take a deep breath. "Have you ever lost anyone?"

"Almost." He's got what's left of his straw wrapper folded between his fingers like an accordion. "Cadence. She's anorexic. Been in and out of hospitals for years."

"Shit."

"Shit, indeed." Archer blinks. "About two years ago, it got real. She was between hospital stays, but she was struggling to follow her care plan. She wasn't answering her phone, and I knew her mom was at work, so I stopped by her house." Another heavy blink. "She was unconscious on the couch."

He sets his accordion straw wrapper on the table. "She's getting by now. Healing. But her parents, her doctors, her psychologist, even Cadence... even me...we all thought it best for us to part ways." Archer looks up. The bottoms of his eyes are shiny. "It's interesting how a love you haven't experienced before changes you."

I want to reach over the table and touch him. I want to tell him that it isn't the love so much as the loss that does the changing. I want to run the pads of my thumbs over his jagged cuticles, and to watch his cheeks flush at my touch. I want, I want, I want.

Rather, I grip my hands together in my lap. "Yeah."

Bill drops our food off with no ceremony, the porcelain plates dingy gray from thousands of identical cheeseburgers. The fries gleam from the hot grease.

Archer takes a generous bite of burger. "Will you tell me something about you? Something silly?"

Gladly. "Do you want good silly or ugly silly?"

"The good. Always the good."

"My dance team did a routine last winter to "Levitating" by Dua Lipa. We performed at half-time during football games. We wore purple spandex bodysuits and the seniors got glittered hearts on our butts."

"Wait." Archer puts his burger down, his lips pursing with questions he doesn't have words for yet. A pickle is slipping out the side of his bun, someone sinks a pool ball in the back, and I feel the crinkle of his eyes sinking into the folds of my brain where I store my permanent memories. "A bunch of Midwestern girls dancing to Dua Lipa."

"Nay." I wave a fry in the air. "Seductively dancing to Dua Lipa. With sparkly hearts on our asses."

Archer points to the jukebox that's extremely unlikely to hold any pop music at all. "Care to recreate your dance team moves?"

I laugh. A genuine, loud laugh. It feels good. It feels beyond good. It feels...like I might be alive, again, someday. "No."

Archer sends me a playlist he enjoys when he's in a retrospective mood. "Does it have your music in it?" I ask, thumbing through it as we get close to campus.

"No. I want your introduction to my tunes at the showcase. Wowed by my stage presence, enraptured by my voice in person." He flips the blinker to the street in front of my dorm.

"You're really selling yourself."

Archer grins. "Somebody's gotta."

As I get out of the Bronco, he recommends Brandi Carlile's cover of "Heaven." "Sublime," he says, revving the engine as he pulls away.

Annabella's still in class, so I grab my earbuds and hit play on the playlist. Sufjan Stevens, Brandi Carlile, Alexi Murdoch, Lana Del Rey, Dalton Rogue, Bob Dylan, David Gray. Singer/songwriters up the wazoo. I prop my head up with a pillow on the futon and start at track one. Plucky, warm guitar strings, mixed with sad, floaty lyrics. Each song boasts a distinct personality, but molds into the next to tell a story. The story of Archer, as if he wrote himself.

I love it.

My phone screen flashes, yanking me from peace.

UNIDENTIFIED NUMBER: This is Chris! Is this Lou?

LOU: How did you get this number?

CREEPY CHRIS: A friend of a friend ... of a friend.

LOU: I need names.

CREEPY CHRIS: ...

The dots come, the dots go. I stand to stretch the ick away.

CREEPY CHRIS: My roommate's cousin's girlfriend is on your cross-country team. She got it from the team roster.

What. The. Fuck.

CREEPY CHRIS: I know I probably overstepped.

"Probably?" I pull my earbuds out. I don't want to associate the dreaminess of Archer's playlist with this mess.

CREEPY CHRIS: Let me take you to dinner to make up for it.

LOU: Absolutely not.

CREEPY CHRIS: Please?

LOU: Definitely not. Stop.

When Annabella gets back, I show her the texts. "Ew." She makes a face as she yanks her windbreaker over her head. "Guys are gross."

"Not all of them." I regret it as soon as I say it.

Annabella elbows me with a grin.

~

Meghan scans my phone screen as I hold it up to her. Her lips press into a thin line: I am vindicated.

"Well," Meghan curls her feet under her, her rose-colored, crushed-velvet, pointed-toe flats tucked beside her chair. They're new, I think. "Not a route I would have taken, but ... he did."

"He did." I click my phone off and shove it behind the yellow throw pillow.

"What are you going to do?"

"Ignore him. I told him to leave me alone. So what if we fucked once, you know?"

Meghan nods. "Sexual agency is important. Just because it happened one time doesn't mean it has to ever happen again."

"Why doesn't he get that?"

"I'm not defending him," she starts. "I don't love how he got your phone number—your teammate should not have done that—but people process rejection in a myriad of ways. He'll figure it out. In the meantime." She stares at me. I resist a smirk. "You are under no obligation to teach him how to accept no. Or do anything but say no, or ghost him, or say yes. Whatever you want to do."

"I've never had an adult give permission to ghost someone."

"I'm giving you permission to do what you want." Meghan's voice is mellow. "You owe nothing to anyone. Be careful with your body and mind, be respectful of his, have fun, do what you want."

That could open a thousand bad doors. I don't say it though. There's something bigger happening inside me anyway. It's been weighing in the back of my head to the point that sometimes I think I'm about to tip sideways. "Can I ask you something?"

Meghan nods, scooching her teacup to the middle of her end table.

I picture myself approaching the starting line, missing the start, and falling face first. "Am I depressed?"

Meghan's fingertips float from her teacup to her lap. "Yes, I believe so. I think you're suffering from acute anxiety and a bout of depression. Both are why I put you on Xanax. Still no side effects?" I shake my head as she shifts in her chair. "What do you think?"

My cheeks burn at the D-word. Depression. "I think you're right."

"Does that scare you?"

If anyone else asked me, it'd be like they stuck a fingernail in a peeled back scab to poke around. Meghan and her sunshine-soaked office and her blueberry tea and her velvet headband studded with fake pearls... I don't know how she'd know to find a scab, let alone peel it away.

"Do you want to think, and talk more about it next time?"

I nod.

She moves on like her diagnosis won't send me into a shame spiral. "Before we're done today, how did your homework go?" She sips her ever-present tea.

"It didn't." She's talking about my worksheet (WHO ARE YOU WHEN YOU'RE ANGRY?). "I blew it off."

"Tell me why." Still, with the super mellow voice.

I shrug. "I'm not here by my own volition. I guess this is my stand up to authority."

"You know I'm not grading them."

"What hinges on me doing them or not?"

"Lou," Meghan leans forward. Her foot oh-so-comfortably nestled under her thigh slides down and grazes her area rug. "This is part of treatment. It's part of the agreement."

Treatment. Agreement. Buzz words. "This isn't court-mandated. I have a larger say here." My blood begins to froth.

"You absolutely do," Meghan agrees. "But, again, this is part of treatment. You can't pick and choose, and decide when you're healed."

"And you can?"

Meghan tucks her bottom lip between her teeth. "Let's talk about why you don't want to do your worksheets. We can pivot to other directions of treatment."

"No." Steam rises in my ribcage. I hate this. All the times I hid my feelings. Tucking my mother into bed every night for a year. Dry heaving into my toilet with Milo's promise ring squished under my mattress. Pretending Dad's in Cincinnati and not across town with his secretary. "I want to do one thing my way. On my timeline. Just once."

"You have a scholarship, Lou. That goes away if the team goes away. And the team goes if you don't participate in treatment."

"So take it away!" And I don't care. I really don't. My skin is on fire, fueled by the blood boiling. I could ignite and burn down Student Health. Reduce it to ashes. I take it back: Meghan knows how to peel back scabs.

"Lou."

"Meghan. I. Don't. Care."

"What do you care about?"

Annabella.

Archer.

Running.

Ginny.

Not being alone.

Keeping my promise to Mom.

"Not these stupid worksheets," I say.

"We'll revisit our treatment plan next week," Meghan allows, and masterfully redirects the conversation. As if she took my body off the stovetop, my blood cools. She's quiet and I'm quiet and my emotions teeter back to the calm side. Meghan is kind with her dumb yellow curtains and yellow pillows and yellow flats. She's trying to help me. "Doing anything fun for Hobo Day? Going to the parade with Annabella?"

"Archer's showcase is tonight." I look out the window. The trees are rainbows of cheerful oranges and maroons. When I walk back to the dorm, I'll hear the marching band practicing for tomorrow's parade and football game, the thumps and horns whistling through the air. The drumline will crash through my lungs, puncture my heart and slop back out again without breaking stride. Perfect homecoming aesthetic.

Meghan folds her fingers together. "Can you try a new thing this weekend?"

I look at her. "What?"

"Find one thing that brings you peace," she says. "Lean in. Let it happen to you."

~

Peace. Lean in. Let it happen.

Sure. No problem. I step up the curb to cut through student parking. A wayward horn squeals from the football stadium, and I'm deeply thankful that cross country isn't supported by marching band.

My phone buzzes in my jacket pocket. I swear if it's Chris—

COACH: Come to my office. ASAP.

I swivel and jog to the Wellness Center. It would be a flat sprint, but knock-off moto boots slow me down. For a woman who hates the idea of teamwork and abiding by Coach's rules, I sure skid past the rows of lockers and crash into Coach's office door in a hurry.

Coach is at her desk. She's pressing her fingers into the back of her hands so tightly I can see the white imprints. Her wife's picture even glares at me. "You missed Wellness 101 yesterday."

I did not. I was there...long enough to leave. And probably make a commotion of it. I don't remember.

"What was more important than class?"

I want to say:

Avoiding graphic memories of my mother's death that sit under my eyelids.

Flirting with my roommate's best friend.

At a bar.

What tumbles out: "It won't happen again."

"Every class, McKinnley. Every. Class." Coach looks torn in half and I know what's happening.

"No. Please."

"Every class. It was the deal."

I scream and scream for my dad.

Later, after her body is gone, and the bathtub is drained, we sit elbow to elbow on the couch in the dark. I can't move to turn on the lamp right next to me. Dad twirls his wedding ring. "How long were you just standing over her?"

"I wasn't. I was screaming."

"You were not." His words are sharp, clipping into my numb bubble. "You were half in the tub, holding her. You should have left her and gotten me."

Dad stands. Leaves.

My bubble leaks from where he cut it open, all the feelings seeping out at once.

Coach's lips disappear. "I'm sorry. You're out, McKinnley."

I hate this. I hate her. I hate her. I deserve a chance. A place.

"Clean out your locker." Coach looks down, her hands still tied together.

Tears spill down my cheeks. Old Lou would hate this version of us. This crybaby. This sniveling mess.

Coach closes her office door when I trip backwards into the locker room. I sink to a bench. Girls crowd the mirrors drying their hair and misting too-sweet scents to their necks. I put my forehead on my knees, squeezing my nails into my palms. Angry crescent marks carve my skin. Something peachy sneaks into my nose and I curl tighter into myself. Squealed laughter rings off the concrete walls. Showers splash on. A hair dryer drones out words.

My head is too light. It could detach and float away. My tongue tastes like metal, my breath leaves me, glitter crowds my vision, and the panic takes over.

CHAPTER 9

I DON'T TELL ANNABELLA.

She's applying mascara and laughing with Zoey on Facetime when I walk in. She doesn't notice my lips are raw from my struggle to breathe on the gross locker room floor. She wouldn't know my teeth ache from clenching my jaw to muffle my sobs.

Coach got me water, at least. Told me she'd have my things ready for Annabella to bring me on Monday. She waited for my breath to come back, and sent me on my way.

Annabella curls the ends of her hair and moons over Zoey's face on her screen. I pull on black jeans and an old high school track team t-shirt and roll up the sleeves. The black moto boots go back on, I don't bother to comb out my hair knots, and I wait until Annabella blows a kiss at Zoey and announces she's ready.

Downtown, Annabella parks a block from the venue, a place called Gallerie, and we walk.

Past a sports bar, Annabella pauses at a black door right next to Gallerie's door front. Black paint peels off the wood like shedding skin. The brass doorknob is dingy from too many hands on it. She points up to the windows on the second floor. "Arch lives up there, over Gallerie. A tiny studio."

"Yeah?" I keep walking.

Annabella clocks my surliness. "When you open the fridge, the door knocks into the bed. His parents hate it. Thus its appeal."

"At least when you get sick of your roommate, you have a place to go."

She sets her jaw. "Excellent point."

The lights are down inside Gallerie, the first band blasting bass and not much else on the stage. Archer is backstage, and the crowd is marginal, but it's early. He scheduled himself at the end of the night to maximize exposure.

My phone lights up at the same time as Annabella's. Archer started a group chat.

ARCHER: You here?

ANNABELLA: In our dancing shoes.

I put my phone in my back pocket.

Annabella looks at me. I pretend I don't notice. "Nothing? Okay. I'm getting water." She disappears.

It's for the best.

I bite my lips. The metal taste drips into my mouth. Don't cry in public. Don't cry. Do. Not. Cry.

The band ends their set, and a duo filters on stage with a cello and a microphone and introduce themselves as Cello Again. More people cram around me. Annabella reappears, and hands me a water bottle and texts someone. Probably Zoey. I hope it's Zoey. I hope she isn't telling Archer she has second thoughts about me.

I wouldn't blame her.

Time passes. The floor feels far away. How much would it hurt if my knees buckle and I crumble to the ground? I hope my head doesn't smack first.

More people crowd in.

Cello Again wraps up and they're chased off the stage by an energetic girl quartet named AeroSwift who only performs Aerosmith and Taylor Swift acapella mashups. It's strange as hell, mixing Taylor's early princess metaphors with Steven Tyler's vocal riffs. I text Archer.

LOU: I didn't know mashups count as new songwriting.

SwiftAero's set ends. I wait for my phone to buzz, but it stays still. He's busy, I rationalize. Managing this must be exhausting.

Annabella's phone lights up. She laughs at whatever's on her screen.

Halfway through the second to last set (three boys with a guitar, keyboard, and tambourine), as I eye an empty piece of wall to slide against and sit, a hand lands on my shoulder. I whip around. "What are you doing here?"

"I'm on my way to a party and thought I'd check it out. Those eye-searing lime green fliers were everywhere." Chris' hair is spiked and shorter tonight. He probably has a standing stylist appointment every other week to keep it high and tight. His oatmeal cable knit sweater clings in the right places, but an ugly-as-sin Puka shell necklace knocks the hotness down to at most an 8.

I should tell him to buzz off. But I don't. I let him shift between me and Annabella, and pretend not to notice how the angle of hips slowly divides me from her. The band wears on.

People stop to talk to Chris, clap his shoulder, punch his arm. Songs tick by. His hand drifts to my tail bone. The weight is nice. It keeps me upright.

If I feel this, his hand on me, it will shove away feeling anything else.

The band wraps up. As the cheers die, Annabella pivots our way. "Hi." She sticks her hand out to Chris. "I'm Lou's roommate. You are?"

"Chris. Hey there." He lifts his hand from my back to meet her. Annabella watches his hand slice through the air. Her eyebrows spike up as his fingers wrap around my hip after their handshake.

"You good?" Annabella shifts her glare from Chris' hand to my face.

I can't look at her. "Yeah."

She frowns and turns back to the stage.

Archer comes out to loud cheers, crossing the stage to a microphone stand. Matilda bounces with every step he takes, as if she can't wait to be swung around and put to work. I realize I haven't seen her out of her case since I flung chamomile tea all over them. Archer's hair is characteristically uncombed and he's wearing a black t-shirt, Docs, and black jeans. I see his pear tattoo, a green dot on his wrist from the back of the crowd. My fingers ache to trace its outline and feel his skin against mine. Purple light washes over him as he adjusts the mic to his lips.

Somewhere in the crowd, a girl's whistle trills against the pitch-black walls. Hyena-esque giggles split open the hush.

Annabella jiggles her water bottle. "I hate his groupies."

Focused and unbothered, Archer holds Matilda and begins to strum. His guitar pick catches each string and sets the note alight.

As he plays, Archer moves across the stage as if he's caught in a lazy breeze. There's no end destination, no fancy footwork to follow; it's simply Archer, moving, where his energy takes him. He listens to the melody as he makes it, his eyes closed, his head resting on his shoulder, lost in the making. Matilda is part of him. His heart outside his body. Words might fail him, but music won't.

My own heart wobbles as Archer begins to sing in a sweet tenor. "I knew I'd follow you everywhere, that very first day."

You don't deserve him.

"You squinted into the sun, and I didn't, I didn't."

You blew your chance on the team. With Milo.

"And when you took flight, I tried, I tried."

Annabella. Me.

My nose burns with the effort of trapping my tears in my eyes. Annabella doesn't notice. Nor does Chris.

Archer does.

On stage, a million miles away, but right here with me, we lock eyes. He shifts his shoulders to me. "Straight to the sun. My dear, straight to the light...the light...the light."

Chris squeezes my hip. "I'm bored," he says loudly. "Want to get out of here?"

You don't deserve happiness.

I rub my eyes with my fingers. If there's a time to see clearly, it's this second. I pull Chris to the door. "Let's go."

Archer's voice notches up a key as he watches me leave clinging to another guy.

"I'm sorry," I whisper, squeezing past the bouncer.

"For what?" Chris is behind me in the cold outside Gallerie. The door muffles Archer's voice. A memory, already.

I look at Chris. "I didn't say anything. Take me to your place."

My ass smashes against the doorknob as we tumble into his room. Chris' hands are everywhere: my hair, fumbling my bra hook, caught in his oatmeal sweater as he tries to get out. I shove him backwards and he bounces on his mattress, his feet over his head. "Hey!" he protests, until he realizes I yanked off my t-shirt.

"Shut up." I climb into his lap, my knees locked on his hips.

His eyes are dark as he scrambles out of his sweater. My fingers slide under his Puka shell necklace; if I break it mid-thrust, I'm doing the world a favor. His tongue presses into my mouth, my hips grinding into his groin. Lean in, Meghan said. This will feel good. This'll work.

"Am I at least gonna get breakfast this time?" I ask as Chris nips my neck, still struggling with the bra hook.

He shoots me a wolfish grin. "I'll give you more than breakfast." He flips us over with more grace than I anticipate, given his fingertips are under the button on my jeans. "Let's get you out of these first."

Why do you keep doing this?

Because I want to. Chris wiggles my jeans past my knees.

Orgasms are great. What about after?

My jeans crumple next to my boots on the floor. Chris kisses the inside of my thighs.

His lips only tickle. The ache to arch my hips up to him is missing. Chris isn't deterred; he probably doesn't notice. His fingers march forward to my underwear with the confidence of a guy who's watched a lot of porn and thinks he knows the best sex moves.

Lou. What about after?

No Gin, no Annabella. No Archer.

No amount of running will save me if I don't have a place to go.

And I do.

I lurch up, ramming my stomach into the top of Chris' head. I swipe my t-shirt off the floor, and my hair is popping through my t-shirt before he realizes I'm not playing anymore. Chris stills as I raise my leg over his head and roll off the bed. "What's happening?"

"I gotta go." One leg in my jeans, both boots in hand, I fight the other pant leg to get my foot through.

"I wasn't joking—I'll make you breakfast." Chris is still on his belly starfishing the mattress.

"Remember for your next random." On the steps, I tug my boots on. Chris' bed creaks, a sure sign he's getting up. "Thanks for trying," I call and stomp down the steps.

I don't know if he follows. But it doesn't matter. I'm already gone.

~

Gallerie is deserted, except for the cleaning crew and bartenders, wiping down counters and stacking crates. "You missed the show," one guy offers.

On the street, I pull my hair up, breaking a sweat from running. Bars signs glow in the dark, string lights dangle from poles, smoking areas light up. The sidewalks are packed: Hobo Day homecoming crowds swarm around me, a living, breathing maze of too much cologne and hormones. Students stream by, calling to friends and full of hugs and complaints about homecoming cover charges. Two food trucks set up on the curbs, their generators pumping, ready and waiting for the drunk crowds.

If I were Archer and Annabella, where would I be?

They could be anywhere.

What if this is it? What if they're cutting me from their collective memory right now? Bidding me good riddance. It wouldn't be hard; I've known them for a matter of weeks. They can rewrite this chapter. I'm easy to cut. Coach. Gin. Walking proof I'm not wanted.

People push by and I squeeze against the building. The ridges on the brick hold me up like Velcro. I force air into my lungs. It's okay, I think. You're okay. What would Meghan ask right now? What grounds you?

Archer has the funniest sideways shuffle. He tilts to the right when he walks, like a little old man. The pear tattoo peeks out under his hoodie sleeve, and I know that's only the beginning of his ink. I want to know why he picked each tattoo. I want to hear Matilda rumble from his hands. I want to know why his eyes glint when I speak.

And Annabella. I want to meet her sisters and listen to her laugh and lay in the Meeting of the Minds and hear her breathe in her sleep and race her and feel her have my back even when she races past the finish line inches in front of me and know I'm not second, even when she's first.

I want them.

A metal door slams shut a few storefronts down, next to three girls squealing their faces off about a guy named Hunter. My eyes latch onto a flat brass doorknob. A place for Annabella to go when she's mad at her roommate.

Inside the door, I scamper up the steep staircase. It smells like trapped cigarette smoke from the nineties and knock-off Tide. I hover outside a scratched-up door. Quiet hangs like a bad dream after you wake: no voices, no lingering television noises. Bartenders clank glasses downstairs, and farther out I can hear Hobo Day clamor, but up here, there's nothing.

But then, I hear him.

Or rather: her.

Matilda.

I press my ear to the door like a creeper. His voice rises and pauses like a heartbeat with the strumming. It's a different song than what he sang tonight but I can't hear the words. I knock.

The strumming pauses. I knock again. "Archer, I hear you. Please don't hide."

Floorboards creak, the deadbolt flips, and Archer opens the door, his fingers wrapped around the guitar's neck. He's still in his stage clothes, but his boots are gone and his snow-white socks are jarring. I couldn't see when he was on stage, but he hasn't shaved in a few days. His beard is light red, and coarse compared to his curls. "I'm not hiding." Archer shifts in the doorway. "I'm in my apartment."

"Is Annabella here?"

"She is. She's asleep." Archer's hand drifts to the doorknob. "What do you need, Lou?"

"Don't do that," I reach out, only to pull back. I don't have the right to stop him from doing what he wants. "Please don't."

"You're the one cutting yourself out." He turns his fingers into a pair of scissors. Snip, snip.

"Coach kicked me off the team today." It spills out easier than I expected.

Archer jerks his head up.

"And I got in a fight with my therapist. A one-sided fight. Obviously, she was calm and listened, and I'm the one who lost my shit, but still."

He nods, making eye contact with lint from Chris' floor on my shirt.

"You need an apology, don't you?" My palms tingle from the effort of holding back.

"You left in the middle of my set, Lou." He's still, his restraint impressive. "You knew how hard I worked on the showcase, and that song was about who I was before— " He cracks his neck. "It was the first time I performed it, and I wanted you to hear it. I want you to know these pieces of me, all of them, including the shitty parts. Like I want to know yours."

I hate that I made him look at me like this. "I'm not a good friend. I fucked things up with you and Annabella. And Ginny."

"See?" Archer sets Matilda against the wall. "Who's Ginny? I have no idea. I'd like to."

I nod. "I'm sorry I left tonight."

Archer opens the door for me to come inside. "I was kinda pitchy anyway."

"You were not."

"I know. I was pretty great. Your loss." His chuckle is a dream. He waves his arm like Vanna White through his living room. Past his tiny navy couch, crammed up against a bookshelf-turned-room-divider. Records fill the top three shelves, packed away in their envelopes. I spy Thriller and Billy Joel cases propped up next to the record player. The corner of his mattress is covered in a rumpled gray quilt. A narrow stove and sink are across from the couch, next to a table shoved under a window looking over Main. Three wooden chairs crowd the table, their seats worn from decades of butts sitting to eat supper. A couple flannel blankets are strewn about the couch. Lamplight glows from the bed's end table and lights the room.

Archer shrugs, his shoulders bunching at his ears. "I like it. I don't need much."

It feels like Archer. It feels like a home.

He looks at me. "Can I show you something?"

Archer. You can show me anything. "Yes."

"Don't take off your shoes," Archer slips his feet into the most worn pair of tan moccasins I've ever seen. He is such an old man. "Follow me."

He leads me past his bed to a tight, short hallway. "Bathroom." He waves at the only door. But that's not what he's showing me.

One window looks over the alley and into the building next door. Its screen is popped out. Archer bends in half and climbs through to the fire escape. "Come on."

I peek out. "Are you gonna push me over?"

"Not tonight."

I crawl through the window. We climb upwards, the alley below and homecoming sounds swirling. At the top of the ladder, Archer hops on the cement block lining the roof. "It's intimidating," he says. "But worth it." I follow his move: butt on block, swing legs, land on tar roof.

It's worth it.

Archer strung golden string lights, and they cross above us, cutting up the night sky like a puzzle. I walk to two plastic lawn chairs and a metal table with a succulent in the middle. Past the roof, the street below is alive. A band plays on a patio with a throng of people crowding the stage, the drumbeat stretching up to us. The food trucks down the block whir with people at their windows. Bouncers shuffle in bar doorways, streetlights are on, and the voices float upwards in a tangled hum of life. Thousands of students dart across the street, dot sidewalks, mingle and meander, or rush into bars. A thousand Saturday nights, just beginning. "Archer, this is part of your place?"

"Eh. No. I'm waiting for Gus—the guy who owns Gallerie—to realize I figured out the fire escape." Archer cracks a tote lid nestled under an overhang and digs me out a scratchy black blanket. "It's chilly. I keep them up here for AB. Speaking of." He points to a hammock in the opposite corner. There's a bulge in the middle of it, a human curled inside like a caterpillar. The corner of a wool blanket drifts in the breeze below her.

I wrap my blanket over my shoulders. "This is amazing."

"I had a dorm room on campus for like a week." Archer sinks into a chair. I sit too. "My roommate was fine, but he likes silence... and with Matilda and me..." He sighs as if to say whoops. "I heard Gus had this studio open and it's cheap. It's not big, but I can come up here and..." He sighs again. "Process without judgment."

I tuck my ankles under the blanket. "We have a shit ton of baggage."

"Do we ever."

"Do you think it'll weigh us down forever?" My question, long speculated, now spoken. To the only person who might have the answer.

Archer tilts his chin to the stars. I look up too. What's he looking for? What's he not seeing?

"Let people help you unpack," Archer finally says, back with me. "That's what my therapist in high school told me. Find, and let, people help you unpack."

"It sounds nice."

"It's new-age Pinterest garbage. I hate the way it sounds like a quote from a workbook attached to the New Testament to make the Bible accessible."

"When did you leave the Church?" I ask.

"About a year ago."

"It must have been a huge decision."

Archer looks at me. "It was. The immense ... release I felt when I realized that it was okay that it didn't provide comfort anymore, but I wasn't giving anything back, and that's what wasn't okay..." He shrugs. "I'm grateful it's part of what makes Annabella feel whole, but I have no place in it anymore."

Bass thumps like a car backfiring from a bar down the block. Closer, in another bar, a wave of cheers blows to us and drifts away again as a bouncer shuts the door.

"You've seen a therapist?" My voice is quiet.

Archer nods. "For most of senior year. I started after Cadence's second stint in a treatment program, but as that started to...oh, I don't want to say heal, but scab, my therapist helped me unearth other things I had to address." He smiles, with no humor. "GAD. Generalized Anxiety Disorder is the official diagnosis. I've always been on edge, and learning music helped curb it, but then life kept piling on..." Archer bites his lips into a straight edge and wrinkles his nose. "Yeah."

I think of my diagnosis: newly faced, and now, a little less feared. I picture tree roots. The underground pieces of his story and my story, the anxiety that drives us, reaching for connection. Put like that it's easier to fathom sharing anything. "Mine's depression," I say. "Persistent depressive disorder, to be technical, likely triggered by a few steady years of undiagnosed general anxiety."

"Anxiety buddy!" Archer holds up his hand for a high-five.

I slap my flat palm against his and pretend tingles don't race up my wrist, a reverse carpal tunnel. Romance and mental health. What a mix. "Have you found a therapist here?"

He shakes his head. "My last one in high school cut me loose with a hearty namaste and wished me grace and continued healing." Archer sees my horrified eyes, and laughs. "The guy's method is out there, but he's a PhD and the go-to referral for young adults. He was weird and his approach was weird, but I liked parts of it."

"Are you?"

"Am I what?"

"Healed."

Archer looks out into the middle distance again. "I've been thinking about that. It's evolving, mental health. It's like water. It's always here, changing, morphing. Sometimes it presents as rain, sometimes snow, sometimes fog, or dew, or an ocean wave. And there are educated guesstimations and all the science in the world to support the cycle of a water drop, but at the end of the day..." He shrugs, spent. "It's kind of left up to nature, you know?"

I watch Archer, spread limp in the lawn chair like Stretch Armstrong. Full of lyrics and melodies and etymology facts and theories on cognitive development, and still keeping his shit mostly in check.

Had to be hard. And lonely.

"There's probably truth in it," I say. "The new-age Pinterest garbage your therapist recommended. Letting others help you unpack your baggage."

"Yeah, probably." Archer looks at me. "How's the unpacking going for you?"

I feel like I can breathe up here. "My luggage is still in the car."

"Mine too."

We laugh on the roof together. The ends of my hair lift in the breeze. And I feel lighter.

A little.

CHAPTER 10

"YOU'RE GONNA WAKE HER UP."

"Shut your pie-hole, Arch."

A frying pan clatters hard against the stove top. "Stop. She had a bad day that turned into a really bad night."

"And you didn't? Watching her slink off with some frat boy douche canoe?"

A coffee maker I didn't see last night gurgles.

"Arch. You were mid-set when she disappeared."

"Stop. We're not married."

"You're not even dating."

"Thanks for the reminder."

I open my eyes and follow a crack on the wall from my pillow up, up, up to the ceiling.

"You know I like her. She's my roommate. Thank god I like her," Annabella hisses. The floor creaks and I picture her standing next to Archer as he moves eggs over the frying pan. "But you're my priority. You are always my biggest priority."

My heart folds in half. If Ginny hadn't abandoned me, is this what we'd be?

"Maybe I don't have to be," he whispers.

I inhale. Swing my legs out from under the blankets and scoot past the pillow still dented from Annabella's head last night. Annabella sees me first, frowns, and sits at the table, pulling out her cell phone. She's wrapped in a huge black hoodie, her thumbs shoved through hand-ripped holes at the cuffs. Her hair's frizzy, piled on her head. It looks as pissed as its owner.

Archer moves a spatula over the eggs. He's in hacked off sweats and a t-shirt thinner than my resolve with their youth group name stamped on the back. (The Finders Keepers.) A black music note is inked into his calf. I haven't seen that one.

He looks at me and smiles. "Good morning."

Annabella stares at the phone in her hand like it's a lifeline. I slip behind Archer and sit gently next to her at the table. Her anger vibrates off her in cartoon waves, like Pigpen and dirt.

I thought I'm scary when I'm mad, but nope. Not like this.

"I have coffee," Archer offers.

"He's being bashful," Annabella twists away from me. "He's got chamomile tea too. And milk. And a frother. For you. In case."

He drops the spatula on the stovetop. It bangs against the frying pan. "AB!"

"Forever your wing woman, darling." She doesn't look up from her phone.

Archer's cheeks flush and I pretend it's the heat rising from the eggs. "I'll put the water on."

"Thank you," I say. I put my hand flat on the table next to my roommate, an olive branch with fingers. "Annabella, I'm sorry for last night. I was a total bitch."

Her phone slants away from her face. "You weren't a bitch."

"I was." I mean. I was. "Truly. I'm sorry."

She scrubs at what's left of last night's eyeliner. It streaks halfway to her ear. "I heard what happened. I'm sorry too."

The few minutes I forgot I was cut were fun. "Thanks."

She looks at me for a long moment, weighing whatever she needs to make sure I'm the real deal. Or am now.

"I ran here," I say quietly, twisting my knuckles together. "When I realized what I wanted—what I want—I sprinted."

The space between Annabella's eyebrows creases. Behind her, Archer peeks at us. His bottom lip is stuck between his teeth, but the corners trend up. I said the right thing.

A quick nod, and Annabella's mind is made up.

She touches my arm. "You're freezing. I'll get you one of Arch's sweaters." Annabella's gone and back in a flash with a pilled black V-neck from the dresser under Archer's bed. The cuffs are split from sliding over guitar strings a million times. "Next, tea."

Archer watches me slip his sweater over my head and pull my hair from it. He goes back to cooking the eggs. To Annabella, he says, "You two will triple my laundry pile."

"Good thing we're charming, right?" She drops a tea bag into a mug and brings it to the table while we wait for the water to boil. When Annabella hands me the mug, she smiles.

And I'm back in.

Annabella plops next to me on Archer's couch. Story is that they gifted it to him in hopes he would stop sleeping on their nice one in the living room. The fabric is woolly and sticks to my palms when I shift to cross both feet under my thighs. "I'm going to the late service, but maybe we could hang out here later?"

"I'll be here." Archer dries a dish and stacks it on the shelf over the sink.

"I'm stopping at the dorm. What do you want me to grab?" Annabella asks as I reach for my cold tea mug. "Sweats, your running shoes, homework?"

"That would be great." Going out into the real world—leaving Archer's—is too much to bear yet. His blanket and pillow he'd used to sleep on the couch are folded and stuffed next to me. I want to unfold the creases and slide inside.

She glances at her phone. "It's ten. I gotta go if I want to hit the eleven AM service." Annabella shifts to Archer. "Safe to assume you're not coming?"

"Entirely safe," he says. His hair is more frizz than curls this time of day. I picked that Archer Fact up in Wellness, over a quiz on the difference in muscle mass and muscle strength that I blew off to track his curl pattern. "Say hi to Jesus for me."

"I'll be back." She slides on her shoes, waves, and is out the door. Her steps thump down the stairs in the hall.

Archer turns my way. His face drains of color, like he never expected this moment to arrive: me, on his couch, in his beat-to-shit sweater, sipping chamomile tea he bought for me.

Or I'm the one who didn't expect it. But this is too important. He's too important. "Will you sing me your song?"

Archer's smile is that first bit of sunshine after a storm. "Yes."

He settles Matilda on his knees beside me on the couch. Archer feels the prats, and begins to sing. "I thought I'd follow you everywhere, that very first day..."

His voice is quieter than last night. He looks at the guitar strings as he sings, not that he needs to, but like he's watching them do what they're meant to do. It's fluid, natural. Part of Archer. Almost all of him.

"You squinted into the sun, and I didn't, I didn't. And when you took flight, I tried, I tried."

Archer's closed his eyes now, his sweet tenor like honey. Maybe he's remembering the minutes, the hours, that inspired this melody. Perhaps he's back with her, reliving the way their fingers might have tangled, or the way her lips tasted when they kissed in the rain.

"The way the shine caught your hair, my dear. It was too much, too much."

It's like watching a magic trick, or a tornado spin. Mind-blowing to see up close. As Archer's words combine with the notes, and he's giving me this gift—it's lightning in my bloodstream. Energy straight from the tornado.

"When I fell, did you look back? I still see you, all the way up there, up there."

His last note is bittersweet. Archer blinks as if he emerged rudely from a dream he'd burrowed back into. What's it like to write a song, see how it can contribute to the world, and then be forced to revisit it over and over?

Does he ever get to mourn it and move on?

Do any of us?

I shove away the concept of never fully escaping the worst moment of your life. "Thank you."

"Thanks for asking to hear it." Archer clears his throat and sets Matilda on the coffee table. I stare at her polish, flat on the tiny table separating us from the kitchen. No wonder Archer prefers to write on the roof. Up there, he can feel the worst of it, and let it blow away. Inside, it lives with us, the memories of what he suffered with Cadence and Cadence's suffering, weaving between his guitar strings and into the hollow. He doesn't want it associated with Matilda, but, like everything, it's intertwined. These weeds growing, climbing, connecting.

"Is she still in a treatment program?"

Archer cracks his knuckles. "Yeah. I haven't heard from her in awhile, but she checks in with AB from time to time. I think she's okay right now."

His hands, empty without his guitar, sit awkwardly on his thighs. I reach forward and wrap his fingers in mine. They tangle and rest on his knee. "I'm glad you told me about her."

He knocks his shoulder into mine. "Remember what I said last night? I want to know you. I want you to know me. Cadence's part of my story. She always will be." His sigh fills the apartment. "But now you have to tell me something good again. Like seductively dancing to Dua Lipa."

Ginny. She was my something good. "I had an Annabella too. My whole life."

Archer tilts his face towards mine. "Ginny?"

Her name is always on the tip of my tongue, but it's nice to think about getting past her name. "She loves coffee, summer, and writing. She's a spectacular writer, and she knows it, which was fun." I smile. "She writes these beautiful short stories. Made me see things I already saw—because I was there—in a new way. Her way." Bonfires, nights on the lake, watching me fall in love with Milo. She was our record-keeper.

"Sounds incredible," Archer says.

"It was." I take a deep breath. "Is. For other people now."

"What happened?"

I bite the inside of my cheek. "I needed her. And she wasn't there. She didn't see me drowning and jump in too."

Archer's finger bumps into my knuckle and he flips his hand. Our palms press together, and I swear my heart hopscotches right over at least three beats. "I'm sad that happened to you."

My tea is cold. I move to stand to put my mug in the microwave, mostly to lift the spotlight off me and let my sunburned skin recover, but Archer holds on. "Not for nothing, I see you. And you can't stop me from jumping in."

Our hands slide against his and my fingertips brush his pear tattoo, finally. It's warm. A souvenir stamped on his skin to keep Cadence near. His pulse hammers away underneath, and mine attempts to match his beat.

His face flushes to his eyebrows. "I mean, Annabella sees you too."

"I know." I squeeze his hand once, twice, and a third time. He's magnetic, and I'm empowered. A piece of me is back, my own bit of the swirling tornado. The part that reaches out, and lets others in.

Archer's eyes grow round as I let him go. I hope it isn't regret, as I stand to take my tea to the microwave.

~

Among running shoes, fresh sweats, and her Bible, Annabella shoved my therapy folder and Xanax next to my laptop in her bag. As Annabella and Archer bicker next to the tiny oven over dinner options, I pull out the top worksheet. Meghan snuck a new one in as I glowered out the window at the end of our last session, with a Post-it stuck on the top corner. "If you feel like it – I really am open to discussion. See you Tuesday."

"Sundays are for crock pots. You know this, Arch," Annabella says as I stand.

"It's gorgeous outside, and yesterday was Hobo Day—we're grilling," Archer has the fridge open, a plate of pressed hamburger patties in hand. "We can crock pot after the snow flies."

"You sound like an eighty-year-old man."

"Who's to say I'm not?"

"Annabella," I interrupt. "I need a pen."

"Lou—crock pot or grilling?" Annabella pulls open a junk drawer.

"Pizza," I say. "Always pizza."

She produces a pen from the back. "We'll never eat."

I click the pen open and go back to the couch. Their squabbles fade as I begin to write.

For my next session, I walk into Meghan's office, Archer's pen looped over the top of my worksheet.

Meghan greets me at the door. "You're early."

I give her the worksheet, filled out top to bottom. "I'm leaning in."

She takes my worksheet and turns it upside down on her desk. "I've had success with patients trying other therapies. Want to talk about a few options?"

"I'm scared." I flop to the couch. My yellow pillow slips to the floor, and I pick it up and toss it against the other couch arm.

"Of?" Meghan leans on her desk, folding her palms together.

"Feeling like this forever."

She nods. "That's where our conversations come in. You tell me what's got you anxious, we feel around together—you're never alone—and get to the bottom of it. And your meds support all of this, of course."

"I know, but it's more than that." I wish I hadn't tossed the pillow away.

"How so?"

"Of what depression means. The diagnosis is...expected. It can run in families. I get that. But in a bigger way..." I look around this tiny office on the third floor of Student Health, snuggled inside the trees and the birds, far away from the people wandering campus. This is bigger. So much bigger. "What if this dictates who I am?"

Meghan rises from her desk and pads around to her chair. She's tossed an afghan onto it since I was here last. It looks like it belongs on The Golden Girls set. "Depression is a disease, not a definition."

"What's the difference?"

"The difference is inside of you, Lou." Meghan tilts her head to the side. "You're the difference. The choice to care for yourself, however it may look. And I know—I promise—how difficult that is. Depression knows no bounds on who it impresses upon, but the choice to measure your life in five-minute or five-year increments is only yours."

I think of Mom on my first day of sixth grade, in bed with gray circles stamped under her eyes. Ginny's dad braided my hair that morning. He gave me his special back-to-school blueberry scone, and posed me and Ginny together in both of our front yards. "Depression isn't a choice."

"Nor is free will," Meghan says. "If all a patient can manage is to brush her teeth and go back to bed, I'm incredibly proud of her." She shrugs. "Depression is a disease of the brain, and obviously, yes, the body's command center. But our hearts?" Meghan pats hers. "That's a fixed point. If it's still beating, it's still trying. You're still trying."

"But Mom." It's a full sentence, and my throat closes.

"It sounds like she kept trying for a long, long time." Meghan sits next to me. "And it sounds like because of her, you were never alone."

I see her fuzzy white slippers on the kitchen floor. Feel her nails drawing stars on my scalp. And Meghan's right. I was never alone.

Orange leaves burn to crimson. Diminishing, delicate and clinging to branches for literal life.

I take to swallowing the Xanax with my chamomile right before Archer pops up at my side. We meet now even on mornings we don't have class, just to walk. The pill bottle lives in my backpack, tucked away in a pocket on the side. I never even hear it rattle.

I go to every class. I do my homework, attend my geography labs and care about foundations of rock in south central Colorado, and I fill out pastel worksheets for three hours a week with Archer, waiting for his pretty smile to spread across his face. When Archer smiles, it's like the sun is peeking from behind a cloud, and I forget (briefly) about taking the tattletale TA to her knees by stringing a fishing line across the classroom's doorway.

Leaves curl at their crimson edges. Pulling in. Preparing to let go.

"EMDR," Meghan says. "It stands for Eye Movement Desensitization and Reprocessing. It's a type of psychotherapy that helps people address and heal from emotional distress and traumatic events."

"Are there wires?" Her use of 'psychotherapy' is enough to send me to the stairs.

She's already shaking her head. "Absolutely not. The closest thing I can compare it to is therapist-led meditation."

My heart screeches back to its normal thumping pattern.

Meghan puts her feet flat on the floor and straightens her spine to a stick. "If you decide this is a method you want to try, it looks like this." She crosses her arms over her chest so each hand rests below the opposite shoulder. "We'll pick out moments, a catalyst of a situation you've survived—I call them the latest, or the greatest—and you'll focus on your memory—keeping one foot in the present here with me—and I'll pause you, ask you to rate your level of acceptance on a one-to-ten scale, and we'll process it as you tap your fingers against your body in a fast succession."

Tap tap tap go her fingers on her purple wool crew sweater.

Questions pop and crowd my brain. "Latest and the greatest?"

Meghan relaxes into her chair again. "I have an idea of what yours are, but we'll continue talking and together we'll decide if you want to tackle your dad's abusive disinterest or your mom's suicide. Or if there's something else."

The heart pounding is back. This is where Ginny should poke in with her dumb frizzy bun and ratchet my anxiety sky-high with a pointed side-eye. She knows what she's doing now, I think. Holding out when I need her. Hiding out in the dark rather than coming out so I can present her as proof.

I need to tell Meghan about her.

Instead: "I don't see how this helps, Meghan."

"I get that a lot." She nods. "What it does is help the person reframe the situation that rooted this anxiety within them. It shines a brighter light on why what happened wasn't your fault, or yours to carry alone."

"Meghan, I—" Do it. Do it. Tell her about Ginny. I look at my fingers, clustered in a knot on the yellow pillow. I pull them apart and rub my thumb into my knuckles. "How—why, I guess, does the shoulder tapping help?"

"It's called bilateral stimulation," Meghan says. "It's a self-regulation tool. Very good for calming when you feel panic rising."

"But why?" I try to distract her from my knuckle massage. "I know you have a textbook explanation for me."

"It stimulates both sides of our brain and sends a signal to our brain that we're safe."

My knuckle is beet red under my thumb. I shake out both hands. "Safe?" I repeat.

Meghan nods. "Safe."

ARCHER: IDK You Yet. Alexander 23. Listen to it.

I'm mid-sprint on a Wednesday afternoon outside the engineering building when the first leaf unhooks from its branch with a sigh. It floats to the dirt under the tree, with zero fanfare.

On Halloween, Annabella brings home cat ears and a fuzzy tail and we collapse in laughter trying to duct tape her tail to her butt. Properly tailed, Annabella sits me down and charcoals the crap out of my eyes. I dig out Dad's ancient Rolling Stone t-shirt—the one with the tongue everyone has—and grab Annabella's scissors. The sleeves gone, I tug the shirt over my hair (huge because Annabella backcombed it to death and offered her curly hair mask for my deep-fried ends). Once I'm in my pleather leggings, Annabella rips two more strategic holes in the shirt at my shoulders and around my ribs.

"You need one more thing." She sorts through my makeup case. "This'll do." She holds my red lipstick tube. "May I?"

I haven't uncapped it since graduation. My makeup had been done that morning, but not yet the hair. I say yes, my heartbeat ringing. Can Annabella hear it? How can she not hear it? She glides my old signature lipstick on my lips.

I used to do this with Ginny, with a muted pink shade.

"Forgive me if this isn't perfect, but you're going for a rocker look after all." Annabella gracefully sidesteps any anxiety she feels in our room. "My sister, Catherine, gets dolled up before going out. She loves red lipstick. Mom hates it." Annabella pulls back, capping the lipstick. "You look hot too. Red might be your color."

The NCAA Regional is next week. If I could draw Annabella's uptick of steely focus as she packs for Oklahoma against Emily's smarmy shoe squeaks and cocky crows of race times as she passes our door on a line graph, both rises would be as epic as my trip from competitive cross-country grace.

Instead, I track times, names, standings from the university's sports Twitter while Archer's Spotify playlist hums from my phone. And I price new cleats.

Leaves drift past our dorm window, one here, one there, flipping, twisting to sidewalks. Blowing through the dead grass, their scrappy edges hooking them together. Caught in alley corners, and smashed under tires in student parking.

I keep running.

Midterm grades are posted. I come in at Bs, with one A: Wellness 101. That night, Annabella tells me it's the only test Archer passed.

LOU: It's Nice to Have a Friend. Taylor Swift.

Dead leaves pile in the quiet stairwell to my geography lab. They twist, caught in doorways next to garbage cans and cigarette butt holders.

My psychology textbook is heavy and open in my lap. Archer putters around his kitchen, draining water from the sink and checking the oven timer. The air smells like dish bubbles and frozen pizza. Annabella is meeting us after training, but she's probably still a half hour away. Outside, clouds cling low in the sky. It's always cloudy now. At his record player,

Archer slides a Sufjan Stevens album from the sleeve. He sets the record on the player, adjusting the needle with such care a lump collects in my throat.

Needling guitar ticks fill the space, followed by a haunting, but warm, melody before the lyrics start. Archer hums and cracks a knuckle. As he watches the record spin, I watch Archer. He finger-combs his hair and his curls turn to puffs. "I'm going to hop in the shower." I nod, and Archer is around the corner, gone.

Sufjan sings. "Amethyst and flowers on the table. Is it real or a fable? Well, I suppose a friend is a friend. And we all know how this will end."

I shove my textbook to the empty cushion. Feet flat on the floor, arms crossed over my chest, I place each hand on the opposite shoulder. Archer's shower turns on and the curtain hangers clang together and apart as he gets in. Annabella's nowhere near yet. As safe as they come, I think. My eyes drift shut, my fingernails curling into my hoodie.

Runs get cool, then cold. People quit hanging out outside. Students drag their shitty yard couches under awnings and onto shittier porches. Bros replace their mesh shorts with thick gray sweatpants and their hoodies with Jackrabbit stocking hats, the bright yellow fuzzy balls bouncing down the sidewalks. Girls layer leggings and Uggs like somebody hit copy/paste over campus. I pull a black stocking cap on (sans the fuzzy ball) and off I go, my hair in pigtails instead of high ponies. Hills of leaves crunch under my soles, and when I sprint, they billow up behind my heels like a cartoon. I like how my footsteps echo in the quiet. A name every stride. Annabella. Archer. Meghan. Mom. Ginny.

Ginny.

Where did you go? Why can't I hear you?

She's leaving me, again.

ARCHER: Somebody to Love, Kacey Musgraves. It's AB's favorite. (She said I could tell you.)

There are other sounds to pull in, I realize as I run. To keep me from floating away. Annabella's laugh twinkles like wind chimes in June before a thunderstorm. Archer's chesty "hmph" that peeks out when he's amused and doesn't want to be. The way Annabella reads random lines from her textbooks aloud, because she wants to remember a passage, and reading it aloud helps.

A gust of wind blasts past my shoulders. Trees on the edge of the green shiver, and together, hundreds of branches let their summer go, leaves surging to the air. Orange, golden, brown leaves tumble like confetti. The wind and the leaves crash, rise, and fall like a set of lungs, breathing life into the end of the autumn. Breathing life into me.

I stop to watch, thinking the leaves will settle, and there will be an end to this spectacle. But the swirling goes on, unpredictable, as the wind blasts and eases in the shadow of campus. Cold sneaks in under my fleece and I need to go and I do, without looking back.

CHAPTER 11

ANNABELLA NEARLY KNOCKS HERSELF IN THE HEAD as she pulls her suitcase off the top shelf in her closet. "When are you heading home?"

I look up from my phone. More cleat shopping. It's a problem. "I'm not. I thought I told you." I don't want to dig the innards from a turkey and Dad doesn't want to be there at all, so we did what any aggressively grieving father/daughter duo with no relationship would do—we canceled Thanksgiving dinner.

"I didn't think you were serious. Won't you miss pumpkin pie? Your dad?" She flips open her suitcase and chucks sweats, t-shirts, and pajama pants inside. She's casual about it, asking about my family. When people know how Mom died, or even when, their brows press into deep Vs. Their voices lilt softer. They tend not to be smashing an obscene amount of clothes into a too-small suitcase.

Archer hasn't told her how it happened. And I was kinda banking on him doing my dirty work.

"No. He'll be fine." I answer her question.

Annabella pops to her closet for an extra pair of running shoes. A girl after my own heart. "You're coming home with me."

"What? No." I have a tasteless Hungry Man frozen dinner picked out at the student convenience store.

She drops her shoes in her suitcase and crosses to my closet. "Where's your suitcase?"

"Annabella."

My roommate teeters on my desk chair, scoping my closet's top shelf. Suitcase spotted, she yanks it down more gracefully than she did her own. "Listen, if you don't want to, cool. But my mom's cinnamon pecan sweet potatoes are legendary." Annabella pulls a pile of clean, folded laundry from my hamper. She holds it over my open suitcase, hovering closer and closer. "Yeah?"

I nod. "Yeah."

~

Annabella's Toyota beater isn't representative of her family's financial situation—I don't know why I'm surprised. Her dad's an obstetrician, inspiring Annabella's nursing major and her sister's residency at Mayo. "My dad wanted pharmacy for me," Annabella says as we buzz down I-29. Wind whistles around the car's jiggling joints. "Better hours. But I don't want that level of continuing education. The FDA approves new drugs constantly."

"How's it different from nursing?"

"There won't be a counter separating me from patients." Annabella navigates the late afternoon holiday traffic stream going for central Sioux Falls. Her top knot of curls brushes the car and frizzes like a Muppet at the point of contact.

I crack my wrists. I'm going to get early-onset arthritis. "Any topics to avoid? I mean, besides the obvious?"

Annabella taps her fingers on the steering wheel to the song on the radio. "Everything else is fair game. I'm an open book with my family. Except for ..."

"Your favorite person."

"Pretty much," she sighs and turns into her neighborhood.

Annabella slows to a stop in front of a traditional two-story, snow-white colonial with black shutters lining every window. A brick arch swoops over the front door. The yard rivals a football field. Oak trees and a literal white picket fence complete the real estate package like a dream. My dad would consider murder to get his hands on this house. "Geez, where's the tire swing?" I joke.

"Dad takes it down around Halloween," Annabella says, distracted, putting her car in park. "Three, two, one..."

On cue the front porch door swings open and a short, slightly rotund and well-put-together woman trots down the steps. Pearls gleam at her throat, and her apron floats at her knees. We're sliding into Leave It to Beaver territory in a hurry. "Darling girl!"

"Hi Momma." Annabella is out of the car and circles the hood to hug her mother. "Why do you smell like sugar? Did you start cooking a night early?"

"Early? Your father had to stop me from starting last night. That was early." Mrs. Harris squeezes Annabella's face, bunching her cheeks up to her eyes. Annabella laughs, her fingers dangling from her mom's wrists.

I wish my mom was here to hug.

"I brought Lou home too." She points her mom my way as I get out of the car. "Her family didn't have plans, and I wanted to show Lou around."

"Louise." Mrs. Harris releases her daughter and comes at me, arms up, ready to hug.

I stick my hand out in a hurry. I can't hug her. I don't even know her, but I'm afraid I won't let go. "Lou. Hi. Thanks for welcoming me into your home."

She closes my hand inside hers, her other hand draping over our handshake. Her skin is smooth like a silk pillow. "Any girl friend of my daughter is welcome."

Holy anvil.

Annabella blinks. She looks at the house. "Are we the first home? Where's Cat?"

"Still on her way from Rochester." Her tone is clipped while referencing her eldest.

"Is Jake coming?" Annabella presses, holding the door open for me. As I slip by, she winks, confirming she's ribbing her mother.

"I would assume. Why are you anxious?"

"Looking forward to having the whole family home." Annabella smiles serenely at her mother's back in case she turns around. But Mrs. Harris heads to the kitchen, and Annabella's face evens out, sinking back to normal.

Annabella's got a strange family dynamic of her own. It seeps from the walls and through my friend's sigh. Good thing I brought all that Xanax.

Annabella's childhood bedroom is babydoll pink. Pink canopy bed, pink frilly bed skirt, curtains with embroidered roses. Lace pillow shams. The whole room accented to death in wicker. I spin and look for a hint of the chill, non-frilly human I've lived with for three months.

I find her on a lone bulletin board over a scalloped Victorian-era writing desk. Race ribbons, a maroon and cream plastic rosary draped over a corner, and approximately one thousand Polaroids. I lean closer. Annabella and Archer in matching Pokémon Halloween costumes circa sixth grade. Annabella and Archer at their first communion, based on Annabella's white lace veil with ruffles like her bedding. Annabella and Archer at a concert a year or two ago. Annabella's hair is fluffier. Archer's curls are tighter, like a Chia pet. They're bookended by two people: Zoey, two feet away from Annabella in the picture, and a pretty brunette girl with a lip ring and conflicted eyes. She leans against Archer. Cadence.

"Sorry." Annabella yanks off her boots. They bang into her desk leg. "I like to get under my mom's skin when I can."

I sink into her overwrought bed. It eats me up like a cloud. "Your mom doesn't seem to love Jake."

"Not even a little." She begins to braid her hair. "Cat's gonna be a doctor. Boys are distractions. Jake is cute and charming and a legit good guy, but Mom just sees trouble."

I nuzzle a pillow, pushing a weird lace sham to the floor. I'd nap all day right here.

"Me on the other hand?" The rubber band snaps at the bottom of her braid. "Nursing isn't as intense, so I was to excel at classes, date a nice boy, marry the nice boy, and carry on the Catholic tradition of populating the earth."

I open my eyes. "You can still repopulate the earth. Just with a little more science."

Annabella snaps her fingers. "I'll remind her of that over the turkey tomorrow."

Downstairs, the front door clatters open. Bags smack to the floor. "Mom!" a woman calls.

"Mom, we're home!" Another voice. A male voice.

I snort. "Jake calls your mom 'Mom'?"

"He has no boundaries with her, and it's my favorite thing about him. Come on." She grabs my hand. "Let's watch."

I thought we'd linger at the top of the stairs, not seen or heard, but Annabella pulls me down the steps, leaping down the last two right into Catherine's hug. "Seester!"

"Seester!" Catherine laughs and wraps her arms around Annabella. When they part, I see her cross necklace lives in the hollow of her throat too. It's tiny and strung on the chain from the long ends of the cross like Annabella's, but Catherine's is black stone and rounded at the corners. "Long time, dorkface. Why haven't you Facetimed me?"

"I'm busy." Annabella hugs Jake and waves me over. "This is my roommate, Lou."

Catherine twists to her sister. Annabella pinches her arm. "Just roommate."

"Hi." Jake envelopes me in a hug and whoa. Cute for sure. Cute in the crew-cut, Free-People-model way. Cute in the I-make-myself-at-home-with-your-mom-and-call-her-Mom kind of way.

Mrs. Harris emerges from the kitchen, drying her hands on a crisp, white towel. Food smells waft out after her and I'm mesmerized. If it smells this delicious the night before Thanksgiving, what is up her sleeve for tomorrow? "My darlings." She is gleeful, pulling both girls to her chest. "… and Jake," she adds, an afterthought.

Jake doesn't care. He hovers over the three women and hugs everyone. "Smells great, Mom. Is it too early for Doc's spiced pickles?"

"Yes." Mrs. Harris's curt. "Come, Cat. You never call. You need to catch me up." Mrs. Harris pulls her into the kitchen. Catherine looks back, her eyes shooting us an SOS.

Jake snorts as Catherine disappears behind her mother into the kitchen. "Anna, I'm gonna get us settled in and let them catch up. Don't want to incite your mom too early."

"You're a trooper," Annabella calls to his back as Jake scurries upstairs. "He is," she tells me. "They live together in Rochester, but Mom and Dad make him sleep in the guest room when they're here."

"Aren't they engaged?" I mean, the Mom thing. I can't get past it.

"Nope. Even if they were, according to our mother, a diamond doesn't mean squat in the eyes of God." Annabella walks into the living room and flops onto the couch. The news blasts on, and Annabella flips it to a streaming service. "Cat and Jake bug Mom with the whole relationship thing, but she's serious about her career and Jake's a teacher at an underprivileged school and is basically aiming for saint status. They're career-focused."

Catherine peeks out the kitchen door. "Anna. Get your ass in here." Behind her, Mrs. Harris is talking non-stop, steam rising over her head. "Lou," Catherine says louder. "Do you know how to roll pie dough?"

"Yeah. I do." Mom showed me how a few Christmases ago. Did she picture it as a holiday tradition, or as the beginning of making sure I was prepared without her?

Catherine waves me in. "Get in here. Drag my sister by her hair, if you need. I do it all the time."

Meghan said to lean in. Today, that means twirling Annabella's curl around my finger with a grin that isn't entirely forced until she yelps, slaps my hand away, and follows me into the lion's den of one Mrs. Harris.

~

I wake to the sound of a coffee grinder.

"She's killing me." Annabella groans and pulls the comforter up over her head next to me.

The bedroom door cracks open and Catherine slides through. She gets into bed on her sister's side and cuddles in, the big spoon to Annabella's little. "She's luring us with fresh coffee to turn us into her worker bees."

"It'll work too." Now Jake is in the doorway. Are we in a sitcom? This is a sitcom. "I can't believe you're cuddling with your sister over your banished-to-the-guest-room fiancé." He nods at me. "Good morning, by the way."

"Hi."

"I like Anna more," Catherine mumbles, snuggling in harder.

The coffee bean grinder blasts on again. Annabella snorts and together we go downstairs in our pajamas. On the way, we pass four crosses in varying sizes and shapes displayed in different places. The cross next to the bathroom features a wood-carved, gruesome depiction of what the man suffered on the cross. Annabella doesn't blink twice, but I look away. Jesus is around every corner here.

The kitchen decor leans less religious. Cornflower blue skies are framed in the kitchen windows as Mrs. Harris folds more dough into itself on the wooden island. The scent of peeled apples and spices mixes with raw sweet potatoes. If this is the heaven Annabella believes in, sign me up.

No one is allowed in the kitchen without an assignment. (And no one is allowed coffee without going into the kitchen.) Annabella runs the food processor, whacking whole pecans into nutty dust, and then crumbles through two cornbreads for stuffing. I'm handed a knife and instructed to chop literally everything shoved my way; I slice tomatoes, cube potatoes, sliver onions. Corn is husked from cobs, pits pulled from avocados. Jake comes downstairs and brews coffee, and Mrs. Harris isn't fully annoyed by his presence, so he's put to work on the chop brigade with me. Catherine shows up later, rubbing her eyes, declaring it nice to sleep in. Annabella isn't the only child who enjoys ribbing her mother.

I'm turning in my pitted avocados to Mrs. Harris when Dr. Harris comes in the back door, stuffing leather gloves in his pockets. "Sorry, family," he starts.

"Patients!" they yell, another family tradition.

"Dad!" Annabella jumps around the island, her arms up for a hug. Dr. Harris delivered twins overnight and he never made it home. "They're named Gobble and Wattle," Annabella had joked earlier over the dull roar of the food processor pulsating.

"My Anna." Dr. Harris hugs her, and his arms envelope her whole torso. I look away. "Have you gone for your run yet today?"

"Not yet. Dad, this is Lou. My roommate." She points to me over all the heads. I force myself to look up and wave. His smile is toothy, like both of his girls' smiles, and his eyes are clear blue. Annabella said his bedside manner earns him the best patient reviews in the hospital. I see why.

"Lou. Anna's told us so much. Welcome." He drops three kisses on her head and Annabella positively swells. "When you go for your run, tell me. I'll join you. Just let me get a quick cat nap in."

Annabella beams, cracking open a can of creamed corn.

"Good morning, sweets." Dr. Harris pecks his wife on the lips.

She gives him a bemused nod and shoves a towel into his chest. "Speaking of sweets, you need to start your pie if you want your dessert before midnight."

"My marching orders," he laughs, and reaches for his apron on a hook in the pantry.

Lunch is served precisely at 1 pm in the formal dining room. High backed chairs, lace table cloth. Mrs. Harris has put on a shinier set of pearls, Dr. Harris enjoyed a whopping 45-minute nap, Jake tried to teach me about football, and Annabella and Catherine bickered about place settings.

"Mom and Dad met while Dad was at John Hopkins," Annabella says as we change from our pajamas into chunky sweaters and yoga pants: half comfortable, fully Thanksgiving-appropriate. "When he was done, they married, he matched here, Cat was born, and they bought this house because it's blocks from the hospital."

"The house is beautiful," I offer, still spooked by the crosses. Another one crept up on me outside the pantry this morning while I snooped through the Oreo stash. Jesus glared—I swear it's always a heavy-lidded glare—and I backed away from the cookies, a crook caught.

"It is," Annabella agreed. "A dream to grow up here." She bites her lip and her freshly applied lip gloss disappears. "Comes with a lot of expectations."

I step next to her in front of her mirror, and twist around as if I'm checking my reflection and not just watching hers. I want to touch her elbow, rest my cheek on her shoulder. Show some sign of solidarity. I don't.

Annabella jams a pin in her bun. "Cat's got it worse. But still."

"Cat's story doesn't negate yours," I watch her in the mirror. The second pin is slid in, rather than jabbed. Its progress.

On the way downstairs, Annabella is still messing with her hair. "By the way, Arch's coming for dessert later. It's tradition."

Archer. Despite enjoying the Harris family dynamic by tracking each eyeroll, elbow jab, and loving shoulder pat, pins and needles erupt under my skin whenever someone enters a room. I'd half expected Archer to pop into the house or to look up and see him on her couch next to Jake, his stocking feet side-by-side on the coffee table.

"Oh," I say.

Annabella smirks and waves me to the empty spot between her and her mom. Across the table Jake is watching Catherine fuss with the cloth napkin in her lap. Annabella kicks Catherine's chair and cocks her head. Catherine looks away.

At the end of the table, Mrs. Harris assumes position: elbows on table, fingers woven like a basket, forehead on thumbs. The family follows suit. I fold my hands under the table.

"Gracious Lord, thank you for this food," Mrs. Harris says. "Thank you for the opportunity to be with my family, whom I love more than life, and to welcome new people to our table." She cracks an eyelid, zoning in on her husband. "Sweetie, do you have anything to add?"

Dr. Harris is wearing a huge, content smile. Maybe that's what completeness looks like. "Succinct and true. Amen."

We look up, as if emerging from a cozy nap under a blanket to marvel at the spread: cornbread stuffing and green bean casserole, a scalloped corn casserole, and homemade bread that smells like a gift and feels like a cloud. More turkey than anyone can fathom eating, and three pies cooling in the kitchen. Conversation explodes over the clatter of forks scratching plates, spoons squelching out of Mrs. Harris's famed sweet potatoes and mac and cheese dishes. Dr. Harris laughs, Annabella passes me all the food before I'm ready. Jake drops bad jokes like it's his job and Catherine rolls her eyes as if it's hers.

Mrs. Harris hands me the plate piled high with rolls. "Louise, I don't want to see an inch of empty plate in front of you."

Two people are going to call me Louise, I guess. I don't mind.

Jake passes me the scalloped corn. Yellow corn dots the top of the creamy casserole as I scoop it to my plate. "Lou, I assume you've met the extremely passionate Archer."

"I have." I take in my plate—Mrs. Harris will be pleased. Not an inch uncovered. I have no idea where to start.

"How many songs has he written about you?" Jake persists, grinning. Knowing. Needling.

For the first time, possibly ever, I blush. I blush hard. It burns as it rises to my cheeks. I press my lips together, willing the wave to flatten, but it's too late—I'm as bright as a fire engine.

"Jake!" Catherine yelps. "Leave her alone."

"I'm sure she has a few," Annabella says casually, knocking her ankle into mine under the table. "I have 63 at last count. He writes plenty of platonic songs too."

I know she's trying to redirect the flame in my face, but it doesn't help.

The truth is: I want a song. I want a hundred songs. Something I can listen to when the darkness is too impossible to navigate and I'm spinning like a broken record, a second from getting lost, at least then I'll have Archer's song.

Proof anyone is thinking of me.

Proof he is thinking of me.

"Archer is still processing what happened to Cadence," Mrs. Harris murmurs, buttering a roll. Jake's smile slides off his face. Catherine's empty fork hovers over her plate in a pause.

My blush prickles, a doppler of red and pink. A regular storm cell right on my cheeks.

Mom!" Annabella's voice sounds like a shout, but it's because I'm sitting next to her. "Archer can move on. They broke up a year ago."

"Annabella." Mrs. Harris looks exhausted, and it's not from baking bread since four am. "I ask that we give him time to recover. There is no timeline for that kind of trauma."

All this food on my plate may as well be sawdust. Tell me more about grief timelines, please.

"I'm curious." Dr. Harris pauses cutting his slab of turkey. "How many songs do we think Archer has written about me?"

"Probably at least one," Jake chimes in. "I think he's jealous of your stately gray."

"Yes, I agree." Dr. Harris winks at me, Annabella snorts over her mashed potatoes and I gulp my drink and the moment passes.

Conversation turns into a ruckus again.

Annabella mouths an apology me. Jake sweetly piles more mac and cheese onto Catherine's plate and she shifts, weirdly, it seems to me, but I look away. Mrs. Harris forces more food on all of us. Dr. Harris says the twin girls are actually named Stella and Grace. Catherine fidgets more. I look at the front door every two seconds and demolish another helping of sweet potatoes.

I slide my fork into the corn, and catch Jake's fingers squeezing Catherine's left hand on the lace tablecloth. He bites his lips, and she nods.

Her hand sinks into her lap, and when she rests it back on the table, a diamond ring gleams on her left ring finger.

"Guys," Catherine says. Then, louder when the family keeps yammering. "Guys."

I poke Annabella's shoulder. She waves me away and talks to her dad about a course in Minnesota that has a hill steeper than a bell tower.

"Family!" Catherine yells over the din.

Mrs. Harris is the first to look up. An arrow to a bullseye, she zeroes in on the bauble on her daughter's finger. "What is that?"

The edge in Mrs. Harris's voice makes the table quiet.

Catherine takes a deep breath and wraps her fingers over Jake's hand. Light bounces off the solitaire diamond. "We're married!"

Annabella's spoon clunks over her sweet potato and crashes into her water glass.

Jake's vibrating like a kid's toy, his left hand lurching up. A gray, shiny band sits on his finger now too. "Married, guys!"

No one moves.

"Are you pregnant?" Mrs. Harris hisses.

"Mom!" Catherine recoils. Her cheeks drain to a pale pink. "No!"

Jake jumps in. "With our schedules, we thought it best to go to City Hall and have a larger celebration this summer."

"City Hall?" Mrs. Harris repeats in a strangled whisper. "But Father Smith. Sacred Heart. Where you were baptized."

Catherine reaches over the lace tablecloth and the basket of rolls for her mom's hand. Mrs. Harris springs backwards. I look at my plate, trying to figure out how to ooze into the floor and get out the door. "Mom, I wish you were there. All of you. But with just us, it was ..." I peek up. Her eyes have gone soft, looking at her husband. The heartiest of heart eyes. "Romantic."

Annabella stirs from her trance and stands. Hesitantly, she steps around her mother and hugs Catherine. "I love you," Annabella whispers. "You saved me from wearing a hideous bridesmaid dress, and I forgive you."

Catherine's giggles explode through her nose as a snort.

Mrs. Harris slams her fists on the table so hard my glass tilts and water sloshes on the tablecloth. I will my bones to hurry up on the oozing process. "Richard. Thoughts?"

Dr. Harris is putty in his chair, his muscles molding around the arm rests. He looks like a melted crayon. "I wish I could have walked you down the aisle, Catherine."

The screech that leaves Mrs. Harris's lips is half angry lion, half motorcycle leaving tread at a green light. She crumples her napkin over her turkey breast and peels off for the staircase.

As Mrs. Harris flies by the front door, Archer walks in with a bouquet of orange and cream roses in one hand, and a boxed pie in the other. "Happy Thanksgiving." Archer's voice trails off as she hurries past him and upstairs, her hand gliding up the railing and out of sight. A bedroom door slams.

Catherine gasps, joy escaping her body like a popped balloon. Jake brings her ring finger to his lips and kisses her knuckle. Dr. Harris pushes his chair back and heads for the stairs, but he pauses, and sets his hand on his daughter's shoulder. He squeezes three times, and goes after his wife.

Archer holds his bouquet upside down, managing to keep the pie box upright. "What happened?" He's looking for Annabella at the table, but finds me first. "Lou?"

How does my name sound so special when he says it? "Hi."

Annabella sinks into her mother's seat. Archer slides into Annabella's chair and sets the pie on the table. Annabella peeks inside Archer's pie box. "Apple? Thank god. Cat and Jake got married."

"What?" Archer's face splits into a grin as Catherine holds up her hand again. Her tears gleam as bright as her brand new diamond. "Congratulations!"

"Holy crap." Annabella yanks Catherine's hand to her over their mom's half-eaten plate and brings the ring to within an inch of her nose. "Holee-smokes. This thing is gorgeous."

Jake's arm winds around Catherine's waist. "I've always known she's the one, so I had time to save."

Still watery-eyed, Catherine nuzzles Jake's jaw.

"What's tradition?" Annabella muses. "It's a year's salary, right?"

Jake lazily air-slaps Annabella, and she dissolves into giggles that I don't really hear. Next to me, Archer pulsates heat. He's a wood burning stove. I want to curl up next to it. To him.

Like he knows, Archer slides his arm over the back of my chair, tilting in. Goosebumps nibble my skin like he touched me. "If I knew you were here, I would have worn a nicer hoodie."

The hoodie he's wearing is faded gray from ten zillion trips through the washing machine. The cuffs are predictably sliced up. It looks like a blanket. I want to take it off him. Wrap myself up in it. Wrap us both up in it.

Oh, hell.

"You look good, Archer," I say.

Jesus the Statue, in the hutch behind Jake and Catherine, cocks an eyebrow in my direction.

"So do you," Archer whispers. His foot bounces against the leg of my chair. The beat of it is all I can focus on until we give up on the pretense of dinner.

CHAPTER 12

MRS. HARRIS NEVER RETURNS TO THE TABLE.

Dr. Harris comes back after an hour. Catherine meets him on the stairs and hugs him. She cries, Jake hovers, and Dr. Harris pets her head and says he loves her, he loves her, he loves her.

Archer looks at Annabella and they do their best-friend-shared-brain thing and take the heaping bowls of green beans and sweet potatoes to the kitchen. I follow with a stack of picked over plates. We pull tinfoil from the roll and slap lids on Tupperware and rearrange the contents of the fridge in the saddest game of Tetris. Jake filters in with more leftovers, and we keep storing, moving, shifting until everything fits.

Dr. Harris follows Catherine in, and says he'll finish clean up. Whatever passed on the staircase between Catherine and Dr. Harris wasn't enough for Catherine; she watches her dad over the growing pile of dirty dishes, her huge eyes begging him to look up.

It is devastating. I have no business seeing this.

"Thoughts on a movie?" Archer proposes as Dr. Harris turns on the faucet. His eyes dart from Annabella to me. "That monster remake just opened."

"The one with awful reviews?" Annabella asks. "Let's go." She claps her lid on noodle salad and we file out the front door, leaving Catherine and her huge, sad eyes behind.

Outside, Annabella stops on the front steps and inhales the cold air as if winter is new for her. The low sun lurks through the trees in the park across the street, breaking the dead grass into a million shadows. I stop next to her. "You okay?"

Archer turns, already halfway to the Bronco parked behind Annabella's car on the street.

"I can't believe Cat's married," she breathes. Her eyes are far away, as if she's picturing wedding scenes she won't get with her big sister.

Archer comes back and reaches for Annabella's hand. "I can."

As they walk to the curb, Annabella rests her head on Archer's shoulder. I trail behind, my hands bundled in the vest I grabbed on our way out. Annabella veers to the backseat door behind Archer, pointing at the front passenger door for me. "Take shotgun. I'm calling Zo."

We're half a block gone when Zoey answers the call and Archer and I listen to Annabella spill the entire story. Zoey exclaims at the right spots and Archer, hearing it in full for the first time, lets his jaw fall slack. "That's all your dad said?" Archer looks at Annabella in his rearview mirror. She nods vigorously.

We cross through neighborhoods, and I relax, watching Archer's hands manage the steering wheel. Annabella's voice, her tone back to its relaxed octave I'm used to, rolls over me. We stop in front of a house that belongs in the neighborhood I grew up in. A little less historical-park-adjacent, a little more cookie-cutter double stall garage. Archer parks.

"I'm here. Give me two seconds." Annabella hangs up. "Thanks for the escape, Arch."

He waves off her hair rustle. "Call us when you need a ride."

Annabella touches my shoulder. "Enjoy the movie." Annabella relaxes, stress seeping from her body. Zoey is waiting; everything will be easy for a few hours. She dashes from the Bronco and jumps up the front stoop, walking right into Zoey's house, slipping out of her coat as she shuts the front door.

Archer checks the mirrors and pulls back into the street. "We have a code when we're home and she needs out."

"Want to see that movie?" I smile.

"If it's got bad reviews, it's a hell yes, get me out now."

The golden hour drifts over his face as we merge into heavier traffic. "You have this down."

"A decade of friendship will do that."

"I know," I want to say. It's on the tip of my tongue.

But the honey light spins in his hair. He turns a corner, and the glow slants over his face, kisses his eyelids, and I can't look away.

Everything before doesn't matter. I'm here. And I get to watch the sunlight weave on his two-day old beard, and how he clutches the steering wheel tighter when he clocks me studying him.

"Can I show you my favorite place in town?" Archer asks.

My answer is immediate. "Yes."

Archer parks in an empty lot next to a bike path along the Big Sioux River, grabs a blanket from the backseat, and we start down the path. The trees get thick and absorb the city sounds as we get closer to the river. Soon, all we've got is leaves crunching under our toes, and the rush of the river flowing around the rocks. Golden sunlight cuts through branches. I stay close to Archer. Without touching him. On purpose, anyway. I can't help when our arms brush. The blanket looped through his arm is the only thing keeping our hips from knocking like bumper cars.

"We're here," Archer says, next to a tree with roots bending and curving out of the dirt like angry knuckles looking for a fight. We're on an island. A Lou-and-Archer island of misfit toys and varying levels of mental health. He touches my back to direct me down the riverbank, the tree's branches sprawling over the water. An abandoned train track bridge stretches higher into the sky than the trees rooted at the bank. Wood rots from the bridge, waiting for a strong breeze to turn it to toothpicks. I picture Archer launching his body up it, dangling over the river like it's a set of monkey bars.

I miss his hand as soon as he lifts it from my back.

Fall's long since folded itself into the roots of this tree; her leaves are piles at the base of her trunk. I sit and shove my ankles into the piles of crispy leaves like a little kid. We're hip to hip, and Archer's Vans end just south of my ankles. The river sloshes over rocks and mud, and a pair of geese that haven't migrated dip into the stream headfirst. "I came down here a lot when I was younger," Archer says. "And…again, after everything."

Mrs. Harris's words from dinner ring between my ears, and all my yearning boils into guilt. Again.

Let him talk about Cadence, I think. If he wants.

But Lust does what she does with Archer—she peeks up. She's all "hey—listen, I have questions for him." I'm not proud. But she makes the air crackle, and I like the sizzle in my belly. "How many tattoos do you have?"

Archer's eyebrows bounce skyward.

I shrug, and Lust settles in with a cackle. "Give me the tattoo tour."

"Well," Archer unzips his hoodie. He has a black sleeveless shirt underneath. Shit. This is a bad idea. Such a bad idea. "I might freeze, but let's count."

"You don't know how many you have?"

Goosebumps dot his skin from the crisp air, but he seems unbothered. "I went through a phase—the tattoo needle, the buzz, the sting, was the only thing more powerful than everything else that hurt." The way he says it, casually, like he hasn't had to sew his heart back together himself, breaks mine. Lust twists her lips together in what would be shame, if Lust understood the concept.

"I've shown you the pear." Archer skims his fingers past it and travels up his arm. A four-leaf clover sits on the tip of his shoulder, the leaves rounding to his neck. The ink is dark on his pale skin. "I come from a long Irish lineage. Granddad had the same curls I do."

I gasp. "You're Irish?"

He shakes his hair. "Shocking, right?" I scoot closer, and regret it. He's the core of the sun, about to explode.

Oblivious to the fact that he's a nuclear accident about to detonate a crater into southeastern South Dakota, Archer innocently points at the inside of his elbow. It's a single line, looping to his wrist in the shape of the top of a dog's head: ear, wavy fur, ear. "This is Buddy. He's my first dog. A golden retriever. He died in his sleep when I was seven. I learned to walk while holding his tail."

Archer twists his arm to the side so I can see his elbow. An astronaut in full gear sits inside a crescent moon. His hands sit on his thighs, his feet hanging into space, as if he's waiting for the bus on a bench rather than rotating the earth. "I like the paradox of ol' Neil finding his own gravity," Archer explains as I study the tattoo. "He found the gravity, and the gravity found him. Third Law of Motion and all that."

"You mean how Earth pulls the moon with gravity, and the moon pulls on Earth in the same amount?" Science bores, but this tattoo does not.

"The equal and opposite reaction. Even sitting here, we're pulling the Earth up with us, with as much force as gravity is keeping us here." Archer untwists his arm and the astronaut is hidden. "Tale as old as time."

A beat passes and Archer swivels his hips from me and tugs up the back of his shirt. The expanse of his skin is shocking white and even in the twilight, I see veins crisscross and sew his muscles together as his back arches forward. Dark red, coarse hair frizzes at the nape of his neck, and I itch to feel it under my fingers. But there's a reason his shirt is half off: a solid black cross is etched into his skin between his shoulder blades. It's dignified. Majestic, really.

And hot. It's hot.

Lust claps in glee. I cannot make eye contact with any of the Jesuses in the Harris home tonight.

Archer looks at me over his shoulder and pulls his shirt down. "What's that? Five?"

I grunt my confirmation.

"Let me see..." Archer notices none of my turmoil and continues to focus on his body. My mind may as well buy property in the gutter. "Oh yeah." He bends and pulls up the hem on his jeans, squeezing the denim as far up his calf as he can, showing off what I saw at homecoming weekend in the kitchen. "My music note."

"Symbolic or decorative?" Thank god his leg isn't as sexy as his back. As sexy.

"Symbolic. First note of my forever favorite song."

"Which is?"

Archer wrinkles his nose. "I don't know if we know each other quite well enough for that."

"You're stripping in the woods to show me your tats." I pull my knees to my chin. "Do you need a personal fact about me?"

"You know? Yes!" Archer pulls his pant leg down. "What's your favorite song?"

Of course he considers that the most intimate thing about me.

But, I mean, I guess it kind of is.

"'Cleopatra.' The Lumineers. It's always ..." I dig into the leaves under me. "It feels like a heartbeat, the song." As far as heartbeats go, it was one I could sync mine to.

Archer hums the melody, and his fingers float into what's left of the golden hour, like he's playing piano. "And I've read the script," he recites. "And the costume fit."

"So I played my part." That lyric pulled me through every one of the blackest nights this summer.

We share a smile.

"Now you have to tell me yours," I say.

"You can't make fun of me."

"I would never."

His sigh is epic, probably rustling birds in nests across the river. "'Can't Help Falling in Love.'"

Well. That's unexpected yet...right.

I crunch a leaf; bits of dried summer rain through my knuckles. "It's a beautiful song."

"I like the melancholy of it," Archer says. "He knows he shouldn't be falling in love, but he is anyway. The 'only fools rush in' thing. All that." He smiles, but looks far away, past the river and the old railroad bridge, seeing memories on the other bank. "It's pure poetry, packed into three minutes and two seconds."

I look where he's looking, but don't see a thing. "Do you have any more tattoos?"

"One more," Archer twists, facing me. A solid black plus sign rounds the tip of his other shoulder. "I got it one day when I was desperate to add anything to my life that made a difference."

His skin is still pink, free of scabs around the ink, but I can tell the edges of the tattoo are still crisp, the ink blacker than the rest of his work. Archer tilts my way by about a centimeter, grazes my arm. Permission for me to trace the outline of the plus sign, to brush my finger past its middle and leave my fingerprint, no matter how invisible. "When did you get it?"

"The day of the showcase. It was the tattoo shop, or your dorm." Archer's voice is soft. "Regardless, I was walking through a door."

That day, I was in no place mentally for a conversation, let alone romance, but still:

I picture him framed in our doorway, looking for me, and not Annabella. We kiss like we've done it forever, fast, a habit, but something we never want to be dull, and he fills the dorm room with music while I study and lust might start to morph into something more poignant and life would be natural and real, and not at all just a daydream for either of us.

Archer watches my fingers graze his tattoo. I pull away. "It would have been anticlimactic if you'd knocked on my door and Annabella answered."

He chuckles, pulling his sweatshirt down. The tattoos hide away. "It would have been."

We sit in the park until it's too dark to see the river. At some point, Archer drapes his blanket over our shoulders; at some point I scoot my left hip against his right. When it's time to go, Archer pulls me up, both my hands in his, and holds on. His fingers press into my palms. Once, twice, a third time.

It's better than a song.

~

I'm not sure a Saturday departure was always the plan—Annabella had packed us both enough sweats and t-shirts to last through December—but after Catherine and Jake's bombshell, the Harris home necessitated tiptoeing, literally and figuratively. The newlyweds left early Saturday, claiming Catherine was on call that night, but it was the first mention of her schedule, and Catherine didn't make eye contact with anyone over breakfast. Not that her mother was available to be lied to; Mrs. Harris has remained tucked in her room.

"What's she up to?" Annabella said to the ceiling as if her mother was knitting or watching *The Price is Right* in the room directly above our heads.

"She's praying the rosary for my soul," Catherine had grumbled.

Annabella opened her arms wide for Catherine. "Stop. We all know it's Jake's soul she's worried about, what with his picture-perfect charm and love for plain cheese pizza. You're going to defile his innocence."

"I love *stuffed crust* plain cheese pizza, thanks. That makes it special." Jake walks from the kitchen, looking at his phone. "Your dad's at the hospital, babe. Had a delivery. Said to give you this." He cups Catherine's cheek and places three quick kisses on her forehead.

The crease between Catherine's eyebrows deepens. "Right." She hooks her bag on Jake's outreached hand. "Shall we?"

No sooner did their car disappear down the street did a bedroom door upstairs open, accompanied by steps down the staircase. Mrs. Harris shuffles behind us, tissue stuffed in the cuff of her sweater, her eyes swollen, but her voice even, if forced. "Does anyone want turkey sandwiches? I can warm things up."

When Annabella and I leave a few hours later, Dr. Harris is still at the hospital. No one is watching the television, but it's still blasting a movie about a dog who can't die (take that Marley). Mrs. Harris trails us outside much like the dog in the movie who is fated to forever wander the earth. She looks about as lost.

"Thank you for hosting me," I say as Mrs. Harris hands me two plastic bags full of Tupperware containers of her legendary sweet potatoes and almost an entire apple pie. She'd spent an inordinate amount of time with a tiny dough cutter stamping out cartoony apples and delicately placing them over the pie lattice Thanksgiving morning. The guilt I'll feel eating all this later is real, but I'm still eating it.

Annabella holds her arms out to her mother. "See you at Christmas, Mom."

Their hug starts as a normal side-arm hug but Mrs. Harris tugs her daughter closer, and it morphs to a cling. Mrs. Harris's fingertips turn white under the pressure she exerts onto her daughter's shoulders. "Whenever you have someone special in your life, we'd love to meet her," she whispers.

Annabella nods tightly, like her head is on a spring. "Maybe soon."

"Yes?" Mrs. Harris's face glows. How long did it take her, as she holed away up in her California King, to dream up this subplot for Annabella, and invade the dreams she's been nurturing on her own?

"We'll see." Annabella releases her mother and backs away. Her voice is scratchy like cheap wool socks. She walks towards me, and the car, her eyes as wide as plates. "Oh my god," Annabella mutters, as she passes me and rounds to the driver's side door.

My wave and over-cheerful grin are obnoxious as we buckle in and Annabella pulls away from the curb with one swift pound on the accelerator. I sit beside her, a pile of Thanksgiving leftovers wafting their holiday smells up to my nose, and study my roommate as we speed to a major thoroughfare to get us to the interstate, and then home. I'm trying to decide if I want to wait until the interstate to speak—Annabella's eyes are nearly crossed in her fury—but she beats me to it. "You know what pisses me off?"

"Tell me."

"Mom has these unrealistic visions, these perfect plans, for us, and Cat keeps breaking them, or doing her own thing which is, naturally, against our mother's. Who cares if she eloped? She married a good guy. Like, a perfect guy." Annabella's clutch on the steering wheel tightens and her knuckles turn pink. "She did what made her happy." Her eyes are flashing, and my stomach gets queasy. Why did I let her drive?

"And isn't happiness every parent's dream?" Annabella's voice is reaching screeching proportions. "And Cat is happy. So happy, Lou. SO HAPPY."

"Yes, she seems happy," I slide in, having known her for all of 48 hours, but Annabella is wound tight, and it's time to let her spin.

"And now, just because Catherine's dreams differed from Mom's, mine need to match Mom's exactly. There's no straying. Mama Harris gets what she wants on the second try." The front car tire hits a curb as we drift up to a stoplight. We both yelp varying vulgar expletives.

"Okay." I grab the wheel, even though we're going about two miles an hour now, and Annabella stops us at the light. "Want me to drive?"

Annabella gulps and shakes her head. "I got this. Sorry."

"No apologizing." I release the steering wheel, and Annabella's fingers crawl up to ten and two. The light flips to green, she taps the accelerator, and we move forward calmly.

The car stays quiet well after we turn north and towards Brookings. Annabella props her elbow next to her window, resting her head on her open palm. "Do you think..." She sighs. "Do you think she wants to meet Zoey, or do you think this is just the next logical step to controlling my future?"

Oh, fuck. My lips flap open, too fast to let my brain figure out an answer first. "I think," I say, not thinking at all. "I think that I don't know your mom well enough to answer that question."

Annabella's frustrated sigh is louder than the sound of tires spinning up the interstate.

"But," I interject. "But I'm getting to know you. Pretty well. And I wonder if while you say you're protecting your mom going through the judgment of others...your mom just feels left out of your lives."

"How…" Annabella looks at me, steering us into the rumble strips on the edge of the pavement. She over-corrects the car back into the lane with a vicious swerve. Thank god no one is around. "How did you figure that out? You were in my house for two days."

"Jesus," I want to say to deflect as feelings rise up my throat. (He'd snuck up on me outside the guest bathroom this morning, his eyes following me down the hallway.) But that would hurt Annabella, and there's no way I will hurt Annabella. So I say the next best thing: "You."

"Me?"

I nod. "You care hard about the people in your life—you pulled me from a long weekend full of nothing except for a Hungry Man turkey dinner—which will still be a delicious dinner in a few days after we take down your mom's apple pie—to be with your family. To take me home. You had to learn that from somewhere." My voice cracks on the last word, as I watch the Interstate disappear underneath her front bumper.

Annabella swallows. "I'm glad you talk now." She moves her right hand from the steering wheel, and it lands in mine, resting on top of Mrs. Harris's Tupperware. "You aren't alone either."

I catch her fingers and hold on.

CHAPTER 13

I CAN'T THINK ABOUT HOW THIS IS MY FIRST CHRISTMAS without Mom. It snows most days now, and it's not magical confetti. Dad doesn't know the special story behind every tree ornament. He won't ask what I want for Christmas, or watch *It's a Wonderful Life*. I don't have a mom anymore. I won't have a Christmas. I'll be a spectator this year, and from now on. If I refuse to feel it, it can't—it won't—hurt me.

With that decided, it's much easier to watch Annabella and Archer bicker about theirs. And all of their traditions.

Annabella and Archer's friendship is steeped in tradition. Code words to sneak out of crowded kitchens. Strawberry milkshakes with smashed Oreos on Tuesdays and every Arbor Day. (I haven't gotten a straight answer about that one yet.) Annabella does seventeen jumping jacks before every 8K, and only 8Ks, because in eighth grade, she only did sixteen jumping jacks before an 8K at a meet, and Archer fell off his bike and broke his arm that same afternoon. Archer won't drive by the corner on 10th and Phillips Avenue in Sioux Falls because he saw Annabella's doppelganger there in 2018. ("Make fun of me all you want," he'd said. "It was like seeing a red balloon float from a storm sewer.")

And then there's their Christmas tree.

It's a broken-branched, bare, and shorter-than-Archer clearance tree from when Glee was still on the air that spent their formative years getting swapped into each bedroom every other December. I picture the two of them with chubbier cheeks and in Archer's case, no patchy beard, sparring over who tangled the lights last year, cutting snowflakes from notebook paper and tucking hand-me-down felt ornaments into what are basically pipe cleaner branches. Annabella falling asleep after Archer's gone home, the Christmas lights weaving through the fake needles and paper snowflakes to make her room glow in holiday magic and fire hazard vibes.

The easiest part of this to picture is the bickering. They're so good at it.

"Arch, if you insist on the white lights, we're using the angel theme," Annabella says as I walk into Archer's apartment. I quit knocking a few weeks ago, and I'm not sure either of them noticed.

Archer sighs; this is not the beginning of this fight. "You know how I feel about angels."

"I do. And I'm using it to get what I want." Annabella waves a box of color lights in one hand and the white lights in the other at me. "Lou. Weigh in here."

"Color lights." I kick off my boots and line them up next to Annabella's against the wall. It's snowing and ice is crammed in the tread. "They're dreamier."

"Seriously?" Archer watches me scoot past the only open bit of wall space in the studio—which now contains the tree—from the couch. I feel him watching me all the time now, even when I look up and he's not. I like the idea of him knowing exactly where I'm at in any given room, like I know where he is. "You've thought about the difference in white vs. color Christmas lights?"

I shrug. "White lights make everything feel untouchable. Like all the presents underneath it will be underwear and socks." I leave out how my mom used white lights, and it will be like swallowing glass to have the safest place I know right now contain a tree that even resembles the one I grew up under.

Annabella spins to Archer, her wool socks making her turn zippy. I can smell her shampoo when she flips her hair into a ponytail. “You don’t want a tree that inspires socks.”

“I like socks,” Archer defends. “We can use the color lights. But you’re stringing it all.”

“A compromise I can deal with.” Annabella rips open the color lights. Cardboard chunks and plastic drift to the rug as Annabella whips out the light strings. Plugged in, the room is cheery with the Christmas colors webbed on the floor.

Archer streams holiday music as I step over his legs on the coffee table and settle on the couch. Bing Crosby’s voice wafts from the tiny speakers.

Annabella is muffled behind the wiggling tree. All I see is her crooked pony sliding halfway down her skull. “Bing was a raging racist and a womanizer.”

Archer touches next on the phone screen. Michael Bublé replaces Bing.

I stick my heels into the cushion I left between me and Archer. This is our go-to seating arrangement now: space between us, protecting the other from our unhealed wounds, but not far enough away to make the other feel alone. Archer adds a mini wave. I lift two fingers from the sleeve knot I wound together to conserve body heat.

Annabella moans underneath the tree and pops up. “Half the branches are missing. It looks like a bald man back here. I’m checking the closet.” She’s gone before she’s done talking.

“She’s wound tight today,” I say as the closet swings shut next to the bathroom. “Is she still freaking out about her calc final?”

“I suggested we do this—” Archer waves at the tree “—to make her take a break, but I think all I did was redirect her anxiety.”

“Maybe if we help her?” I suggest and burrow deeper into the cushion.

"We could." Archer bends his head back. His curls at the nape of his neck are getting crushed. I want him to hold my freezing fingers and let me warm my toes under his thighs. My hair stands on the back of my neck imagining it.

He watches me; what's littering his mind? Longing? Lust? Sex-filled daydreams that take place on the table next to the tree?

Nope.

"How many gifts of socks and underwear did you get under your tree as a kid?"

I try to dislodge the fantasy of his fingers molding around my hip bone, my lips pressing against his whiskers. Unsuccessful, I knock my foot against his knee. Flirting like a third grader. "I'm freezing, so not enough."

Archer squints. "We can't have that." He produces a giant gray knit blanket with a sapphire stripe down the middle from his side of the couch. Archer flaps the blanket and it billows over my legs.

I stretch out, like the blanket is an invisibility cloak, and press my feet against his thighs. Electricity zings straight into my nervous system. He feels it too, based on the smile on his face. "We've rented out Gallerie for a show on New Year's Eve. An open mic night," he says. "You should come."

Disappointment thuds in my chest. "I'll still be at home."

"Oh."

"Even if I did come back, I wouldn't have a place to stay. The dorms will be closed."

He dips his chin and delivers the most scathing side-eye of my life. Of course I'd have a place to stay. Of course.

It doesn't help that Archer parks his hand on my ankle under the blanket. He brushes his thumb over my ankle bump, and settles his fingers on my skin. My leg lights on fire.

There's nothing left at home that makes me feel that kind of warmth. I lean my cheek to my shoulder, in what I hope is a flirty pose, but I have no idea anymore. "Will I at least get the good pillow?"

Archer grins at what I think are his knuckles under the blanket. "You'll need to talk that over with AB."

Annabella is back, arms full of plastic tree branches. She looks like she's ripped a bush from the landscaping outside the dorm. "You two gonna help me?"

Archer pinches his lips together and shakes his head. I burst out laughing, and so does Annabella. "This is the actual tradition," she says to me. "I do the work, and Archer lays underneath the tree at the end and takes credit."

"It's my favorite part of Christmas," Archer says. "Admiring your handiwork. I can't argue with perfection."

"You're full of it," Annabella jams the lost branches into the tree base. "How'd your trig final go?" She's talking to me; Archer's clearly on the do-not-talk list for at least five minutes.

"It was okay, I guess." I shrug.

"You were smart to not take calc," Annabella mutters. Her eyes are on the tree like it's an equation in need of solving.

"I'm not smart enough to take calc."

"You are," she corrects, brushing her hair from her eyes.

After Thanksgiving, she ghosted her mom, afraid to say yes, afraid to say no. Afraid to do anything that will hurt anyone she loves. Her insecurities mingle with her heart, which is way bigger than mine. I'd say it's like looking in a mirror, watching Annabella these last weeks, but at least she has people to love outside of this room.

Damn. Have I come to love the people in this room?

I can't let her decorate this tree alone.

I toss the blanket to Archer, though the feeling of his hand on me will linger as I slip to sleep tonight. He frowns, and I hope it's because I'm walking away. I want to kiss him, so badly it keeps me up at night—every night—but I need Annabella too. I need to be a best friend again.

I fish out the second string of color lights from the pile of ancient ornaments Annabella has spread on the kitchen table. "Let me help."

The tree, packed full of box-store, glossy green balls and white sparkly snowflakes and Santa hats and buffalo check stars and candy canes and more twinkly lights than a six-foot-tall, skimpy tree cocked slightly to the right needs, is done.

Annabella pretends to blow into a trumpet and plugs in the silver-tinsel-wrapped star tree topper. Bright and garish, it pulls every color in the universe, and not in a festive way. It looks like what a Wellness 101 worksheet would describe as an acid trip.

I nod fake approval. Archer snorts from the couch.

"We got it in middle school," Annabella explains. "Arch's mom gave it to us when they bought a new tree topper. It's the one his parents used on their first Christmas together."

Archer joins us around the tree, the blanket draped over his shoulders like a cape. "Every year I'm shocked it works." He rubs his hands together. "Ladies, it's time." He flips the lights off and the room falls dark, save the streetlights illuminating the floating snowflakes outside. We're in a snow globe.

Archer crumbles to the floor and slides past our socks underneath the tree. Shades of red and golden and blue splash his face. "You two are missing true majesty down here."

Annabella cozies in under the tree with him, their shoulders touching. He stretches his arm out and she uses it as a pillow. "Not bad." She arches her arm up, her hand open to me. "Get down here, Lou. We're not doing this without you."

I settle on the floor next to Annabella, push my hair behind me, and look up. It's a sea of overlapping color, peeking past the plastic needles and bouncing off the shimmery snowflakes. Sparkles and fat glitter chunks, and wobbly branches that threaten to snap off any second. How is it so broken and beautiful at the same time?

I know Archer is watching me over Annabella's head, but I keep my eyes pointed upward, taking in the branches, the ornaments and more lights than I can count. When I feel his fingers in my hair, curling around my ends around his knuckles, my chest warms.

"You two need to get a room," Annabella sighs, content at last.

~

Twinkly lights line Meghan's office windows; she shares an affinity for multi-colored strings with Annabella. I nestle my favorite yellow pillow into my lap.

"You look relaxed." Meghan plops into her armchair. "Xanax still treating you well?"

I nod. "Meds are fine. My last final is tomorrow morning. Annabella's last final, calculus, was yesterday. She's gone home now." Her grade was posted an hour after she turned in the test, and the way she walked into our dorm, her shoulders slumped, her eyelids heavy, I thought she failed, but she didn't. Ninety-three percent. I suggested we call Archer, and get celebratory milkshakes, but she was already crawling up her loft, on the phone with Zoey.

"When will you see her next?"

"Hopefully on New Year's Eve. Archer's hosting an open mic night."

"Is he done with finals yet?"

He's home now too. He bailed right after our Wellness final on Wednesday. I can't be sure, but I don't think he took all his tests. This morning, after Annabella headed home for break, I climbed back to bed for the sole purpose of imagining Archer beside me under my quilt. His lips grazed my forehead as he held me, his breath mingling with mine. The top of his thighs were soft under my fingers.

ARCHER: I'm working on a new song for the open mic night. I can't wait for you to hear it.

It's taking everything I've got to not crash his parents' house and insist he plays it for me right now.

And it's a distraction for what's waiting for me at home: pretending there's no Christmas. Pretending Mom is just on a road trip. Pretending Ginny's golden desk lamplight isn't stretching across our dark street from her bedroom to mine. Pretending this Archer attraction is short-lived. Pretending this aching to press my palm against his chest where his ribs turn to stomach is just the output of a silly, weird little crush.

It's a Christmas full of unattainable goals.

"Same," I answer Meghan's question.

"Have you thought more about EMDR therapy?"

I nod.

"Any questions? What are you thinking there?"

I bite my lips into a line. "I'm thinking I'm still thinking about it."

"Fair." Meghan reaches for her teacup. "What's keeping you awake right now?"

In the literal sense, Archer. But also: "I'm worried about Annabella."

Meghan nods, her tell to continue.

"She's stressed." This morning, after ten hours of sleep, Annabella admitted it was the minus part of the A that made her sad. "Finals took it out of her, and even Archer and Zoey can't shake her mind free." I think of

Zoey's voice, far away in Annabella's cell phone last night. Annabella cried into her pillow trying to muffle it from me, while Zoey struggled to dam the tears from three hours away. I grabbed my laptop and moved to the lobby until I thought she might be asleep.

"Okay," Meghan says, after I tell her the story. "Annabella is struggling right now. She's scared to not live up to expectations her family has set upon her."

"That's probably right."

"What does that have to do with you?"

I look from the tree lights glowing like little festive ghosts behind Meghan's sheer curtains. "What?"

"How do Annabella's struggles affect you?"

"I'm her roommate," I sputter, merry lights forgotten. "I can't watch her suffer. I won't watch her suffer."

"Have you listened to her?"

"Yes." Thanksgiving made me realize it, sure, but if I'm honest, I'd listened to every word Annabella uttered since she helped me during that meet. I'd tried to do right by her, ever since.

"There must be something else I can do. I can call Catherine," I say. "Call Zoey. Archer's out of ideas, but the girls might not be."

Meghan doesn't move a muscle. "You can. But why?"

My feet swing to the floor. "Are you joking? Why not?"

"What's wrong with redirecting that energy—not all, but some—into you?"

Saliva pools in my mouth. "Maybe I care about her more."

Meghan places her teacup on her desk. "Lou—"

"No, seriously." Anger weaves through my rib cage like a weed. "You're a therapist. You can't be suggesting I don't help my friend."

"Is that what you think I'm saying?"

Somewhere in my brain, light flashes: common sense, Lou. Common sense. "No."

"Listen, Annabella and Archer are becoming real pillars of your support system. Am I wrong?"

"No."

"And you want to do whatever you need to do to help them—"

"Yes," I interject.

"What I'm asking," Meghan rests her elbows on her knees. "Is there a way to take half that energy you devote to your friends and reinvest it in yourself?"

I comb the tassels on the pillow still in my lap. "I don't know how."

"Then let's work on it when we come back."

~

My trig final is over. I probably passed. I'm headed home in the morning. I could've gone home tonight. But to what?

With Annabella, and everyone on our floor, gone, the crushing hum of humans has vanished. I don't miss them, but I miss my roommate. Wind rattles the screen against the window. There's a blizzard brewing, but it won't hit for days. That's how South Dakota storms work. Buildup, days of it, stillness sets in, and: bam. The real show begins.

I intended to make the most of Annabella's absence and planned to let my mind wander to Archer (again), but the vibe is off and I pull my fingers out of my underwear.

I flip over my phone to shop for cleats to sleep (I have my eye on a hot pink pair), but I navigate to Annabella's text from earlier this afternoon.

ANNABELLA: I can't believe I never sent this – my bad.

ARCHER: You forgot the attachment.

ANNABELLA: Sorry. Double bad.

ARCHER: You text like a grandma.

ANNABELLA: At least I don't look like one ELBOW PATCHES ARE OUT OF STYLE ARCHER.

ARCHER: Hipster grandpas would be your thing. And you still haven't sent the pic.

ANNABELLA: Hipster grannies will be my thing. In approximately 54 years.

ANNABELLA: Here's the picture - to be clear, I'm only sending it now because I still like Lou.

I roll my eyes (again), and save the photo. Annabella snapped a selfie of the three of us under the Christmas tree the night we put it up. She's cheesing, Archer's grinning up at the camera, his smile bigger than almost any other I've seen in real life. I'm cozied into Annabella, my chin on her shoulder. Archer's fingers are still in my hair. Our foreheads are a kaleidoscope of splotches: yellow, red, blue, mingling.

We look happy.

That's enough.

CHAPTER 14

THEN I GET HOME.

No one is here.

I know what Mom would be wearing, if she was here. How she'd greet me—the same way she always did when I came home after practice. Buttery pastel pink skinny jeans. Probably a white t-shirt knotted over a belt loop. It's Christmas, so a heavier cardigan. A mug of tea in her hand. Her hair is curled, her berry lipstick perfect. She was tiny like a baby bird, but her hug was bigger than time itself. "I missed you on Thanksgiving," she would have said.

But she never would have said that because I never would have missed Thanksgiving. Not if she was still here.

Now she's not. But I am, and alone in the doorway of the house I grew up in, three days before Christmas.

On the kitchen counter, Dad left a note. It takes a second to register his handwriting. It's not like he ever signed the birthday cards or my field trip permission slips.

Ran out. Back later. Cash in drawer. Order a pizza.

I sigh and take my bag up to my room, closing their bedroom door on the way. The house feels down-to-its-bones-cold, like no one has slept here in days. Weeks? He could have at least lit a candle. Sent one of his firm's staging people over here to fluff a curtain.

But that's Dad. Chronically incapable of caring about anything, or anyone, at all.

On my second morning home, as I swallow my Xanax with a swig of Earl Gray, Gin's house is a magnet through the window, my eyes drawn to the dormant lilac bush by her garage. The windows are dark. Her car's missing from its spot in the driveway.

Dad didn't come home until about midnight. I called hello to him from my bed so he wouldn't grab the shotgun in the night if I had to pee, and he just murmured a quiet hello back, passing my bedroom door for his study.

There's one new development: Marissa, his old secretary, is now his out-in-the-open girlfriend. At least he has the common sense to not bring her around here.

I need to get out of this house. But there's nowhere to go. Stippled clouds press over Aberdeen, light gray but plenty foreboding like at Dorothy's house as Miss Gulch speeds up on her bike to collect Toto. I watch Ginny's next-door neighbors pull in and get out of their car, their wrapped gifts and coats lifting to fly away in gusts of wind. The grocery stores are sold out of everything, and Dad even claims to be coming home early tonight. The storm is imminent.

I go to my room, pull the curtains to block Ginny's house, and wish Dad would stay at Marissa's.

ANNABELLA: Did you know blizzard claustrophobia is a real thing?

ARCHER: We grew up in the northern tundra. We've experienced it.

ANNABELLA: Yeah, but blizzards used to be cozy. Movies. Popcorn. Hot chocolate with marshmallow fluff.

ARCHER: You spent last winter begging to scale drifts in the Bronco.

ANNABELLA: Blizzard claustrophobia made me go mad. Lou – how's home? Is it snowing up there yet?

ARCHER: If the blizzard lasts too long, don't chance it. Just stay there. No pressure.

ANNABELLA: He's lying.

ARCHER: I'm not.

ANNABELLA: He is.

Day three. Kitchen window. Clouds skim the treetops, spitting tiny snowflakes into the gusts of wind. Xanax. Cold Earl Grey. Swallow, gulp, turn from window. Dad's home, and mad about it. Holed up in his study, like I'm about to be holed up in my bedroom.

ARCHER: Hope you're okay.

The meteorologist narrows our Christmas blizzard timeline. She says it'll kick into high gear Christmas Eve as thick ice flurries and wind and transition to multiple feet of snow over several days. The cloud mass on the radar is about to park itself right over us like its home. Ms. Meteorologist says she's optimistic the storm will fade by New Years, but her grimace is deep and doubtful.

"Hm," Dad says, watching the news with me. He hasn't sat down and instead is rocking on the balls of his feet.

I have my own "hm" dialed up on my tongue, but it dies on my lips. I sink deeper into what I've adopted as my blanket, even though Grandma made it for my parents' wedding twenty years ago. Grandma is long gone, and now so is Mom, but she spent a lot of time under this blanket, picking at it, unraveling the yarn.

Ginny would appreciate that metaphor. Her car is parked in its spot now, but it hasn't moved in days, even as her dad has come and gone.

The weather report switches to coverage of a hockey game in Sioux Falls. Dad sighs his way out of the living room and to his study.

I snake my hands out of my burrito blanket situation to knot my hair up on my head. Done, one hand lands on top of my other wrist. And I squint, wondering what it's like to have lines there, like Mom did.

ANNABELLA: It's so weird here. Cat and Jake just got home, blaming the storm even though it hasn't started yet besides the wind. Mom won't look at Cat. And everyone is over-polite.

We don't have a place to bury her.

At least that's what I assumed.

"We have a family plot," Dad tells the funeral home director over the phone. He glances up and sees me across the kitchen, picking at a bowl of cereal. It's dinner time. But neither of us feel like cooking. "But cremation was her preferred option." Dad answers whatever question was posed, and turns his back to me, as if I didn't just plan half the service that afternoon while he stared out the window.

Dad hangs up, and I speak before he can escape. "We have a family plot?"

"Well. Yes." Dad looks startled I don't know this.

I am startled. "Why?"

"In case something happened. To you, mostly." Dad slips his phone in his pocket.

"In case something happened to me?" Blood drums in my ears, and I stand hoping the dizziness fades, but it just gets worse. "Was something going to happen to me?"

"Of course not." Dad jerks his head side to side—he's done. Ready to go. "It's just a thing parents do, Lou. We make these plans in the event of the unthinkable."

"Like this."

He won't look me in the eye. "Yeah."

Now that he's here, opening up, even in one syllable snippets, I want more. I need more. I need to make him stay with me. "Are you gonna be buried there?"

"I can't talk about this with you—"

And it smacks me hard. Marissa is real. So was the Marissa before her. And the Marissa before her. The administrative assistants that never stayed long—they either quit or were promoted quickly. All of those trips to Cincinnati. Whoever he's with when he drops dead will be who he's buried with.

Mom will be long scattered to the wind. Alone.

Dad sweeps away and the click of his study door closing echoes to me.

Who am I kidding? Mom was always alone.

I blink out of the memory, and I find I've wandered into my bathroom. My toothbrush is already in hand, and I don't know what time it is, but muscle memory takes over and toothpaste worms onto the bristles and I scrub away at my teeth like they've done me wrong.

I spit my toothpaste out, exhausted by the act. My bed is so far away. Too far. I sink to the floor and press my cheek into the freezing floor.

She was never alone. She had you.

Ginny. Relief crowds my lungs, shoves all the air out. I don't care that I lose my breath. She tethers me to this world. The world where my mom's still gone, but I'm still here.

Early Christmas Eve morning the blizzard swirls in like a banshee as I try to sleep.

The heat is too high, but it's too cold to open my windows. Besides, I don't want to hear Ginny come home, or risk hearing her real voice float from her driveway as she kisses Milo goodbye. Snow would rest on the wool hat I gave her two years ago for Christmas. It's mustard, her favorite color, with a giant pompom on the crown. She wears it as she serves coffee at her dad's coffee shop, the nerdiest, cutest barista the world ever did see.

Sleet crashes into my window panes, twinkling, then banging like sandpaper determined to scrape through the glass.

My phone lights up in the dark.

ARCHER: You ever feel like our lives are blowing by us?

ARCHER: Don't answer. That first Christmas is impossible. I get it. I might be talking to an echo chamber, but there's a romance in sending an SOS into the night. The modern message in a bottle.

ARCHER: I feel like it sometimes, life blowing by. Like whatever is 'normal' or 'right' doesn't fit my skin the way it should, so I shrug it off, and I feel free – but then I want to know: what else am I missing? What am I not fast enough to see, or strong enough to do? What am I missing because I'm scared?

ARCHER: Sometimes I can't write fast enough. Or the right melody doesn't come. And I think about when I was a kid, and my mom took me to this donut store in the neighborhood, and we'd always get the powdered sugar donuts and fuck Lou, they were good. Everything a kid could idolize forever. And when I can't find that melody or the lyric is stupid, that's what comes to me. Those fucking perfect donuts and how the sugar tasted when I licked it from my finger and Mom's smile as she watched me suck down my chocolate milk and what if I've already lived my perfect memory?

ARCHER: This is probably preposterously dumb. Blizzard claustrophobia, right?

ARCHER: All this to say – thinking of you.

ARCHER: And now those amazing donuts. Dammit.

My phone slips to my lap, and I see M&Ms. M&Ms spread over a tied-end fleece blanket. A pile of red candies over a hot pink fleece heart. Greens clustered on a blue star. Lumpy yellows roll in Ginny's hot hand. Shiny browns on my trig notes. Gin is talking about the last Nicola Yoon book-turned-movie, and my eyes trace the path her hand swings through the air as she pops yellow M&Ms in her mouth one by one.

The interstate closes. Drifts measure at three feet tall and growing, curving over cars and up to our house windows. Ice lurks underneath the snow, a literal death trap. I can't see our curb through the white-out, let alone Ginny's.

Dad eats the chicken noodle soup and grilled cheese lunch I cobbled together. He shifts his gaze from the whiteout window back to the phone scrolling. Like he'll sell a house on Christmas Eve. "Really coming down out there," he says.

ARCHER: If the snow ever stops, Gallerie will be unlocked to set up at 6 on NYE.

ANNABELLA: If the snow ever stops.

ARCHER: It will. KELO's reporting interstates will open Saturday morning.

ANNABELLA: Doubtful. The blizzard claustrophobia will be my end.

ARCHER: Try to trust that good happens sometimes.

ANNABELLA: I'll pray for it.

ARCHER: Jesus-y sarcasm. And on his birthday. Bold.

ANNABELLA: He gets my sense of humor.

ARCHER: Lou, are you okay? We haven't heard from you in over a week.

Christmas morning. I'm up, and I pad to the kitchen for my pill and tea. I stand over my mug, the steam dancing off my nose, and I think about how I'm going to tell Meghan what's happening here. And Annabella. Archer. How I need them. Not to fix me, but to be with me.

How to ask for help.

I take my tea into our living room. Neither of us put up the tree. Santa never came. It could be the middle of July, based on what this place looks like.

It needs a mom.

I'm not anyone's mom, but I can try.

I'm in the basement a minute later, yanking giant, over-filled storage containers off the shelves. The tree—or rather, its bag handles—brush the top of my head from the top shelf, as if to remind me of its location, but

I'm not putting it up. I'm not ready to unzip the bag and smell Mom's White Diamonds from last Christmas, and every Christmas. Nor am I looking for our traditional ornaments: the white lights, the clay ornaments featuring Little-Lou handprints and lopsided glitter clumps that Mom carefully wrapped in bubble wrap last December, assuming she'd be here this December.

No, I'm looking for Dad's Christmas stash—the only decor he ever cared about, because if the neighbors think you look good, obviously, you're good. Plus, as the top-five selling realtor in town, your personal curb appeal is just good marketing.

Of course, his stuff is in the last storage container. "Yes," I mutter, hoisting the container to my hip, and turn for the stairs.

Twenty minutes later, I snuggle into Mom's pristine snow-white couch and pull Grandma's blanket into my lap. Plugged in, Dad's roof lights took over the living room, the red, golden, deep blue bulbs snaking over our bookshelves in the corner, dripping to the carpet, and skyrocket up to the framed daffodils in watercolor Mom redecorated with two years ago. The lights stretch to the television, drape the screen and move onto more art, a shelf full of pictures of me as a kid, and touch the ground again, zig-zagging over the floor like a river looking for the ocean.

It's not perfect. It's nowhere near. But it's bearable.

I slide my phone from my flannel pants and snap a picture of my favorite part, where the string of lights reaches for the TV like The Creation of Adam. I kind of love it.

Dad comes downstairs later, his robe grubby. I've turned on Home Alone, and Kevin is accidentally stealing a toothbrush. "What is all of this?"

I don't turn at the sound of his voice. "It's Christmas."

ARCHER: Wait, by Alexi Murdoch. It's pure and it's magic.

New Year's Eve. The highways are still closed.

I pull down my stocking cap, put my phone on silent, and am out the door when the guest room shower blasts on; night training post-blizzard is best done when your dad doesn't try to talk you out of it as you lace up your traction cleats. Lamplight streaks from every living room on the block.

Snow swaths arch and wane on the street, untouched. The night is silent, save the wind blowing wet snow clumps from branches, plopping into the fresh powder, twinkling like faraway stars.

The air is crisp. Fresh. I can breathe again and want to suck every bit of this perfect clear air into my lungs and keep it forever. At a red light, I jog right through it, and I go farther than I'd planned when I left.

At least an hour later, I circle back to my street. My house is the only dark house on the block, sitting in the shadows, but I doubt anyone expected anything from us this year. Neighbors turned on their Christmas lights, colors swinging from the arching eaves while I run past. Decorated trees glow in windows, and behind the decorations, families exist in their rooms.

Ginny's living room window is lit up, finally, brighter than anything else on our street. Anyone can see right in.

Inside the window, Summer waves wildly at someone in the kitchen. Her leg is bent on the cushion, as if it will launch her off the furniture if it would get her to whoever she's talking to faster.

Then I see her. Ginny, framed in the kitchen door, holds two mugs. I don't have to be in the room to know it's her dad's hot chocolate recipe. Her rosy cheeks are the giveaway—she had to stir the chocolate for exactly twelve minutes for peak creaminess. Ginny gives Summer a mug. Two hot chocolate mugs, two sets of hands, two grins.

This open window is a fucking humble brag.

"You can come inside, you know."

I jump. I didn't notice his snow-covered truck on the street. Or him in it. "Milo."

"Hey." Milo gently shuts his truck door, to not bring his girlfriend sprinting to her front door yet.

"Braved the travel ban?" I'm back to watching Ginny and Summer. Summer's lips move a mile a minute, and Ginny keeps splicing into Summer's words with mad giggles and weird little karate hand chops. They look like a sitcom from the nineties.

"I'm not the only one." Milo crosses the street and points to my traction spikes. "Those new?"

"Coach recommended them." I leave out that while Coach recommended the spikes to the squad, Annabella had to tell me. "I shouldn't be creeping on Gin. Don't tell her."

"I won't." Milo hikes over a snowbank, the snow eating his legs. We're out of view from Ginny's window. We won't be spotted.

His hair looks short under a fleece beanie. "Did you just get back from Michigan? How are Nana and Pops?" I spent a handful of holidays driving to Michigan with Milo's family. In the evenings we stashed ourselves in the far backseat under a blanket, pretending to sleep. How his family never clocked the illicit movements under the blankets is beyond me.

Milo stomps his feet in the snow. "Getting old. Every year, I worry it's the last."

"Did you take Ginny?"

"No," he shakes his head. "She wanted to stay and spend time with her dad. Plus, she needs to pack."

"Pack?"

"She got into Iowa. Moving into Summer's dorm next week."

Goosebumps pool on my arms. Iowa. Her dream school. "That's... incredible."

Milo beams, every bit the proud boyfriend. "It is."

When Milo visits, they'll cram in a twin bed, but it's fine because they probably still fall asleep touching. Summer will make soupy mac and cheese in the microwave and decorate their dorm door for every social media holiday. They'll buy magnetic poetry for the mini fridge, and take turns picking out ice cream because only one carton fits in the tiny freezer. They'll speak in their shorthand that only they know. Ginny will lose days and nights to writing in her unmade bed and I won't be in any of the stories anymore.

There are pieces that I want. But only pieces.

"Come inside. Please." Milo reaches out, his gloves grazing my Sherpa.

My head jerks into a hard shake. "She needs to ask me."

Milo pulls his hand back. "Can I tell her I saw you?"

Through the window, Ginny looks—is—happy as she talks to Summer. She didn't call after Mom. She never crossed the street again. As I disintegrated to ash, I felt her watching me from her bedroom window, safe, and never saying a word. And words are her specialty. "She can ask me first, Milo."

He can't help himself; his hand lands on my shoulder. I pat his fingers, as if that's my role here now: comfort the boy. His smile peeks out. Safe. Charming. Full of straight teeth. The first love for two girls. It's not a bad track record.

I'm in my garage by the time Milo gets to Ginny's house. He knocks—why, if not for dramatic impact, and I look as Ginny springs off the couch, whips open the door, and crashes so hard into Milo they nearly topple off the stoop into a snowbank.

That's what he expected when he gave me that godforsaken promise ring.

Next to the lawnmower, I check my phone. One text chain, three names.

ANNABELLA: Lou. The interstate is plowed and open. Get down here.

ARCHER: Please? (But be careful.)

ANNABELLA: We want you here.

ARCHER: I want you here.

ANNABELLA: He does. Like, so bad. It's gross.

ARCHER: It is. And I do.

Ginny's door slams shut. I don't know who shut it. It doesn't matter. It might tomorrow.

But tonight?

LOU: I'm on my way.

CHAPTER 15

DEEP GROOVES OF SNOW LINE THE HIGHWAYS, STILL untouched by plows, but already forced open by restless farmers. My tires skid over bridges, the black ice another booby trap to stop me from getting to Archer and Annabella. I should turn around, go home.

I don't.

By eleven, I'm outside Gallerie, shaking my hair free of sleet and slicking down my fingers to tuck the loose frizz around my forehead into something not chaotic. It doesn't matter. I'm chaotic. Every second without Archer plucks my veins as if to say get closer.

The floor is full, the bar is open. A circle of rugs is flopped in the middle of the floor with a mic stand, Archer's speakers on the concrete and a spotlight shining off the tops of heads. People hold drinks and surround the rugs as a woman sings an acoustic cover of a song I should know, but don't. A set of girls carry their heels, as if the night is old.

It's a blank slate. Ready for new memories to embed within these walls. For me to become part of this energy that never fades, not entirely. We'll always be here, in the air, in the memories these walls keep. I feel like I can reach out, clasp it, keep it.

I've been here before, but not like this.

Fingers squeeze past the fluff of my parka on my elbow. Annabella. Relief floods to my toes as I hug her. Next to her, Zoey waves. "I'm sorry I'm late."

Annabella grins. "You're right on time. He's up next."

The woman singing ends her song—I still don't know why it's familiar—and she backs away from the mic. Archer comes out of nowhere, like he's summoned from the folds in the rugs. Energy fizzes under my skin and pulls me forward; I need proximity. To see if his thumb nail is still cracked. The dusting of freckles that's thicker on his left cheek. I need him to see me.

Archer strums Matilda and tunes a knob at the handle. His flannel has maroon lines with gray-green squares, like he'd put it in a blender and mixed the colors up. I know it smells like laundry detergent and black coffee. The cotton is smooth after getting beat in the dryer a hundred times and from moving mics and speakers to the Bronco and putzing around his tiny apartment, flipping grilled cheeses and rolling the cuffs up his forearms. The collar is missing a button, the thread still in the cotton with nothing to hold together. I noticed it while we pretended to study for the Wellness final, our stacks of pastel worksheets ignored. The thread obliterated every thought except for how his skin would feel against my knuckles if I told him to stay still so I could yank it out.

His fingers, calloused from practicing until pain fades, pause on top of Matilda. His gaze dances over every face, looking for mine in the crowd.

And when Archer sees me, every pull in me steadies.

The edges of Archer's lips curl up. He steps up to the mic. "Last minute audible. I'm doing a cover. It's a gamble but, um, I think it might be worth it."

Archer picks at Matilda's strings, her sweet hum vibrating between my ribs. He takes a deep breath, and sings. "Wise men say, only fools rush in."

I squeeze between two guys in the front row. I'm close enough to touch his mic stand, but my hands, under their own volition, fold at my belly button. Archer sways with the melody. His eyes are on me and my hair slipping from my ponytail and the t-shirt I grabbed off the floor in my bedroom in my hurry, and I don't care that I'm a mess. I had to be here. I had to see him sing this song.

"Like a river flows, surely to the sea. Darling, so it goes. Some things are meant to be."

Archer looks down at his fingers strumming, and smiles. "Take my hand. Take my whole life too. 'Cause I can't help falling in love with you."

Applause swallows his last note. Archer releases Matilda and she swings it to his back. The crowd's claps fill my ears, but my chest is full of the song, desperation multiplying in my lungs. His eyes are fire, and I know that while gravity pulled me to right here tonight, he'd felt it towing him to me at home.

The equal and opposite reaction, each of us pulling to the other with the exact same force, time and space be damned. It is what it is.

So when he kisses me, we just are.

~

"How were you a stranger four months ago?" I think, following Archer up the steep stairs to his apartment. His fingers thread through mine at the base of his spine.

"Why are you not looking?" I wonder, as I shimmy out of my jeans. I'm not as restrained; I watch when Archer takes his flannel and t-shirt under off. The black cross between his shoulder blades makes my heart stutter, but my heart has had palpitations for hours.

"How did I get here?" I ask aloud, as weak sunshine tiptoes into Archer's windows the next morning.

"We came up the stairs?" Archer answers, twirling a chunk of my hair between his knuckles. "Or are we talking on a more existential level?"

His scruff is a translucent peach in the morning. "Thanks for asking me to come back."

"I begged. It wasn't my finest moment."

I sit up, last night's t-shirt wrinkled like tissue paper. "I mean it. Thank you."

Archer touches my chin, his thumb brushing my bottom lip. It's a heady feeling, one I've never experienced, a spark that comes with every single shift of his body. Like it's all a secret to unlock, and magic only I get to see.

Last night, when the open mic singers tapped out, someone turned on their Spotify retro playlist and acoustic night shifted into a dance party. Backstreet Boys and Ace of Base and Spice Girls. Annabella, Zoey, Archer, and I danced, matching shimmies to shakes. For all of Annabella's natural athleticism, she dances like an inflatable wave woman outside car dealerships and new car washes, bending and twisting with the wind. She owned it. Zoey's stare was pure, but her grip on her water bottle was anything but.

And I had to be touching Archer. Had to. Like a lifeline. My palms itched when they weren't pressed against him. He knew, and weaved his fingers through my belt loops, his whiskers sweet on the skin under my neck. I folded into his body, and every song after became a slow song even when it wasn't.

Two minutes before midnight, Archer climbed on the bar, waving everyone to the clock on his phone. Together, two hundred of our closest friends counted down, screaming by the ten second mark.

With three seconds to go, Archer jumped down, his boots landing between my Keds with a thud. "Three! Two!" His hand drifted to the top of my head, his eyelashes close enough to count.

"One," I said. And I kissed him first.

"I'm glad I'm here," I say now.

He smiles. "Are you hungry?"

Before we head to the greasy spoon across the street, Archer darts to the bathroom to brush his teeth. He spares me a squirt of toothpaste, that I rub furiously across my teeth with my pointer finger. While he rinses and spits, I peek at the record player: Explosions in the Sky.

The street in the morning after a major drinking event is quiet. We pass a bar that's a shell of itself without the booming bass and the bouncer and his tiny ID-checking flashlight. A beer bottle sticks from a drift like a flag, and Archer grabs it, dumps it in the garbage can. He walks backwards, his knuckles peaks and valleys in his pockets, smiling.

"What?" I laugh, gripping my coat shut.

Archer reaches for me. "This is just something to see. That's all."

"The omelets, right?" Last night's singer line-up, scribbled on his forearm, peeks out from under his sweater sleeve.

"Yes." Archer holds the diner door open for me. "Obviously, the omelets."

The servers are loopy, counting the tips drunk customers left behind. Archer and I order omelets and tea for me, coffee for him. I shed my coat, glad I grabbed one of Annabella's hoodies she forgot bunched up on Archer's couch. "Where did Annabella and Zoey end up?"

"Zoey surprised her with a suite at a hotel. Way fancier than anything Mama Harris would ever allow the Doctor to shell out for, so AB jumped at the offer." Archer fishes three creamers from the bowl on the table and lines them up. He split open the first lid. "I hope this romantic getaway helps her get her head back in the game."

"I know," I say.

In goes the second creamer. "Speaking of being off." Archer peels back the third creamer's lid. The milk swirls into his coffee. "I worried about you while you were in Aberdeen." He glances up. "I'm still worried about what happened to you in Aberdeen."

"I..." My gaze flutters around the diner. Our server is flirting with the cook through the pass window as he fries our omelets. An old guy flips through a newspaper in the restaurant's window, and behind us, there's a table of four people, probably grad students, in stocking caps and boots, stacking mini packs of jellies and peanut butters like they're playing Jenga. I look back to Archer, his gray eyes gentle and focused on me. "I had a hard time," I whisper, the last words scrambling in my brain so messily that I'm not sure they came out in order.

But Archer's nodding, so even if they didn't, he still understood.

"A really hard time." I look down at my knuckles, grinding against each other over the table. Consciously, I pull them apart, and spread my fingers out next to my silverware. I've got Mom's hands—she always said so, but even if she hadn't, I would see her hands in mine now. The same nail beds. Our pinkies share the same slightly wide curve on our right hands. How our veins pop out just a little bit more on our left hands.

That's what I'm thinking about as Archer puts his hand over mine. His square cuticles, the blue lines shining through his porcelain skin. "Is this okay?"

I nod, and look back up to him.

"What can I do to help?"

I'm not surprised he's the first person to ever ask. "Spend some of your free time with me?"

He presses his lips into a line that I swear he's trying to stop from turning into a smile. "Just some of my free time?"

As quickly as the shadows had taken over, a little light cracked through. "Please tell me about your Christmas."

He keeps his hand over mine, and uses the other to dip his spoon in his coffee. "Fine. Mom and Dad were fine. Too many presents. Didn't give me too much grief when I skipped midnight mass. Honestly, I'm lucky they're mine."

I want to know his mom's name. Study his dad's smile to see if lifts on the right side first, then the left, like Archer's. Read the books on his end table. I want to see the posters in his childhood bedroom, sit in his closet and peek up through the sleeve holes for the shirts he ditched at home. So different than what's left of my family. The kind of light that chases all the shadows out.

He stirs his coffee again, and watches the creamer spin. "Cadence called. She asked if I wanted to meet for coffee. I said no."

"You could have."

"I know," Archer says quickly. "Don't take offense, but I said no for me, not for you." He squeezes one eye closed. "I said that terribly. You know what I mean."

"I do."

Archer nudges his hand under mine and raises our palms together, tenting over the empty creamer cups. My fingers are as long as his, but his are riddled with tiny, hardened ridges from the guitar strings. More pen ink streaks across his skin like paint. I know without asking he'd been writing before the open mic.

"I'm working on that baggage," he says. "Pinterest garbage or not, it's time." Archer squeezes my hand again and releases me as the server drops off our steaming omelets.

I hate that he let me go, but my stomach growls, reminding me why we're here. My fork tilted to cut into the omelet, I inhale the breakfast smells. "You've at least gotten your baggage out of the car?"

Archer laughs. "It's unzipped. You?"

Cheese oozes from my omelet. "Wide open. The wind is scattering my dirty laundry over the front yard. It's embarrassing."

He snorts and stabs a piece of egg with his fork. "Do you think we're healthy enough to be doing this?"

"Doing what?"

Archer looks at me over our breakfast. His eyes gleam. "Kissing."

He makes me smile. It's strange, having all the feelings over breakfast, all this smiling, mixing with the rooted sadness. But maybe that's just who I am now. A sad person filled with starlight. The pinpricks of hope in the endless black sky.

"We're friends who kiss. I don't think it needs a doctor's note or anything." I don't point out that he was the one who said love in a song over and over last night.

"Lou," he smirks. "Your tongue was in my mouth a half hour ago."

My tongue, currently navigating a too big bite of omelet, stays silent as I ball up my napkin and throw it at Archer's head. He bats it back with his fork and I laugh, trying not to spray the table with half-chewed egg.

"Seriously." His fork is positioned over his plate for another scoop, but it dangles from his fingers like the omelet is the last thing on his mind. "I'd like to be more than friends who kiss. With you."

I press the tea bag into the mug to keep my hands busy, so I don't leap over the table and into his lap. "Me too. With you."

Archer's face glows like the sun rose inside him. "So we keep unpacking."

I nod, stoic. "I need to get my underwear out of the flower bed anyway."

"See." Archer points his empty fork at me. "We're talking about underwear already. This is promising."

~

Back at Archer's, I dump my suitcase into the washing machine down the hall. Archer goes downstairs to clean up the equipment we ditched after midnight before Gus gets too pissed. He insists I stay comfy in bed, claiming he'll be devastated if he comes back and I'm doing anything but relaxing. I appreciate what he's doing, but the quiet is almost enough to crawl into my heart and upend the hopeful calm Archer spent the day kissing into my skin.

I nestle into Archer's pillow—the good pillow—and listen to him bang around downstairs. First the single speaker, I imagine him heaving into the back of the Bronco. Then the mic stand and boho rugs rolled up and shoved into the storage room behind the stage.

Then I hear...Matilda. A faint melody hums up through the floor and the walls. The needling in my rib cage ceases under the groove of his fingers picking at her strings, and I relax and listen.

Annabella swings the door open, duffel over her shoulder, hair more frizz than curl, and in last night's clothes. I dart up in bed and grin. She drops her bag on the floor, snaps her fingers and points at me, a clear 'don't even.'

I pay no heed. "Hey there, Ms. Walk of Shame." I tent my fingers like a cartoon witch. "Have a good night?"

"Shut your mouth you." Annabella pulls a t-shirt from her bag and swaps shirts, yanking her bra out of an arm hole with flourish. "Rich from a woman still in bed."

"How's Zoey?"

Annabella flops dramatically onto the bed beside me. "Great. We stayed at this new boutique hotel downtown on Philips. It housed contraband alcohol during Prohibition, and it's a vibe."

"I heard." I scoot into her view. "Every room has a huge whirlpool tub, no?"

If watching a human turn red faster than a stoplight was on my bucket list, I could check it off with flourish. "Lou—please."

"I mean." I give her a seductive wiggle. "Jets. In the right places, you know?"

"*Lou*!"

"Like the release—"

"LOU!" She curls her knees to her chest and squashes her chin between the two. "Well, it wasn't the jets, but those didn't hurt." Her giggle is delightful. Zoey and an orgasm. Solves, or at least eases, a lot of problems.

Annabella keeps laughing, pulling a fleece blanket around her shoulders. "Please don't tell Arch. He doesn't need to know…every single thing about me."

I draw a cross over my heart.

"What about you?" She plucks fuzz off the blanket. "I don't want details but did you two…?"

"Nah." I roll to my back and stretch until I feel my back cracking. "He says my tongue was in his mouth. A lot." I pause in the memory of our ankles intertwining under the table in the diner. Which led to the walk to Archer's place with me inside his coat as he kissed the back of my neck. Which led to us barely getting up the stairs, and lips under blankets as morning became afternoon, then evening over downtown Brookings and we didn't notice the streetlights pop on because his tongue and my fingers and his biceps and my nails and his hands wrapping my ass and, well.

Annabella shrieks. "You need a filter." She folds into herself tighter in laughter. "You look happy."

The haunting, for tonight, is paused. "I feel a little happy. It's nice."

Annabella snuggles into her blanket. "Same."

CHAPTER 16

"YOU WERE IN ABERDEEN, RUNNING, TALKING TO MILO, and he invited you inside his girlfriend's house." Meghan's kicked her navy velvet flats to the floor. Snow boots with neon pink laces and faux fur dry on the floor mat by the door. Sleet pelts her windows like a cat begging to be let inside. "You've hardly mentioned Milo—once, I think? He doesn't seem to be a stressor for you. How was he the last straw to bring you back here?"

A pillow tassel is tight around my pinky, the nail cold and purple. "It wasn't Milo." Deep breath. Get the underwear out of the bushes. "It was Ginny."

Meghan processes the new name. "Who's Ginny?"

I pull the tassel tighter. I hadn't intended this when I slopped across campus for today's appointment. "She's my best friend. My ex-best friend. We grew up together."

Silence from the armchair. Meghan wants me to keep going.

"We stopped speaking at the beginning of the summer."

"Is Gin here yet?"

His eyes dart up—normally a perfect shade of moonstone, close to navy. "No," he whispers.

I shift my body forwards. Mom's urn is on the table next to the altar. "When will she be here?"

Milo's hands tremble on the back of my chair. "She isn't coming."

I nod, keeping my eyes steady on Mom's urn. Steady as she goes.

"I can sit up here with you," he says, already squeezing between chairs. "I'm here."

"No." I whisper, knotting my hands together in my lap. "No, thank you."

The tassel pops off my finger and unwinds like a ball on a tether. "I don't want to talk about her."

"Okay."

"I came back because I feel wanted here."

"How so?"

I resist the urge to yank my phone from my backpack and scroll for proof. "They literally said it."

Meghan adjusts in the chair. A whole semester in now, I know when she shifts, she's preparing to dig in. Like when a massage therapist plants her feet on the floor to push her elbow into the tissue under your shoulder and shove the ache to the surface. "When have you ever felt not wanted?"

Every day of senior year, *that's when*, Meghan.

First, when Summer transferred into our homeroom. Summer was new and artistic. Summer had a photography side gig and fifty-three thousand followers. Summer fell in love with Ginny's dad's hot chocolate and could sit at the coffee shop for hours after school, while I had to train.

When Milo gave me the ring—and if he'd paid attention to me at all, he would have never.

When Mom began sliding. Farther away, deeper in, and I couldn't stop her.

When, instead, she stopped herself.

There's only so much to say for getting all the underwear out of the yard right out of the gate.

Meghan squints like a light is too bright. She's chewing over my silence, piecing snippets of me together.

It's driving me crazy.

"What are you thinking?" The words trip off my lips. "No, I know what you're thinking." Dead mom. Daddy issues. Anxiety morphing into depression. All true. But lots of things can be true at once.

Meghan reaches for her teacup. It must be cold by now. We've been at this for a half hour. "I'd rather know what you're thinking."

It boils over.

"I'm angry Ginny didn't come to my mother's funeral. That she never came across the street to see if I was okay, even though she knew there was no way in hell I was okay. That she stayed holed up with her new best friend, even though I needed her, and she could keep her abandonment and her space, if she'd just been at the fucking funeral."

"Where do you feel in your body?"

I blink. "Right now?"

"Yes."

My hand folds into a fist and drifts to underneath my left ribs. "Here."

"Do you remember what it felt like that day?"

I nod. I'll never forget it. "Like an itch. On the inside of my skin. That I couldn't do anything about."

"I'm sorry you experienced that."

"Thank you." It comes out a whisper. The air is heavy, and I hate it. I can't stand how it feels sliding over my skin, no matter how good the outburst probably was for any sort of healing I hope for.

Ice chips scrape Meghan's windows.

"I have a theory," she says. "Can I share it with you?"

I nod.

Meghan drums her arm, ruminating on how to present her hypothesis. "I think," she says. "You value your friendships more than anything in your entire life. And the loss of a friendship is extremely traumatic for you. You may overcompensate in other parts of your life to fill a void."

"Like with running."

"Yes." Meghan nods. "Compound the loss of a deep, valuable friend with the irrevocable loss of your mother, and starting college three months later, it became impossible for you to self-regulate."

"I need you to speak in English, please."

"You can't find your pace."

A chuckle comes from nowhere. I lean into my open palm, wiped.

Meghan looks at me for a moment, then speaks. "Think of it like this: you're running a race. On a harder course than you trained for, but you keep going because there's no turning around. But there are branches and holes from forest animals and a tree fell down and no one noticed but you. Everyone leaps over it like it's been there for years, even though you know it hasn't. You'd start to feel overwhelmed, right? And then your pace is shot because you're distracted and it's all too much. It has nothing to do with your effort. It has everything to do with your surroundings."

I press my fingers into my closed eyelids. "You've summarized all of my broken pieces. What now?"

"You keep thinking about EMDR. We develop and agree on a plan of attack."

"But how?" I push my fingers harder and see stars on the other side.

"Hey," Meghan says. "Look at me."

I peek between my fingers.

"You do what you do best," Meghan's eyes are stern, but kind. "You show up. And you keep showing up."

~

Fluffy snow explodes from the sky like cotton balls as the diner door swings shut behind me. The hostess clicks her gum and points me to Annabella's booth. She sits behind her laptop with her earbuds poking from her ears, grinning at the screen.

My boots squelch on the linoleum as I toss my hat and coat into the booth, wave to Zoey on Zoom, and slide to my side of the table. I open the menu, and blink. I can't make letters out for words; the letters swim and lose meaning.

"Zoey, I gotta go," Annabella says. She waves goodbye to her girlfriend on the screen. Her eyes are heavy but burst with blissful waves simultaneously. The juxtaposition was startling before Christmas, but might just be Annabella now.

"You didn't have to hang up," I say as Annabella pulls out her earbuds.

"You and I are having dinner." She slips her laptop in her bag and tucks her earbuds in their case. "What are you getting?"

Annabella's little cross, bright against her collarbone, shines.

I hope it's a good sign.

"Meghan thinks I've moved into depression."

Annabella doesn't move. "Okay."

"I want you to know." My hands rattle on the table. "Some of it's because of my mom's death. Some of it's because of my old best friend and how our friendship ended and it all happened at the same time and was really traumatic, and I never acknowledged exactly how traumatic and now I'm here, and I feel guilty and ashamed, but also human, and—"

Annabella swings to my booth so swiftly it's like she's there the whole time, hip to hip, arm woven under mine. "You'll never have to talk about it if you don't want to, but if you want to, I will always listen."

Around us, voices layer into a dull hum. Plates clank, the cash register dings, Blues Traveler crackles on the speaker next to the bathrooms. Diner noises circle like it's a hurricane and we're in the eye.

"My mom called me Birdie," I say, suddenly. "She said I came out sprinting, and as soon as I figured out walking, I was running. Flitting around the yard like a baby bird." I look at the stack of menus. "Flying at my meets." I glance at Annabella. "Sorry. That came out of nowhere."

"You're grieving your mom in every way that makes sense to you." Annabella tilts her chin to my shoulder. "Tell me more."

Tears burn my eyes. This isn't fair. The heartbreak that stems simply from living. "I wish she wasn't gone."

"I know. And it's not the same, but at least we have each other." Under the table, Annabella parts my fingers with hers and holds on.

~

The Wellness 201 classroom still smells like pencil shavings and sweat, with a hint of rubber from the closet of basketballs next door. Archer and I enrolled in the same section. First day of class, I claim our chairs: front row, tucked off to the right side of the classroom.

Archer blows off class, with no warning or explanation.

At the end of the hour, my Keds planted on the chair, reserving it as Archer's, my phone buzzes next to my worksheet (KUMQUATS: THEIR VALUE AND HOW TO BUY THEM.)

ARCHER: Meet when class is done. In the place we met.

Seriously? After all this, he's dumping me? Can you dump someone you only make out with? How do I keep Annabella in the not-a-breakup?

LOU: Are you breaking up with your kissing friend?

I count to nine before he replies. In my opinion, it takes him too long.

ARCHER: I would sooner sell Matilda.

My heart calms but doesn't stop me from barely making my name legible as I slap my worksheet on the TA's desk and race out of the classroom, past Coach's office, and to the Union. Outside the Union, I slow and tighten my ponytail. Archer hasn't earned the freaked-out girlfriend look. Not yet.

He waits on the floor twenty feet from the coffee shop. Students and faculty form a squiggly line back to where he sits, his shoes jammed under his knees. Matilda's in her case, tilted against the bench. He's an Irish Buddha in meditation pose. I'm pretty sure he forgot to comb his hair. I see myself planting in his lap, crossing my ankles above his ass, and doing things that will cause the baristas to call UPD and report indecent exposure.

Instead, I tower over Archer and Matilda. "What the hell?"

Archer pops his eyes open. His face does that melty thing, where his smile ticks up and his cheeks relax and I know he too is thinking smutty things. "Here." He hands me a steaming cup. "Chamomile. Sit."

I cradle the tea and tuck my legs under the bench, my back to the line. "I literally ran over here, and for the like the third time in my life running wasn't fun. What's going on?"

"I dropped out this morning."

"Dropped out of what?"

"School."

The tea nearly slips from my grip. "You did what?"

"I'm not leaving," Archer's hands are up in defense, or to comfort me. I can't tell.

"We've made out every day this week and you couldn't fit this in between sessions?"

He shrugs. "That was more fun."

I put the tea down and hide my face in my palms, hot from the tea. "What is happening?"

"Hey." Archer wraps his fingers around my wrists and I let him pull down my guard. "It's about the baggage. And making room for you. I need you to trust me."

My hands stiffen in his. "You're not gonna tell me why?"

"That's where the trust comes in, sweetheart."

I let him go and move away, so my knee isn't touching his hip. So he can't reach me or have easy access for a kiss. His "sweetheart' pinpricks right into my heart, and hightails to my arteries to spread the good word throughout my body.

I don't get to decide how he deals with his baggage. "You promise you're not leaving?" My voice squeaks and it's mortifying.

Inherently bad liars in my life have the same tells. They suck in air like a guppy and their eyes dart to the right. Ginny did it the last time she told me she loved me. Dad did it on Mom's last birthday before a closed-mouth kiss, after she opened her diamond solitaire necklace. Milo did it over that ring in the snow.

I wait for Archer's eyeballs to dart right. For the gulp of air. It doesn't happen.

"Not yet, anyway." It's not a lie, but it's not not a lie either.

I pull him to me. I kiss him recklessly, my fingers in his orange hair, my tongue in his mouth. His fingers crisscross my back like a Tic Tac Toe board. Neither of us can breathe or get enough—there isn't enough—and I feel the *want* bubble into *need* to have Archer against me.

A fool whistles from the coffee bar line. Archer smiles against my lips, and I sink deeper into him.

Let them call UPD.

~

Archer convinced us to go to the rooftop. In the dark. In January. It's only eight, and the sun's already been down for four hours.

"Here's the thing." Archer flips on a portable kerosene burner on the metal table he dragged to the hammock for wind protection. Rust cobwebs over the metal tabletop. "There's shit bumming all of us out right now. Legit shit."

Annabella shivers inside her parka. I loop my arm through hers and pull her close.

Archer swings his backpack off and produces the only three foods that should be at the top of the food pyramid: chocolate, graham crackers, and fluffy marshmallows the size of tiny pillows. "But we *are* making s'mores on the roof in the dead of January."

"Even my bones are cold, Arch." Annabella wrinkles her nose.

He rips open the marshmallows and one springs from the plastic. Archer catches it and pops it in my mouth. It fills up the inside of my entire cheek. He grins and turns back to Annabella. "That's why I put blankets on the hammock. Just let me do this for my two favorite people, you fun-hater."

Our parkas squeak as they rub against each other as Annabella and I nestle into the hammock. Archer lined the bottom with the wool blanket he lent me the first night he brought me up here. I yank down the side of Annabella's stocking cap over her ears and she sticks her tongue out at me.

Archer drapes the fleece blanket from his bed over us, ducks away, and reappears with a plugged-in electric blanket. Annabella's eyes about fall from her face as he puts it over her head, and tucks me in. "Fine," she huffs, delighted, emerging from under the cotton. "You got me."

He shakes her ankle under the blankets. "I've always got you." An eyebrow notch comes my way. "You too."

The buzz that spreads through my bones like honey has little to do with the electric blanket. "Did you just have a hankering for starry night s'mores?"

"Yes," Archer says simply, a marshmallow speared with a tiny metal stick. "And to spend time with you two without distractions. Like phones or—"

"Or guitars," Annabella supplies.

"Matilda is always welcome, especially at the world's tiniest bonfire."

"Only if the songs are about us," she continues, as her nose wrinkles. "But if they get sexual, I'm out."

"If things get sexual, I will personally escort you out." Archer smushes the hot marshmallow between two graham crackers on his knee. "First dibs, ladies?"

"You always give the first s'more to your lady," Annabella says.

"True story." I rock the hammock forward and reach for the s'more. My fingertips brush Archer's and I shiver, thinking of the same fingertips on me later in bed. Judging by his current lip bite, he's picturing the same thing. Annabella might be bouncing early tonight. "So are we gonna round-robin our malfunctions, or how do you want to do this?" I ask. Chocolate oozes down my finger, and I lick it off.

"Round-robin," Annabella agrees. "You're up Arch."

"Nope."

"Well, you're the one who spontaneously dropped out of school this morning."

"It was hardly spontaneous." Regardless, Archer stabs his second marshmallow like it owes him money. "There are dreams that keep me awake at night. They take energy. Energy I don't have when I'm doing things that don't serve said dreams. AB?"

She puts her head on my shoulder and I'm careful to not get crumbs in her hair. "I'm in love with the perfect woman. And she's in love with me. What if my mother's insistence on meeting her is more about controlling the situation, and less about accepting me? You saw her on Thanksgiving, and that was about a guy Mom knew would propose to Cat eventually anyway." Annabella huffs down into her parka. "At least when my family disowns me, I have Zoey's family. And you two."

Archer hands Annabella a s'more. The marshmallow is burnt, and I bet it's on purpose. He knows her s'mores order. Of course he does. "You are high off your bonkers ass if you think Catherine is disowning you for anything."

Annabella crunches into her s'more.

"You're up, my dear." Archer looks at me.

"You two ever heard of EMDR?" I ask, scraping a bit of marshmallow off my thumb with my teeth.

"No," says Annabella.

"Yes," Archer says at the same time. "It's a calming mechanism."

"Sorta?" I say. "Meghan describes it as therapist-guided meditation."

"Is this why you haven't had a weekly feelings worksheet?" Annabella holds her half-eaten s'more up in the moonlight to plan her next bite attack. "I miss those."

Archer turns his marshmallow; the part I can see is totally black. "Have you tried it?"

"Not yet. Did you try it with Dr. Namaste?"

"Yes." Archer turns his marshmallow a nano-inch. It's about to light on fire. "It was weird as hell the first time, and the constant check-ins from the Doc—on a scale of 1-10, where does this sit pain-wise now—was annoying, but he explained to me after that a tiny part of that was just keeping me in the current day."

"Did you worry about sinking away too far?"

"I mean, a little. You reprocess the most traumatic shit you can come up with, and I can't imagine getting stuck there for too long."

Annabella yelps. "This sounds terrifying."

"It is, and it isn't," Archer insists. "I don't think Meghan would have suggested it if she was worried about doing more harm. Doc said he uses it on PTSD patients all the time."

"I hear 'PTSD' and feel guilty. It's not like I was in a war."

"I did too," Archer finally takes his marshmallow out of the flame. "Dr. Namaste said I should try to remember how my situation doesn't diminish anyone else's. My story is worth something too."

"So, reframing it," I say.

"I like that. Reframing." Her s'more gone, Annabella snuggles deeper into my shoulder. "Does this mean we get to reframe all the bad stuff that happens?"

Archer cracks off chocolate hunks and layers it inside his graham cracker. "I think that's the way to survive sometimes."

CHAPTER 17

IT SNOWS EVERY DAY NOW. FLURRIES OR SLEET OR A MIX OF both slap our cheeks and tangle our hair on the way to class. Annabella and the girls are forced inside on treadmills. Sunny days are colder without the cloud cover, but the girls bundle up, strap on their spikes, and run the dirt roads on the north side of campus between the horse barns and Highway 14. When I hit the same trail hours later, as the sun sinks into the line where the ground starts and the sky ends, their cleat pockmarks are frozen solid in the trampled snow and they propel me forward.

The third Saturday in January, it's so snowy Annabella and I can barely make out the curve of our building out our window. She pulls sweats over her mesh shorts. "I'm going to train." On cue, her phone rings, and she rolls her eyes. "No, I'm not." She answers and switches to speaker phone. "Hi. You're on speaker in my room and Lou is here. I'm going for a run."

"Oh, in this weather darling?" Mrs. Harris's voice twills from the speaker. "Hello, Louise. How are you?"

"I'm great, thank you," I call from my bed.

Annabella shoves her foot in a boot. "What's up Mom?"

"Just calling to invite you girls and Archer to a get together celebrating your father's retirement."

"Wait, what?" Annabella drops her other boot on the floor.

"Yes, after Christmas, Dad and I had a long talk, and he decided he's ready. Wants to see more of the world. Be more present for you and Catherine."

I pop my head up over the bed like a groundhog. Annabella looks up at me, confused.

"Honey?"

"We're here, Mom." Annabella ties on her other boot and stands, shoving odds and ends into her backpack she doesn't even need at the gym: her mouse. A ruler. A pack of gum. "I'm confused. I didn't know he was thinking about retirement."

Mrs. Harris's laugh is floaty, like she can't believe it either, but that she very much wants to. "Life is short, I guess."

I flop back onto the mattress.

Annabella gets the details from her mother: the day after Valentine's Day, their house, seven pm. "Bring your gal, honey," Mrs. Harris ends it with. "We'd love to meet her."

"Yep. Bye Mom." Annabella hangs up and drops her phone on her desk with a clatter. She steps onto the futon and pops her head up next to me. "'Wants to be more present for you girls' is code for 'you're too busy and that's why Cat eloped and Anna won't bring her gal home.'"

"Really?"

"No." Annabella hops down and stomps to her gym bag. "I'm projecting." She sweeps back around to me. "My legs need to move. This weather makes me so pent up."

I don't have to be near the window to know the blizzard is raging. I can hear it howling as it swirls between all the dorm buildings. "At least there's the treadmills."

"Sure are. Let's go."

At the gym, we peel off coats and hats in the locker room (I use a guest locker I must seal shut with my student ID—a real insult) and we go to the treadmills. Maddie and Sara are on the weights – one doing a chest press, another with her earbuds so far in her ears she's expediting inevitable hearing loss. Emily is MIA. Sweet miracle. They nod at Annabella and ignore me entirely.

We claim a pair of treadmills next to the windows overlooking campus. The Campanile flashes her red SOS through the blowing snow.

Annabella gets to work, her indoor shoes pounding on the belt like thunder. I look at the control panel like I've never seen a treadmill before. Stupid. This is stupid. I shake out my limbs, tighten my pony, and hit the start button, jabbing the arrow up until I find my pace.

Out the window, students scurry to the library two buildings down from the Wellness Center, like they've never walked through a blizzard before. I think of Archer on his couch with weak blizzard daylight slanting over the scratched-up floor. His guitar is on his knee, a notebook open in front of him. The page bleeds black ink. I bet it would drip if he picked it up. Has he written a song about me yet? Last night, we watched a movie in his bed. His thumb traced circles on my thigh and my head felt like a balloon and I kissed him until his lips chapped and the corner of my mouth was pink from whiskers-on-skin friction, the movie credits rolled, and we didn't stop kissing and got under the covers instead.

Annabella's treadmill shifts; she jogs into the cool down. I jam my speed up two clicks higher to stretch my legs out. I imagine Creedence Clearwater Revival spinning on Archer's record player. Snow billows down Main Street as he strums that thumb he touched me with over his guitar strings. And I'm here, sweaty, but breathing again.

Coach walks by, stops at Sara and gives her advice on form. Sara nods like Coach is God's gift to competitive running, all wide-eyed and yes ma'am. Coach's file folders tip but don't fall from her crooked arm and she continues on, her parka still unzipped. She sees Annabella and gives her a thumbs up, sees me, and stops.

I know what I would say about me. Trying too hard, sprinting on a treadmill. Cool story, suck up. Ponytail swinging from the crown of my head, my ragged breaths coming in even puffs. I can feel Maddie's eye rolls and Sara's glares over the barbells.

Fuck it. I don't care. This is where I belong. This is what I'm best at. And I can follow Coach's rules all day, but if she can't see my dedication, that's on her. Not me.

And with or without the squad, I'm going to keep running. I promised.

We make eye contact. Coach nods.

I nod back.

And Coach goes on her way.

~

"Two minutes." Archer holds the door open for me at Gallerie. Flyers taped to the wall for student art shows and concerts and a writer's circle at Haven drift up at the corners. "I need to grab my amp and talk to Gus." On top of being his landlord, Gus is Archer's new boss—since the New Year's Eve show, people asked Archer to organize more shows, so he and Gus are having conversations about bands in the area. Archer's eyes glow when he talks about local music.

Selfishness pricks at my ribs. I hope this is enough to keep him in Brookings.

"Take your time." I slide onto a barstool. My workout is in for the day—on a treadmill strategically close to Coach's office. Classes are done. I'm tagging along with Archer because, well. Gravity.

Archer teeter-totters between my knees, torn between the music and me. He kisses my cheek and his breath rushes into my ear and I want to weave my fingers under his jacket and feel the curve where his back becomes his ass in my hands. I haven't told him—and won't—that this morning, I spent the better part of French class ignoring the subjugating verbs lesson and daydreamed about straddling his hips and brushing my nails over the cross on his back. Moving my thumbs over the ink. Feeling his muscles constrict and relax under my pressure. I haven't seen that tattoo since New Year's Day. The want is real.

So is the sacrilege.

"Come get me if I'm not back in five," Archer says now. "You don't need to wait for me all day."

"Okay." I blink, pausing the daydream.

"Okay." Archer steps away and immediately presses back against me. "Why can't I stop?" he whispers, kissing my lips. "You're like candy. One kiss is never enough."

We stay like that, my arms under Archer's flannel, his hips between my legs until the bartender clears his throat. Archer breaks the kiss. "Right," he says. "Gus. My amp." Archer presses his forehead against mine and I go cross-eyed meeting his eyes. "I'll be right back," he whispers, and scurries to the back offices.

My phone buzzes in my pocket, pushing the daydream of Archer entirely out of reach for now. It's maddening. I want the fantasy at the tip of my fingers.

Still, I look at my phone anyway.

PhotogSummer is live on TikTok: Freshman Ginny C. at her first reading.

I jack the volume up and lean close to my phone flat on the bar to listen.

The video slides up. There she is. Ginny. Blond curls gone wild like ditch weed. Crisp green eyes. She's on a low stage, possibly in a basement, with lightbulbs on wire crossing the beams barely above her. A microphone in front, and a stool behind her. Summer tilts the view to see a packed house in the small space. People on the orange couch in front. A hundred armchairs, more teetering stools, all full.

"Hi. I'm Ginny, freshman creative writing. I'm here to read to you from my first novel, *The Right Kind of Light*."

My heart cracks open. She wrote a book. Ginny wrote a book.

But then. Ginny begins to read her work. And I hear her loud and clear.

> "I look into the sea of mortarboards and think: I should be able to write this. I should have the color of blue on the tip of my tongue and know instinctively how to describe the way the yellow tassels are more golden than mustard as the strings get caught on earrings. How the four corners of these silly hats are throwing weird shadows over all of our faces, and how we all have to tilt our heads just a tad unnaturally to see the podium as we all pretend to care. I should also know where Lou is. And I don't."

Holy shit.

Holy damn shit.

She wrote a book. About me.

The ice starts in my toes. It rises upward, capturing my ankles, my legs, and moves north to freeze my hips, elbows, shoulders. If I could cry, the tears would turn to literal snowflakes sparkling on my cheeks. Glitter and guilt meld into one.

I'm the perpetual ice queen. Almost thawed. But not quite.

She will never stop using me. I'm just a character.

Just a story for her to write.

I mute Ginny (it's nice to have a mute button) and scroll through the comments. A million names I don't recognize. A million people I can't defend myself to.

WEEBLEWOBBLE: This Lou character is fascinating, but not entirely clear yet. Look forward to more.

SASHAM: The imagery! You're meant for this.

Then, names I recognize:

PHOTOSummer: Stunning! Heart eyes!

MILO: That's my girl. Love you.

"What are you looking at?" Archer's elbows land on the bar on each side of me, his chin on my shoulder. Ginny's still muted, but her mouth is moving. Saying my name over and over as if it's hers. Archer glances at my phone. "If it's not posted on TikTok, did it really happen?"

I cram my phone in my pocket. "Even if it ends up on TikTok, did it really happen?"

"So existential, sitting at the bar in the middle of the afternoon. We better get you out of here." Archer waves to the bartender and holds my hand as we walk to the door. Outside, I blink into the light and tent my fingers over my eyes. We were inside for ten minutes. How did my tolerance to the sun change so quickly?

"This is what matters," Archer is saying, bringing our hands to his chest, over his heart. "What's never posted."

I want to agree, but I can't push the words up my throat.

~

"Sparkles or no sparkles?" Annabella holds up a black dress on a hanger, and she cocks her hip to model another dress, a super sexy deep burgundy number with a tight skirt. The black dress has long sleeves and a tulle skirt full of sparkles that'll catch the light on the roof like stars. Valentine's Day is Friday, and Zoey's visiting for a rooftop date. Saturday is Dr. Harris's party that we're all—all—going to together.

From our futon, I study Annabella's options. Archer's thigh is pressed against mine, his laptop on my knees as we talk about marketing his first band at Gallerie. Afterglow is an electronica band out of St. Paul. It's a big get. When Archer got the call yesterday, he lit up like our Christmas tree.

"Your ass looks great in the tight one," I say to Annabella.

Archer waves my words away. "I can't say it. But what she said."

Annabella looks at the black dress on the hanger. "I need to try this one too. Arch, avert your eyes."

He buries his face in my neck, and nuzzles in. I roll my eyes for Annabella's benefit and wrap my arms around his shoulders.

"I'll tell you when you can look!" Annabella calls from half inside her closet.

Archer ignores her and starts lining my collarbone with tiny kisses.

I tug on a curl. "Archer!"

"Shush, I'm busy," he murmurs against my skin. His tongue brushes my skin and I tug harder on his hair. Archer laughs, holds tighter, and tilts his chin up. "Yes, darling?"

"Do we have plans for Valentine's Day?" Bees buzz in my belly. My sternum is splotchy from his whiskers, but I'm afraid to ask about Valentine's? "I mean," I stammer. "What do kissing friends do on Valentine's Day?"

"More of this, I think," Archer scoots up, his hand on my cheek. He smiles, moving in for a kiss.

Annabella bumps into the wall in her closet; an arm flails out as she wiggles into the black dress. "Will there be dinner?" I ask. "A lady can get hungry."

His eyelashes flutter and I can count each one. "I'll whip dinner up. Then kissing."

My lips graze his without kissing him. "All night."

Annabella bursts from her closet, sweeping the curtain to the side. "Arch! You're free to adore me and this fantastic dress now!"

His forehead crashes into my shoulder. "You two will kill me."

I snort, but only have eyes for my roommate. "Oh my god. Annabella."

"Right?" Annabella twirls in front of us. The skirt drifts up like a cloud, and the glitter is subtle, but perfect. She paired it with my black moto boots and is holding her brown hair up in an impromptu ponytail. She swings around, her grin sunnier on each twirl.

Archer sits up and stares. "That's the winner," he says quietly. Annabella beams, swinging the skirt back and forth like the Campanile bell. He stands abruptly and kisses me quick, like he has a million times, like it's the most natural thing ever. "I gotta go. Cold shower."

On his way out he squeezes Annabella's hand. "Wear this one. If you don't, I'm canceling our friendship."

"Noted." Annabella spins back to the mirror to admire her perfect self.

Archer shuts the door, and I watch Annabella preen in the mirror. "Archer mentioned that Zoey is going to your dad's party."

"She is." Annabella's moved to her desk now and is holding a red lip stain up next to a pink gloss. "I left it up to her. She thinks we're ready."

"Are you?"

Annabella twists her lips together, and nods. "Yeah. I am."

I smile, and nod to the red tube. "It's Valentines. The dress is black. Lean in."

She slicks on the cherry red and hops up to check in the mirror. "Whoa," she says, checking herself out, and darts out the door. "I need to figure out shoes."

With a snort, I look back to Archer's computer. For all his bluster about hating social media, Archer admitted we need it for marketing. The ad I made is rudimentary, but it has a message (Live Music! COME!) and is clean and bright enough to jump out of the noise online. I tweak a color, turn off the bleeds, and pull up Gmail. He's signed into his account, so I send it to him from himself.

"Do you know what the forecast is for tomorrow night?" Annabella's swapping my boots with Maddie's ruby pumps from across the hall.

"I'll look," I answer, knowing she'll want my boots. They're fleece-lined, she'll need leggings, and it's February, in South Dakota. I move the mouse away from Archer's email to the weather app and stop.

There's a read message at the top of the queue. My gaze darts to the right: the email preview is still up. Zach Harris, Bad Jasper Records. "Archer, thanks for the demos you sent us last week. They were phenomenal."

Demos?

Last week?

Archer's email to Zach is the second email in the sent folder with a link to SoundCloud. "Straight into the Sun" is there—Cadence's song. The other: "Lou_Untitled".

I have a song?

How do I have a song I don't know about?

How do I have a song other people have heard and I haven't?

I read Zach's email. "Listen, you have a real talent, and a future in songwriting. But to be candid, man—you gotta move to Nashville. It's where everything's happening."

"Hey." Annabella says, tucking her hair to the side, testing a bun with a pair of earrings. "Weather report?"

I snap the laptop shut. "Wear the boots with fleece leggings."

~

I need the long hair pins. I bet they're in Mom's bathroom.

I stop at the top of Archer's stairs and shove my fists into my eyes.

Keds squeaking on the kitchen floor as she swiped toaster waffles, waiting for me to finish getting ready for school. Always with me. Always waiting for me.

Stop it, stop it.

Her hand is pale and palm-up on the water.

Stop stop stop.

Always with me.

STOPSTOPSTOP.

Archer opens his door and pulls me inside. Unzips my coat, slides it down my shoulders, tosses it on his couch. He's pulsating. Giddy. My mouth responds like it should, like I want it to, sliding my tongue against his teeth and pulling him close. Archer murmurs something at me. I stop kissing him. "What?"

"I'm glad you're here. That's all."

I look around. Archer covered every flat surface with candles. Light flickers from bunches of candle tins next to the sink and dot the oven. The table is basically a bonfire of tiny candles. More candlelight dances on the windowsill by the bed. A million little shadows morph into one glow and tangle in his curls. "It's beautiful."

He shrugs, bashfully, like he didn't spend twenty minutes hunched over the tiny wicks and burn his thumb a hundred times. "Can I give you your Valentine's gift? I've been waiting."

"Okay." I paste a smile on my face like I know he needs and close my eyes.

"I think you know it's not a physical thing, Lou." Archer flips open Matilda's lid on the couch.

My song. All I've wanted for months.

And I'm not the first one to hear it.

"What's it called?" Please don't be the same. Please. Bees flit their silky little wings behind my belly button.

"Ah," Archer swings Matilda's strap over his shoulder, fingers brushing her frets. "I don't know yet. Don't take it personally. Titles are hard."

The bees pop stingers out of their angry, fuzzy asses. "Is it called Lou-underscore-untitled?"

Archer blinks, and lets Matilda slide to his back, against his tattoo. Right where I want to be. But I gotta be out here, doing this. "Did you listen to it?"

I shake my head. "I knew you'd play it for me when you were ready."

The guitar bounces off his spine as he walks to me. "Did you read the email?"

"Yes."

Archer swallows and passes his palm over his chin. "Nashville. Cat's outta the bag."

"I shouldn't have looked."

"Stop." Archer steps closer still. He isn't touching me, and it's the first time in weeks he's pressed this close and hasn't brushed his wrist against mine or found a reason to pull my hand to lips to kiss my skin. "When you used my account to send me that Afterglow ad, I knew you found it."

"Are you moving?"

Archer is quiet.

"You are," I breathe.

"When fall semester starts," Archer allows. He brushes his thumb over my lip. My body is riddled with sparks. "I want to spend the summer with my girls."

Summer, again. I could stay in Brookings. Annabella and I could find an apartment near Archer. I'd have a summer running partner worth her salt. Diner milkshakes for dinner. In the evening, I would drift in the hammock and sleep to Archer strumming under the stars, the hum of his plucking filling my dreams.

"I've been so inspired since we met," Archer is saying. "Happy stuff again. Stuff that doesn't make my parents call my shrink. Stuff that would sell, Lou." His eyes are wide. Shining. Alive.

Always with me. Always waiting for me.

Stuff that would sell, Lou.

All I am. Means to an end for someone else's dream.

I stumble backwards. "I need to go."

Archer's eyes crinkle. "What? Why? I need to tell you something else."

I know what he needs to tell me. I feel it. I want it. But not like this. I shake my head, throwing my coat back on.

"Lou!"

My fingers can't twist the deadbolt the right way. Archer reaches past me and clicks the knob up, giving me the freedom I don't want, and can't stop. "Please stay."

That's the last thing I hear, even though he follows me halfway down the steps in his old man slippers.

I slam outside to Main Avenue. My brain pounds into my skull, knocking for a crack to chisel away at. I make it to the bar I parked behind—the bass thumps for people with no Valentines. Safe in my car, I turn the ignition, but just sit there and let my headlights shine on the bar's brick wall.

CHAPTER 18

"HOW LONG DID YOU STAY BEHIND RAY'S CORNER?" Meghan's got her legs crossed in her chair and her eyes set on me.

"I don't know." I comb my pillow's tassels into parallel lines. "Maybe an hour. Or three."

"What happened then?"

"I went home. Went to sleep."

"And did you? Sleep, I mean."

"Yes." I sampled Annabella's melatonin and woke up so groggy I didn't move except to pee, but it worked—until I noticed Archer's calls. Sixteen in a row.

There's more underwear in the bushes now. Super.

I look at Meghan's feet. Cherry red toenails, the left big toe has a white heart painted on it. Of course she has holiday-themed pedicures. "We're going to revisit your mom's death. But I'm not forcing it today."

I sigh. "EMDR therapy...can it help me process everything with my mom?"

"It certainly may," Meghan nods. "No guarantees, but it'd be a great thing to try to address your history of trauma related to abandonment. And I'll be here every step."

I take a deep breath. "Let's try it next time?"

"You bet. Now, what's under your skin today?"

I scratch my forehead. "Ginny is a writer," I say. "Got into University of Iowa."

Meghan frowns in that exaggerated way that really means mega approval. "Prestigious."

"I know," I say. "Someone posted her first reading. It was the first chapter of her book. It's about me. The book is about me. Us, probably. I don't know. She didn't tell me it existed. She hasn't told me anything in months, but she's running around Iowa claiming my life as fiction. Meanwhile." I take a big gulp of air. "Archer wrote me a song. He wrote me a damn song, Meghan. And that song might be his ticket to Nashville and I'm tired of my life being inspiration for art."

Meghan presses the tip of her pen into her notebook hard; there's probably a blot of ink bleeding through the page. "To summarize. You don't want to be anyone's muse again—understandable—and Archer wrote you a song?"

"And he wanted to play it for me, and I couldn't let him because all I could hear was Ginny reading about my shoes squeaking in her kitchen as I didn't knock on her front door because I thought I had the right to pop by—which I did, by the way, no one, even her dad, ever said anything—and I stopped the guy I'm really into from singing. Me. My. Own. Love. Song. In candlelight. On Valentine's Day."

Meghan's pen is poised in the same place. The ink blot will be big enough for her to use in psychoanalysis.

"I'm not a work of fiction. I can't do it. She has no idea who I am now. Not anymore." I make myself pause for breath.

"Do you think Archer knows who you are?"

I think of kissing him in Gallerie on that random afternoon. How he kept coming back for kisses, as if there wasn't enough of a day to get enough. Like we don't have enough time. Maybe we don't.

And I miss him. It's been the longest fifteen hours. "I hope so."

Meghan caps her pen. That blot has to be the size of Rhode Island now. "Do you know the real Archer?"

I squint, crack my knuckles. I'm figuring out the constellation of freckles on his neck, and how his candidness is a coping mechanism stemming from secrets and worry and history repeating somehow. I know why he toasts his Pop Tarts like a heathen—he likes the gooey stretch of the marshmallows. I think I know how he loved Cadence, and how part of him will for some time, but I'm not scared of it. I see his commitment through Annabella, his drive through his music. His heart in his smile. His passion through Matilda.

Yeah. I know him.

I nod.

"How are you going to tell him?"

I see Archer's kind eyes, as he sits twitchy and proud on the floor in the Union next to our bench. Our fingertips brushing as he presents my tea. Archer knows what goodbye looks like, the oxygen-stealing, future-robbing loss that takes people to their knees. He got up.

I am too.

"I'm going to tell him I'm more than inspiration. I want to be with him, but I'm more than that."

"Bingo."

The air is brittle like ice. It catches me off guard as I cross Medary at the Campanile across the street from Meghan's office. Archer's phone sends me to his full voicemail. Probably full of Nashville producers.

Stop it, I think, and pound out a text, my thumbs skimming the letters.

LOU: Call me. ASAP.

My phone lights up with a call. I hit the green button and bring it to my ear. "Sweetheart, I'm so sorry – "

"McKinnley, I don't know who your sweetheart is, but it sure as hell isn't me."

I skid to a stop. A lone street light pops on down Medary. It blinks out an SOS and steadies on. I try—and fail—to filter the shock from my voice. "Coach?"

"One and only. Come to my office."

"I—" I stick my pointer finger in my other ear, desperately confused. "Now?" I squeak.

"Yes, now." She rustles papers in the background. "And make it snappy. My wife's making vegetarian lasagna for dinner and it's my favorite, so if you ruin this for me, I will be pissed."

She hangs up. And I sprint.

I shoulder-check Coach's door hard enough I'll have a bruise on my arm. My breath is ragged, and my right boot Annabella returned while I was knocked out is untied. Snot pools under my nose and I wipe it with my sleeve. The picture of class.

Coach looks up from her laptop. "Hi Sweetheart."

She is such a pain in the ass. I'm here for it.

Coach looks at the only chair on the other side of her desk. I sit.

"What's your 1500-meter time?" she says, looking at her computer screen. A spreadsheet is reflected in her blue light glasses.

I blink. "4:35:41."

"And your 5000-meter."

"17:23:02."

"Your 10,000 meters?"

"I think it's 35:42:824."

Her eyebrow flicks up, but she doesn't look from her computer. "You think, or you know?"

My lips curve up. "I know."

"That's faster than when we scouted you," Coach says.

"Is it?" It is.

"Second in the division too."

Behind only Annabella. I'm aware.

Coach snaps the laptop shut. "I want you seeing Dr. Stellan again."

"I never stopped."

She looks like her brain skips a beat. My fingers itch as Coach's eyes my ruddy cheeks, my dumb boots. The holes in my jeans. As if they tell my whole story.

She blinks, and I see something new. It looks like the first glimmer of ...trust.

"You're back, on probation," Coach says, finally, drawing her words out like they aren't the opposite of a death sentence. "You start training for track tomorrow."

My chest swells. "Thank y—"

"Get out."

Out, I get.

~

I erupt into our room, sweaty from jogging across campus twice in ten minutes.

Zoey is zipping up Annabella's dress in front of the mirror. Annabella's hand is on Zoey's cheek, and a lazy grin inches to the right side of Zoey's face. They swing my way at the commotion when I bust in, in untied boots, completely destroying the vibe.

Annabella steps my way. "What's wrong?"

I open my mouth but nothing comes out. Zoey slips behind me and knocks the door shut.

Annabella scrambles to unwind my scarf and pluck off my stocking hat. "You need to speak."

I look at my friend. Her eyes are darting all over my body, looking for a protruding bone or blood or an invisible tragedy I don't have words for. But I do. I have the words. "Coach called. I'm back on the team."

Her eyes turn into flying saucers. "What?"

I nod.

"Lou!" Her arms fly around my neck. "Zoey, she's back!" Annabella says, as if Zoey isn't a foot away.

Zoey waves her hands like fireworks.

Annabella clings to me like she's a panda and I'm a tree, rocking us back and forth. I squeeze her back, and notice how good she smells—like freesia and fresh air. And her hair is particularly bouncy in curls. And Zoey is sexy as hell in open-toed heels and a hunter green pant suit and oh—

"Fuck." I wrench backward, and take in Annabella. That dress Zoey zipped up is a floaty cocktail dress in cream with gauzy balloon sleeves. The retirement party. "Give me two seconds!"

"You're fine," Annabella calls as I fly to my closet, smacking hangers, looking for anything appropriate to wear. "We've got time."

"I don't want to make it more stressful." Dress found, I yank off my clothes and step into a black, low-cut sleeved dress that's too short, has an open back, but the frills seem to over distract from the skin. I bought it for Homecoming senior year. Mom said no. Fifteen months later, I'm wearing it to a retirement party.

"You aren't making anything stressful," Zoey assures, handing me her still-hot curling iron as Annabella zips me up.

"Makeup in the car." I wind a few curls around my crown, and wish for more time, but it is what it is. "Is Archer still going? He's not picking up his phone."

I see Zoey glance at Annabella in the mirror. "Yes," Annabella takes the curling iron and grabs a strand to curl. "He's already on his way down. I assumed you were with him."

"Everything's fine," I say, fully implying it's not. I step back into my boots. "I promise. I just..." I funnel oxygen in through my nose and out through my mouth. "I just need to talk to him."

I keep my eyes closed for a long beat, so I don't have to see the two of them exchange a knowing look. When I peek out, Zoey is opening the door, ushering Annabella out, and waiting for me. "Let's go then."

CHAPTER 19

ZOEY AND ANNABELLA DROP ME AT THE CURB—ZOEY decided on the way that she wants to bring flowers for Mrs. Harris. After I squeeze Annabella's shoulder in solidarity, I book it up the front walk and hope I don't look like a drunk raccoon from my car eyeliner.

We passed the Bronco down the block. Archer's here.

I ring the doorbell, and wait. Mrs. Harris went all out—I can see the buffet table in the family room through the window, and every light in the house is on. It's a home, it's alive, and people inside it actually love each other, and—

Jake swings the door open, that big, kind grin radiating off his Free People face. "Louuuuuise!"

"Lou," I remind him and cross the threshold. Inside, the impression I pulled from outside is magnified. Caterers in crisp, black uniform. Golden mood lighting. Strategically placed cocktail tables. "Where's Archer?"

Jake twists his face together in thought. "I think he's in the wine cellar helping Doc bring up wine?"

"Thanks." I scoot past Jake, realizing I have no idea how to get downstairs. "Where is the wine cellar?"

"Closed door next to the Jesus bathroom off the kitchen."

I skid around the corner from the kitchen, where I spy Mrs. Harris micromanaging a caterer, and all but slam into the only other door in this hallway that doesn't have a slightly judgy Jesus staring me down. (He was fond of wine, after all.)

The door swings open on its own, and Archer pounds through, a box of reds in his hands. He sees me, registers it's me, and yanks his jaw up from the ground. "When did you get here?"

"Hi." I lift the wine box from his hands—fuck, its heavy—and put it on the floor. I kiss him, wrapping my arms around him. His lips are freezing, and I picture him out walking in the winter sun before he got here, collecting words and melodies in the city noise.

"Hi," Archer says, the words shaping against my mouth. He kisses me back, pushing me up against the hallway wall. His hands are in my hair, and mine in his, and his lips trail up my jawbone to my ear. "I missed you."

"You're not mad?"

Archer bends back just enough so I can see his whole face. It's almost too far away. "My feelings won't disappear just because you're a total weirdo for one night. I'm not angry. I am, however, damn curious." He leans over me in the hallway, brushing his thumb on my forehead, keeping us in our safe, little alcove. I don't deserve this kind of warmth after I ran out on him.

No. Wait.

I do. Yes, I fucking do.

My fingers tiptoe over his gray button down, and up his black tie. I didn't know he even owned a tie. "I've been calling you for two hours. Why weren't you picking up?"

"Jake called. Said the Harris women were driving him nuts, and to get down here ASAP. My phone died, and I don't keep a charger in the Bronco."

My god. Some things really are that easy.

He tucks hair behind my ear. "Are we gonna talk about this, now or—"

"Gin wrote a whole book about me," I blurt. "A whole fucking book about what happened to me last summer, and now she's doing readings in every cute bookshop basement in the state of Iowa."

Archer's eyebrows shoot up. "She did not."

"She did." The tight-skin thing is happening again, even inside our bubble. "That's why I freaked out. I have this song that you think is good enough to sell, that I haven't even heard yet, but some dude in Nashville has? It ... felt not great."

Even in all my words, I watch realization flicker in Archer's eyes like a firefly. "Stuff that sells."

Thank god this wall is here to lean on. "Don't hate me."

His hands find my cheeks. "Don't hate me."

"I don't," I insist. The kitchen sounds are louder—more people must be arriving for the party. Clanking silverware and voices instructing. I need to get this vulnerable look off Archer's face before it sticks and haunts me at three am. "You just deserve to know why I sprinted."

His eyes crinkle around the edges. "I am never, ever going to be able to hate you. You could murder a litter of kittens, and I'd understand that their sweet little meows were just too cute."

"Archer."

His fingertips trace my jaw, and while his right hand lands under my ear, his left arm cuts through my hair and crawls up the wall above me.

Good lord.

"You could park a whole convent of nuns on a train track, and I'd testify in court that it's not fair how many miracles they were bestowing," he whispers, the words tangling and knotting their way to my ears. "That they had to share some of the miracling."

"Arch."

I'm not sure if I angle up to him, or if he swoops to me, not that it matters. Because his skin against mine, the way his tongue lines the bottom of my teeth, the way I'm picking up that he's wearing cologne and it's slight, but it's musky with a hint of cinnamon, makes me cling to him like the sun won't rise come morning. A moan escapes his mouth, so quietly

I wouldn't have heard it at all of my senses weren't on high alert. Kissing Archer is sheer perfection, and all I want to do. There will never be another moment, another night like this, another kiss, and all I care about is him. Him, him, him. Him.

"What in the world am I gonna write songs about now?" Archer draws back, his shoulders heaving as he breathes in as much as he can. I can tell by the way he's looking at my lips that he's not done kissing me.

I pinch an earlobe between my fingers and wonder what sounds he'd make if I sucked it between my teeth. "Like, how sunlight ripples off puddles or whatever."

Archer swallows, and leans into my hand. I guess I don't have to wonder too hard. He shifts a leg between my knees and I almost bite a hole through my lip. I guess he doesn't have to wonder either. "You think that's what writers draw inspiration from?"

Lust clutters my vision. "You can write about me. Not everything. I don't want to get a big head."

"Can't have that."

"And I have to hear them before any bigwigs in Nashville."

"Absolutely."

My fingers are threaded through his belt loops, pulling him flush against me. "I'm sorry I read your email."

Somehow, his eyes hold room for sexy and warm forgiveness concurrently. "Water under the bridge, Lou."

We're kissing again when the door to the wine cellar swings open. I startle, but Archer holds tight, and looks blankly at Dr. Harris framed in the doorway, his tie crooked, his glasses on his forehead, and a matching box to what Archer had hauled upstairs five—no, ten? —minutes ago. Archer snaps to attention, and slides the case from Dr. Harris's grip, with muttered sorries. "Lou just got here. I wasn't expecting—"

The doctor's smile is wide, as he slips by. "Just don't let the missus see you. She'll have to disinfect the hallway." He squeezes Archer's shoulder three times, and offers the same hand to me for a brief shake. "Welcome back, Louise."

"Thanks," I whisper.

As if her ears are buzzing, Mrs. Harris careens around the corner, her heels clacking away on the hardwood. "Oh dear, where have you been? Anna and Zoey are due any minute." She grabs a cocktail napkin from a passing caterer, and dabs at her husband's forehead where his hairline begins. "Don't get any more wine from the cellar. The caterers can navigate those stairs."

"Of course, darling," he says, taking the napkin from his wife, folding it, and sliding it in his trouser pocket. The two of them drift around the corner like Homecoming King and Queen, leaving me and Archer in the hallway, unspotted. We look at each other, and burst into gut-splitting laughter.

We drift into the living room, as if on a cloud. Our fingers are knotted, my hand is gripping the inside of Archer's elbow, he's grinning like a lovesick fool, and a bit of my lipstick is smeared above his eyebrow. I resist the urge to wipe it away; Catherine and Jake are perched on the couch, staring at our sideshow here to distract from the main event.

Jake elbows his wife, waving his hand in our direction. "You owe me ten bucks."

"We both saw this happening. Don't even." Catherine waves Jake's open palm away.

Archer sinks into an overstuffed leather chair next to the fireplace, and to my surprise, yanks me down into his lap. I try to tone down my grin as I smooth my skirt over my thighs and swing my feet over the arm. Catherine smirks and Jake mimes a heart with his hands in our direction. Archer raises his eyebrows, but I can still see a mix of pride and glee in the corners of his eyes.

"Excuse us," Mrs. Harris's voice is in the living room before she is. I watch her separate her husband from a handful of presumed colleagues that just arrived through the garden.

"Are they here?" Dr. Harris, I swear, stands up straighter, and touches his bow tie, making sure it's straight.

His wife nods, and he takes her hand, turning back to his colleagues. "Sorry, I must step away. Our daughter is finally bringing home her girlfriend." He beams, like sunlight hitting daffodils in the spring, and I make a note to tell Annabella later.

"This peanut gallery needs to skedaddle." Mrs. Harris, meanwhile directs her attention to all of us in the living room, towing the doctor to the front door.

"Not a chance, Mom," Jake chirps, settling into the couch with a dog-eared copy of *Nursing Today*. On cue, Catherine pulls out her cell phone, furrowing her brow with exaggeration.

I lean into Archer and use my thumb to comb his sideburn up. A blush floods his cheeks as his grip tightens on my waist. "We didn't come prepared with props."

"We'll just have to make out."

Jake peeks up from Nursing Today. "Gross."

I laugh as the front door opens, and bite my cheek to pipe down. Annabella comes in first, Zoey's hand fully clasped within hers. Her face is flushed pink all the way down to her dress's collar, but a nervous smile is plastered on her face, and I take that to be a good sign. Zoey's calm, with the bouquet of daisies in her free hand.

Mrs. Harris is basically vibrating, sort of like a chihuahua. Dr. Harris is a little more chill—a little—and holds his arm out to hug his daughter. "Glad you're here, sweetheart."

"Hi Dad," Annabella murmurs, leaning into his hug, and holding tight to Zoey. Annabella glances at Zoey, and I watch Zoey's face relax, reminiscent of how Archer looked minutes ago next to a too-heavy box of red wine bottles. Annabella's face opens, genuine, wide, peaceful. "Mom. Dad. This is Zoey. My girlfriend."

"Zoey, welcome to our home," Dr. Harris says, reaching to shake her hand. There's a flower-holding-shuffle of hands that ends with Annabella clutching Zoey and the bouquet, as Zoey shakes hands with the doctor.

Gently, Zoey untangles the flowers from Annabella, and she passes them to Mrs. Harris. "Ma'am. For you. Thank you for inviting me tonight."

"Daisies." Mrs. Harris smells the top of the flowers, and looks up to her daughter and Zoey. "They're just gorgeous. Thank you. Please, call me Carol."

"Carol?" Jake pipes up from the couch. "I didn't get to call you Carol until my third Christmas."

"Oh, hush you," Mrs. Harris turns back to us for a second, and Jake holds up his copy of *Nursing Today*, but upside down. Annabella looks at the lot of us, watching in the living room, and bursts out laughing, cutting what nervous tension is left.

Dr. Harris looks to the ceiling, clearly mulling something over. "Archer?"

Archer turns from where he'd been nuzzling my ear, the meet and greet forgotten.

"What's that goofy nickname you gave my youngest child again?"

"AB, sir."

A sly grin creeps across Dr. Harris's face, as he turns his attention back to the women in front of him. Annabella's eyes widen, as if she's anticipating her father. "If you two adopt a couple nickname, may I nominate 'AB&Z'?"

"Oh my god, DAD," Annabella groans and flies at her dad for a hug. Mrs. Harris steps closer to talk to Zoey, but her words are lost in the commotion of all us moving again. Catherine is rushing to hug Zoey, Jake is high-fiving Annabella, who then throws her head back and dramatically crashes her forehead into his shoulder. Zoey hooks her pinkie through Annabella's, and Mrs. Harris is crossing the family circle to hug her daughter, gently, without an agenda or need.

"Were you nervous?" I lean closer to Zoey to be heard over the hoopla of the Harris living room. I had no idea hospital staff could party this hard—wine is flowing, the servers aren't making full laps through the crowd without running out of appetizers, and every fifteen seconds or so, laughter surges from wherever in the room Dr. Harris happens to be holding court with his closest colleagues of the moment.

Zoe nods furiously. "I was freaking out. I've never met parents before."

"You did great," Archer chimes in. "Carol can be ... unapproachable."

"You get to call her Carol too?" I elbow Archer, and he catches me, and holds me against him.

"Lifelong bestie comes with the first-name perk."

"My loves." Annabella rushes up, holding a catering platter. Four glasses of wine slosh around in stemless glasses, and the shininess in Annabella's eyes suggest she's already sampled the wine in the ten minutes she spent away, searching for soda.

"Whatcha got there?" Archer asks as if he wasn't the one to drag most of the wine upstairs.

Annabella poses with the platter balanced on three fingers, and Zoey fans herself. She hands me a glass, which I accept, and then one to Archer, then one to Zoey, and keeps the last for herself before handing the empty try to a passing server. "Mother said we have her implicit blessing to imbibe this evening, as long as we promise not to drive."

Archer looks down into his swirling wine, as if he's a sommelier and not a Keystone Light connoisseur when he does drink. "When did Momma Harris become liberal with the wine?"

I told my own glass up the light, the rotundness of the glass throwing me off. Being given a glass of wine is wholly different from sneaking shots with Ginny from Dad's liquor cabinet, or holding lukewarm Coors in a mildewy basement. "There's a communion joke in there somewhere, Arch."

Annabella's nestled under Zoey's arm, and I'm caught by the way Zoey's fingers curl off Annabella's shoulder. It's an old intimacy, I realize. They've stood around coffee shops and bookstores and concerts and our dorm room like that a thousand times. I want that. I want that badly.

"Well, you know." Annabella takes a long swig of her wine and smacks her lips. Yeah, she definitely snuck a glass back in the kitchen with Jake or Catherine. Probably both. "Life is short, darlings." And then she giggles into her wine glass and Zoey kisses her hair and Archer and I clank glasses and his grip on my waist pulls me closer to him and I lose any other thoughts except for him and me and us and this.

More doctors show up sporting tassel shoes and glossy hair and bags under their eyes. Nurses sweep in, fresh out of scrubs, in sneakers nicer than my running shoes. Catherine camps in the corner with us, balancing on the arm of the overstuffed chair Zoey and Annabella are tangled up in. Zoey hands over her wine, pledging to be the sober driver, and Catherine takes it down like it's a glass of water. Jake passes by, asking Archer to confirm lyrics to a Foo Fighter song before he's swallowed into the crowd again. I stay tucked next to Archer on the couch, only moving when he volunteers to go find drinks that are more cocktail in nature, or at least beers. He reappears with red beverages for the girls, and a closed Coors tucked away in his back pocket. He hands out the drinks and cracks open his can, relaxing into the couch, pulling my legs into his lap again. "Ah," he breathes. "This is more like it."

Annabella is holding her drink at eye level, studying the way the liquor isn't mixing with the mixer. "What is this?"

"A Dirty Shirley, babe."

Catherine sips it, and nods, flashing a hearty thumbs up. "It's sweet. You'll like it."

"Hey, I was just chugging wine."

"Not the winning endorsement you think it is." Catherine tugs her sister's hair, and sticks her tongue out. Annabella twists the same face back and tastes the drink, then smiles and sinks into Zoey like she's lost the bones in her body.

The next time Jake comes by, it's to tell Catherine they've run out of ice. Catherine's now on the couch too, melting, leaning into my arm. "Send the caterers," she says.

"They were done at ten," Jake says, as the front door opens and another set of scrubs walk in, just off their shift.

"It's not even nine."

Jake brings his watch to his face so closely it's comical, and I can't stop the bubbles from curling in my chest. "Listen, I haven't drank that much, but I'm pretty sure it's after ten."

Zoey, bless her patience, peeks at her phone. "It's about twenty after ten."

"Huh." Annabella looks up to the ceiling. "Cat—did you know we have a light on the ceiling?"

Catherine looks up to the overhead light. "You mean the one that's been there our entire lives?"

"Carol hates overhead lights," Jake helpfully adds, for Zoey's sake, and likely mine.

"Lamps or bust!" Annabella announces, thrusting her fist skyward.

Zoey's lips skim Annabella's forehead. "I think it's time we cut you off, love."

"What about the ice?" Archer brings the conversation back.

"I'd go get it," Jake said. "But Carol would murder me if I drove right now."

"I'll go," Zoey volunteers, standing and shaking her trouser legs down. Annabella slips sideways into her girlfriend's empty spot, staring up at her dreamily. "Impress the future in-laws."

Annabella's eyes go from dreamy to delighted saucers beaming in my direction. "Future in-laws?" Her voice is raspy and girl-whispery.

"Come on," Zoey offers her hand, then her elbow to hold as Annabella does a tuck and roll to stand. "You need fresh air."

"I need you." Annabella preens, and Archer snorts as they head to the front door.

Dr. Harris sees them moving to leave, and Zoey waves at him, her keys in her empty hand. "We're going to get ice."

Annabella does her best to cosplay as a sober human. "Be back in a jiff, Dad."

"You haven't been drinking?"

Zoey shakes her head. "No, sir."

"I have, Daddy," Annabella blurts.

Doctor Harris's smile cranks up a notch. "I could barely tell, my darling." He looks up at Zoey. "Hurry back. I want to hear more about your biochem lab. I've heard Dr. Maree's a real bear."

I watch Zoey's eyebrow notch upwards, and a blush fill her cheeks. "She is. A bear, I mean. We'll be back soon."

"So. Soon." Annabella thrusts her pointer finger in the air as if she's an authority on ice-related errands.

Dr. Harris catches his daughter's errant finger and leans past it to drop three super-fast kisses on her crown. He waves to Zoey, and they're out the door, into the night.

"Anna's so drunk," Catherine announces to no one, rattling her glass of melty ice into the air as if she's expecting a server, or Jake, to whisk it away. She grumps, stands, and wanders off.

"And then there were two," Archer mumbles, the tips of his fingers pressing against the fabric on my waist. I run my nails over where his childhood dog's tattoo starts, the golden retriever's ear disappearing under his cuffed-up sleeve.

I'm still looking at the spot where they stood with Dr. Harris, who has melted back into the crowd already. "They're totally gonna make out."

"If Annabella doesn't pass out."

"Zoey is on a mission anyway." I swing my gaze back to Archer. "The in-laws."

"Caught that," he murmurs, looking at my lips, and Annabella and her family are a distant memory. "Speaking of making out."

"We should..." I zero in on the way Archer's stubble meanders up his jawline and disappears underneath his wily curls. "But where?"

"Not AB's room," Archer vetoes immediately. His fingertips have migrated up my spine and are drawing out tiny hearts on my neck.

I lean in and prop my chin on his shoulder. I hope it looks like an embrace, even though I've snuck my finger under his belt buckle. My skin meets his, just below his belly button, and I feel him suck in his breath. "The pantry is too close to the party."

He gulps, as I trace my own shapes over his hip bone. "I admire your commitment to classiness, Lou."

"The Jesus bathroom," I say, striking on genius.

Archer leans back just enough to get my whole face in his line of vision. "I don't know what's more strange—that I know what you're talking about, or that I heartily, one hundred percent agree to it." He pops up, yanking me with him, our fingers laced together. I hang on, giggling, giggling, giggling.

We dodge a group of strangers, laughing at something Jake is saying, with Catherine on the other side of the group, shooting her husband the patented what-an-idiot-holy-crap-I-love-him side-eye. We turn into the kitchen, and I see Dr. Harris emerge from his own circle, pulling his wife close, kissing her tenderly next to the kitchen sink, overflowing with dishes the caterer is still cleaning up. Mrs. Harris takes in her husband, and I feel it in my bones, the trespassing on this candid, quiet moment of what a good life looks like.

Jesus is lit from within, but we slide right past him until Archer pauses. "Should we sneak in so we aren't weird about it?"

I peek over my shoulder. There's literally about a hundred people like ten feet away, but not a soul has noticed us.

"Nope." I nudge the door open with my hip, grab his perfect black tie, and yank him in with me.

Archer's lips are everywhere, immediately. In my hair, on my shoulders, the sweet spot in the hollow of my throat. My hands match his, tugging, pulling, sliding at his tie, my dress zipper, his buttons, the laces on my boots, flinging the thick soles to land upended next to a towel closet.

My tongue finds Archer's ear and he backs me into and up on top of the sink counter. I wiggle my hips backwards and wrap my legs around Archer's waist, locking him against me.

"Oh my god," Archer whispers, and I suck in a long pull of oxygen. He looks at me, really looks at me, and I don't mind. The light is still on, I realize, plus the vanity mirror framed in antique gold is right behind me, showing Archer every single angle of my almost-naked top half. My dress is rumpled at my waist—yanked down and piled up. Archer is naked, his shirt and tie long gone and pants crumpled at his ankles. His tattoos dot his skin like confetti. My mouth waters, itching to trace the plus sign with my tongue. For all of our making out, we've never had this much skin exposed—even if layers were discarded, we were still under blankets.

"You are fucking beautiful," he says.

For the first time in a long, long time, I actually feel it. I lean in and kiss him, and try to push off the notion of lining his collar bone with kisses. "The only thing that would make this more perfect is to hear my song when we get home."

"Matilda is in the Bronco." Archer moves to whip his shirt from the floor. "I'll go get her."

"Not a chance you're leaving me right now." I tighten my legs around Archer like a vise, and he smirks and it's so sexy I want to float away into a land of blankets and pillows and skin and the way his lips curve around the tip of my shoulder and stay here forever. I work to stay grounded, or this will be too quick of a trip to the Jesus bathroom. "Wait. You have your guitar here?"

Archer's smirk turns smoldering. "Darling, every party is a potential stage."

I burst out laughing.

"Seriously though," Archer whispers, and I resist the very real urge to shut him up with my lips. "I'm down for whatever you're down for, but are we...doing this here?"

"What?" I bat my eyelashes at him, and his fingers betray him by pressing dangerously high on my thighs. "Because this is a retirement party for our best friend's dad, and I'm a little tipsy on legit Napa Valley wine—"

Archer peppers my jaw with kisses, and combining that cinnamon-y musk with his whiskers dusting my face is nearly enough to do me in. "...and in the Jesus bathroom," he murmurs against my earlobe.

Giggles bubble up and out of my chest. "Buzzkill."

"Apologies, Louise," Archer whispers. My full name falling from his lips does something to me I don't think I'll have words for, for years. "I promise I can make it up to you." I let my eyes drift shut, and feel his lips trail down my shoulder, nipping as he moves my bra strap down my arm. I press my face into his open palm on my cheek, kissing each line, each path and hint to what his soul looks like. He unhooks my bra and slides it off my arms, and I pull his belt off and unbuckle his pants.

"Lou," Archer whispers, barely loud enough for me to hear. "I lo—"

There's a boom. Like a body slamming to the ground. It rattles the house.

A scream. Feminine. High, desperate. Terrible.

Glass, breaking. Shattering.

And more screaming.

We learn later, from Dr. Harris's physician, who happened to be walking up the front sidewalk when it happened, that it's a widow-maker that takes him. There was nothing to have been done. People, particularly men of a certain age, don't survive that kind of heart attack even in the hospital, hooked up to machines because they're so fucking quick. There was almost zero chance Annabella's dad was ever gonna beat the odds.

But we don't know that yet.

Archer helps me slide from the counter. He zips me back into my dress and himself into his pants and whips the bathroom door open. Dr. Harris is on the floor, surrounded by people but, through the crowd of legs, I can see Catherine kneeling over her father, her fingers laced and pounding his chest. Sweat is already beading at her hairline. Mrs. Harris is horror-struck and inside Jake's arms, being held back. Someone kneels next to Catherine and whispers to her; she lifts her hands from her father, and the other person takes over compressions with a detached, focused stare.

Next to me, Archer is frozen. I want to reach to him, to touch his skin—just warm, and probably now ice cold. But I'm frozen too. Stiff. Stuck.

I need the long hair pins.

I open my mom's bathroom door, eyes set on the vanity.

I know she bought them.

I'm moving bottles around on the vanity, hunting behind a flowery-scented deodorant, her favorite retinol, past the extra moisturizer she always has on hand, just in case, when my movement catches my eye in the mirror. She's in the bath. "Oh crap, Mom. I'm sorry. I didn't realize you were in here," I say. "Where are the bobby pins?"

She doesn't answer.

"Mom?" I set her tiny bottle of eye cream down. "Mom?"

Her hand is pale and palm-up on the water.

My body becomes unstuck.

I walk past the crowd, but Mrs. Harris's screams follow. As do the chest compression counts. The hush of everyone else. I walk through the dining room, past the Jesus statue from Thanksgiving. The living room, the entryway, and land on the third step up.

Sirens cry in the distance, slicing through the winter night.

I stay on the third step as the ambulance squeals to a stop on the street. As the red lights spin through the living room window, separating what was from what is. As Archer sprints to meet the first responders, as Jake holds the door for the two women and one man who move the stretcher into the house. As Mrs. Harris's wails become nightmares I'll hear again and again in the middle of the night. As the siren is silenced, and as Catherine sinks to the living room rug when her legs give out, as Jake takes Mrs. Harris to the chair I'd been in with Archer not three hours ago, watching Annabella introduce Zoey to her beloved parents.

As two becomes one.

As Mrs. Harris's screams become hoarse, and show no sign of fading.

As the paramedics load Dr. Harris onto the stretcher.

As they cover his face, and leave.

CHAPTER 20

"BABE, BE CAREFUL OF THE GLASS." SWITCHING A BROOM to his other hand, Archer takes my elbow and guides me to the kitchen where there's no smashed Fostoria ground to glitter on the hardwood floors.

Jake's taken Mrs. Harris and Catherine upstairs. Archer disappeared upstairs immediately thereafter with an arm full of bottled waters and the only box of tissues I could find downstairs. He came back to the kitchen quickly, his face blotchy, the light in his eyes flat. I don't have to ask. The ceiling is doing a shitty job of muffling the sobs.

I blink and I see Mom. So I just can't blink. "Let me help."

"No," Archer says, quietly, as he gets back to sweeping. "Thank you."

He sweeps the broken glass into a dustpan and dumps it into the garbage bin, ties the bag closed, and takes it outside to the trash. Archer's gone less than a minute, but it's too long to be alone in this kitchen where a daughter just watched her dad die. I wait until Archer's back, locking the door from the inside. "Do we try them again?"

"Yes." He's in my arms, pressing his forehead into my neck. "No."

"Yes," I whisper, pulling his phone from his back pocket. Archer lends me his thumb for a password, and I call Annabella again. Six rings, then her voicemail. Zoey. Same.

Archer is still pressing his face into me. "I can't stay here. I can't leave without her."

"We'll wait on the front steps," I decide, not looking at the part of the kitchen floor where Dr. Harris collapsed. "Come on." We slip out of the kitchen and through the living room like a pair of ghosts. I grab a fluffy blanket and Archer makes sure the door clicks as we slip outside.

The steps are cold, and the night air is collecting every drop of water to weave a layer of crunch over the dead grass and what's left of Mrs. Harris's fall mums. They'd been purple at Thanksgiving, if I remember. A deep, queenly purple.

Archer shakes out the blanket and offers me half. We huddle together on the fourth step, his head on my shoulder, slipping to my lap. I let my nails trace shapes over his skull, the tension in his shoulders cutting into my tummy like a knife. "Arch—"

"Don't stop," he says. "It's the only thing stopping me from screaming."

I nod, and search the streets for headlights. Any headlights. Onto Archer's skin, I draw hearts, seven million hearts, over and over.

Branches in the park across the street start to creak in the wind as the temperature sinks again. The breeze echoes way above us, creeping through the trees like a maze. Where are they? Where are they? I fold my lips between my teeth and bite down, trying to stop myself from asking him if I should call her again.

Headlights, finally, turn onto the Harris's street, several blocks away. They start as white pinpricks in the night, and get bigger, and brighter, until Zoey's car slows to a stop in front of the house.

Archer sits up, unwinds from his half of the blanket and pulls it tight around me, arranging my hair to fall over my shoulders. I hear Zoey park, but I can't take my eyes from Archer. Golden lamplight from the living room warms his face, his right cheek flushed pink from where he'd nestled in my lap. His tie is gone. His face is gray, his eyes jumpy. His curls are as lopsided as his frown.

He can't do this. He can't have this sully his bond with Annabella. It'll change them. The Christmas tree, his songs, the strawberry and Oreo milkshakes, inside jokes and lore and weirdness and perfectness that makes them them. I stand. "I'll tell her. You can't—I can't let you."

Archer was shaking his head before I'd begun speaking. "I'm gonna tell her. I have to be the one to tell her that her life, that my life, is..." Archer presses a kiss on my forehead that's more about him than me. Past him, Zoey circles the front end of her car, grasping a giant bag of ice, opening the passenger side door for Annabella.

"...is different now," Archer murmurs. His eyes search mine, and I know. "I'm in love with you. That's what I was trying to say earlier."

Every bit of air is squeezed from my lungs, and then rushes back in a flood. My lips part, and I know what I want to say, but he shakes his head, kisses me while pulling the blanket together again over my chest, stands, and turns.

I am in love with Archer.

And I understand why he has to be the one to tell Annabella.

"What are you two doing out here?" Annabella's voice is hoarse, but full of song. Zoey's slung her arm over Annabella's shoulders, still clutching that fucking bag of ice.

I can only see the back of Archer's body, but his arms are crooked, and I imagine him pressing into the guitar string scars on his thumbs. "Annabella."

"You never call me that. What is it? Third grade?" Annabella stops on the sidewalk, and looks up at her house. Clocks how the party is over. How the street is empty. How Zoey parked right in front. "Where'd everyone go?"

The paramedics rush past me through Mom's room to her bathroom and crowd over the bathtub. One paramedic leaves a perfectly captured boot mark in Mom's spongy carpet. I watch, I wait, I wish for it to spring back up.

"We've been calling you. Zoey." Archer's voice turns up like it's a question. Zoey's eyes go round, and I watch her hand on Annabella's shoulder unfurl, pressing all five fingertips into the cloth on her girlfriend's party dress.

"Archer." Annabella steps closer to him. "What the fuck is going on?"

They've hauled Mom's body from the water. I think they're doing CPR? There's counting. I can see her wrist, her hand. Her fingers curled up like she's waiting for me to slide my hand into hers.

I clutch Mrs. Harris's fleece blanket around my shoulders.

"Your mom, Cat and Jake are upstairs," Archer whispers. "They're okay."

Her nails are freshly done. Pale pink. Her favorite.

"Did Dad get called to surgery? That doesn't make sense. He retired."

"AB—no."

Her hand jerks up and smacks to the linoleum. It's the CPR. Once. Twice, a third time.

"Archer, where is he?" Annabella's voice is high. Terrified. And already on the other side, where her life is different now.

I slip past Dad in the hallway and am nearly to my room when I hear someone say they can't find a heartbeat.

"He had a heart attack," Archer is saying. Already, Annabella and Archer feel too far away. "There was nothing they could do."

Annabella's face stills. "You're a fucking jerk. This is an awful joke."

"Honey, it's not—"

"No." Her finger rams straight into his chest. "Stop. Zo, come on."

I leave my sundress in a cotton puddle on the floor, kick past the heels I set out last night and dig out shorts and a sports bra.

Zoey's let the ice bag slip to the sidewalk. It hunches over like a troll. "Anna, I don't think it's a joke."

My favorite running shoes, the ones with the pink laces, knot perfectly like they always do.

"It's a joke." Annabella's eyes are lit with fire, but she blinks, and there's a new Annabella. An Annabella with a mom and a sister, a childhood of memories, and a dead dad. Archer sees what I see, and steps to her, his arms open wide, his eyes overflowing. I think she's going for his hug, but she slaps his face, hard. The crack snaps down her street. "Of course it's a joke."

Archer doesn't flinch, and yanks Annabella to him as her knees buckle under her ruffled skirt. Her head hits his chest and her first wail erupts from her lips. Archer opens his arms to Zoey, and she slides in behind Annabella, holding up what Archer can't.

I pass the empty stretcher at the door. The ambulance, its lights and siren off, faces west.

His cheek pressed against Annabella's forehead, Archer looks for me. I'm on the edge of the lawn, my fingers knotting the loose ends of the blanket together. Archer raises an arm to me, and I want to. I need to. For him, for Annabella. Even Zoey. For me.

I turn east.

I know that.

And I run.

But I run.

Part 2

...TO A KID BURYING A PARENT

CHAPTER 21

IT'S FIVE AM. MADDIE AND EMILY HAVE NO CONCERN FOR others sleeping (or not sleeping) on our floor.

"Can you believe it?" Emily is saying. She sounds nearby. They must be leaving for training. "I hate that girl as much as the next person, but her dad? At a party?"

I'm curled up tight in bed, but hollow dorm doors do nothing to mask sound. They can probably hear breathing in here. Alone. Guilty.

"Stop it," Maddie says as they pass my—our—dorm room door. Her keys jangle as she locks their room across the hall. "You don't hate her. You're jealous as fuck of her endurance and time, but you don't hate her."

"I'm jealous of her, and I hate her," Emily corrects. "But losing her dad already? Not jealous of that. At all."

They keep talking as they head out and I lose their words, then their voices. I straighten my legs from the ball I'm in, but the stretch doesn't feel good. Nothing feels good.

My phone buzzes again—for the millionth time in the last four hours—and I flip it over. It's only my alarm this time. Training. My first back, and I should be following Emily and Maddie out. I crawl from my bed and untangle myself from Mrs. Harris's blanket. I pretend it smells like Archer, but it doesn't.

It's a quick walk to the Wellness Center. I reclaim my locker next to Annabella's by unceremoniously throwing my bag inside it. I fish around inside for my pill bottle. Archer's texts run on the marquee in my brain as I swallow the pill dry. He'd sent a dozen ranging in concern to shock. The worst:

ARCHER: You just left us.

ARCHER: Are you serious right now?

ARCHER: The Bronco is gone. I'm guessing that's you. Please tell me you got home okay.

ARCHER: Please.

LOU: At dorm. I'm so sorry.

That was three hours ago. Silence since.

"Welcome back." Coach is at the end of the row, shrugging off her coat.

"Thank you." I resist the urge to hide my pill bottles.

I feel her note my smeared eyeliner and the sparkly clip Annabella had shoved in my hair at some point before the ice run, but after the drinking began. "You heard, I assume."

I nod.

Coach adjusts her gaze to somewhere over my left shoulder. "I was planning on pulling all the girls together before we start to say something. To cut off the gossip."

I nod again.

Coach blinks and nods too. "See you out there."

~

Coach pulls the nine of us together in a quiet corner of the gym. Says she'll organize a bus to Sioux Falls for the funeral when she hears more. How this is tough and unexpected, and we need to allow Annabella space and grace. All the things you say. Sara suggests we pray, and leads something I don't listen to, but I bow my head anyway. I try to close my eyes and just see darkness, but my brain flashes a reel of my mother's fingertips and Dr.

Harris's hands still at his waist on the floor. I throw my head back, eyes wide open, and catch Coach, as Sara finishes the prayer, already watching me.

My presence is hardly noticed, except for Emily's sneer in my direction in the locker room. Coach makes no indication that my presence is weird, and for the first time in months, I line up with the team for stretches and set off to claim a treadmill.

Our miles in, the other girls hit the showers and I stall at my locker, peeling off my layers. My phone has no new texts.

The showers turn off one by one, and girls start filtering back into the locker room. Sara walks up to me in her street clothes, still scrunching water from her brown hair. "I'm glad you're here," she says. "How is she?"

"Um." I lean into my locker to hide my panic. I don't know. I have no idea how Annabella is.

"Zoey is with her," I say. "And Archer. They're at her family's house."

"Your boyfriend?"

"Her best friend."

"Oh. I thought...I always see him with you." Sara begins to braid her hair, under the guise of caring, waiting for me to spill.

"He is. We are," I stammer before I bite down on the inside of my cheek hard enough to clear my brain. "Archer is where he needs to be right now."

Sara nods. "Of course," she says quickly. A tiny bit of satisfaction grows when her layers start to pop from her braid. "When you talk to Annabella, tell her I'm thinking of her."

"Sure," I mumble, and grab my shower bottles from my bag. I jerk my thumb over my shoulder in the direction of the showers. "I'm gonna..."

"Yeah, totally, sorry." Sara waves me off, and I escape.

My favorite stall is open. I slide in and yank the knob to hot. I don't undress, or even step under the water. I stand, and let the steam rise.

That's where Coach finds me, later. A minute, an hour, the entire morning? I don't know. The shower curtain swooshes open like a breeze caught it, with only Coach's shiny white Nike running shoes poking under. I expect Coach's scary face, the one she used outside the med tent last fall when I threw up all of my stomach's contents in the bushes.

But Coach is ... soft. Worry changes the shape of her face.

A cry rips from my throat.

"Whoa." Coach turns off the water and pulls me to sit on dry shower tile. "Tell me. Now."

I tell her everything. Annabella and Dr. Harris. The bowl Mrs. Harris was holding splintering to glitter on the floor. Catherine's trembling hands on her dad's chest. Mom. The bobby pins and the boot print in her carpet. Archer. Ginny. Mom's funeral and how alone I was, surrounded by people. All the words I've shared with Meghan, all the words I haven't, and tucked away to ruminate on alone, to chew over and over and over, to let eat me alive.

I'm a sopping mess. Tears turn into snot trails and I can't sniff fast enough.

Coach goes to the supply closet and returns with a box of tissues. She settles next to the shower, her back pressed against the tiled wall with me, and rips the box open. "First. It's too much for one person to handle alone. I'm so sorry."

Hurt pings under my sternum like waves, threatening to explode if I say anything. I press a tissue into my eyes.

"Deep breaths," Coach's comfort voice is velvet. I wouldn't think it fits her, but it's natural. "In through your nose, out through your mouth. Deep as you can get."

I flatten my shoulders against the wall and look up. In. Out. In. Out. Next to me, Coach matches my pattern, looking up too. "Wow," she says after a while of listening to our breaths fill the stall. "We need to paint these ceilings."

I grunt.

"Ah, there you are." Coach offers me another tissue. I wipe my cheeks.

"I should have stayed last night." My voice is as scratchy as my throat feels. "Or I never should have been there in the first place. I never should have gotten involved at all."

"Listen, I don't know Annabella like you do, but I know her a little," Coach says. "And knowing her even a little means you get her heart. She's rare. You were never going to live in that dorm room and not become her best friend. It's who she is."

Those words. That label. Best friend. "I was never good enough for her."

"Stop." Coach holds her hands up. "I never want to hear that from you, ever again. You know what I see when I look at you?"

I shake my head.

"I see bravery. I see fierce."

"You do not."

"I kicked you off the team because you were too fierce for a team sport," Coach says. "And you couldn't follow my rules. I'm still not sure you can, but I know you're gonna try like hell to prove me wrong." Her voice goes soft. "Why don't you prove yourself wrong too?"

"I'm just not a good friend." I want to collapse on myself like a dying star.

"Think of it like training, friendship. Training is all you've been doing since you got here first semester."

"Stop. You know it's not the same thing."

"As usual, you're right about exactly half of it." Coach has a small smile on her face and it's jarring, but also comforting? "Running is a solo sport. You get your two legs and your brain and your heart and you do what you can. But McKinnley—life isn't solo. You don't get to do it alone."

"I don't know what to do for her. I don't even know what to do for myself." I flash back to how black and white it all was. Archer's pale face, Annabella's black hair. The bag of ice, how the dark attached itself to Zoey's hunter green pants. The fleece of the blanket to the harsh crunch of grass with each step I took. Mom's hands. Stay. Go.

I'm in love with you, Lou.

He had a heart attack.

This is a sick joke.

Coach hands me another tissue and I press it against my eyes until I see stars. She's still beside me as the stars fade and the tears subside. "You want breakfast?"

I twist my neck to look at her. "Breakfast?"

"I'm in the mood for hashbrowns."

I clear my throat, and ball all my tissues together. "I could go for some orange juice."

"That's the spirit." Coach pops up, and offers me a hand up too.

~

My phone lights up in the dark.

"Hi," I answer, pulling it to my ear.

"Sweetheart." Archer's voice is more of a sigh than a word. "Hi."

I roll, bookending my phone between my cheek and the pillow. It was a stupid decision. All I see is Annabella's empty desk and closet. "Where are you?"

"On my way home. Zoey's spending the night at the house with AB."

I close my eyes. "Good."

A car door shuts, and I hear keys rattle in Archer's hand. He must be back already. "We miss you."

I press my fingers against my eyelids. Collapse into that dark hole I pictured back in the shower. "You don't have to lie. I literally sprinted away from the worst moment of her life."

"It was more of a weird waddle thing with that massive blanket," he says, trying for a joke.

"Arch."

"Lou. We all miss you. But I miss you the most." Archer says. "It's like what light was left is gone."

"Stop." A tear trails down my cheek to my earlobe.

"It's true," he says. "You pulled all that underwear out of the bushes and stuffed it back in your suitcase."

"We're killing this metaphor."

"Wait, your underwear isn't actually in the bushes? This is a real let down."

A snort bursts from my nose. He laughs too, hushed, walking wherever he's walking.

"Will you maybe come over later?" I ask.

Archer makes that *hmph* sound in the back of his throat that I used to think sounded like a grandpa back in our early Wellness 101 days. "How's now?" On cue, knuckles rattle on my door. I roll sideways off the loft in my haste to get to him.

I whip open the door, and there he is, back lit by harsh fluorescent hall lights. He smiles, carefully, like he hasn't gotten to use those muscles in the last day, and I restrain myself from throwing myself into his arms. "You came for the Bronco."

"I came for you, you weirdo." Archer shuts the dorm door behind him, doesn't bother with similar restraint, and yanks me to him. Every place he kisses feels like wildfire. I swear I hear sizzling. His tongue in my mouth, his hands messing my hair, his heart pounding against his ribcage and into mine. I can't breathe, and I don't ever want to again.

Archer slows the kiss, tucking hair behind my ears. "I missed you," he says, twirling the end of my ponytail between his fingers. "And I'm heartbroken about Dr. Harris. And AB. And Cat and Carol. And I'm so pissed at you I can't see straight."

Inky dread flows through me and I look down to his shirt. It's yet another flannel, one I've never seen. Probably lifted from his childhood closet in Sioux Falls. Hunter green and navy with gray lines. Soft against the tip of my nose. "I know."

"Running like you did on Valentines Day was whatever because you were hurt. And I'm working on forgiving you for leaving like you did the other night, and I will, I promise, but babe?" He slips a finger under my chin and gently redirects my gaze up to him. "Annabella wasn't the only one who needed you."

"I know," I breathe. "I'm really, really sorry."

His eyebrows curve to each other over his nose. "Thanks for saying that."

We're staring at each other now, in my dark room. His eyes are bottomless, but, and I realize this now, that gives them room for every feeling to ever occur to exist inside him. Love, of course. Forgiveness, hopefully. But there's also pain, and hurt, and worry. Fear. Heartache. Struggle. And everything his eyes have had to see this week, that mine didn't...he deserves to know why.

And I deserve to talk about it.

"Can I tell you about my mom?"

I'm curled into Archer's side when I run out of words. I tell him of finding Mom, of how her nail color came back to me in Annabella's front yard. Of the boot print in the carpet and Principal Smitz's stupid Hallmark.

Of running away from my house and not coming back for hours. Of Mom's funeral. Of the shape of her urn. Of my lonely summer. Of coming here, and not speaking, and failing right off the mark until I got into therapy, and then there was Annabella, and then him, and I thought I was healing but I don't think I am, not like I thought.

Through every word, Archer holds tight to my hands, his guitar string scars pressing between my knuckles and tethering me so I don't float into the night.

"Lou," he murmurs, pressing his cheek into the top of my head when my mouth finally stills. "I get it. I can see how that was an impossible moment for you."

"Grief is stupid," I say quietly. We never did turn on a lamp, but Archer had tugged a blanket off my bed until it fell at our feet like a cotton avalanche. I snuggle in harder.

"Grief is the fucking worst," he agrees, kicking off his Vans, and relaxing into me. "I can't take any more stupid shit about how if there's grief, that means there was love. Grief means an end, and it's fucking brutal."

"Someone should needlepoint that into a pillow." I listen to his chuckle rumble in his chest. He begins to twirl my hair around his fingers, and I let my eyes drift shut. "I heard the funeral is on Wednesday."

"It is." The twirling doesn't stop. "I know how hard it might be for you, given your mom's." He pauses. "But think about coming? Even just sitting in the back."

"What if I can't?"

"Then you can't." Archer drops the piece of hair he's holding, and a kiss lands on my head. "No one is going to hold it against you."

I take a long, deep breath. "Ginny wasn't at my mom's."

"Do you hold it against her?"

"I mean." I sigh. "Yeah. She was my best friend. And my dad is … my dad. I was alone."

"I hate that for you. I hate that it happened like that. But if you don't go to Eric's funeral, AB won't be alone," Archer says. "I'll be there, Zoey. Her sister. She won't have the same experience you did, no matter what you choose. I need you to take care of you."

"How do you always know what to do? What to say?" I prop my chin on his shoulder to see his face.

"First, I don't. Second, therapy. Extensive, life-altering therapy. Third, and this is specific to recent events: I'm trying to listen to my gut. AB's got a radio signal right into my cell structure. My gut knows what to do, even when my brain and my heart are clueless."

"So. I should listen to my gut."

"Or your heart. Your brain. Whatever body part you most prefer direct your decisions."

I look up at him through my eyelashes. "When you put it like that."

Archer's laughter fills the room. "Yes. All the yes. But first, tap into your gut or whatever. Try to listen."

"Fine. But don't watch." I settle into his shoulder. I take a big breath, and exhale.

It's weird to be without my voice, or his. I feel Archer breathing beside me, and beyond the walls of the room, I hear the other residents moving around. Someone's clacking loudly on a keyboard. A shower starts, then a toilet flushes in the bathrooms. Voices, farther away, shriek at something and dissolve into giggles. People, living their lives, paying no mind to me.

I squeeze my eyes shut and listen harder.

It comes to me in colors. A red circle from the tree lights in Annabella's hair. Green and golden splotches splayed on her neck. Archer is on her right, watching me. Annabella stares up through the Christmas tree branches, the ornaments and lights nestled in molting plastic branches, layered up to the ancient tinsel-rimmed star flickering like a broken lightbulb.

I'd wavered above Annabella and Archer, nervous to infringe on their sacred tradition.

Annabella waves me down. "Get down here. We're not doing this without you."

I open my eyes and stand. Archer has moved to my desk. "Sorry," he says. "You were humming a lovely melody and I had to try and get it down before I forgot it."

"What did it sound like?"

Archer taps out a beat on my desk with his fingertips. A sweet hum comes from his lips, and he scribbles something else down in my notebook.

It's the first music I've heard in days.

CHAPTER 22

IN THE END, MY GUT TELLS ME TO GO TO THE FUNERAL.

My gut tells me to park my car far from the hearse, on the other side of St. Michael's parking lot, and to hurry in, keeping my eyes focused on the top of my black boots. I sign the guest book, and take the program handed to me at the door. I sit in the back pew, next to the extra pile of programs for when the ushers run out. I do not read the obituary printed right inside, nor do I look at Dr. Harris' picture at the top. I avoid looking at the sanctuary all together, knowing I'd see family pictures and flowers on flowers on flowers.

The pews begin to fill. Hospital staff I recognize from the party. People our age who must be old classmates of Catherine or Annabella. An older couple, who, I think, are Jake's parents, based on how he shows them to a pew near the front. Coach leads Emily, Maddie, Sara and the team down the middle aisle like a line of ducklings.

People continue to file in. Even the back pew is tight, and I'm forced to scoot to the aisle next to a stack of extra programs. The backs of people's heads start to lose detail, and everyone begins to overlap into one. Like a watercolor, or the stained-glass windows we all sit under now.

I try very, very hard to not think of how full Mom's service was at the funeral home. How so many loved her. How her nails were that soft pink, and the gashes on her arm were bandaged over the last time I saw her before her body was cremated. How Milo's fingers rounded my shoulder as I sat in the front pew, and how they're slipping over my same shoulder now.

It's not Milo.

“Hey.” It’s Jake. He’s squeezed in next to me.

I focus on his face, and I’m fully in Sioux Falls. Mom’s ashes are split between an urn in the living room and under her favorite tree in the backyard. Dr. Harris’s casket is somewhere behind me in the lobby. I blink hard. “Hi. Jake.”

“Hey,” he murmurs again. “Listen, we’re about to start, but if you want, you can move up to the second pew. Zoey, Arch, my parents, and other family friends are sitting up there.”

My gut tells me to get up and walk out the door.

I shake my head, and thank him. Jake disappears back into the lobby.

Organ music begins in the balcony. People stand. Doors open, pallbearers, led by Jake, roll Dr. Harris’s casket down the aisle. Mrs. Harris follows her husband, clutching Catherine and Annabella’s arms. They all stare forward as if they see what’s happening, but aren’t processing it.

I get it.

Harris family cousins and aunts and uncles file in behind them, and it feels like the family processional goes on forever until I see a man with red hair in a suit he had to buy for today. He nearly passes by, until my hand springs out. Archer stops, waves for Zoey to keep walking, and kisses my nose, then my lips. “Thank you,” he whispers.

I kiss his cheek. “Go.” He does.

The processional ends. An opening prayer is prayed. The priest tells us to sit.

We sit.

We pray, again.

I watch the front two rows.

If one of the daughters begins to cry, the other does too. Jake keeps his arm steadily around Catherine. Zoey’s got her arms around Annabella’s shoulders from behind. Her lips move against Annabella's hair, and I can't tell if it's kisses or comforting words. I shouldn't be watching it, but I am.

There's a hymn, and we rise. Archer doesn't bother with the music because he's got it memorized. His lips move with grace and ease, but his eyes are anything but calm. I know his face after hours of staring at it in every kind of light he'll let me stare at him in, but right now, I can't make it make sense. He's a Picasso, a piece of art, but I don't recognize him.

I'm halfway up the aisle before I think too hard about it. I step into the pew, and pull Archer's face to me. He crumbles against my body, and I hold us both up, until the hymn ends, and we're told to sit again. We sink back to the pew, and Archer lifts his head. His eyes are rimmed in red. Is this the first time he's allowed himself to cry this week? I hate that I don't know.

Our fingers slip together and land on his leg.

Those who are Catholic are encouraged to kneel. Archer and I bow our heads, without pulling out the stool, and I squeeze my eyes shut to not see the coffin, flowers, or pictures of Dr. Harris, happy with his family. Blood pounds in my brain and—

Mom's funeral director leads us through The Lord's Prayer. Her urn gleams. It looks warm, but no one has touched it in hours. I can't touch Mom if she—it—is as cold as ice. My feet twitch toward the aisle. Three steps.

"For thine is the kingdom..."

My hips rise to vault me out, but Dad's hand lands heavy on my leg. I look at him, and his eyes are hard, looking at the funeral director. He isn't thinking of Mom. He isn't praying either. He's making sure I stay right here, the good daughter. The appearance of the two of us coming together in crisis.

I want to go. I could run. Calmly walk back to my seat, or sprint from the church.

I could disappear.

Archer shifts and lowers his forehead to our clasped hands on his knee. His eyes are closed, and his lips move with the words reaching for the rafters.

I still. And I hang on tighter.

CHAPTER 23

"HOW ARE YOU?" MEGHAN ASKS. HER GRAY SOCKS ARE embroidered with tiny four leaf clovers. The toe is green, like she dipped the tip in ivy-colored paint. "Talk me through the funeral."

"It was awful. I wanted to run away the whole time."

"But you didn't?"

"No."

"Have you talked to Annabella since the funeral?"

"No."

"Doesn't that complicate living together?"

"She's staying at home with her mom. She's taken leave for the rest of the semester." Archer told me outside the church. He'd lent me his jacket because I was shivering in the weak sunlight.

"Why haven't you called her?"

I squeeze my eyes shut. "I'm ashamed."

"Of what?"

I unscrew an eyelid. "I don't know how to do this. Or sit in this with the people I love. I never mourned my mom. I buried it and hoped that was good enough."

Meghan's chair squeaks as she shifts her weight. "It never is."

"Yeah, I know that now."

She puts her pen down. "I think it's time to talk about grieving your mother in a more head-on fashion."

"Am I ready for that?" I think of Archer on the roof weeks ago, smashing marshmallows between graham crackers, and waxing poetic about how crucial it is to keep one foot in the present while you grab your sword and storm the life of Past You.

"You've been ready for it the whole time." Meghan's eyes are warm. Warmer than normal. She thinks I'm healable. I'm still doubtful, but parts of me are so shattered that what's left whole needs protecting, I guess.

I take a deep breath. "You're good."

Meghan smiles. "You are too."

~

I stare at the stain above my head on the ceiling. I stare at it so long it starts to look vaguely like Australia.

"I don't miss climbing six feet into the air just to get into bed." Archer hoists himself over the end of my loft, folds in half, and Army crawls up my mattress to meet me on my pillow.

"It's not bad," I say. "I liked Annabella close. I was never alone up here, but I could feel like I was, if I wanted."

"Screw being alone." Archer's fingers meet mine under my pillow. I roll to him. His stubble is soft under my palm. We might be able to call it scruff soon. "I'm here," he says.

The question that's been on the tip of my tongue for weeks. "For how long?"

"Things are different. Here." Archer boops my nose to try to elicit a laugh. It doesn't work. "I guess it's kind of a live-while-you-can-thing now." His hand is solid—for now—on my back. "I'll be here for as long as you'll let me."

Saturday morning run. Thick, gray clouds tumble low and crowd the Campanile and swallow the top of her tower. I head down Medary, farther from home. When the wet snow starts, it's fluffy as it flies around me. I know it won't last long—it never does this time of year—but I still flip up my hood and focus on my breathing.

My blow dryer is louder than my thoughts, and it's a relief. The locker room is almost empty; most of us have gone to class or back to bed.

Coach walks by the mirror bank, tapping on her phone. I imagine she's trash talking NDSU's coach, and I want to text Annabella but do not. Coach and I lock eyes in the mirror. She puts her hand on my shoulder and taps once.

I nod.

She drums her fingertips into my skin and continues on.

As he sleeps, Archer kisses my wrist. His lips feather against my skin. He puts my hand back over my belly and snuggles his face between my shoulders. I brush my fingers over where he kissed me, swearing he's seeping under my skin in that exact place.

I'm studying, cross-legged on the futon. My music is extra loud to drown out the silence. I don't hear the door open and I jerk up when Annabella walks into her closet. I dig my ear buds out.

"Sorry." Annabella looks anything but. She's got a pile of clothes on her desk, the hangers tangling into a plastic nest at the top.

"It's okay. This is your room."

She looks at her pile. "I needed more clothes."

"How are you?" I blurt, shooting to my feet, and almost conk my head on the bottom of my bed.

She narrows her eyes and opens her mouth, like the thoughts are fast, but the words are slow to come. "I've been better."

I know. I understand. I'm here. I care. I love you. Whatever you need. That's what I should say.

Instead, I knot my fingers over my belly button and nod as if I'm solving a calc equation.

Annabella crosses the rug she bought for our room. A pair of cleats she never uses is tied at the laces and slung through her elbow. She pulls her pile of clothes into her arms.

"Let me help," I manage, reaching for the top hangers.

Annabella shakes her head, her neck coiled and tight and I drop my arms.

Her keys jangle in her grip and she struggles to shift her clothes to see her key ring that she's already twisting apart. "Here," Annabella says, freeing the only key on her ring that matches mine. "I don't need it anymore."

My heart crashes to my abdomen. "Annabella."

"Hey," Archer careens into our room. "I'm early, sorry." He sees Annabella, and his face lights up. "You didn't tell me you were here."

"I'm not." She sets the key on her empty desk.

Archer looks at the key. "What's going on?"

"She can use the rest of my stuff until the end of the semester." Annabella speaks to Archer like I'm a ghost, lurking over the two of them. "Bring it home after finals for me, please?"

"Annabella." His voice sounds far away. "Don't. This is silly."

She blinks, swallows hard. "Lou needs her space. She's got it."

Annabella exits as quickly as she arrived. Her hangers click against each other down the hall.

Archer crosses the room to me. His fingers skim my own, still clutching my ear buds. "Go," I say. "She needs you."

"Lou."

"Please. I'm okay." I nod my head like I am.

We both know I'm not, but neither is Annabella. "Go."

He hesitates, and I sit with my textbook and laptop, putting on a show of studying, as if my world isn't ending, again. Archer sinks to his knees in front of me, and cups my face. He kisses me three times. Short, soft kisses, like he has no intention to ever stop.

And then he rises and goes, shouting his best friend's name as she leaves the hall.

Outside Meghan's office, I step over a stream trickling to the storm drain. Thawing water gurgles, scrubbing ice melt and dirt from the curb. Neon green grass spikes through what's left of the ice crunch in the lawn. I hate it.

Archer's got me walking around campus. He says the fresh air and the sun, even when I'm not running, will help. Getting out of bed was okay, but tying my shoes for a simple walk was nearly too much. Meghan told me to start paying attention to where I feel it, my depression. She said it's important to identify it as any other part of my body that could get sick. So I pay attention: my depression has claimed its usual residence in my forehead, sometimes arching around my temples like a pair of the ugliest earmuffs. It made me feel top-heavy, bending over tying my laces. I could have stayed like that all day, bent in half.

I look at Archer shuffling next to me, his hands stuffed in his pockets, his head in the clouds. "I have a weird question."

"My favorite kind." He takes my hand.

"When you don't feel great, and you know it's your depression, where do you feel it? Where does it live in your body?"

"That is a weird question. I like it." Archer moves my hand to his lips and kisses my third knuckle. "Mine tends to start as anxiety that flares under my ribs. It sort of feels wild."

"Wild?"

"Yeah. Right here." He moves our hands again, this time to cover his left lung as we walk. "I've always sort of pictured it as this bird that wants me to move, but he can't figure out which direction or where to go so he—the bird—freezes, and then so do I. Sometimes hours pass." Archer shrugs. "A weird answer for a weird question, I guess."

"No," I say. "No, I get it."

Running. Clouds. Heavier, grayer, rain-filled in the west. A weighted blanket, except one that wishes to soak me rather than lull me to sleep. I wish I were asleep. My whole head aches, and it's beginning to feel like the hurt won't lift at all.

I get to the gravel road we train on. Proof that we're here, all the time: millions of cleat marks pock the dirt. I dig in, and head straight for the storm.

Fresh spring air, warm and sweet, drapes my lungs and I run faster.

Swish. Tap.

Swish. Tap.

Swishtapswishtap.

The clouds open and I sprint straight into the waterfall. Heavy drops splatter my face and smear down my bare legs as I pump my cleats into the gravel. Rain pounds the new crops, flooding the field into a black mud pit no tractor will get into for days.

Thunder cracks like a bookshelf tipping. Water sneaks into my cleats and pools at my arches. I'm losing my time. My endurance. My breath.

I don't stop.

How the sweet turned sour. Violence, unleashed. Anger crashes in the clouds, furious at spring for making it warm enough for rain.

It's relentless, this rain, smacking my cheeks and sneaking up my nostrils. Our pock marks disappear as the gravel turns to the color of rust and my cleats gunk up. I stumble to the clay, and pebbles stop me from sliding.

Water streams from my ponytail to my eyes and I roll to face the sky. Tiny rivers carve through the mud against my body, flowing into my sweatshirt and shorts.

I don't want to get up.

I could sleep here.

I could give up. Stay here.

Archer will go to Nashville. He'll write more songs about me: the one who got away. He'll win big awards and write for superstars and live on a ranch with his own recording studio and he'll find love one more time and it will be for good.

Annabella will run, graduate with honors, and work at Mayo in the cardiac ICU for her dad. She'll marry and have two girls, just like her parents, and she will love, and be loved, endlessly.

I'll be here. Let the rain pound my skin to welts. Let night fall and watch the stars shoot light to me that's older than the dirt under me. Let the sun rise again, and again, and I'll never move, and I'll roll to the weeds and no one will find me, and it'll be fine. maybe

That's not what you want. Momma.

Why wasn't I enough to stay for, Mom? Why wasn't my love enough?

I feel light. Unencumbered, as if I can float. As if I already am.

Finally.

Stop. it

Gin, leave me alone.

No. This isn't what you want.

Maybe it is.

You won't find us, no matter where you look. We're already gone.

I miss you. I miss my mom.

I know. But it's time to get up now.

I open my eyes, and can't tell where the tears end and the rain begins. My head is a rock for how heavy it is. I shiver, soaked, though the storm has lightened to a sprinkle.

What do you want, Birdie?

I want to know Annabella's girls and see if she ends up with Zoey or the next woman, or a woman five women down the line. I want to race her, and beat her, and race her again and lose, and get her advice and have an ornament on the tree and know her voice like I know Ginny's.

And I want Archer. I want to hear my song. I want our language we haven't written yet. I want his frizzy curls and my smile described in his lyrics and a family spaghetti sauce recipe we pretend is fancy, but just comes out of a jar. I want his tattoos and his leftover guitar pics and his lips on the back of my neck before he drifts off every night.

I want me. I want to love myself, and be loved by them, endlessly.

I get up.

CHAPTER 24

"MENTAL HEALTH ISN'T LINEAR." MEGHAN'S VOICE MIGHT lull me to sleep.

It's still raining, and her lamps stretch light to the darkest corners of her office. I'm curled against the couch, clutching my favorite pillow in my lap. My insides feel scraped empty, like a stand-mixer bowl post cookie dough.

"I wish it was," Meghan is saying. "We all do. But there are dips and spikes."

I want to press my face into the pillow. "I'm tired."

We both know it's not that kind of tired, but Meghan chooses to focus on the less delicate first.

"Remind me: what's your sleep routine look like?"

I explain: stretches. I'm back to Key West, Alaska, Sydney. Then it's teeth brushing, pajamas, and Archer gets there within the hour. I don't tell her I love the smell of boy sweat where his neck slopes into his shoulder. That he's the string keeping me from floating away. That's too much, so I'm not telling him either.

"Good." Meghan nods encouragingly. "Routine is key. Is Archer there every night?"

"I feel better with someone sleeping in the same room." After Mom's funeral, I moved into Mom's room, a little girl again. Mom's side of the mattress dipped lower than Dad's, like she slept in a canyon, and I pretended it was because Mom spent so much time in bed, and not because Dad spent none there. Of course, none of this made me feel better, and I moved back to my bed.

Then I had Annabella, our pillows touching in the corner. She usually fell asleep reading her Bible. I fell asleep to the thin pages wisping by like butterfly wings.

"Whatever is healthy and makes you feel safe," Meghan says. She rubs her hands together and shrugs like we're about to start an arts and crafts project. "It's time we get started. If you hate this, we can find another method of treatment, but I strongly believe that this might help you shake loose some of that gridlock." She poises her pen over a loose piece of paper balanced on her notebook. "Do you agree that we're going to review your situation with your dad?"

I clear my throat. It's louder than I want. "Can we talk about what happened after the paramedics took my mom's body away instead?"

Meghan looks up, nods. "Sure. Ground rules are the same. You find a comfortable spot, pat your shoulders for the bilateral stimulation. I want you to focus on how your body feels during this. If anything aches or alternately, feels too light, tell me. I'll pause you to check on your acceptance level ratings: one to ten, ten being the least accepted."

"Okay." I wiggle between the seams of two cushions, and my pillow flops sideways. I put it back on my thighs. Fingers posed at my shoulders, I close my eyes. I exhale.

"What do you rate the day the paramedics took your mom's body away, ten being the least accepted."

"Ten."

I hear Meghan begin to tap her shoulders. My taps match her speed. "Tell me about that day."

My brain sinks, as if traveling through quicksand. "The paramedics were there. Mom's death was declared. I couldn't be in the house. I was running." I'd run forever, I think. Across town, and back. Turning in the direction of home felt like a prison sentence, but I had to go back. Houses

I passed had graduation parties in living rooms and spilling out of garages. Every other house it seemed had blue and yellow balloons tied to mailboxes, bouncing in the breeze. "I was almost home. Just a few houses away. A car on the street slows as it passes me, and turns into Ginny's driveway."

"Good. Keep going." Meghan's taps pick up, so mine do too.

"Dad flies out our front door. Bright red cheeks, fists clenched like he's looking for something to hit." Feet away I can see how his fingertips are turning white from lack of blood circulation.

Where did you go? You need to stretch your legs? Keep your trim figure? You left me alone with your mother's body!

The paramedics were here. They're still here.

Still parked right where I left them, facing west, and blocking traffic for the whole block. "Ginny's getting out of the car. She's holding her graduation cap, and she's got a curl going the wrong way from how the hat sat on her head." I never even put mine on. "Her dad is walking to us, staring at the ambulance."

Joe. Sorry to interrupt. What's going on?

Dad claps his forehead like this is slapstick, and spins to the front door.

Her mother just...she...

I can't look at Ginny's dad. *We're fine.*

"Ginny's at the end of her driveway. I can feel her." Like when you accidentally walk through a spiderweb. You feel it, the invisible thread, but you can't scrape it away with just your nails. I know she's there.

"My dad laughs and it sounds like a pig's squeal. I am horrified. Ginny's dad's hand is on my shoulder." *Lou, respectfully, I don't think everything here is fine.*

Dad spins, and like a magic trick, he turns into the realtor version of himself. Full stature, driven eyes, fake smile. *Fine? Nothing has been fine here in years.*

Taptaptap. "Good work," Megan says.

"I look over. Ginny's crossing the street. Her dad waves her back. She stops." I want someone to wave me back. I want to never go back into my house, and that's what I have to do when everyone else goes home. *Dad. Stop.*

"He sneers at me." *Daddy. Stop. You've always been a momma's girl.*

"I want to tell him to fuck off. To leave for good." No one has to try and pretend now. And I'm about to say it, when our front door opens.

"A paramedic comes out, navigating my mom's body, covered in a white sheet, strapped tight on a stretcher, out the door." Another paramedic is at Mom's head, lifting the back wheels up and over the threshold. Ginny's dad curses. Ginny's at my side, clutching my elbow. Dad spins away, his knuckles digging into his eye sockets.

"And you, Lou?" Meghan's voice tiptoes into my memory. Saving me. Like she promised.

"I'm standing there, watching it happen. It's in slow motion. Like I'll never fully move again."

"Pause." Meghan stops tapping. I peek my eyes open. The everywhere-yellow is garish against my clear-as-day front yard setting. "What do you rate the day the paramedics took your mom's body away, ten being the least accepted."

I don't think long. "Eleven."

"The goal is for the number to sink. Let's keep going." Meghan positions her hands. "Deep breath, tap."

"Ginny's fingers are too tight." I shake her off, and she has the gall to look hurt. Her dad walks away from the ambulance like death is catching.

I was looking for hair pins. For my mortarboard. Mom had the long ones we bought for today. I found her. In her bath—

Louise. Enough.

I swing to Dad and his voice. He's stalking across the yard, his fists wide-open palms. Like that's something to be scared of now.

I didn't talk about how sad Mom was, all the time, with you gone on your business trips —

Louise! "He's closer, swiping at me, grabbing for a hand or an elbow."

With Marissa in Ohio or Indiana or— I'm spinning away, just out of his reach.

I said stop IT. Dad stretches for my arm and comes up with only air.

I stop moving, having circled the whole yard away from where we started. I'm a bull, ready to fight. If Ginny were to wave a red flag, I'd lunge at him and gore my dad to pieces. *Or at the new Holiday Inn Express out on 6th, wherever you could fuck your girl of the week without Mom knowing.*

ENOUGH.

Dad's roar rips down the block. It makes the paramedic driving the ambulance, who'd been waiting while his colleagues finished up in the back, get out of the rig. Ginny hustles across the yard to me, her dad shadowing her, standing between us and my father.

And Dad. He pants like the old man he is turning into. After a long time, he speaks.

Fine. You know everything. You figure this out.

He goes to his car, pulls out in front of the ambulance, and drives away.

Ginny's dad is in my face, trying to read my eyes, holding my shoulders, even shaking me before Dad's down the block. I watch his car get smaller and smaller, and something in me just...ends. Or stops. Or something.

Whatever it was, it's over.

Ginny's dad is still trying to talk to me when the Brown County Sheriff pulls up. He walks across the yard, nods at the ambulance, and heads for me. He says he needs to settle a crime scene investigation, and asks to see the scene.

Go home. I'm okay. I say it to Ginny and her dad. I wave the Sheriff into the house, and shut the front door tight.

"Stop tapping," Meghan says. I do as she says, and open my eyes, relieved to find this dumb yellow room. "Are you here with me?"

I nod. "Can we take a quick break?"

When I come back from the restroom, my water bottle is filled with water and her teacup is steaming again. We get right back to it.

"Anything feel weird or uncomfortable in your body?"

I shake my head. I'd done an inventory as I washed my hands: my lungs are tingly, but that might be relief.

"And you feel firmly placed 100% back here, in this room, with me?"

My lips crack into a weak smirk. "I hate how much you love yellow."

"Good." Meghan sets her pen and paper aside. "I have a theory. And you can tell me I'm wrong, but hear me out."

I nod.

"I think that the one time, the first time you felt confident enough to talk about your mom and her depression and what it led to, you were silenced. Your dad made it abundantly clear you weren't to be heard from."

"Seen and not heard." It was Dad's favorite mantra, starting back when I'd sit at his desk at his first realtor job and ending in an absolute shit show in the front yard.

"How does that make you feel?"

"So angry I want to scream."

"What's stopping you?"

I raise an eyebrow. "I'm in the middle of a college campus. I raise my voice too loudly and someone complains to an RA."

"There's no RA here."

"I'm not screaming. It was a metaphor."

"Fine. But you need to express that energy. Get it out of your body."

"That's why I run."

"Yet you still want to scream."

I shove the butts of my hands into my forehead. Out the window, the tiniest of buds are starting to dot the branches. Green little dots in the sunshine. "Ginny never came back."

Meghan's head dips to the side. "What do you mean?"

"After that day. She never came back. She never crossed the street again. Even her dad managed the funeral." I knew because I saw his name in the guestbook. "She was my best friend, and how ..." Meghan slips from her chair next to me on the couch. Up close, I can see a zit on her cheek underneath her concealer. How clear her eyes are. "How could she just never come back?"

"I don't know Ginny. I can't speak to her action. Or, inaction, as the case suggests. But I can tell you this: It's okay—healthy, even—to mourn Ginny, and that loss. It will be a beast separate from mourning your mom, though they're intertwined. Grief, like mental health, isn't linear. But there's a silver lining."

"Oh yeah?"

"Archer's in your corner. I'm in your corner. Coach Stevens loves you, though she'll never admit it." That makes me smile. "You are deserving of love, Lou. You are deserving of friendship, of mentorship, of comfortable mental health. We're your team. We've got you."

"Archer's moving to Nashville," I say.

"That's a problem for tomorrow."

"I want to be there for Annabella." Cotton chunks in the pillow shift under my nails.

"And we're going to work on it, while we work on protecting you through it." Meghan clasps our hands together on the yellow pillow. "Do you believe me, at least a little?"

I look at our fingers in my lap. Every session, I find the pillow fluffed and ready for me to deform on the couch. Smushed and covered in arches of soggy mascara today, it looks different. It almost looks like hope. Kinda.

"Yeah," I say. "A little."

"I'll take it." Meghan rises and slips back into her chair. She grabs her pen and looks at me. "What do you rate the day the paramedics took your mom's body away, ten being the least accepted."

I dig my nails into the pillow. I swallow hard, I fill my lungs with air, I fidget and grind, and picture my mom, not in the bathtub, but at our kitchen counter, sipping tea. "Nine," I say. "I rate my acceptance at a nine."

CHAPTER 25

"EMDR FEELS A LITTLE SKETCHY UNTIL YOU'RE IN THE thick of it, right?" Archer's saying, as he's unlocking his door.

I slip my backpack off my shoulders. "Maybe even like magic. Some sort of voodoo until you feel things..." I drop my bag onto Archer's table. "Click isn't the right word. None of this is clicking. Or healing, yet. Just..." Where's Ginny when I need her and her words?

Archer piles his winter stuff on top of mine, kicks off his boots and yanks me to his bed. We drop into a heap and crawl up to his pillows. He's a mind reader. I've been waiting for this moment all day. "But it sounds like you're willing to try it again."

I sigh. "I'm willing to try again."

"I'm happy for you." He turns his head to press his lips into my hair. I snuggle into him and breathe deep; underneath my hand on his chest, I can feel his heartbeat, and listen to the way his inhale pulls air in. I revel in it, the pieces of the puzzle that do the hard work to keep us going so we can focus on things like dreams and mental health and falling in love.

Speaking of.

I make my eyes drift open again. This feels like an eyes-open conversation. "I was wondering if you'd be up for playing me my song, finally."

"What song are you talking about?" Archer actually giggles when I pinch his chest under his ribs, and flips to his side so hard the mattress feels like a waterbed for a second. "I will play you any song in the whole wide world you wish to hear."

My heart pounds, though I'm ready, though I've been ready for a while. "Even 'Can't Help Falling in Love'?"

Archer's smile is like water, skimming between rocks, taking the path of least resistance. "Especially 'Can't Help Falling in Love.'" He finds my hand on his chest, brings it to his mouth, and kisses my middle knuckle three times.

"What's that mean?" I blurt and hold up our hands, our fingers overlapping at the joints. "I've seen Annabella and Zoey do it. And Dr. Harris, a bunch. You did it too, Thanksgiving, as we were leaving the river. The three squeezes."

"You did it first." Archer's eyes are shining. "The morning after the showcase, after I played you that song. You stood to warm your tea and you squeezed my hand three times."

For what it's worth, I see you, he'd said. I remember.

My heart aches, but it's good—a reminder that now a new part of my heart is being filled, I have something to lose again. How unfair that as I'm filling in my puzzle pieces, Annabella lost her biggest corner piece.

"Dr. Harris started it when we were little, and he had to leave in a hurry for an emergency," Archer murmurs. "He'd take the hand of whoever he was with at the time, squeeze three times and tell her to pass his love to her sister. AB shared it with me. Three squeezes on a shoulder or fingers. See?" Archer squeezes my hand with each word. "I. Love. You." He clears his throat. "In this case. In our case." He folds our fingers together, and shifts his truly magnificent gaze back up to mine. "Well. You know."

I wiggle close, tilt my head, and brush my lips against his. "I." Another kiss, this one longer. "Love." One more kiss, lingering, and I whisper. "You."

Archer's face is open under that flop of hair, and I swear, if I peer hard enough, I might see sunshine.

"How did I get so lucky?" he whispers, as he envelops me, his hand on my head where it turns to my neck, my hair tumbling down his arms. He shares this space with me, filling it as much as I need, careful to never take too much.

But now I want him to take it all. Just take it, and hold it safe in you, sweetheart, I think. Let me fill your cracks, smooth over the rough edges too, like you do mine. Let's rip open our suitcases and mix my underwear in with your t-shirts and mismatched socks until we lose track of who owns what and just figure this out together.

We kiss until we sway, both dizzy. Until I remember. "Archer. My song."

Archer's cheeks glow like his hair as he cups my cheeks. "I need Matilda."

I sit up and cross my legs while Archer runs the ten feet across the apartment for his guitar. "So many firsts. My first song. My first time being fine with my boyfriend declaring he needs another woman..."

"She's my first love. I don't know what to tell you." Archer beams and crawls onto the bed with me, settling Matilda in his lap. "This is for you. I named it 'Still a Way.'"

He takes a deep breath, nicking the strings. "She asks me about my tattoos. She asks me to count. She asks me to connect the dots I never wanted to before now," Archer sings. His eyes gleam. "She asks me to go. She asks me to stay. She makes me want to never fade away."

I put my hand on Archer's knee. Matilda's hum vibrates through him to me.

"And she's the first reason I've had. In so long I can't say," Archer sings, blending a higher key to a stronger strum. "To hang on, to sleep, to dream. Now she's showing me. That there's still a way."

The chorus again, over and over, and Archer flicks the last cord, deep, gorgeous, and I want that energy to pulsate the air between us forever. The electricity that's specific to Archer—the core of Archer. Whatever makes up the fine matter in Archer and the fine matter in me is one now, permanently, and will spin into something stronger than a memory. As if I can pluck it from the story of our life, and live in this moment, whenever I want, forever.

That's why Ginny writes, I realize. It's why Archer looks at me sometimes, as if the words are already connecting behind his eyes. And it's not perfect, loving an artist. But it is worth it.

He leans over Matilda, and kisses me. "I love it," I say between kisses. "I love you."

"That's something to hear." Archer's face dazzles this close—not a new view, but a different light. The swirl of his stubble, heavier on his chin than his cheeks. I want to match his freckles to the stars. I want to know every guitar string scar on his fingers. I want to read his palms and know his hands better than mine.

Our mouths take it slow, the guitar between us. Archer moves her to the corner and comes back to his bed and we crawl to the pillows, his chest pressing into me. My shirt goes first, then his. I let my fingers trace the cross. Even though I can't see it, I shudder, picturing my nails over it. Archer drops a kiss onto my neck to mask a laugh.

"I know it's terrible," I whisper. "That tattoo is beyond hot. It's been a thing since Thanksgiving."

"Give me your left arm," he says. I hold it up, and Archer turns it, pointing to a birthmark below my shoulder. "That birthmark is shaped like the Eiffel Tower. You were wearing one of your strappy tank tops the day in Wellness when you finally told me your name. I couldn't stop staring at it. It's consumed days of my life, Lou." Archer places a whisper fine kiss on the mark. "You know how many songs I have about it? Like ten. And they're terrible."

"I'm going to need to hear all of them."

"Never."

I muffle a laugh against his chest, and he tilts my chin up to his mouth and we're kissing again, Eiffel Tower birth marks and sexy tattoos forgotten.

Soon Archer's pants are gone, and then mine are, and so is our underwear, and we're under the covers, and when Archer rolls to the nightstand for a condom, lightning bolts strike my rib cage. Sex has never felt this charged before. This real. This goofy, or sexy. This...fun.

Archer's back, the silver packet pinched between his fingers. "One more thing." The flush rises to his hairline. It's the singularly cutest reaction I've ever seen in my entire life. "Is there anything you like? Want me to do for you? To help you..."

I take the packet. "Archer. I just want you. Now." I want your skin against me. I need your hips between my knees and to press my lips against the softest skin under your ear and to feel you there, before I lose it, out here.

His grin is about as love-drunk as I feel. Archer's hand finds its way to my face, and traces my profile from my chin to bury his fingers in my hair. It's hot as hell and my brain starts to forget how to tear foil wrappers.

We manage the condom together, and my hands on him, he mutters something that's lost in his throat. He takes my hand, and squeezes my fingers together, one, two, three. He kisses me slowly, with care, and I'm flying.

~

"I've noticed an uptick in several of you worrying about stride and pace." Coach's voice booms off the metal lockers. Dark ash in the vague shape of a hastily drawn cross, but more gray blob, streaks Sara's forehead, and I keep glancing her way. I forgot it's Ash Wednesday. I wonder if Annabella went to a service at the church where the funeral was, or if she picked a different church.

Coach raps her nails on the whiteboard where she wrote "EFFORT" in caps with squiggly lines shooting out that look vaguely like my high school biology book's drawing of a sperm swimming to an egg. "Ladies, your priority in this off season is that you master controlling your effort level. Not every step needs one hundred percent. But you need to maintain. Sustain. Over time, that becomes your guide."

I unwind my bag from my shoulders and rub my eyes.

"Lastly," Coach says. "We have the spring invitational here at home against NDSU on April 28th. We're permitted three people, and as usual for this meet, I'm taking the current top three best times." Coach makes a production of reviewing at her clipboard, like she didn't already know those three people are Emily, Sara, and Maddie, in Annabella's spot.

Coach clears her throat. "We're changing it up. It's Emily, Sara, and Lou."

Somebody gasps. Loudly.

It's me. I gasped loudly.

Heads swivel back to me. My sweatshirt is half on, my face turtling out the neck hole. Coach makes eye contact with me like she did in the mirror—same "you okay" question mark, but this time with more "WTF" at my hoodie-turned-straitjacket moment.

Coach flips her clipboard down, taking the focus off me. "Outside. I want you to maintain. Sustain. Let's go."

A herd of women amble past me. Coach whacks me on the arm with her clipboard, the last person to pass. "Let's go," she says again.

~

Archer's a quiet typist. First semester when we pretended to study and spent more time flirting, his fingers danced over his laptop keys. I speak from experience now that no matter what Archer is holding – Matilda, his laptop, me, his fingers are feathers, soft, but they get you to where you're going.

There's a chance I have an unhealthy attachment to Archer's fingers.

Anyway—tonight, Archer is clamoring on the keys. Attacking the backspace button with his pinkie like it stole his guitar and tried to light it on fire. The clacking fills my dorm room and rings through the emptiness Annabella left. Forget Matilda—I want to light his keyboard on fire. "You're...aggressive with those keystrokes tonight."

Archer looks down at his blessedly still fingers. "I'm trying to finalize bookings for Gallerie."

"What's the hurry?"

He sucks his lips against his teeth.

I try to keep my feelings off my sleeve. "I thought we had until the end of the summer."

"We do," Archer says. "Come here." He pats the futon and brings up a voicemail. "I got this while you were in class today."

"Archer!" A man's voice booms from the phone speaker as I crash to the foam seat. "Listen man, I wanted to touch base with you. We're still interested. I'm in Omaha the last weekend in April, so I'm thinking I could meet you in Brookings, listen to you perform and we can talk after. Let me know."

I watch Archer while the voicemail plays. Pink swirls underneath his skin and it turns him into a gleeful tomato. It's the cutest I've seen him yet. "What's his name?"

"Zach Diaz. He works for Bad Jasper Records." Archer mutes and pockets his phone. "I reserved Gallerie. I need people there."

"I'll help." I take Archer's chin and turn his face to me. "Congratulations."

"Thank you," he whispers against my lips.

Time. There isn't enough.

CHAPTER 26

"THAT'S EXCITING FOR ARCHER," MEGHAN SAYS, LIKE IT'S the least exciting thing in the world.

"It is," I agree. Her lacking response curdles under my skin.

"For Archer. Yes."

See?

I walk to the window. With the leaves budding, it's like we're high up in a treehouse, abandoning the world and starting our own society: Tree People with Healthy Brains and Great Pedicures.

Meghan rustles her notes behind me. "You said earlier you're going to the spring invitational. What's your 10,000-meter?"

"32:27:32."

A low, impressed whistle springs from Meghan's lips. "I'm proud of you."

"Thanks."

The paper rustling stops. "How did that make you feel?"

I follow a gold line in Meghan's rug and match my toe to my heel, like in a sobriety test after a cop pulls you over for swerving down the road. "I'm excited—I've worked hard to ..." I sigh. "To contribute to this, for myself, I guess, and to the team and my time, but it's still an empty success."

"How?"

Toe to heel. Toe to heel. Toe to heel.

Meghan watches me walk and crosses her ankles. "I can see you're agitated. Let's postpone our EMDR session to next week."

"No." I plant my ass on the couch and position the pillow in my lap. "You said last time that we were going to deal with more Mom stuff, so let's do it."

"Okay," she says. "Ground rules," Meghan says. "Pat your shoulders for bilateral stimulation. Focus on how your body feels. I'll pause you to check on your acceptance level ratings: one to ten, ten being the least accepted."

"What do you rate the afternoon after your mom's funeral?" She touches her shoulders.

"Hard ten."

"Start tapping."

Dad's ditched me with Mom's urn. Everyone's gone to the reception area on the other side of the worship space, where women I've never met and Mom never talked about made funeral sandwiches and potato salad and stacked cookies on paper lace placemats next to daisies for the mourners. It's just me now, in the sanctuary. With Mom.

This is yours now. The funeral director stands next to me outside the pews, but it feels like he's looming. He's got Mom's urn, the bottom flat on one hand. The brushed brass, I swear, looked more gold a few days ago when I'd picked it out.

Mine?

The funeral director nods. His brows are crammed together like a caterpillar. *Your father left a bit ago, and I...* He sighs. *I'm not sure he's coming back?*

Oh. I stand.

"Tell me what you see," Meghan says.

"The funeral director is handing me Mom's urn." I mime clutching it to my chest.

He pauses and steps to me. *May I?* The funeral director helps me hold the urn comfortably, securely, sliding my hand underneath the urn, as if I'm cradling a newborn. *Do you need help getting to your car?*

I shake my head. We walk to the front door. What's left of Mom's funeral programs are strewn on a tablecloth underneath a bouquet of roses I don't want. Her face, cropped from a family picture from when I was six, looks up a dozen times.

He opens the door. *Again, Ms. McKinnley. I'm so sorry for your loss.*

"I don't know what to do with her. With it." Fingers tap. "I put it in the front seat, and buckle it in so it won't tip over." I cry. I scream. No one hears me. No one saves me. Sunshine catches on the maroon paint inside the carved crevices that I thought Mom might have liked. I want to look more, to travel the sides of the urn like a maze, but I have to keep my eyes on the road.

I'm home. I don't know what time it is, but it must be mid-afternoon—the elm's shadow is stretching clear over the front yard. Mom's marigolds are starting to bloom around the mailbox post. I pull into the driveway, and take up both spaces. Dad isn't here.

But Ginny is.

My palms itch, like bees have turned my skin into a hive.

"Tell me what you're feeling," Meghan says.

"I don't want to see Ginny. I don't want her here."

Lou. Ginny pops up and is across the yard in a flash. *I couldn't. I'm so sorry, but I couldn't.*

It's fine. I need to get Mom—no, Mom's urn—out of my car. Did she know her marigolds were days away from blooming?

My fingers brush my shoulders. Tap tap tap.

Ginny's face melts like butter. She almost believes me that it's fine. *Thank you for saying that.*

I very much need to get Mom in the house.

It's been hard. Oh, she's still talking. *Remember when she helped us make those friendship bracelets? We picked out the colors because it looked like the sunset?*

Tap. Tap. Tap.

I'm so heartbroken. For all of us.

TapTapTap.

She was like a mother to me.

"Shut up! Shutup! SHUTUP!" The words rip, burn my throat, as I plant my face into the yellow pillow. "Just STOP."

Meghan sinks into the couch beside me. "Lou. Kiddo." Her voice is low. "Come back to me."

I jerk up, the pillow dented from the valley my face left. My lungs heave like I'm sprinting.

"Tell me what happened."

I feel Meghan rooting around in my brain, unwinding the layers and peeling away like I'm an onion. What's the last thing she doesn't know?

"I hear Ginny," I blurt.

"What do you mean?" Concern laces Meghan's voice. Frantic concern. Like the Campanile is crumbling and tumbling bricks are polka-dotting the green and I'm standing at the foot of the steps, waiting for my brick to take me out.

I stare into the yellow cotton and pick a string, as if I can trace it all the way to the end of its tassel. "I hear Ginny."

"What does she say?" Meghan's hands enter my frame of vision as she crouches in front of me, filling the blank space at the end of the tunnel.

"Stuff she never said in real life." *It's still all about you.* "Makes me the inconvenience."

I can tell Meghan nods because the ends of her brown hair bob against her shoulders.

"But also—" My voice catches. "She was on that gravel road in the rain when I was training, asking me to get up."

"Tell me more."

"She makes me feel not alone. Even when I am. Even when I want to be."

"Is she intrusive?"

"Not in the way you're asking."

"Does she ever feel like she's controlling you?"

I look at Meghan, hovering at my knees. Her eyes sparked in worry, and reading my face like a book. Real or imaginary, Ginny never stood a chance at controlling me, even with the best of intentions. "No."

"Has she ever told you to do something that would be harmful for you to do?"

"No. What is it when people hear voices in their head?" I ask. "Schizophrenia?"

"That's one diagnosis, yes. There's been research in recent years about generalized auditory hallucinations in people who aren't experiencing more well-known psychosis."

"It's not that." I suck in air. "I've never felt threatened. Pissed, but never scared," I say. "She's just there. My conscience."

Meghan leans back on her heels. "I think what's happening here, after getting to know you, Lou—this is your brain in mourning. In letting go and moving on, you're holding on in the only way you can."

Mourning. That word, as a concept, unbuckles my spine. I sink backward into the couch. "I'm not irreversibly fucked up?"

"I don't think anyone is irreversibly fucked up." Meghan moves back to her seat. "We are going to check in with Ginny's voice, what she's saying, from now on. Thank you for telling me."

I nod.

Meghan arranges her face into Neutral Listening Mode again. "What do you want to do about her?"

I think about Ginny—and her real voice on TikTok, reading her piece about me. Keeping her version of me in her bubble where she gets to define me. To take my story and tell the world on her terms. I have my own version of her, tight in my bubble. My own narrative of her. "I think I need to accept she wasn't capable of being who I needed."

"We're going to come back to that next time. Now," Meghan props her chin on her fist. "What do you feel in your body right now?"

I check in with myself. My fingers are cold from clutching the pillow. And my heart. Oh, she's trying to squeeze out between my ribs. I tell Meghan.

"Do something with me. Take the biggest deep breath of air you can."

"What?"

"Just, all of it." She sits like a queen now, her ankles crossed, back straight. Her hands flutter around her diaphragm, her fingers moving like she's playing piano keys. "Breathe in the world. As much as your lungs will carry."

I mimic her position, down to her fingers at her belly. My eyes drift shut and I feel like a balloon, my chest rising first, and then my shoulders and chin pointing to the ceiling. And I feel good.

But more than that, I feel goodness. Coursing through each pocket in my lungs, spreading to my bloodstream, and filling me with grace down to my toes.

I exhale after Meghan. She's watching me. "A little better?"

"A little."

"Do that exact thing, whenever you need."

~

Sustain. Maintain.

Coach wrote them on the white board again this morning. Her "s" looked like a five. She forgot the second "i" in "maintain" in her hurry. Maybe it was on purpose, because the sun is down, and I'm still thinking about the words at my desk and waiting for bedtime.

Archer strums his guitar and hums the beat to lyrics that don't exist yet. I watch him disappear into his head, twirling a chunk of red hair, with an elbow propped up on Matilda's curve as he scribbles in his notebook. I have no idea what he's writing or thinking, but I feel his energy in my belly. Like the lyrics he's writing will turn me inside out and I'll still come out a little spit shined.

Maybe even better.

I give Archer room, more time to create, and pull a small velvet pouch out from my desk drawer. My ancient friendship bracelet waits inside, and I pull it out. At some point as a kid, I wiggled my bony wrist out of Mom's triple knot, so it's still intact. I pick at the knot until it gives—all eleven years of it—and pull the neon pink, orange, and purple threads so they fall from one to three again. Next I take Annabella's key from where I tucked it in the drawer and tie the loose neon pink thread to the top of the key, and the purple thread to the bottom of the key, carefully hooking a sailor knot around the rough ridges. I tie the orange thread to the end of the purple thread, relieved that time hasn't done much to weaken the threads.

"What are you doing?" Archer's up and setting Matilda on Annabella's empty desk.

"Help." I pinch the orange and pink ends together over my pulse. I can't make a knot one-handed.

Archer pulls the ends together, asks twice if it's too tight (it's not), and ties the thread together. I raise my arm and look at the key flat on my wrist bone. When I rest my arm on the desk, her key pings on the wood.

"Again, I'll ask." Archer moves to put Matilda in her case for the night. "What even?"

"Effort."

"Is that a cross-country thing?"

"I think it's a life thing."

CHAPTER 27

SPRING BREAK.

I'm sitting at Archer's table, staring at an email. Flipping an idea around one last time.

Archer emerges from the bathroom, his hair wet. When he shakes his head, droplets scatter like a sprinkler. His arms are heavy and warm, and I feel safe, but I also feel like doing unholy things in his lap. "What should we do today?"

"You need something to take your mind off Zach Diaz."

It's true. He hums through dinner. While I write my freshman comp paper over the span of three nights. While he brushes his teeth in the morning. Pencil cocked over his ear, sliding through his hair to scribble a lyric on a gum wrapper in the diner.

This morning, I woke up alone. I wrapped his comforter around my shoulders and slipped out the still-opened fire escape window. I heard him before I saw him. On the roof, Archer angled out of a lawn chair so Matilda's round base had the room she needed. The air was turning cornflower blue as I wrapped myself into a ball in the hammock and let his melodies put me back to sleep.

Archer tucks my hair away now. "I didn't want to wake you. It was kinda perfect blinking out of my haze and finding you up there with me though."

"You're perfect," I say, kissing his nose. Because he is. "But you need a break. Just a brief one, today. I made two appointments at your favorite tattoo artist."

"Two?" Archer sits up straight. He points at me. I nod. "When?"

"In twenty minutes."

Archer's hands land on his cheeks, slack jawed. "How are you real?"

He pulls me into the tattoo shop like a kid flings his friend into a candy store. We crash into the front counter. Crowded Polaroids of tattoos gleam under the glass and I bend to see. Fantastic, huge chest pieces of lions. Sweet deep white roses, outlines of mountains, the Joker on a playing card. Eagles, American flags. A wedding ring on a ring finger. A couple with matching sternum tattoos: one owl holding a lock, the other holding the key. A jet-black cross between shoulder blades over freckles and skin so pale the camera flash catches the blue veins crossing under the skin. Red hair trails above it, like someone needs a haircut. "That one looks familiar."

His kiss lands on my shoulder. "I can't imagine why."

"Archer. You silly goose." Mae, Archer's favorite artist comes out of the back.

"Mae!" Archer springs, embracing her with a tight hug. She doesn't look surprised and hugs him back.

Mae squeezes out from under his arm and extends her hand. "Hi. Nice to meet you, Lou."

"You too!" She's got a septum piercing, a sharp black bob, and an arm full of violet daisies and fairies. She exudes warmth. I trust her.

Mae taps her short nails against the counter full of her pictures of her work. "I know Lou's got a plan. What are you doing today, Archer?"

He blushes. "I have an idea, but I need to draft it out, see what you think, and let you do your thing with it. Lou should go first."

Excitement surges under my skin, close to how I feel at the starting line. "You'll still sit with me?"

"Are you joking? I'd never miss this."

Mae supplies Archer with a sketchpad and a Sharpie, while I change into a pair of mesh shorts behind a curtain. Back in the main area, I hike up the hem on my left leg and Mae kneels, shaving the area, and transfers our design onto the front of my thigh, about three inches under my pelvic bone. “Check it out in the mirror, girly.”

I swing to the full-length mirror. The tattoo—my almost-tattoo—is lined in purple. It’s one long string of a girl mid-stride. The line starts as the ground, moves onto her shoe, up her leg, puffs at her curves and shapes out her arms. Her ponytail flies in the wind like fire, loops down her profile, draws out her other foot in mid-step, and travels back to the first foot, rooting her back to the ground.

I am in love.

Mae’s table ready, I climb up and lay flat on my back. Mae readies her equipment, and Archer grabs his paper and Sharpie, settling on a stool to my right. I resist the urge to yank my ponytail tight. There’s no one to intimidate here, but that move was always more about me.

Archer slips his hand into mine and squeezes three times.

The tattoo gun buzzes to life, and Mae pops up in my peripheral vision. “If you’re ready, I am too.”

I nod, she holds my leg, and the ink pricks into my skin.

“Almost done,” Mae says, sliding a wipe over my skin. She lifts the gun farther from my body and peeks at my face. “How are you?”

“I’m fine.” I really am. It doesn’t feel great, but it’s nothing worse than scratching an unending itch raw. “I’m curious about what Archer’s working on up there.”

“Same.” We both look at him as his Sharpie scrapes the paper. More than once, he ripped paper off the spiral, balled it up and tossed it in the garbage before consulting his phone again. Mae lowers the gun to my skin again. “Archer,” she says over the noise. “Can you give us a hint?”

“Music,” he grunts. Sun slants into Mae’s shop right into his hair and turns it orange like fire light.

“Shocking,” I tease.

“Sassy,” he replies, not looking up from his paper.

A few minutes pass, and Mae sits up and turns off the gun. “Let’s disinfect it, and you can see.” She spreads antibacterial foam over the ink, and in one long swoop, Mae wipes my leg clean.

Archer drops his paper and bounds to the mirror. I join him, holding my hem up high. My reflection shows a woman in old running clothes. A crooked top knot yanked into place twenty minutes ago when I realized my ponytail wouldn’t let my head lay flat. Beaming at the tattoo of herself, running into what I imagine is a storm. Spine straight, gait strong. She’ll make it out. I know it.

I look at Mae in the mirror. “Thank you.”

Mae squeezes my shoulder.

After Mae packages my tattoo in tattoo-grade plastic and briefs me on the rules (no scented soap or lotion, no touching, no sun), she disinfects her equipment and the bench, and Archer hops up. I swear he catches air. On her stool, Mae rolls to Archer. “It’s time. Gimme.”

Archer pulls the paper from his t-shirt’s front pocket, where he’d torn it off the pad, folded it into eighths, and shoved it into hiding.

She unfolds it and tells him to pull up his pant leg. Mae walks her fingers over the back of his calf where the first note of “Can’t Help Falling in Love” sits, studies his drawing and back to his leg. “I like it,” she says. “Let me draft this against your music note to make them cohesive. Give me fifteen minutes.”

"Sure thing." Archer fist bumps Mae and she heads to the back of her shop.

I scoot onto the bench and wiggle my left leg. A sting set has set in, but it's not bad. Reminds me, more than anything, of the refreshing exhaustion from a hard workout. "Are you gonna tell me or shall I wait with bated breath?"

Archer pulls his phone out. "I snapped a picture while she bandaged you up." I reach for the phone, and he presses it against his heart. "No laughing."

"I would never."

"You might." Archer scrunches his nose. "You're not a sappy person."

I fling my wrist into the air. "I'm wearing an abandoned room key on an old friendship bracelet on the slim chance that Annabella comes up to me and says "Hey, former roomie—you blew me off in my biggest time of need, but we should be roommates again."

"You're right. You're a little sappy." Archer hands the phone over.

In Archer's drawing, his original tattoo, the music note, is held in a hug by a new music note. It wraps itself around the first in protection. "It's cool. I don't get it."

Archer sets his chin on my shoulder. "You know the smaller tattoo is the first note from my favorite song. He outlines the marker lines he drew. "The new tattoo is the first note from 'Cleopatra.' That way you'll always be with me, no matter what happens next week."

~

Archer's making spaghetti and I'm packing my bag. Mazzy Star—at their most melancholy—spins under the needle. Classes start tomorrow for the downhill glide to summer. Annabella and Zoey are on their way from Sioux Falls. Zoey's dropping Annabella here to take real life on a test run again. Archer's showcase and my meet are in six days.

And Annabella still won't look at me.

I'm running out of time. I can't lose them. Not after all of this.

The door opens.

"AB!" Archer shouts, though there's no reason to. A spatula clatters to the stovetop and I see a flash of flannel streak across the room to hug her from the corner of my eye. "Zee," he adds, muffled. He must be hugging her too.

"Zoey came for dinner." Annabella drops her bag on the floor. "I told her you were making spaghetti."

"You know I cannot resist hastily boiled noodle clumps and canned Prego." Zoey sees me at the foot of the bed, hovering against the record shelf. "Hey, Lou." Her voice is warm.

Annabella makes eye contact with me. She looks away.

I want to sink into myself like a black hole.

Archer motions for me to come over. "Show them what you did yesterday."

I step out, feeling the air as if it can tell me when to bounce. "They don't care."

"I'm intrigued." Zoey plops onto the couch. I spy her split-second glance at Archer, and his glance back, and I know. They traded texts as I packed, and Annabella drove Zoey's car up the interstate. One shared half-smile confirms it.

Too bad Archer's phone didn't tumble into the bubbling spaghetti sauce.

"I'll show and tell." Archer props his leg up on a chair and points to our music notes on his leg.

"You got a tattoo," Annabella sighs. "Shocking. Looks nice though."

"Mine is not the surprise, you raging skeptic."

Annabella's left eyebrow arches. She looks at me. "You got a tattoo?"

I nod.

Zoey claps. The ring of skin-on-skin bounces off the kitchen cupboards and slaps into my brain. "Can we see?"

I wiggle the waistband down on my windbreaker pants, Annabella's key warm on my wrist. I'd peeled off the plastic and tape an hour ago and slathered it with scent-free lotion, so it's extra moisturized and puffy. My little runner woman—she looks perfect upside down to me, and on her way to somewhere else.

"Wow." Zoey moves closer to see. "That's so cool. I love the minimal single line design."

"Thanks," I say.

Annabella stays across the room but looks at my leg. "How's Mae?"

"She's good," Archer says, back to stirring the spaghetti sauce. "She's ready whenever you are."

Zoey swings to her girlfriend. "Wait. Are you gonna do it?"

"Doubtful." Annabella's head shake is tight, like she's wound up.

I don't—I won't—I can't—ask.

Later, over clumpy noodles and sauce out of a jar (with just a little too much oregano added in—we'll work on that), I sit across from Annabella at Archer's way-too-tiny table. Zoey's between us, and Archer stands, leaning on the sliver of counter space not taken up by dishes. "Guests sit," he'd said as we dished up.

"I'm not exactly sure who a guest is here," Annabella had said, but I know what she really thinks.

Zoey glances at my wrist, too casually. "I like your bracelet, Lou."

"Thanks." One look at Archer and he stares at the ceiling.

Annabella pulls her knee up to her chin and spins noodles on her fork like she has intention to eat them. "You two don't need to do this. We don't need interference."

Zoey ignores her girlfriend, and bends to inspect my shoddy work. I haven't removed the bracelet since I asked Archer to tie it on, and already, the thread colors are fading. The key is flat gray in this lighting. And when I woke this morning, the metal ridges left swollen ripples on my wrist from where I slept on it.

But Zoey acts like it's made of pure gold. "Seriously Anna. It's kinda great."

"Stop, please," I say. My wrist may as well be under a microscope or a spotlight at the circus. Gather 'round—the girl who fucked up who doesn't know how to make it right. Watch her try to adult and fail miserably!

Zoey settles in her chair. "Sorry."

"No, I —"

"For heaven's sake." Annabella pitches her torso over the table. For all my shyness, I haven't moved a muscle, and her eyes land square on the top of her key. "Quite the fashion statement."

"Thought I'd keep it handy," I murmur. "If you want it back."

Annabella sinks back into her seat, and looks away. "Oh."

Archer, removed from the scene, slurps a noodle next to his kitchen sink. "Oh," he repeats unhelpfully.

CHAPTER 28

THE WEEK IS LONG. LONELY.

Archer stays home, practicing into the night. When I do see him, his gaze is fixed in the middle distance, and he's flipping a guitar pick between his fingers nonstop. Coach keeps me tied up with Emily and Sara, running, pacing, pushing, as we prepare for the invitational, but Annabella's face is what I see when I run. I slather my tattoo in lotion whenever I think of it. Keep up with French adverbs and pastel worksheets and rural Colorado rock formations for quizzes I will never remember a thing about. I eat bowls of mac and cheese in Annabella's ditched microwave before drifting to a dreamless sleep every night.

I look forward to training with the girls. Well. With Sara anyway.

After an afternoon 10K, a blow dryer roars on by the mirrors and a set of shoes squeaks across the room as I turn off the shower. Emily's blow dryer. Sara's street shoes. I want to hide in the shower and wring my hair dry strand-by-strand to avoid them, but I'm already late for Archer's sound check. Coach kept us running until the three of us were breathing ragged and tongue-tied in the dusk. She must sense my pent-up energy, waiting for sparks to erupt from my fingertips. Momentum is what's kept me moving lately. Like I'm on a treadmill and the world keeps moving, so I must too.

I'm afraid of what happens when everything stops. Maybe Coach senses that too.

My towel tucked under my armpit, I leave the shower stall. Sara sits on the sinks watching Emily's terrible form with a round brush and the hairdryer from hell. I open my locker, slip my shorts under my towel and pull on a bra.

The blower dryer finally clicks off. I pinch my ear, wondering if I've lost any hearing.

"I don't blame Annabella for moving out. I mean, living with Lou was probably total hell—I can't even," Emily says.

"She's shacking up with that Archer guy in that shit hole above Gallerie," Sara sighs like it's a conspiracy and not just crazy cramped.

"At least Lou doesn't have to worry about Archer hooking up with Annabella."

Emily's voice drips with so much sass a fog could roll through. "You sure about that?"

My heart picks up speed.

"What are you trying to say?" Sara's laugh tinkles like bad elevator music.

My t-shirt slips from my fingers when I round the lockers. Sara sees me, and kicks Emily—too busy with a mascara wand to notice. "Yeah, what are you trying to say, Em?"

Emily doesn't shift from her mascara. Her eyelashes look like baby spiders already. "What are you trying to hear, Lou?"

She's right. I put my hands up, wishing I'd put on my t-shirt before I popped out. "Forget it."

"No, really." Emily caps her mascara and brushes the back of her nail over a lash to nab a clump. "Are you sensitive about your best friend and your boyfriend living together?"

I step farther from my locker. "Why would I be?"

"Don't be obtuse."

"Her dad died." I emphasize the last word. Sara looks down to her shoes. "What does her sexuality have to do with why she's staying with Archer?" I step closer. "I mean, why do you care?"

Emily rolls her eyes. "Whatever."

I'm at the mirror bank and wedge my hip between Sara and Emily. If someone touches me, I'll explode. "I don't understand why you have it out for me. And if it's just me, I can take it. What in the actual hell do you have against her?"

"Fuck off, Lou."

Up close, I see how clear Emily's skin is, like a porcelain doll, or a mirror. Not a blemish to be found. "You are fucking insufferable."

Emily spins, and pushes me away. "I'm fucking insufferable? You bailed on us all season and now you're back and Coach's favorite."

Her shoulders feel tiny underneath my palms when I shove back. "The reason you got noticed at all is because I was distracted."

Sara tries to get between us, but Emily bats away Sara's hands as she crams my thighs against the sinks. "Oh, poor you," Emily spits. "All of us have anxiety, and yet you get special treatment for it while the rest of us —"

I can't let her finish that sentence. "Back off," I push Emily off into the bench by the lockers. She lands hard on her ass. "You have no idea what I went through. Leave Annabella alone."

The locker room door swings open. Coach has a pep in her step, until she reads the room. Emily's sprawled on a bench, her boot laces weaving over the tile like worms. I'm heaving in the air next to the sinks, and Sara's wide-eyed and spread like an X between us. "What the hell is happening?"

Remind me to never use Sara for an alibi. Her voice squeak is enough to convict us. "Friendly competition!"

Coach's gaze flicks to Emily, who nods, then to me. I look away. "Everything's fine. We're fine."

Coach's glare bores under my skin and creeps between my vertebrae. God, that t-shirt would be awesome. I'm exposed in a multitude of ways. "You compete tomorrow," Coach says. "Keep your shit to yourselves, and take it out on the race. If this ever flares up again in my locker room, I will bench all of you."

Emily pops up and slams her locker door. "Are you joking?"

"Want laundry for a week too, Reid?"

She mashes her lips together.

Coach looks at me. "Understood?"

I nod.

"Keep your shit to yourselves," Coach calls. She backs into her office, and slams the door.

Emily lets loose a guttural yelp that sounds somewhere between a Girl Scout crying that someone beat her cookie sales record and a moose giving birth. She rages from the locker room. I catch her reflection in the mirror; she's blotched and pink. Sara looks to the floor and hurries behind.

After that, I can't get it together. I tremble and drop my toothbrush into the sink. Toothpaste arches like a blue rainbow under the faucet. I almost smooth my face moisturizer into my hair, admit defeat, twist it into a hair claw, and leave. Coach never comes out of her office.

Gallerie is buzzing. Gus wanders with a clipboard, chirping orders to anyone who will listen. The bartender is stocking the soda and locking up the liquor. Soundboard Guy is fiddling with lights flashing down to Archer, who's center stage in a dusty gray flannel and Chucks, twisting Matilda's tuning pegs. My breath steadies for the first time in hours, seeing him in his natural habitat. I spin, looking for Annabella.

She's perched on the bar, her feet balanced on a stool. Archer's lights reflect off her face as she shifts her gaze to anywhere I'm not. I wave to the spot next to her. "May I?"

Annabella crosses her arms on her knees. A subliminal fence. But she nods. And I hop up, leaving enough space for another human between us.

We sit and watch staff scramble to duct tape down cords and lock up the booze. Archer wanders the stage aimlessly, strumming his guitar in the chaos. I pick up the chorus of "Brown Eyed Girl." He sees me watching him, and grins, heading for his plugged-in microphone. "My blue-eyed girl," he sings. "Do you remember when we used to sing..." He winks, and focuses when the lighting guy calls his name.

"I've never seen him like this, ever," Annabella murmurs.

I'm afraid to move and scare her into silence again.

"I've watched him prepare for this moment for a decade. He's ready. More than ready. But when I see him on stage a part of my heart runs up there with him."

I remember myself propped on the edge of a stool at Ginny's dad's coffee shop every time she read her work to a crowd. I'd dive and take the bullet. Keep her from rejection. Keep her safe.

"He's so much stronger than I give him credit for." Annabella sighs. "He doesn't need me to protect him all the time."

I glance at her profile, and note the way her nose slopes down. Corkscrew brown curls burst from behind her ear. The way her lips still want to turn up at the edges, even though her heart is broken. "He's leaving."

Annabella looks at me. I try not to dwell on the immense amount of effort it took for her to turn her head. "I know how close you've gotten. I'll miss him terribly too."

I squeeze my eyes shut. I can't watch Annabella walk away after I say what I say next. "I'll still be here."

There's no sound of a stool scraping on the concrete floor as Annabella makes a stealthy getaway. I open my eyes.

She's watching her best friend on stage again. Archer's kneeling, talking to the sound engineer and waving at his earpiece. "Oh yeah?"

The lights make Archer's hair tangerine, frizzing from constant nervous curl twirling. When he stands, he looks up and sees his best friend sitting next to me, and his smile is radiant. Extraordinary. Completely—completely—earth-shattering.

I look at Annabella. "I'll be here for as long as you'll let me."

CHAPTER 29

MY ALARM BLASTS ON AT SIX AM. I GET READY AND HEAD to the gym. Coach's car is in the parking lot. I'm glad she's here already.

Emily and Sara arrive, we sunscreen up and stretch in silence (at least we can unite in one activity), Coach comes out of her office, and we head out as a unit. The 10,000-meter is up first, so we can race while other events are underway. I line up with my competitors. Their inhales come in like the breeze: predictable. My blood surges, warming my insides.

I think of my starting line tradition. Of tightening my ponytail to unnerve the other runners. Of Ginny's voice tripping me at the gunshot. I give in and tug the ponytail tight. And I wait. She hasn't shown up in weeks, but she will. She's always under the surface, ready, waiting. Always.

"Get it baby! You are a *beast*!"

This voice is real.

I don't have to shift my eyes away from the track. It's Archer, yelling from the parking lot, standing on the Bronco's hood.

Pop.

I march next to the track, pressing bumps from my ponytail down with my sweaty palms. Archer's still in the parking lot on the Bronco hood, though now that my race is done, he's scribbling in his notebook, and smearing lead on his cheek when he shoves his pencil behind his ear. His show starts in six hours. He won't leave until I do. And I'll be done soon. But not soon enough for me.

But being on a squad means I must support my teammates. Respect others' feelings. Celebrate others' achievements. No matter how my tether is pulling me away. (Even if they don't want me here.)

I grind weeds to the dirt with the toe of my shoe as Emily takes second in the 1500-meter. I march around and flip my hood up and down as Sara runs the 5000-meter.

Coach tracks my pacing, as she yells support at Sara, running across the track. On my millionth pass by, she grabs my wrist. "You did well. Relax."

"I'm just cold," I lie, as if the sunshine isn't baking my shoulders.

Coach holds on to me. She glances at Emily talking shit with a distance runner from NDSU next to the hurdles and turns her attention to me. "Relax," she says again. "Deep breaths. Everyone is safe. Everyone is okay."

I nod and look up. She pats her fist into my shoulder, and releases me.

"That 1500 fucking sucked."

"Stop. You came in second to the best in the country, Em. You can't beat that."

"Of course you can. By beating them."

I follow my teammates into the locker room. Sara looks back at me, and props open the door with her shoe. "You looked great out there Lou. Congrats."

Emily nods as I pass by to my locker. "You were fine," Emily grumbles. Her locker door bangs into the next locker. "I mean, not as great as me."

"I don't know. Lou won her race." Sara ducks as Emily throws her towel at her.

I smile.

I mean. I did win my race.

~

The sun is eyeball-searing bright over the Wellness Center as I wrangle my wet hair into jagged pig-tailed braids and run to the parking lot.

Archer slides off the hood, looking every part of a main lead in an eighties rom-com. All he needs is a boombox. He pockets his writing notebook. "You look like a gazelle when you compete."

"Why are you still here?" I corral him to the driver's side. "Your show starts in four hours."

"Lou." Archer sets his hands on my shoulders. "I have to change from one flannel to another. I'm fine."

"But for preparing or whatever—"

"Stop." He's shaking his head. One hand has slid next to a pigtail, and he's pressing the three chunks of hair together as if it's a precious rope and not just my hair. "I just want to be present today. I just want to be with you, right now, after you killed that race, and think about how I get to sing songs about you and all the people I love tonight. Is that okay?"

I press my lips between my teeth, but the grin sneaks through anyway. "I guess I can allow that."

"You know what part of being present, right now, means?"

"Tell me." I do not need to be told at all.

"It means." Archer closes what little of a gap is still between us. His lips brush mine, then he speaks. "That I just want to kiss my girl in the sunshine. It feels right, on a day like today."

CHAPTER 30

ARCHER'S CHILL LASTS FOR THREE HOURS, WHICH IS TWO hours and fifty-eight minutes longer than mine would have. (Fine. Fifty minutes. We were being present for ten minutes next to the Bronco in the sunshine.)

"What time is it?" Archer paces the dressing room, cracking his neck repeatedly, like churches ring their bells at noon.

I peek at my phone. "Seven-thirty-three." He doesn't go on until eight.

"Is Zack here yet?"

Archer showed me the guy's picture on the agency's website more times than I can count, including once more an hour ago. At this point I know the shape of the guy's chin, and the height of his Cillian-Murphy-circa-Peaky-Blinders hair.

I also know he isn't here yet. "I can look again."

"No, no." Archer toes a crack in the concrete floor by the ratty, green couch we hauled from a retiring professor's office. When Archer decorated the dressing room over the winter, I don't think he imagined he'd be one of the first people to use it. An Elvis poster hangs next to a framed Lumineers show advertisement from Omaha.

Well, maybe he did.

Archer sinks to the couch, unbuckling Matilda from her case, even though he'd just put her away a few minutes ago. I don't dare shift from my place on the couch's arm. Archer moves his fingers over the strings and something guttural, far from a melody, rumbles from Matilda's core. He snaps up to put Matilda back in her case. "Actually—"

"On it," I slide out the door and shut it gently behind me. "Zack, I swear to god," I whisper rounding the corner off the stage to check the crowd of people gathering.

I find someone better than Zack.

Annabella is crossing the stage on her way back to us. To Archer, really. "Is he okay?"

"No." We walk back to the dressing room together. I push open the door. Archer's eyes are closed, his fingers in the air drawing out what I imagine are musical notes in the air like a dream.

"Arch." Annabella peels off her leather jacket. Her car keys crunch into her phone in her pocket. Archer's eyes pop open at his name. "Big breaths," Annabella says. "You are you. No one has what you do."

I stop in the doorway. Not in the room. Not out.

She takes Archer's face and pulls his forehead to hers. Their eyes shut.

I should look away. But I don't want to. It's magic right in front of me. Annabella takes every bit of his stress, flips it, and only peace remains. She sucks his worry away, and with a grace I can't begin to manifest in myself. It's friendship. Love. A million of their prayers, answered.

If it's not a prayer, it's the next best thing.

"Love you," Annabella whispers as the tension in his shoulders sink away from his chin. "I'm so proud of you."

Archer bounces to his toes and back, drawing, growing, solidifying her calm as his own. He stills. His hands land on her wrists and he squeezes. One, two, three.

I slip into the hall. For the first time in months, I reach for my phone to call Ginny and hear her real voice. Would she pick up? What would I say? What is there to say?

What is there left to say?

Rubber tennis shoes squeak on the gross backstage floor. "Lou!"

For a second, I swear it's Ginny.

Catherine walks to me, her hair in a high pony and in a cute white crop top and Converse. She looks older than I remember from even February. The kind of older that signifies someone has seen, and survived, some shit.

"Hey," I say.

"I haven't seen you since the funeral." Catherine pulls me into a hug. "Sorry for this. I've become a hugger. Dad would be so confused. Mom sure is." She pulls away, her smile watery, but strong. "Jake said he talked to you before the funeral started. Anna was so grateful you were there. We all were."

I nod, and try not to look as confused as I feel. What?

"You've been taking care of Archer, so he could take care of Anna," Catherine goes on. "She needed him so badly these last few months, and he could be there, because he had you in his corner."

The buzz of voices from the other side of the stage curtains morphs into static in my ears.

"And this is a nice touch." Catherine reaches for my friendship bracelet with Annabella's key. "You're wearing her down."

"I don't want to be wearing her down—" Rocks multiply in my belly. I'm going to have an avalanche to deal with.

"I don't think the words matter here," Catherine doubles down, her fingers following the key's curves. "Grief is horrible. No one does it right. But I guess no one wants to spend enough time in it, to figure out whatever right means." That watery smile grows. "I'm grateful my sister knows you."

I open my mouth to tell her that she has it wrong, that Archer's been caring for me, protecting me, being my biggest champion. And that her sister doesn't need me. She *needs* Zoey. She *needs* Archer.

But what if that's the whole point?

Maybe the only reason I'm in her life, and she's in mine, is because we want to be.

The dressing room door swings open. Archer comes out, searching the corridor, Matilda dutifully dangling from his back. Annabella trails behind, her leather jacket folded over her arm. She sees me with her sister and blinks.

"Cat!" Archer grins, but he's still looking for Zach. "What are you doing here?"

"You think I'd miss your big break after all that off-key strumming in my house for ten years?" Catherine swings Archer into a hug. "You're gonna be fabulous."

"Thank you." Archer's genuine, but his eyes contain the wild until he finds me tucked behind Catherine, and his shoulders sink and relax. He wasn't looking for Zach. He was looking for me.

Archer reaches for me. His lips are sweet nothings murmured at three am. His hands are a story in ink and scars. "We had our first kiss here," Archer whispers, our noses brushing together. "Two of my biggest dreams are coming true in this room."

Screw being needed. I've never felt more wanted in my life.

~

The show begins as Annabella and I slide onto stools in the back of the crowd by the soundboard. A spotlight sets Archer aglow, erasing the nerves from his eyes. He steps up to the microphone, shifts his hip to pull Matilda around, and opens his mouth. His first song is a jam about a girl with a birthmark shaped like the Eiffel Tower. "She paints her lips red and swings away," he sings. "And I stumble behind/my fingerprint on her birthmark anyway."

To me, it's like staring straight into an eclipse.

The crowd at the stage is ten people deep. Catherine elbowed her way to the front row with her cell phone high in the air so Jake, back in Sioux

Falls, can watch too. A wave of energy passes through the crowd by the second verse, and the head bobbing starts to match the beat. Before the crowd swallows her, Catherine's rocking out, losing herself in the music.

Archer bounces right into his second song, a fun ditty about grabbing omelets on New Year's Day at a greasy spoon. It's got a rad-a-tad-tad bounce to it, and yeah, Archer played it for me a few weeks ago so I know the lyrics, but the people around us, by the bridge, are bobbing to the beat like they've heard it before, even though they haven't.

I exhale.

This is working.

Annabella twists her body my way, without taking her eyes from the stage. "Where's this Zack guy?" she calls over Archer's amplified voice.

I point to a guy standing in front of us, separated from the crowd. I'm glad I can't see his face because I don't want to spend this moment analyzing twitches, clocking yawns, logging tight lips or frowns. But I recognize Zack's hair, and the shadow he spreads behind him. I wonder if Archer knows where he's standing.

Archer's song ends and he launches into a fictional tale about sitting front row at fashion shows. It's a bop. He's finding his comfy spot up there on the overlapping carpets, elevated, alone. His movements flow like water, and when he switches keys or bounces into a bridge, the transition is seamless. Contained, crackling, energy. It's Archer.

I am so freaking in love with him.

As if she can read my mind, Annabella speaks over the music. "What you've done. For Archer." Annabella unscrews the lid on her water, and tightens it again, twisting it tight as it will go. "He's centered again."

"Oh." The word trips out of my face in lack of anything other to say than a syllable. "It's nothing," I eventually spit out.

Annabella looks at me. Purple stage light divides us. "No. It's not. It's everything."

On stage, Archer shifts into a slower song. The crowd changes from bouncing to swaying. For the first time since the show started, Archer and I lock eyes. Slightly, he tilts his head to the right, looking at Annabella. As if he knows the water is warm. "Dreaming and being are one in the same, I swear, my darling, oh I swear."

"Annabella?" I say.

She grunts in my general direction. Lights swing to shine down on the top of our heads.

There's only one thing to say. "I shouldn't have run."

Annabella turns to me, tangles of curls clumping on her jacket. Studying, waiting again, like that morning after Archer's showcase. Thinking. I think. I don't know. "Okay."

"It's not okay."

Her eyes flash, and I could blame them on the show lights, but know it's not. "Lou, that wasn't an apology. I'm not even sure that's what I need." She stares, hard, and I want to sink into Gallerie's concrete floor and fade with Archer's lyrics about Christmas blizzards floating above my head. But I stay present, and accept her stare.

Annabella sighs, and stiffly shakes her head. "Apologies only matter if you stop leaving," she says, finally.

"I will. Stop leaving, I mean." I will. There's something in me now, that's been blooming for weeks. It feels like a root, but also like I can fly, like Mom said.

But I won't fly. Not without Annabella. It's not her problem, and I see that now.

She gives me the grace of looking away, and watches Archer instead. He's swinging around, in the middle of the chorus. "She's real, so real, and I can't believe she's mine all mine."

"Okay." She repeats. I barely hear it over Archer's music. "Please don't leave again."

I try to promise I won't, to make my voice do what my feet have always been too good at doing: working. But my throat is clogged, and all I can do is nod.

Archer's lost in a beautiful, melancholy, and dare I say, jazz-inspired riff, his feet stomping dust out of the stage rugs. The crowd is frenzied, elbows banging, bouncing, the kinetic energy multiplying. I make out the back of Catherine's head in the front row; her hands wave in the air like this isn't the seven hundredth time she's heard some version of this song. A frat-ish boy shoves by us, yelling the new lyrics Archer wrote the last day of spring break as I plated the spaghetti for all four of us that night.

Zack crosses his arms at the back edge of the crowd. His feet haven't moved. The definition of stoic.

Annabella turns to where I'm staring. "Please love him."

~

Annabella and I sit crisscross applesauce on the stamped-down stage rugs. Archer's show is done, and the space smells like sweat and spilled beer and a rogue joint or two. Catherine filtered out with the crowd after hugs for her sister and Archer, and a kind wave at me. Joy floats in the air like firework smoke, reminding everyone of what happened here. And that it was good.

Archer sits at the bar with Zack. Matilda dangles from Archer's shoulders, his security blanket, or a Superman cape. He keeps adjusting the strap over his shirt in a nervous tick. Archer's groupies,a gaggle of fellow undergrads I recognize from my French and Comp classes, teeter by, high on the contact and Archer's romantic lyrics that I can loosely trace back to me. Archer waves good night, and one of the girls literally swoons.

I snort so hard my nose hurts.

Annabella frowns. "I don't enjoy his groupies."

The girls gone, we're still too far away to hear anything, and Annabella and I sit and stare for a rogue lip curve or a slight nod. Something—anything—to give them away.

Zack pushes off his stool first and shakes Archer's hand. Archer nods vigorously; Matilda bops along. Zack waves to us, and leaves.

"Well?" Annabella wiggles, too antsy to wait as Archer takes the stage steps two at a time.

"He said he'll call next week. He has to talk to the principals, but he liked what he saw." Archer sinks to the dirty rugs between me and Annabella. His skin is pink like taffy as he unwinds the guitar strap from his body.

Happiness courses through my muscles, poking the fear back. I wrap my arms around his neck. "You killed it."

Archer peers into the sound hole on his guitar. He plucks strings at random, the purr cutting loose and hanging around his thumb. "What now?"

The question is louder than the note.

I pull my arms to my side, and shrug. Annabella uncrosses her legs, and instantly recrosses them again. Archer leans on top of his guitar, and looks up at the stage lights before settling back on us.

"Well," Annabella straightens her spine up and scratches her ear. "Tomorrow's my mom's birthday. We're having dinner at home. She invited you two."

I'm nodding before she's done asking. "When are we leaving?"

CHAPTER 31

LATE AFTERNOON, ARCHER LEADS THE WAY DOWN THE steps to the alley behind his building. Annabella walks behind him, and I bring up the rear. She gets to the Bronco, and holds the door for me to slide in first. Up and in, Archer shuts her door behind her and rounds the front bumper, squinting into the bright sun, low in the sky. Spring is heavy in the air, wet, like a blanket, but I can see goosebumps pooling on Annabella's arm. I wonder if she's cold. I wonder if she's wondered when she'll ever feel warm again.

Annabella falls asleep before we pass the second exit south on the interstate. I glance at her, legs crossed tight at the knee like a pretzel in the footwell. Her chin's propped up on her fist like she's studying the passing landscape, but her eyes are screwed up tight. Forcing sleep.

Archer nudges my ribs with his elbow. "I did some reading on grief specific to losing a parent right after, and that's a thing, all the sleep."

"I know." I did it straight through last summer. The house would be so still, so cold, and I'd look at the time and expect it to be close to evening, and it'd only be noon. Nowhere to go and nowhere to be, I'd go back to bed and rot until...morning, sometimes. I pretended in all of my sleep that I was a caterpillar, saving my energy for freshman year, for an attempt at putting my missing pieces back together, for whatever molting looked like for a human woman-child who missed her mom so much she couldn't breathe. But I knew the truth, simmering between me and the blankets. It was a simple game: forcing time to pass.

I feel Archer look at me before he turns back to the road. "Sorry. You do."

She looks so uncomfortable, down to the furrow in her brow. I release Archer's arm, and gently tug her hoodie until she tilts her face my way—she must actually be asleep. I slouch enough for my shoulder to be the landing pad for her head. It takes her a minute to relax against me, but then all at once, Annabella sighs in her sleep and burrows into my fleece jacket.

I find her hand curled into a fist next to my hip, and stretch one finger out at a time to relax against her belly. My eyes closed, I feel Archer shift lanes and pick up speed to get Annabella home.

~

Jake walks through the kitchen door ten minutes after we arrive, his hands full of bags of food from Mrs. Harris's favorite restaurant downtown. Catherine helps him scoop the bucatini from Styrofoam into bowls and arrange the breadsticks on a plate that doesn't look like Jake ordered this online this afternoon, but rather was a carefully considered menu fit for a queen.

Mrs. Harris walks in from her husband's study off the kitchen, fresh from an afternoon of reading surrounded by the doctor's things, and I try not to be obvious about studying the way her soft face is kind, and open, despite the hard lines creasing under her eyes now. We dig in, their father's empty chair bookending their mom's seat at the other end of the table. Annabella sits between Archer and me, and I watch his hand crawl along the back of her chair to make her feel close.

Catherine disappears into the kitchen and comes back with a cake glowing under candles. She starts singing "Happy Birthday" as she sets it in front of her mother, and the rest of us chime in. Jake's voice is shockingly baritone, Annabella murmurs her way through (though she smiles at her mom), Archer takes a backseat to the singing, and I forget to sing at all because I'm watching. Mrs. Harris blows out the candles and squeezes Catherine's hand that's landed on her shoulder. "Cheesecake. You remembered."

"We can't forget," Annabella says as Catherine wields a cake knife.

"Forget what?" Jake tees up the question.

"Eric hated cake," Mrs. Harris says. "Detested it."

"Texture," Catherine fills in, sliding a piece of sliced cheesecake to a piece of crystal china. She hands it to her mom, but she just passes it on to Archer, where it eventually finds its way to me. "Always said using 'sponge' as a descriptor was entirely unappetizing."

"When we married, his mother insisted upon an almond cake, as it was all the rage in 1982."

"Ew." Annabella twists her nose in disgust, but her eyes say anything but. It's her line, her role, in this family story, I realize.

"Complete with the fondant and swirls of sugary border," Mrs. Harris is saying, passing plates of cake over the table one at a time now to Annabella, then Archer. "Back then, we respected our parent's thoughts on weddings and related pomp and circumstance—"

Jake shoots his mother-in-law an also-rehearsed side-eye, while Catherine swats, and then squeezes her mother's shoulder. All must be forgiven.

"—and so we ordered the almond-flavored, flowery and frosting monstrosity that delighted Grandma Harris down to her pearly pink toenails for the formal, and demanded, country club reception. But your father..." Mrs. Harris hands Jake a slice of cheesecake, and then finally accepts her own as Cat sits down. "Hated it. In all of Grandma's delight, your father had nothing but disdain. Disgust."

"Dissatisfaction," Catherine adds.

"Dismay." Jake smiles and shoves his fork into the crumbly crust in front of him.

Without looking, I feel everyone else turn to Annabella. She has the next line. Her arms cage around her ribs. I hook an ankle around hers under the table, as Archer's hand drifts from the back of her chair to her spine.

"Dislike," Mrs. Harris fills in her daughter's silence. "He hated that wedding cake, and because he hated it, I hated it. And I couldn't hate my wedding cake. No little girl dreams of that. The week of the wedding, I arranged for a tiny cheesecake, big enough for four slices. Two people. Drizzled in strawberry sauce—your father's favorite. After we cut the monstrosity for the crowd, I grabbed your father's hand and pulled him into the kitchen where the chef had it waiting. We had to be careful, of course—couldn't drip strawberry on my chiffon, but we managed." Mrs. Harris looks down at her birthday cheesecake. "I saw so much love in that man's eyes, and I thought it was the cheesecake. That look never went away. He was so deeply full of love."

Annabella purses her lips and funnels air into her lungs. Goosebumps pool on her arms, and under the table she pulls her ankle from mine.

Mrs. Harris looks up at her children and motley crew of birthday celebrants. "He loved you all so much."

Catherine sits down, rubbing her mom's shoulder. "We know."

Annabella sighs, and it feels bigger than the whole room.

Jake, his fork poised over his cheesecake, pauses. "You okay, Anna?"

"Yeah." She nods. A chunk of her curls bounces loose from her scrunchie, and she nods harder. A flush spreads from underneath her collar and up her cheeks. "Yeah."

"Annabella—" Archer's hand presses into her spine now, as he sits up.

"Stop." Annabella puts her palms up. Archer drops his hand from her back and moves it to the back of her chair. "Stop. Everyone."

I knot my fingers in my lap. Jake glances at Catherine, who's still squeezing their mom's shoulder. Archer's face is blocked by Annabella, but the crown of his head is up; I imagine he's looking at his knees.

"Dad loved us." Annabella's still nodding, her bun loosening and bobbing along for the ride. "I know it. I felt it, constantly. But Mom." She looks to her mother. Mrs. Harris looks back, steadily. "I wasn't even here when it happened. And I was drunk. I barely even remember that night. I don't know the last thing I said to him. Or what he said to me." Her voice cracks. My right hand twitches to hers, but hangs onto my leg. "I wasn't here. I wasn't here for him, or with you guys, or even fully there in my own head. And it's like I've been on pause since." Annabella crams the butt of her palms into her eyes and lets her fingers drop limp to her lap. "What are we supposed to do now? What am I supposed to do now?"

Mrs. Harris stood up somewhere in there, and hustled to our side of the table, but Annabella is faster. She whips backwards out of her chair, her flat palms up again. "No. Momma, I'm sorry I ruined your birthday. I just. I can't." She spins, and bursts from the room as if it's on fire.

Honestly, maybe it is.

Archer is sliding behind me, next to go after Annabella, but I block him with my arm. "Let me try." We lock eyes, and I see everything in his. Worry. Remorse. Love. And trust. He nods and I'm out of my chair, trailing Annabella through the living room and out the front door.

She's on the front steps, her butt on the edge of a row of brick. The spring cold must be creeping through her jeans. I duck inside and grab a cream wool blanket from the living room. When I sit down next to her on the steps, I drape it over both of us like a cape.

Annabella looks across the street to the park. Leaves are beginning to bud on the branches, too small to make a canopy, too big to be ignored. It's a neon green haze in the slanted sunshine, promising warmer days to come.

For some of us.

“I don’t know how to make this make sense,” she whispers.

I adjust the blanket over her shoulders. “The Dead Parent Club is shit,” I say. “There is no making sense of it.”

Annabella sighs, and I feel it in my chest. “I knew that this would be impossible, in this far off way, in the way that you don’t prepare for, because you’re still a kid, and he wasn’t old either, and this wasn’t supposed to happen so soon. Already.” She pulls the blanket over her nose and lips, but I can still hear her speak. “I keep waiting to feel whole again, Lou.”

I want to hide behind the blanket too. But I need to say what I’m about to say, and Annabella deserves to hear it with nothing blocking the way. “I don’t think you will. Not like before.”

I hate watching her eyes go glassy. I hate that I did that to her. She snakes her fingers underneath my arm and finds my hand in the sea of wool, and hangs on tight. “What do I have to look forward to?”

“Oh, some self-hatred, but it sounds like you’re already there.” I fold her fingers beneath mine. “Probably questionable hair choices. At least your relationship with Zoey will keep you out of weird people’s beds.”

Annabella snorts. “What else?”

I swallow, expecting it to be hard, like the words don’t want to come out. I don’t know what it means when the words are poised on the tip of my tongue.

“The hole in you doesn’t close. Rumor has it that it never does, but I wouldn’t know yet. It sort of just shifts. All the time. Sometimes more empty than full, sometimes more full than empty.” Across the street, a couple walks through the park. It looks as though he’s pointing out birds in the trees. She’s smiling. Do they notice how the branches cut the sky up into pieces without the full, fat summertime leaves to sew the sky back together?

Do they think about how the sky is always moving, always changing, and even when the blue looks the same, it's not? It's never quite the same view.

"What else?"

"Meghan's taught me that it's okay if it feels like it's moving, the hole," I say. "Sometimes I feel it in my belly, and other times it takes up so much room in my lungs that it clogs my throat when I try to speak."

"And that's okay?"

"Yeah," I say. "She made it sound like it's your body rejecting the grief, but it doesn't have a place to go. So you just sort of ... live with it. Around it."

Annabella rests her head on my shoulder. "That sounds terrible."

"It does. It is." I lean my cheek against her hair part. "But it isn't, after a little while."

"How can that be?"

"If I loved my mom that much, and I did—I do—I would hope there is a gap in her loss."

Annabella's grip on my hand tightens.

"I remember the last conversation you had with your dad," I say softly.

Her inhale is sharp. "You do?"

"You and Zoey volunteered to grab the ice. You were wine-drunk, and extra sassy and silly and Zoey's eyes were lit up like being seen with you with all she'd ever want. You did this weird little sashay thing past your dad, waving, and he stopped the both of you." I stop as Annabella tilts her face from the blanket to the street. "Your dad told Zoey to be safe and hurry up and get you two back because he wanted to talk to her about one of her profs, somebody he knew from med school."

"Then we left?" Annabella's voice is barely a sound over the breeze.

"He kissed your hair, three times, Annabella. You said you loved him, and off you went."

She nods again. My words float to the park, and beyond as we settle into the quiet. Time keeps passing, like the wind, pulling at the ends of her curls. The bird watchers wander out of sight. I sit on the cold concrete step with my best friend, helping to keep her warm.

I'll never understand the comfort she receives from praying, but sitting here with her, I begin to understand—I believe in friendship. And love. And safety. Inside jokes and yellow M&Ms shared over quilts. Christmas tree stories and songs. Drawings of anatomical hearts. Heavy afghans in the spring and tattoos and wishes made on New Year's kisses. Strawberry milkshakes and emergency friendship bracelets. I believe in Annabella.

And in me, to be here with her.

"Thank you," she says.

"Thank you back," I whisper.

~

I hear Mrs. Harris first, opening the front door a crack, and then enough to slip outside.

Instantly, Annabella stands and dives into her mother's arms. Her side of the blanket floats down next to me. "Momma."

"My lovely girl," Annabella's mom whispers into Annabella's hair.

It's too intimate. Too much of what I needed last spring. I stand, untangle myself from the blanket, and drape it heavily over Annabella's shoulders and drift inside like a ghost.

Or I try to.

"Stop." Annabella grabs my sleeve and pulls me against her, looking up from her mom's shoulder. "Lou could use a hug from a mom too, if that's okay."

Mrs. Harris is already shifting to cover us with the blanket, and holding us both as tight as she can. "To your question earlier, Annabella." Her voice is wobbly, but with a hint of steady underneath. "I don't know what we're supposed to do now. I have no idea. But." She's crying now too. "I think this is a good place to start to figure that out."

Annabella's whimpers turn to weeping, and I burrow in against her, finding her fingers in the wool and holding on tight. Mrs. Harris closes the loop, pulling us in hard to her chest, melting Annabella. And I think of my mother.

I think of her after a random race early on in high school. I'd tripped over someone else's shoe and crashed into the dirt. Mom was there, at the finish line, and later in the kitchen as the stand mixer creamed together eggs and sugar and vanilla for my favorite snickerdoodles. Sweetness filled the air, and already, things were turning around. "Not every day will be this hard, sweetheart," she said.

I remember how Mom led with love. As if she were a tree, and happily opened all of her leaves in the spring so I could grow and bask in the warm air, protected from the sun. I could run and be happy under sweet sprinkles while she took the pounding rain.

And how Mrs. Harris—Carol—is holding Annabella up now.

Good moms are more than the roots. They're the whole damn tree.

CHAPTER 32

PEOPLE ROAM THE SIDEWALKS BELOW, CONVERSATIONS drifting upwards in snippets too far away to hear. The pizza truck opens its windows, filling the air with the tangy scent of pepperoni. A bar door swings open, and the first bit of thumping bass tiptoes out, checks to see if anyone's around, and heads back inside.

The night begins.

"Sit with me." Archer's lounging in the hammock. His old-man slippers skim the tar roof. I sit and curl my knees against his ribcage. Yet another blanket balloons as I tuck us away. It's too far away to hear, but Guster's live album from Omaha twirls downstairs.

"This weekend, huh?" Archer kisses my hair, his fingers massaging my skull.

"Right?" I'd close my eyes, but sleep will come and I want to stay here under the purple-pink sky as long as I can.

Archer pushes his toes against the roof so we drift back. "I got the call today. While you were with AB."

My heart empties, and fills. I sit up. "Zack."

Archer's perfect eyes fill with pride and excitement and a spark of fear. He nods.

"Babe," I breathe, crushing our lips together. Stay present, I think. Memorize how his lips arch against mine. The sweet breeze parting his hair. Archer's wet eyelashes on my face. Him. Me. This. Us.

He swipes the back of his hand over his eyes, glowing in the remnants of sunlight. "I didn't think I'd get so emotional."

"I like knowing what dreams coming true looks like on you." I touch his wrist and press his pulse. The pear tattoo reports back a steady heartbeat. I think of Cadence and shake away the words I don't have the right to offer on her behalf. And he already knows anyway. Some pieces of baggage deserve to be kept.

Archer looks at me, his wiser-than-what's-fair eyes taking in the moment. "Come with me."

I'm shaking my head before his sentence is out.

His face, even sad, is flawless. "Why not?"

"I need to stop running." It's simple, really.

"Metaphorically, of course." Archer tucks a piece of my hair behind my ear.

"Obviously."

"Good," he says. "Cause I know it's not about me, but watching you run is pure art and I will be heartbroken if you deprive me."

"Well." I roll my eyes dramatically. "For you, sweetheart." I slide my hand under his blue flannel, and take a deep breath. "When inspiration starts, you follow. You said it. We won't be apart forever."

Archer's smile is slow to break, but when it does...forget an eclipse. He's the whole damn galaxy.

He tilts forward and meets me halfway for a kiss. We nearly somersault out of the hammock in a pile of limbs and laugh as he hauls me back to safety, stretching out sideways like we should have in the first place.

"I always knew that line would get me the girl," Archer says, his lips on my forehead.

I look up at him and my eyelashes brush his cheek. He wiggles from the tickle. "That day in the Union. What was the inspiration that made you stop?"

"Seriously?"

"Seriously."

His eyes are incandescent. "My shoe was untied. As I tied it, a lyric about knots that don't come undone came to mind. And then, this tall, angry girl mowed me over and splashed her weird wildflowery tea all over me."

"There's a song in there somewhere," I whisper.

Archer pulls me against his chest. "I'm still working on it."

The sky darkens from purple to azure to navy, a real-time watercolor. Archer drifts off, his breathing steady. I close my eyes and start to lose track of what's a dream and what's reality. We float in the hammock over downtown Brookings. Or are we on the river? Water splashes, finding its way through rocks. No, the sound of splashing is me running home through puddles on soggy gravel. I peek behind me, to the clouds black on the back of the storm. Daylight pushes the clouds away.

It's golden.

~

The three of us pile into Mae's tattoo shop.

Annabella hops up on Mae's table, and they discuss where to put her tattoo. Archer and I wander while they talk about placement. Archer's planning his next tattoo—something Sioux Falls-centric. "Maybe something with that spot on the river?" he theorizes, looking at a wall of tattoos with bald eagles.

I sit on the stool next to Annabella's hip. "Will you take a picture for Zoey?" Mae poses, the needle poised but not touching the skin above the stencil behind Annabella's ear. They grin. The picture is great.

"Why a Christmas tree?" Mae asks after they begin. The needle presses into Annabella's skin and she winces. I hold her fingers.

Annabella answers through the pain. "Arch and I have a tree we put up every year. I've been thinking about this tattoo forever but always got nervous."

Mae's tongue slips between her lips as she concentrates on her work. "It's cute. Why not?"

Annabella's gaze flutters to me. "It didn't feel quite...us yet. I felt like we were waiting for one last piece."

~

Finals start in two days. As a going away gesture, Coach hosts a party in her backyard. Naturally, she needed live music.

Well, she didn't, but Archer's sitting on the picnic tabletop with Matilda taking requests. Annabella's flitting around under the tree canopy full of tiny neon green leaves that are starting to unfurl. Everyone is way more interested in her tattoo than her sudden departure from the team. She's even smiled a few times. It'll be a while until the three of us can make a stealthy getaway. I don't mind.

"Old school Taylor!" Emily calls from the buffet card table as Archer wraps up "Sunflower" by Post Malone. "Country Taylor!"

"Speak Now Taylor or Fearless Taylor?" Archer asks, strumming. A peal of laughter breaks free from farther back in the yard.

"Fearless," I say, standing up.

Sara points at me as I walk up the deck steps. "What she said."

Matilda's strumming follows me inside and is muted when I shut the deck door. The air conditioner pumps through the house already, the cold slick on my arms.

I pause on the other side of the door, as Archer launches into the song. "We were both young, when I first saw you..." Maddie and Sara hold their phones in the air with the flash on like lighters. Emily stays seated, her chin resting on her fists, so starry-eyed I almost—almost—understand. I slip my phone from my back pocket.

LOU: Young and Beautiful. Lana DelRay.

Coach's steps are heavy on her porch stairs. Her curls are nearly frizz in the slight humidity. Inside, she rounds the butcher's block and plucks two bottles of water from the caterer's iced stash. She shares one with me. "Tell no one I dare hand you a bottle of water. I can't be accused of playing favorites." She arches an eyebrow at me.

"Thank you," I blurt.

Coach looks at me. "It's water, McKinnley."

"It's more than the water."

Pink tints her temples. Coach sashays in place, wiggling the gratitude away before it settles in her bones. "Thank yourself."

I plunk my hand over my chest and tap three times.

CHAPTER 33

"I THINK WE SHOULD EXIST ONLY ON GUMMY WORMS THIS weekend," Annabella says. She balances on the grocery cart handle, her waves spilling over her shoulder to the baby seat. Her sandals leave the ground, and she rides the cart a few feet into the frozen food aisle before stopping. "Live on the wild side."

Archer cracks our painstakingly curated shopping list in front of Annabella's nose. "You should have suggested that back at Lou's house."

"Let loose, buddy. I've never known you to be such a rule-follower." Annabella knocks her elbow into Archer's arm. He grabs it in fake pain. "But you meet the father-in-law and you walk the straight and narrow."

"Okay, calm down," I say, stopping in front of the fish sticks for absolutely no reason. My heart flutters at "in-law." I know it's a joke, and my father probably won't be in my life by then, but the implication of Annabella's word choice is so alluring my mouth goes dry anyway.

I brought Annabella and Archer home to see my home. After the long weekend, Annabella will continue her road trip to meet Zoey for a week in Minneapolis where she's interning for the summer, and Archer will give off pretenses of sleeping in our guest room—Dad's old office, newly cleared of his crap—while I spend the week packing up the house to get it on the market. Dad called (unhelpfully) during my French final and left me a voicemail with the news that he decided to sell. This week is going to be hard and sad, but at least I have Archer with me.

I pull our cart a couple freezer doors down to sweeter treats. Archer stands next to me as my eyes dart between a chocolate ice cream laced with peanut butter and a hearty Rocky Road. The back of his hand brushes mine under the fluorescent lights and my ribs crack open in equal parts goosebumps and glee. "Rocky Road," he suggests, pointing. "Marshmallow with a crunch. Just. Like. You."

"Never change." I open the door and grab both ice cream cartons. "We should add gummy worms to the list."

Annabella punches the air like she's in a karate class and sprints up the aisle. Archer kisses my cheek and peels off behind her. "Get the rainbow sour ones!"

The squeak of their tennis shoes fades as I wander farther into the frozen food. Per the list, I eye a huge bag of frozen fries.

"I grabbed every cheese puff bag I could fit in the basket, Summer. Storybook Land isn't Storybook Land without cheese puffs," a girl says. "Pop-Tarts too. The raspberry ones."

Sweat breaks through my skin. I'll forever know her voice. Anywhere. Everywhere.

Ginny turns into the ice cream aisle, her phone pressed to her ear, studying the frozen waffle selection like it's her last breakfast on earth.

Ginny.

Ginny.

My throat swells like drying concrete.

"Be at the park in twenty," Ginny says into her phone, and laughs. Burning orange cheese puff bags pop from the basket slung over her arm. Knockoff sunglasses from Target sit on her head like a crown. Rose gold threads through a loose braid slung over her yellow Storybook Land polo. She cut bangs at some point and is growing them out. The fringe is too short to tuck away and her hair floofs out above her ears. Her Chucks are the same pair. One lace is neon purple.

Ginny says goodbye, and slips her phone into her back pocket.

I don't know what makes her turn around. Ice cream? A hum in a fluorescent light? Did she feel me staring, counting the ways she's still the same even though I don't think she wants to be? But Ginny does turn.

And I don't run.

We look at each over an open freezer of shrimp packs and pre-pressed hamburger patties.

"Lou," Ginny says.

My name, in her real voice, moves through the distance we grew between us.

Annabella and Archer pile around the corner like comic relief. Annabella's got a giant sack of gummy worms and Archer dumps a bottle of fudge in the cart with a bag of coals. "The coals are actually on the list." His words echo in my ears.

"What's next?" Annabella pulls the list from my fingers.

Archer steps closer when I don't answer either of them. "Lou?"

It's his voice that breaks my daze. I blink. The world whooshes back. Rocky Road. Sour gummy worms. The three other humans in this exact place, because of me.

"Lou?" Ginny says again. She starts around the cooler but stops.

Annabella looks from the list.

"Archer. Annabella." My voice makes her grand reappearance. It's squeaky. Of course. "This is Ginny."

Archer pushes his shoulders back and flashes his friendliest smile, the one from Wellness 101 when he asked me my name. I don't like sharing it with Ginny. His hand lands on my spine, to remind me he's here. "Nice to meet you."

Annabella tries less hard. "Hi."

"Are you guys—" Ginny stops. "I mean. Obviously. Friends from school."

I feel Archer's fingers leave my back and take my left hand. "Boyfriend," he says.

"Roommate. Pacesetter." Annabella's eyes dart to mine. "Best friend."

Ginny, if her thoughts are anything but polite, I can't tell. The itchiness of not knowing creeps under my skin. Even now. Ginny smiles wanly, her empty hand landing on her hip like she planned it. The Storybook Land logo is embroidered over her heart in maroon.

Forgiveness. How many times do I have to do it before it sticks? For her. Of me. I want to grab her and tug her to the floor with me and cram our knees together like we used to as we shared M&Ms and our homework. Make her tell me why. How. When she quit loving me as much as I loved her.

"We should go," I say instead, turning to Annabella and Archer. The best team a girl could ask for. "The ice cream is melting."

"Lead the way." Annabella sweeps her hand forward grandly, like a game show host.

Archer nods at Ginny. "Nice to meet you," he repeats.

My tongue is heavy. I resort to a half wave and lead my friends from the frozen food, pushing the cart away.

~

I take care to not beat my heels against the cupboard door below as I sit on the kitchen island. Mom hated the scuffs that came from my busy feet. Annabella hops up next to me with ease. She's got her running gear on. "May I make a cookie request before I head out?"

"No." Archer's methodically lining up flour, sugar, all the goods. I've already pulled out the stand mixer from its tucked-away corner by the window to mid-counter. (It'll have to go into storage, but I'm keeping it.)

"Yes, please," I correct Archer, calming Annabella's faux-shocked outrage.

I've thought about what Mom would think of these two, and their monumental imprint on her daughter. I think—I hope—she'd like them, and their weird, little idiosyncrasies and bickering and love, and how they brought me in with their open hearts. She'd like that. She'd like them.

"I vote for chocolate chip cookies," Annabella says now. "Peanut butter chocolate chip."

"Already ahead of you, darling," he says, not turning, but taking great care to hold up the jar of Jiffy.

"My hero." Annabella jumps off the counter, looks at her watch, and pokes a button. "It's 10k today. I won't be gone long."

"Do the loop I showed you," I say. "It's almost exactly a 10."

The screen door slaps shut, and Annabella crosses the front yard to stretch. Calf, ham, glute. Her ponytail flips over her head, the ends grazing the grass. Is this what I looked like all these years, ready to set out on a run to take me away from here? She probably isn't thinking about Australia, or Key West or ripped men looking for alibis. Maybe she's thinking of her dad. Her mom. Zoey. Or she's clearing her head to think of nothing but the sound of her shoes hitting the ground. Whatever is filling her brain as she cracks her neck and rolls her shoulders is good. She's not smiling, but her eyes are getting back their spark. Slow, but sure.

Her dorm room key slipped out from under her shirt as she stretched. Annabella traps it between her fingers and slides it back under her collar as she sets off. It's still hooked to the original thread, though we had to re-do a few knots when we turned it into a necklace.

"Do you want to put it on a chain?" I'd asked the morning after her mom's birthday. She'd found me and Archer asleep on the roof and we went downstairs to the apartment to figure out how to get the bracelet off my wrist.

"Nope," Annabella said, tugging on the thread around her neck, checking its sturdiness. Nothing snaps or breaks. "This will do."

Archer studies Mom's handwritten recipe card, and decides on the Snickerdoodles first, then Annabella's peanut butter chocolate chip. The mixer whirs as it creams salted butter. I watch him work, the way the back of his neck straightens as he watches the beater slice through the ingredients, making these individual things something else entirely.

My gaze shifts from the freckles that curve with his spine and into his hair. In a few hours, after Annabella goes to bed, I'll tiptoe to the guest room and connect the dots with kisses. It's a brain scrambling daydream for sure, but in the hazy, X-rated places my dreams could take me, Ginny's house stays clear out the window in front of Archer.

In her office three days ago, Meghan sat with a leopard-print shoe dangling from her toes. "It's okay that you're not healed yet, Lou," she'd said. "You've gone through multiple traumatic experiences. Healing takes time."

"I know." I picked at my pillow. "But I want to go home and not feel like the only way to handle seeing Ginny's house is to literally run from it. My fight or flight with her was fight for so long that now it's stuck on flight."

"You don't have to keep people in your life who don't add what you need to it. And it's okay to sit in anxious feelings, and not have answers. Breathe through it, like we practice."

I traced the loose threads in the pillow. If I ever heal, Meghan will have to replace it. My fingernails had gnawed countless dimples. "I just..." My lip squeaked between my teeth. "I think part of the reason I heard her is that we aren't done yet."

"Have you heard her lately?"

I shook my head. "Not since she told me to get up off the gravel in the storm."

Meghan tilted her head. "It's interesting her parting words to you in your imagination were words of love."

"Lou." Archer's turned from the mixer to throw a cracked egg shell in the trash. He's looking at me, and I know it's not the first time he's said my name. "Babe. What was your mom's favorite song?"

I smile and shove my hands under my thighs. "She would have told you 'all of them.'"

"What would you say her favorite song was?"

"'Stand By Me.'" Easy. No doubt. *So darlin', darlin', stand by me.*

"It's a good song," he says. He leans in, his lips brushing my temple, and he doesn't have to say it. I know.

He twists back to spoon flour into the mixer. I take a beat to remember Archer right here, humming the melody, mixing flour into pillowy butter, asking me about my mother, in the house where I grew up. The house getting sold isn't the heart-shattering thing I thought it might be. Without Mom, it's just a collection of rooms now.

Besides, the roots I need are found in the people I love, and not places.

And how I feel about any of it, demands to be felt.

I slide off the counter. "I'll be back soon." I drop a kiss into Archer's fuzzy beard, and let the screen door slam behind me on the way out. Tonight, even that sounds like a song.

The walk is muscle memory.

Swish. Twelve steps across the street, up the slight incline of her driveway.

Tap. Dart between the lilac bushes, coming back to life in early summer air.

Swish. I step over the Lock Rock that holds the key I never, ever needed.

Tap. At the door, I curl my fingers together, loose, and knock.

Footsteps pound on the other side, coming from the kitchen. The lock turns and the door swings open. Ginny stands there, in wool socks, black linen shorts, and a ratty Undergrounds t-shirt with a hole on the shoulder I accidentally put there when I trimmed her split ends on a snow day in eighth grade. Her hair is piled on the back of her skull in an explosion and her chopped bangs frame her wide-as-the-sun eyes.

She smiles with half her mouth.

"Hey."

"Hey."

ACKNOWLEDGMENTS

Terry and Cheryl Liebel. I'm a lucky kid.

Spencer Liebel. I'm not me without you.

Amanda Brock. The weeble to my wobble, forever and ever.

Sam Logue. I love you like you love Legos.

Brett Logue. For going to that bonfire.

AUTHOR'S NOTE

You never have to suffer in silence. There are resources, including the Suicide and Crisis Lifeline where you will be put in touch with a trained crisis counselor immediately. In the US, text or call 988. Sending you love.

STEPHANIE LOGUE is a fiction and non-fiction writer living in South Dakota with her husband and son. *Not Without You* is Stephanie's first published fiction novel. Her non-fiction New Adult novella *Yes. Every Single Day.* is available now. Stephanie's commitment to writing about young, strong women doing their best to figure it out is second only to her need to hear Taylor Swift's debut album re-release someday.

Connect Online
stephanieloguewrites.com
stephanielogue_writes

www.ingramcontent.com/pod-product-compliance
Ingram Content Group UK Ltd.
Pitfield, Milton Keynes, MK11 3LW, UK
UKHW041633190726
13854UKWH00006B/2472

9 798218 457686